KBL
KILL BIN LADEN

A NOVEL BASED ON TRUE EVENTS

JOHN WEISMAN

HARPER

An Imprint of HarperCollins*Publishers*

This book is a work of fiction. Although based on actual events, all references to living people, establishments, organizations, or locales are used fictitiously. All other characters, and all incidents and dialogue, are drawn from the author's imagination and are not to be construed as real.

HARPER

An Imprint of HarperCollins*Publishers*
10 East 53rd Street
New York, New York 10022-5299

Copyright © 2011 by John Weisman
ISBN 978-0-06-212787-7

First Harper mass market printing: May 2012
First William Morrow hardcover printing: November 2011

HarperCollins® and Harper® are registered trademarks of Harper-Collins Publishers.

Printed in the United States of America

Visit Harper paperbacks on the World Wide Web
at www.harpercollins.com

10 9 8 7 6 5 4 3 2 1

To the Warriors Past, Present & Future,
Both in and out of uniform,
Who let us sleep safe in our beds;

To all those Warriors, covert, overt, and K-9 too, who have
paid the ultimate price
To protect our Constitution and our Liberty;

To the memory of Lieutenant Commander (SEAL)
Roy Henry Boehm, USN (Ret.),
Who would have given his left you-know-what to be a part of
this operation;

And, to Deb, who keeps me whole.

The only easy day was yesterday.

—U.S. Navy SEAL motto

AUTHOR'S NOTE

I approached this work of fiction as I would any journalistic undertaking: researching using OSINT (open source intelligence) techniques, talking to people involved in the sorts of undertakings described herein, and fact-checking the tactical, political, and intelligence nuts and bolts by utilizing special operations sources who have performed scores if not hundreds of HVT missions in the past half decade in the AFPAK theater of operations, informants knowledgeable in the White House bureaucracy, and individuals familiar with how our intelligence community proceeded with the decade-long hunt for Usama Bin Laden. Any flaws or inaccuracies, however, are mine and not theirs.

KBL
KILL BIN LADEN

PAKISTAN

Courtesy of the Department of Defense

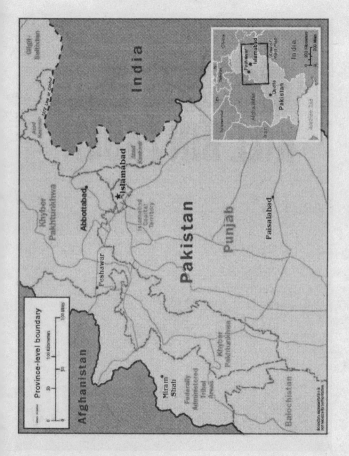

ABBOTTABAD COMPOUND, 2005

Courtesy of the Department of Defense

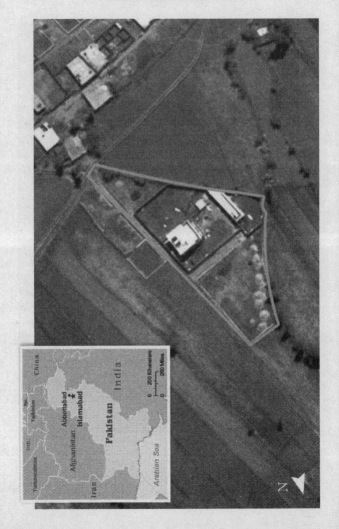

ABBOTTABAD COMPOUND

Courtesy of the Department of Defense

ABBOTTABAD COMPOUND, 2011

Courtesy of the Department of Defense

ILLUSTRATION OF ABBOTTABAD COMPOUND

Courtesy of the Department of Defense

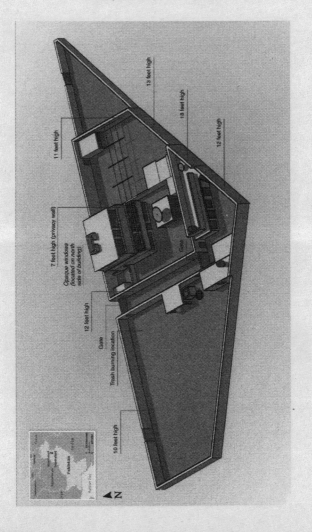

PROLOGUE

The retired Airborne Ranger stepped up to the body bag on the plowed wheat field just as the two young SEALs were about to load it into the big enabler helo. He put his arm up like a traffic cop and shouted over the whine of the big twin idling Lycoming jet engines, "Hey, dude, lemme see him quick."

"For sure, bro." The SEALs lowered the bag back onto the deck, and the baby-faced one unzipped it from the top. The Ranger hit the button on his green-lensed Surefire and peered down. It was him, all right, even though the face was distorted. Bullets tend to do that. Especially Barnes 70-grain TSX fired at a distance of under fifteen feet.

One round had hit just above the left eye. His head must have been turned toward the shooter because it exited out behind the right ear, taking a fair amount of skull and brain matter with it. Between the green light and the Ranger's night-vision equipment, the blood and brain goo registered black. But that wasn't all. The shock and kinetic energy had ballooned the head itself so it looked almost hydrocephalic.

Nasty stuff, those hand-loads.

Even in the green light the Ranger could see that the

corpse's unkempt scraggly beard and kinky hair had turned mostly gray. So the sonofabitch had dyed his hair to make all those videos. That brought a smile to the Ranger's face. He thought, *Wonder what it says in the Quran about using Just for Jihadis.*

He reached down, which took some effort, and pulled the zipper to waist level.

Whoa, Crankshaft'd taken a wholesome burst dead-center mass. Four, maybe five, maybe more rounds. Turned most of his chest cavity into squishy, bloody-colored jelly. Faint fecal scent told the Ranger maybe they'd even nicked the colon.

No way Washington was going to admit to any of that. The Ranger made himself a bet that the official report would read something to the effect of one round to the chest and one round to the head. After all, we wear the White Hats. Turning the architect of 9/11 into hamburger? That would be worse than politically incorrect. It would be . . . inhuman.

Still, the sight brought a smile to his face. The kids did good today. No embarrassing arm or leg wounds.

A clean kill.

The best kind. Next to a dirty kill, that is. The Ranger, he knew all about dirty kills.

He turned toward the young SEAL. Shouted above the jet whine, "He say anything?"

The kid shook his head. "Not a word. Sank like a sack of you-know-what."

The other SEAL adjusted the sling on his suppressed short-barreled rifle as the Ranger hitched up his long, baggy trousers, trousers that covered a quarter-million-dollars' worth of prosthetic legs. The SEAL pointed. "Where'd you lose 'em?"

The Ranger pulled the Velcro tighter on the vest and body armor he'd been given. It was way too big. He'd lost twenty,

twenty-five pounds in the past half year. "Iraq."

"When?"

"Oh-four."

"*When?*"

The Ranger used his hands to reinforce the message. "Zero-four!"

The SEAL caught sight of the Ranger's ruined hands. His expression showed respect. He pointed at the prosthetics. "How they work?"

"Pretty good. They're low mileage, though. Tell you in about ten years and fifty thousand miles." The Ranger gestured toward the women and children, all flexicuffed and sitting against the compound's outer wall atop a clump of wild cannabis. "What are they gonna do with them?"

"Leave 'em here for the Pakis."

The Ranger nodded his head approvingly. "Way it should be."

He pivoted the flashlight to illuminate his way toward the chopper's lowered ramp and half-turned.

Then turned back. "Nice work," he told the SEALs. "Bravo Zulu. Now, go put him on board."

PART ONE

DECEMBER 5, 2010 TO JANUARY 27, 2011

1

The beggar was nervous. You couldn't tell by looking, but he was. Still, he maintained his rounds. He wheeled himself onto the short street just off Narian Link Road right after morning prayers at the Sakoon Mosque. The shops were opening. He made his way up to the sidewalk tables in front of the tearoom, just the way he always did.

He smiled "Good morning, brother" through broken, stained teeth at Waseem, the tearoom proprietor, and accepted gratefully the tiny cup of sweet, dark, steaming brew that Waseem offered him whenever he showed up, sometimes in the morning, sometimes later.

Waseem rubbed his balding head. He admired the beggar. After all, the beggar was mujahidin—he was even aptly named Shahid—a fighter who had lost both his legs and most of four of his fingers when the detested Americans had hit his Waziristan compound with a missile from one of their armed Predator unmanned aerial vehicles that killed Muslims without regard to their guilt or innocence.

Shahid had come to Abbottabad a little over a month ago. From Peshawar, he'd said, and before that Waziristan. On his way to Islamabad. It wasn't far. Maybe he'd get there someday, God willing, to collect the money he was owed by the government, those Westernized thieves.

Judging from the rough Urdu-tinged accent, Waseem figured the beggar was originally from up north, the rugged, harsh mountains close to the Afghan border. Someplace like Drosh or Chitral. Places the government—Waseem considered the president and most of the government bureaucrats in Islamabad to be puppets of the detested Americans—was afraid to go.

They grew them tough up there in the northwest. Thin-air Jihadis who could carry sixty, seventy kilos on their backs all day, humping up and down the passes like mountain sheep. God's warriors, who extracted a good price from the Infidels. And sometimes paid one, too.

"A sweet, Brother Shahid?" Waseem always asked. You didn't want to offend someone who'd put his life on the line defending Islam against evildoers.

The beggar set down the two lengths of wood he used to push the padded furniture dolly on which he traveled. "God bless you, Brother Waseem."

"And you, Brother Shahid." Waseem excused himself and returned almost immediately with a pastry dripping honey sitting on a small rectangle of thin waxed tissue. He stood there in his shirtsleeves, pulled a well-used handkerchief out of his rear pocket, and wiped his forehead as if it were summer as he watched the beggar stuff the treat into his mouth with ruined finger stubs, then wipe his lips with a ragged tunic sleeve.

"Are you well?"

The beggar shrugged and sipped tea. "As well I can be, thanks to God." He emptied the cup and, using both hands, offered it back to Waseem. The beggar looked around conspiratorially. "There were strangers here yesterday. I saw them by the Bibi Amna Mosque."

"Yes," Waseem nodded. "Four of them in Army uniforms. Captains. From Islamabad, I think." He paused. "Visiting the Military Academy, from the look of them."

"God be praised." The beggar picked up his sticks. "I always wanted to go to military school." He tapped his rag-wrapped stumps with one of them. "But God had other uses for me."

"God be praised."

The beggar sighed. "God be praised." And then he swiveled, pushed off, and foot by foot wheeled himself down the street to the corner by the Iqbal Market, where he sat for an hour, sometimes more, his back up against the wall, his wooden bowl in front of him, collecting alms—and intelligence.

■

It was the strangers who'd snagged the beggar's tripwire. Made him more than slightly nervous.

They were Pashto-speakers. Accents? Islamabad, the beggar thought. Maybe. Nah—better than maybe. But officers visiting the Pakistan Military Academy? No fricking way. These guys didn't walk or talk like soldiers. They were Intel professionals. They reeked ISI, Pakistan's Inter-Services Intelligence. And it was well known to the beggar that significant elements of ISI were sympathetic to al-Qaeda and the Taliban.

Moreover, operating under military cover was a common ISI tactic. In 2008 and 2009, some of the top-tier **International Security Assistance Force** (ISAF) units in Afghanistan, units that hunted for HVTs—high-value targets, in militaryspeak—operated with Pakistani "military observ-ers" embedded.

Except the embeds hadn't been military. They'd been ISI officers in uniform, and they reported back to Islamabad on the HVT hunters' sources, methods, and tactics.

And guess what? Shortly thereafter, HVTs in Afghanistan began to change their tactics and methods. And shortly after *that*, not a few of the sources who had led American forces to those HVTs were abducted, tortured, and murdered.

More to the point, the beggar had eyeballed these guys, and they'd been *looking*. Surveiling. Eliciting. Searching for an anomaly in this garrison city of thirty-five thousand souls.

Hunting for something specific.

And the beggar, whose Infidel name was Charlie Becker and whose legs and fingers had been blown off on Father's Day 2004 by an al-Qaeda in Iraq suicide bomber just out-side the city of Mahmudiya, and who currently occupied a GS-15, Step 10, slot at SAD, the Special Activities Divi-sion of the Central Intelligence Agency, knew exactly what anomaly yesterday's strangers had been seeking.

They were looking for a CIA safe house. A safe house that had been set up just about two months ago. A safe house that had been rented from an unsuspecting owner by false-flag recruited, anti-American Pakistanis who thought they were working for the Haqqani Network, a violent Afghani militia based in Pakistan's North Waziristan, where they ran training camps for foreign terrorists.

In point of fact, however, the hoodwinked Paks had rented the property on behalf of their—and the Haqqanis'—sworn enemy: America's Central Intelligence Agency.

Which then filled it with several million dollars' worth of high-tech eavesdropping and communications equipment, which was covertly, painstakingly, meticulously shipped in and set up, piece by piece by piece.

This was Valhalla Base, the safe house for which it was Charlie's job to provide countersurveillance and thus protection.

■

Charlie Becker, a retired U.S. Army Airborne Ranger master sergeant, had spent just over five and a half years in rehab after what he called "the nasty Iraqi incident." And since he had an innate talent for language, and since he had no intention of not working for a living or writing a tell-all book or getting by on a disability pension, and since he was someone who believed in the credo "Don't get mad, don't get even: get ahead," he'd spent that time prepping his mind as well as his body, learning the languages his enemies spoke.

Learning to speak them like a native.

He was currently fluent in Urdu and Pashto, and his Arabic wasn't bad either. Since January 2009 he'd spent most of his time down at Guantánamo working interrogations. He'd volunteered for Gitmo because it was the best way, he argued, to get his language skills where he wanted them. The best way, he harangued, to discuss Quranic law in Pashto and Urdu and get the damn phrases right. The best way, he knew right down to the marrow in his bones, to learn *how to pass*.

Charlie was no fool. He had discovered in Iraq that he could pass for Egyptian or Syrian. Until, that was, he opened his mouth. But now? Now he had all the tools.

And when he learned that CIA had got this . . . *thing* going in Abbottabad, he'd volunteered to play lonesome end and watch his comrades' backs.

So he'd left his prostheses in his Special Activities Division locker, set up in Camp Alpha, the secure compound in a far corner of Bagram Air Base in Afghanistan. The selfsame Camp Alpha compound that sat safely behind four layers of three-meter fence topped by concertina wire, patrolled by

K-9 security teams, and backstopped with a sensor system that cost more than Bill Gates and Warren Buffett made in a year, plus bonuses, combined.

It was the compound where, inside a hangar with a shielded roof that couldn't be seen by any loitering ISAF unmanned aerial vehicle or penetrated by Russkie or Chinese infrared or thermal-capable satellites, a hangar large enough to store three C-17 Globemaster-IIIs, the CIA was keeping some nasty little surprises for its most bodaciously, successfully reclusive HVTs.

Knowing what was going on inside that hangar and getting a peek at the items therein had been hugely motivational for Charlie Becker.

Which was why for six weeks he lived outside the hangar in the same clothes he was wearing now, with nothing but the cardboard shelter he'd constructed himself to shield him from the elements, and consuming the same seasoned lentil stew, *roti* flat bread, and sweet tea diet consumed by most poor Pakistanis. He bathed only occasionally, except for his stumps and hands, which he washed religiously before dawn, morning, noon, afternoon, and evening prayers, prayers he recited with the passion of the Salafist Jihadi into which he was metamorphosing.

He drank tepid Pak tap water and *zam-zam* fruit milk-shakes brought in from Abbottabad until his gut got used to them, which meant he wasn't shitting twelve times in one day or one time in twelve.

He practiced getting around on the padded furniture dolly—built from materials scrounged entirely in Pakistan—until it was second nature, worked on his Pashto until he was dreaming in the language, and radiated Pashtunwali from every pore. Then he ran himself through four weeks of painful, intense preparation until he knew his legend was firm, his cover secure, and his body ready for Show Time.

And it was—all of it, every bit of pain, every ounce of energy expended—worth it.

Worth it because this was going to be huge. Gargantuan. Broadway. Hollywood. The fricking Oscars.

This time, it was Crankshaft. UBL.

UBL. Usama. The ghost. The wraith. The Grail.

And Charlie would have a hand in this show. Not a bit part, either, but a featured role.

Covertly, of course. And anonymous. But still... featured.

If, that is, he survived.

2

Charlie Becker paused, checking the traffic, then pushed himself across Hospital Road, on the uneven edge between Abbottabad's commercial district with its three hospitals, and, to the northeast, the sprawling military complex housing the campus many Paks called the West Point of Pakistan. It was a city that in some ways reminded Charlie of Annapolis, Maryland, home of the U.S. Naval Academy. Not that there was a bay, or boats. But the cities had just about equal populations, and military academies, with their hundreds of young cadets. And Abbottabad was, like Annapolis, a place where denizens from the nation's capital could escape the heat. For those in D.C., it would be to spend summers or long weekends on the Chesapeake Bay. In Abbottabad's case, they'd come from Islamabad for the cool breezes that blew off the mountains to the north and west.

This morning the breezes were a lot more than cool. He'd

completed roughly one-eighth of the route he took every day, sitting in front of the mosques or cadging lentils with chicken, tea, and sweet cakes from friendly store owners with whom he gossiped or traded stories.

His circuit, which covered roughly five and a half kilometers—three-plus miles—varied from day to day. But it always covered 360 degrees. Its epicenter, more or less, was Valhalla Base, the CIA safe house he was watchdogging. One dog leg of Charlie's route often took him through the neighborhood called Bilal Town, clear around the outer perimeter wall of the location the retired master sergeant thought of as GZ. Ground Zero. The irregularly shaped compound that Valhalla Base had been set up to monitor.

The place was formidable. GZ sat surrounded on two sides by neatly plowed wheat fields. Other farmed plots held symmetrical rows of tomato plants, cauliflower, or cabbages.

Charlie took special notice of the perimeter walls, around whose base wild cannabis plants sprouted here and there like weeds. The walls were fifteen, sixteen, even eighteen feet high in some places. Every linear foot was topped by coiled barbed wire. Above and to the side of GZ's twin front gates a security camera had been installed.

Unlike virtually every other house in the neighborhood, GZ had no visible balconies. Neither did it have, unlike most of the other residential compounds in Abbottabad—ompounds that were mostly owned by retired general staff officers, senior government bureaucrats, or former intelligence officials—any satellite TV or Internet dishes on the roofs of its two main and three smaller outbuildings. Nor was there the spaghetti tangle of telephone wires and electrical power cables that were common to houses even in many of Pakistan's best neighborhoods.

In fact, Charlie thought the place looked much more like a

commercial structure, like the warehouses or small factories he'd grown accustomed to seeing in Iraq, than a luxury villa.

But a villa it was. Owned by two brothers, Arshad and Tareq Khan. But Charlie knew their names were aliases. "Arshad" was the brother who lived on-site. He drove a red Suzuki SUV or a white Suzuki van and told anyone who asked that he'd made his fortune as a gold trader in the south.

Mushtaq Sadiq, the gnarled, stooped farmer who grew tomatoes and cabbages on one of the plots adjacent to the compound, had told Charlie the previous week that Arshad and Tareq bought the land and built GZ five or six years ago, and more than a dozen people currently lived there. Mushtaq seemed to recall that they'd come from Charsadda. Charlie had nodded. He knew the city. It was on the North West Frontier, perhaps twenty miles northeast of Peshawar and sixty from the Khyber Pass. It was the location from which Tareq Khan had made a significant satellite phone call to GZ last July.

Charlie had seen Arshad only once, driving past in his red Suzuki SUV, one of his wives veiled behind darkly tinted windows, a young son sans seatbelt in the front passenger seat. Charlie ballparked Arshad to be in his forties. Height? Unknown. Appearance? Neat. Clean-shaven except for the brushlike Pashtun mustache favored by many of his apparent class, which was no doubt upper.

Verification? According to Arshad's farmer neighbor Mushtaq, Arshad's Pashto, the language of Pakistan's northwest tribal regions, was upper-class perfect, the Pakistani equivalent of the Oxbridge accent of British prime ministers. "He speaks like he's a Benazir Bhutto," was the way Mushtaq snidely put it to Charlie. Arshad Khan's real name—well, his war name, anyway—was Abu Ahmed al-Kuwaiti. And al-Kuwaiti was one of two high-level couriers trusted by Usama Bin Laden.

The younger brother, Tareq, had never appeared in the five and a half weeks since Charlie's insertion.

Charlie knew why, too: Tareq was out of town. In the Gulf. Taking messages from UBL to AQAP, which Charlie pronounced *a-kwap* and which stood for al-Qaeda in the Arabian Peninsula. Because Tareq Khan was UBL's second trusted courier.

■

Charlie knew all of this because even though Tareq Khan was pretty punctilious about maintaining operational security overseas, his cover had been blown about three years previously, despite the fact that he never communicated with Bin Laden except face to face. When Tareq Khan used cell phones—which was *v-e-r-y* infrequently—they were operated using a series of prepaid subscriber identity module, or SIM, cards that were bought for him by intermediaries at European locations where no one asked for their names.

It was a SIM card that had led investigators to Tareq Khan, a Swiss-made card, manufactured by a company called Swisscom. He had used the prepaid SIM card in September 2005 to make a single, thirty-second call from Dublin to his villa in Abbottabad to check up on his youngest son, Khalid, who was sick with pneumonia.

The call had been tracked by the British Government Communications Headquarters. Located in Cheltenham, GCHQ is the U.K. equivalent of America's National Security Agency. And when Khan made the call, GCHQ was in crisis mode, recovering from the July 7, 2005, London bombings in which fifty-two people were killed and another seven hundred injured by four terrorists, of which three were of Pakistani origin and two had actually received training in bomb making from al-Qaeda in northwest Pakistan. In those days GCHQ was tracking virtually every phone call from England and Ireland to Pakistan. When it was discerned that Khan was using a Swisscom card, the agency put a big target on his back.

Why? Because between 2001 and 2003, Swisscom SIM cards had been the favorite of many high-level al-Qaeda operatives, including the mastermind of the 9/11 attacks, Khalid Sheikh Mohammed, known to his counterterrorist hunters as KSM. It was, in fact, a Swisscom SIM card that had been used initially to track and locate KSM in Karachi.

By 2007 al-Qaeda operatives had largely abandoned Swisscom SIM cards. Too dangerous. But Tareq Khan used one anyway.

Why had he done that?

Charlie had no idea. Maybe Tareq thought that because the card had been bought before KSM was captured he would be safe. Maybe he was more concerned about his son than operational security. The *why* didn't matter. Khan had made the brief call, and he'd been ID'd.

And happily ever after, thought Charlie Becker, he'd been tracked.

By the Brits, by the Europeans, by the Saudis, and finally, by us.

Then, five months ago, in July, Tareq Khan made two satellite telephone calls. One on the twentieth, from a phone in Kohat, northwest Pakistan. The second from Charsadda on the twenty-second.

To a cell phone located at the villa in Abbottabad that Charlie called Ground Zero.

They lasted less than twenty seconds each. But in both, Tareq used *al mas*, the Arabic for "the Diamond," a known codeword for Bin Laden.

It was Tareq Khan that Valhalla Base was hoping to eyeball. Because if he showed up at the villa, it was oh so likely he was coming to see UBL. Which is why, even though UBL was still the Invisible Man, Valhalla Base had been set up in early October.

■

But now there were strangers in town. Not that there weren't always lots of visitors. Abbottabad's hotels played host to thousands of tourists and military families visiting their cadets. Scores of VIPs from Islamabad would come to the graduation ceremonies held every spring.

But these visitors were different. Waseem had seen four men. It hadn't taken Charlie even a full day to identify four *teams*. They were working separately, but they were all doing the same thing. They were combing the area around the military school and the residential neighborhoods just to the school's north and east, where Abbottabad's biggest villas were situated.

"Combing" was inaccurate; they were executing pattern searches. They divided their areas of operation into quadrants, and each team moved through each quadrant in exactly the same way. They went north to south, then south to north; east to west, then west to east. They drove, and they searched on foot.

Charlie knew exactly what they were doing. They were looking for anomalies. They were looking for things and people that didn't belong. And they were doing it relentlessly.

■

December 7, 2010, 1114 Hours

Charlie saw the Mercedes pull over by the Kabul Café, across four chaotic lanes of traffic shoehorned into the two-lane street redolent with exhaust fumes. He'd stationed himself next to a stand that made the fruit milkshakes known locally as *zam-zams*, to which he'd treat himself if his bowl was filled with enough paisa, anna, and occasional rupee coins to afford a splurge. Charlie lived on what Shahid made begging—nothing more.

He was on the second leg of his journey now, slowly working his way behind Valhalla Base. This was the base's E&E (evasion and escape) route because it led away from the military academy and Abbottabad's commercial center.

It had been a long morning. Charlie's arms and shoulders burned like hell and his stumps throbbed. It was almost lunchtime. He looked forward to chicken and lentil stew, another three hours on the streets, evening prayers, then making his way back to his room, where he would burst the day's report to Valhalla, which would carom it on to Langley.

The car's occupants caught his eye. Shit. It was a fifth surveillance team. There were four of them in the coffee-colored Mercedes diesel sedan, windows rolled down.

The sedan was parked, and no one in it moved. Silently Charlie counted. Thirty, sixty, ninety seconds. Still nothing. The occupants weren't even talking. Instead, they were eyeballing, examining, giving the whole street scene a three-sixty.

The driver, round-faced with a thin mustache, wore a captain's uniform. So did the guy riding shotgun, a big man with full facial hair. Then the rear door opened and a prissy-looking major got out. He straightened his uniform and inspected his trouser creases. Then he scanned the traffic, found a hole, and headed in Charlie's direction.

The momentary break in the traffic let Charlie catch a quick profile of the fourth passenger, a civilian sitting behind the driver, who had just turned to watch the major's progress. And was staring at Charlie. Staring hard.

Instantly Charlie became afraid.

Very afraid.

Oh, my God. Charlie's world went dark for a millisecond.

He sensed the major coming in his direction, stopping traffic with his hands.

And then, all of Charlie's survival skills, the ones he spent all that time at Bagram honing, kicked in.

Charlie forced himself to avert his eyes. Looked down at the few coins in his bowl. Then looked up, away from the Mercedes, smiling wanly, hand outstretched. "Something for a disabled brother, Major? Just a coin or two for a brother crippled by the Infidels?"

All the time thinking, *Jeezus H—I know the guy in the car. But that's impossible. Where the hell would I have—*

Guantánamo. Guantánamo, Guantánamo, Guantánamo.

Light-complexioned. Thick, dark, curly hair under an Afghan *qarakul*. Broad, flattened nose that looked like he'd spent time in the ring. Full, Jihadi beard.

Saif.

Saif Hadi al Iraqi.

Charlie's mind raced.

■

Real name: Nasser Abdulrazaq Abdulbaqi. Former major in Saddam's army. Fought in Afghanistan during the Soviet invasion. Joined al-Qaeda in the late 1990s. Starting in 2003, he coordinated al-Qaeda in Iraq's activities. The cocksucker was Abu Musab al-Zarqawi's boss. Personally beheaded maybe twenty, thirty people Charlie knew about, including four Americans. By 2004, when Charlie was working in Iraq for CIA, he'd heard the name Saif Hadi al Iraqi and knew he had blood all over his hands.

The SOB was picked up in Pakistan in 2006 and ended up at Gitmo. Deported to Yemen in December 2009, thanks to the blankety-blanking current attorney general of the United States, who spent most of his time trying to indict CIA officers for doing their jobs but turned terrorists loose so they could kill more Americans.

The idiot AG'd tossed Br'er Saif right back into the Briar Patch.

Saif Hadi. By trade an al-Qaeda murderer and bomb maker.

Saif Hadi, who'd helped train London's lead 7/7 suicide bomber, Mohammed Sidique Khan, when Khan made a terror pilgrimage to Pakistan in 2003.

Saif was the real fricking deal. A hard-core hater.

Charlie had spent two weeks interrogating the guy. In Arabic, Waziri Pashto, and Urdu.

Face to face.

Nose to nose.

Knows to knows. *He knows me, I know him.* He always had hate in his eyes. Always. Never gave an inch. Well, neither did I.

But now: oh, shit.

■

It was the one known unknown element of his Gitmo mission Charlie had worried about from the get-go. He understood that the al-Qaeda combatants he interrogated were spending just as much time studying him as he was studying them. Knew that most would ultimately return to work with the AQN, the al-Qaeda network, that if and when they were released from Gitmo, they'd spend their initial days, weeks, even months writing reports on every Infidel they'd met during their capture, incarceration, and interrogation. It was their job. To expand al-Qaeda's intelligence files. To build dossiers on their captors and interrogators. So they could be targeted.

Charlie's mind was working at warp speed now, thinking, *What the fuck does he know about me?* I worked under alias. I was Mr. José at Gitmo. Puerto Rican.

Even so: *Can he ID me, despite the beard, despite the grime, despite everything?*

Charlie had practiced good op-sec, operational security, during his fifteen months at Gitmo. Alias, Tito Puente mustache, tinted glasses, nothing personal on his person. A sterile uniform with *nada* but an American flag. Plus, he'd always been sitting at the desk when *they* were brought in, escorted blindfolded by two Marines. No way to tell his height, or know about his legs.

Besides, by the time Charlie began work at Camp X-Ray, he walked like everybody else. He could run five miles, stand all day, climb ladders, even dance. All it had taken was $575,000 or so worth of engineering and plastic surgery, and he was almost as good as new. Better than new. The new and improved bionic Becker.

But had all that op-sec been good enough?

Because here and now, Charlie was scared shitless.

Did the sonofabitch ID my prosthetics? Did he memorize the scars on my face? Draw sketches of my mangled hands for his handlers?

And the most important question: *Why is he here*?

Charlie knew that in intelligence work, there are no coincidences. Things never just happen. And so he knew Saif Hadi al Iraqi was in Abbottabad for a reason. Because ISI wanted him here. Why? To ID Gringos, of course. Infidel spies employed by the Great Satan. Saif had been at Gitmo, and before that, held in at least two black sites. He'd know people. Faces.

And he was being paid to ID them for ISI. Our alleged allies in GWOT—the Global War on Terror. Except they weren't our allies. Not really. Because if they were our allies and our friends, they wouldn't hire people like Saif Hadi al Iraqi, who had almost as much blood his hands as UBL. Who, in fact, knew UBL.

No wonder they'd brought Saif to Abbottabad. Holy mother of God.

■

The major ignored Charlie's plea. Walked past him like he didn't exist and up to the milkshake stand. Ordered four mango *zam-zams*. Charlie heard him speak. A southern accent, Karachi. Definitely not local.

Charlie forced himself: *Do not look at the Mercedes*. Concentrate on being All Shahid All the Time.

Live Shahid.

Breathe Shahid.

Reek of Shahidness.

Charlie kept his face slightly angled downward, so as not to present a profile to the Mercedes across the road. Profiles can give you away faster at a distance.

The major put money into the vendor's palm, collected his change, secured his drinks in their cardboard holder, and then turned toward the street. As he passed Charlie he looked down. Charlie glanced up into the man's dark eyes.

The major scowled. "And where were you wounded?" He had a high, irritating voice. The voice of a bureaucrat.

"Miram Shah, major. Missiles—near the girls school. They killed my son Muhammad." Charlie spat. "They do not care if they kill our children."

"When?"

"Last year. Winter."

The major nodded. Silent, as if thinking. His eyes narrowed. Then he peered at the Mercedes and spoke as if to himself. "The Americans are scum. They suck our blood. They defile our children. They spit on our traditions."

He reached into his pocket, then extended his hand. Half a dozen coins clattered into Charlie's bowl.

Charlie's hands covered his face in a gesture of gratefulness. "Thanks be to God, brother, and to you."

"God is all merciful," the major said, not bothering to look at Charlie. He stepped into the street, his free arm raised to stop traffic, and crossed, heedless of the honking and cursing of drivers.

Charlie counted to twenty-five, not daring to look up, concentrating on the coins in the bowl. Only when he heard the Mercedes' distinctive horn sound twice did he watch the car nose into traffic. Its tinted windows were rolled up.

He waited until they'd driven off, then fingered the coins to make sure they were real and not tracking devices.

Was he being paranoid?

No. He was being careful.

Careful because today the game had changed. Exponentially. *Five* teams. And Saif Hadi al Iraqi, working as an ISI finger-man.

The Paks were tightening the screws. Whatever had triggered their tripwire, it was undeniable they'd sensed something was up. Here. In beautiful downtown Abbottabad. This was not good news. Not for Charlie. Or Langley.

3

Once upon a time, Anthony Vincent Mercaldi, currently the twenty-first director of the CIA, had been a California attorney. He also had been a civil rights lawyer at the Department of Health, Education, and Welfare in the Nixon administration and an eight-term Democratic congressman, which he followed with an eighteen-month stint as director of the Office of Management and Budget. When the forty-second president of the United States realized at the height of the 1994 presidential campaign that he needed a real adult to oversee the unruly adolescents working in his White House, he'd appointed Mercaldi to be his chief of staff.

In other words, Anthony Vincent Mercaldi, who insisted that everybody call him Vince, was one of Washington's maybe half-dozen Big Time, Major League, superstar go-to guys.

Normally at this hour, Call Me Vince would have been doing his daily five miles on a treadmill in the basement gym at CIA headquarters, watching Al Jazeera's English-language channel, CNN International, or the Beeb.

But 0645 in Langley, Virginia, was 1545 in Abbottabad, Pakistan—3:45 P.M. in civilianspeak.

And Abbottabad was on Vince's mind. More to the point, Charlie Becker was on his mind.

He'd met personally with Charlie three weeks before he left for Bagram to do his final mission prep. Invited Charlie for a one-on-one lunch on fine bone china bearing the CIA seal in the private Director's Dining Room that was adjacent to his office. Of course he had. Vince Mercaldi was a congressman at heart. He'd always thought of the House of Representatives as the People's House, and for the sixteen years he held office he'd taken as much time as needed to get together with his constituents whenever they came calling or when he was back home taking the political pulse of his district.

He brought that meet-and-greet tradition with him to the seventh-floor suite of offices at Langley when he became D/CIA. How, he had reasoned, could you ask a man or woman to put their lives on the line and not look them in the eye?

So now he was reading the flash cable Charlie had burst-transmitted as soon as he could after his encounter with Saif Hadi al Iraqi. And Vince was worried. About Charlie, whom he both liked and admired, and about The Operation.

It wasn't the first time The Operation he'd fought to mount had been jeopardized. The previous October, just as CIA's Bin Laden Group (BLG), the successor to Alec Station, the first of the CIA's working groups devoted exclusively to Usama Bin Laden and al-Qaeda, was setting up the Abbottabad safe house, some idiot NATO officer (Vince had his staff run it to ground and discovered the culprit was a pussy-chasing Norwegian lieutenant colonel trying to ingratiate himself with a Brussels-based female reporter) had told

CNN that UBL wasn't hiding in some cave in Afghanistan or the Federally Administered Tribal Areas, but living the life of Reilly in a villa somewhere in northwest Pakistan.

Of course, CNN immediately put it on the air. Who wouldn't have?

At Langley, bells and whistles went off. By October the BLG had more than 250 people working under the cover of CIA's Special Activities Division, but in point of fact it was a stand-alone unit reporting directly to two people: CIA Director Vince Mercaldi and Stuart Kapos, the director of the National Clandestine Service, the successor to the old Directorate of Operations.

A straight line. No middlemen.

BLG was virtually unique at Langley in that unlike most covert units, its existence had never leaked. The whole world knew that there was a CIA Bin Laden unit called Alec Station. Indeed a former Alec Station chief was a constant bloviator on cable news shows, where he pummeled CIA regularly. And everyone knew about CIA's CTC, the Counter-Terrorism Center, originally created by the legendary spy Duane "Dewey" Clarridge in 1986 and still in full operation against America's enemies.

But very few individuals—certainly no one on leak-prone Capitol Hill—were cleared to know about the covert intelli-gnomes who had been working in a secure, cipher-locked suite of offices located in the subbasement of the new CIA headquarters building since late the previous July. The individuals who worked there were listed under their previous assignments. The sign on the door read "Special Activities Division: AFPAK Technical Support Group." And that's how the unit was listed in CIA's internal phone book. But it was BLG—all Bin Laden, all the time.

It was a potpourri of talent, each one hand-picked. There were linguists, analysts, and operations officers from the

National Clandestine Service and its Special Activities Division (SAD); there were intel squirrels, psy-ops specialists, SEALs, Delta Force operators, and other snake-eating individuals from the Joint Special Operations Command (JSOC) at Fort Bragg, North Carolina, and there were Soldiers and contractors from the Army's most nimble counterterrorist-slash-counterinsurgency-slash-unconventional warfare unit, the Asymmetric Warfare Group from Fort Meade, Maryland.

It was a first: BLG was a task force of organically integrated intelligence and operations personnel with an established chain of command and the authority to initiate both long-term and actionable intelligence gathering and then exploit that intel in its own unilateral operations. It was a seamless integration of CIA's intelligence-gathering and paramilitary capabilities and JSOC's unique talent pool. Its budget ran well into ten figures. And it all revolved around one mission objective: to find and kill Usama Bin Laden.

Some of the personnel had been focused on Bin Laden for more than a decade. But the BLG was the first entity that allowed them to work as part of a holistic team. For the first few weeks, BLG had met only at night, so its members wouldn't attract attention. Then, when the information started to build more rapidly, they went full time with Vince Mercaldi's complete support. In fact from the very first days, the director met daily with BLG's chief, Richard Hallett, to monitor the group's progress.

And on the first of September, Hallett told Call Me Vince that they had found UBL—at least they believed strongly that they'd found the sonofabitch. The courier named Tareq Khan, the man who used the phrase *al mas,* "the Diamond," had returned to the villa. The people at BLG were convinced beyond a shadow of a doubt that Tareq had come home in order to deliver a long-awaited message to Usama.

Tareq's return to Abbottabad was one of the reasons Charlie Becker was now in Pakistan. And why Dick Hallett, a supergrade spook who'd come of age in the Marine Corps but spent the past twenty-nine years as an operations officer in some of the world's most nasty places, had, by Labor Day and with the strong encouragement of Vince Mercaldi and D/NCS Kapos, begun some complicated and hugely sensitive advance work. Hallett's efforts resulted in the establishment of a covert CIA safe house 250 yards from the Abbottabad villa in which Hallett and his top analyst, whom he called Spike, believed Usama Bin Laden was living.

Then, on October 18, not ten days after the safe house had been set up, CNN broadcast the NATO-sourced "Bin Laden's living in a villa in Pakistan" story, and back at Langley all hell broke loose. Quietly. Covertly. But very, very intensely.

The reverberations had taken almost a week to quell.

That first day of panic, Vince Mercaldi himself assumed hands-on management of BLG's damage control. He had the presence of mind—the genius, Dick Hallett said later—to immediately call Richard Holbrooke, the veteran diplomat, consummate Washington insider, and the president's special envoy to Pakistan.

Dick Holbrooke had no idea what was going on in Abbottabad because, as one of Washington's most sieve-like leakers, he of all people wasn't cleared to know. Which is why Vince called him and told him in hushed tones, "This is for your ears only, Dick, please! I can assure you that so far as CIA is concerned, the CNN story is pure horse puckey. It's wishful thinking. Irresponsible fiction. NATO's got its head up its ass."

That confidential whisper was passed on to Holbrooke's press corps favorites within minutes. On background, of course.

Vince laughed out loud when he'd read his precise

words—the printable ones, unattributed—in the next day's papers.

These were dicey times, when the Justice Department was crawling all over CIA looking to prosecute someone, anyone because of those so-called enhanced interrogation methods. And congressional intelligence oversight committees were demanding that CIA never lie, cheat, steal, or do anything that Boy Scouts wouldn't do. Which is why Vince's staff had to be goddamn contortionists to come up with on-the-record answers that were misleading enough to put the story to sleep, but not come back and bite CIA on its well-scarred ass when the truth about Abbottabad finally came out.

■

Vince focused on Charlie Becker's cable. Five teams of Paki gumshoes and one Guantánamo knucklehead—a very dangerous Guantánamo knucklehead, to boot—working a city of thirty-five thousand. Shit.

"Obviously, the Pakistanis are worried, right?" He shook the sheet of paper at the National Clandestine Service's top spook. "Stu, whatta you think?"

Stuart Kapos had twenty-eight years under his belt as an officer in CIA's clandestine service. Now he ran it. A big man who'd played football at the Naval Academy, he still ran marathons at age fifty-five. Kapos, who was known Agency-wide as a no-shit guy, sipped his coffee, placed the mug on the glass top of the director's desk, and leaned back in the armchair that faced Mercaldi. "I think what you think, Boss. The Paks are worried that we're doing something." He smiled. "And y'know, they're right."

"We have no proof UBL's in Abbottabad."

"Not yet."

"And we've committed hundreds of millions of dollars to this operation so far—with no real evidence that he's there."

"You know who they used to quote at the Academy? John Paul Jones: 'He who will not risk cannot win.'"

"Easy for you to say," the D/CIA said. "You're covert. I'm the one who's gonna get his ass handed to him in public if I have to tell Congress we've flushed a shitload of the people's money down the toilet."

"That's why you got the big car and all those bodyguards." Kapos scratched his shaved head. "I spoke with Dick Hallett and Spike before I came up here. Let me give you BLG's take on Charlie's cable. They say, Okay, let's say the Paks know—or at least a few of them know—UBL actually *is* in the Khan brothers' compound in Abbottabad. So, the Paks think, what if those stupid Americans might have listened to that NATO guy, and now they're starting to wonder if UBL isn't hiding out in some cave in Waziristan, but living large in Pakistan. And what if the Great Satan is sending the dreaded CIA onto our sovereign soil to check the NATO story out. And what if the Great Satan has spies in Abbottabad, where we know UBL is stashed, and they actually find him. Then we Pakistanis are fucked. Because we've lied to our biggest cash cow."

"Hmmm. And?"

"And so Spike's analysts believe the Paks—or at least those Paks protecting UBL—are sending a full-court press of ISI co-conspirators to Abbottabad to make sure we're specifically not operating there."

The director scratched his ear.

Kapos continued: "Because they're sure as hell not pulling a full-court press anywhere else. Not Lahore, not Peshawar, not Islamabad or Karachi or Rawalpindi. Nowhere but Abbottabad.

"Spike takes this full-court press as a very positive sign. Because you know and I know that when we lay our hands on UBL—and we will—and he's been living in a city where all the top generals and intelligence pashas retire? UBL surrounded by the cream of Pakistan's military and intelligence crop? And if we kill him right under their noses? They'll do more than shit a few bricks. They'll shit Yankee fucking Stadium."

"Hmmm." The director sat silently for half a minute, contemplating the ceiling. Then he said, "Okay, Stu, let's say you're right. UBL's in Abbottabad. So, what do we do to keep the Paks at bay?"

Kapos shrugged and pointed to the coffee cup he had set down on the director's desk. "Follow the instructions on my mug."

Vince turned the mug until he could read what was printed on it: "ADMIT NOTHING. DENY EVERYTHING. FILE COUNTERCHARGES." He laughed. "That's it?"

"Well, in a nutshell, yes."

"Funny, Stu. Very funny." The director's expression turned serious. "Look, if BLG is right, then we have to distract them. Draw their attention away from Abbottabad. From Valhalla. Divert their focus."

"Exactly," Kapos's head nodded in agreement. "Remember Sun Tzu."

Vince's brow furrowed. "Sun Tzu?"

"He wrote, 'All warfare is deception.'" The operations officer sipped his coffee. "Today's Pearl Harbor Day. Remember how the Japanese kept Roosevelt busy negotiating smoke and mirrors while Isoroku Yamamoto's fleet was steaming east to Hawaii? We need to expose the Pakis to some of the same kind of three-card Monte smoke and mirrors."

Vince laid Charlie's cable on his desk facedown and moved his hands back and forth across the glass as if he were shifting folded playing cards. "Keep your eyes on the ace and win twenty bucks."

"Which you never win. Exactly."

The D/CIA stared at his deputy. "And I bet you already have a deception operation in mind."

Stu Kapos hooked a thumb in his red-white-and-blue suspenders and Cheshire-cat smiled at his boss. "You got another ten minutes for me?"

"I've got all day if you need it."

"Ten minutes. It's so KISS." Kapos caught the quizzical look on the D/CIA's face. "KISS—Keep it simple, stupid." He grinned. "You'll love it."

"Do we have to brief the Hill?"

Kapos shook his head. "Nope, players are already all in place. I'll use two teams from our Whiskey Trio targeting program. Whiskey Trio is run out of Special Activities Division. Congress was already briefed. So BLG can keep on keepin' on."

That made Vince happy. No congressional briefings meant no leaks. The D/CIA put both elbows on his desk and interlaced his fingers. "Talk away, Boychik."

4

Boatswain's Mate Second Class (SEAL) Troy Roberts, BUD/S (Basic Underwater Demolition/SEALS) Class 237, finished the eight minutes of stretching he did every morning so he wouldn't cramp up as he ran his eight miles. This morning's course would take him west, around Lake Trashmore, then south and east, where he ran the perimeter of the Bow Creek Country Club. Other days meant other routes. It was part of Roberts's normal operational security pattern.

Op-sec was central to Troy's lifestyle—and his family's as well. Whenever she was asked, his wife, Brittany, would tell people that Troy worked as part of a Navy logistics team that supported the SEAL teams, even though she knew it was a lie. She lied because her husband was a Navy SEAL whose missions, like the actual name of his unit, were classified top secret.

The ability to maintain this bifurcated existence had

been part of the selection process. Troy had undergone a
battery of psychological tests to ensure that he was not a
sociopath nor had any other personality disorder. The results also showed him to be the one in several hundreds of
thousands of individuals who could kill efficiently, brutally,
in any number of ways, then turn the switch and go home to
be a loving father and husband. In other words, he was the
ideal special warfare operator.

That was good, because the ultimate cost of his constant
training would run into the low seven figures. He could pick
locks, hotwire cars, work ciphers, jump out of perfectly
good aircraft, and launch a minisub off the deck of a sub-
merged nuclear boomer. During his short tenure in his current unit, the baby-faced youngster had killed more than two
dozen individuals. Not at a distance, either, but up close and
personal. And yet unlike the SEALs at Little Creek Amphibious Base, where SEAL Teams Two, Four, Eight, and
Ten had their quarterdecks, Troy seldom wore the eagle,
flintlock pistol, and trident device, ubiquitously known to
SEALs as the Budweiser, in public.

That was because except on rare occasions, or when he
was deployed overseas, Troy didn't wear a uniform. He went
to work in civvies, jeans mostly, and long overshirts that
concealed the Glock 26 in its well-used Kydex and horse-
hide Crossbreed holster and the Emerson LaGriffe last-ditch
knife that hung on a chain around his neck, both of which
he carried even when he took his daily runs. Only when he
had passed through the single-lane checkpoint that led to
the Dam Neck Fleet Training Center, a twelve-minute commute from his home, would he sometimes change into some
of the clothing and use some of the equipment the military
had issued him.

There was a lot of it, too. What the American taxpayer

had bought for the twenty-four-year-old, dark-haired Minnesotan whose radio call sign was T-Rob filled a standard twenty-foot dry freight container. That is, a steel box nineteen feet ten inches in length, eight feet six inches high, and eight feet wide. Filled it almost to overflowing.

That container, and dozens more just like it, each containing the equipment of a single SEAL, sat in a warehouse-like structure just east of Regulus Avenue and just north of Lake Tecumseh, at the northernmost edge of the sprawling Dam Neck campus that was the headquarters for Roberts's unit, the Naval Special Warfare Development Group, commonly referred to as DEVGRU.

DEVGRU was the current unclassified designator for the unit formerly known as SEAL Team Six. ST6 had been established in the wake of the disastrous hostage rescue attempt by Delta Force that ended with the debacle at Desert One on April 25, 1980, which cost the lives of eight American servicemen and the United States of America immeasurable loss of stature and prestige among both allies and adversaries. By late October of that year, ST6's first CO, Commander Richard Marcinko, had hand-selected the unit's initial seventy-two SEALs—Plankowners, in Navy parlance—plucking them from SEAL Team One in Coronado, California, and SEAL Team Two, based in Little Creek, Virginia.

Marcinko trained SEAL Team Six hard. The newly minted counterterrorists shot thousands of rounds of ammunition; perfected jumping out of planes at thirty-thousand-plus feet; endlessly practiced boarding cruise ships, tankers, and container vessels under way using flexible caving ladders and pure brute upper-body strength; honed assault tactics on everything from oil platforms to passenger jets to railroad trains. They deployed from submarines and commercial aircraft. They cross-trained with our allies' best counterterror units: Britain's Special Air Service and the Royal Marines' Special Boat Squadron, Germany's GSG-9, and Israel's Sayeret Matkal.

But by the mid-1980s, ST6 had come under a cloud. Despite the undeniable fact that Six's shooters were among the most capable in the world, unit discipline was known to be lax. Excessive drinking was commonplace, and fiscal restraint was acknowledged to be virtually nonexistent.

The Naval Criminal Investigative Service initiated an investigation. Ultimately several of Six's personnel, including its former commanding officer, Marcinko, were indicted, and some were subsequently convicted of felonies. Marcinko himself served a year in the minimum security section of the federal prison complex at Petersburg, Virginia. The charge: "Conspiracy to defraud the United States to commit bribery, Title 18, U.S.C., section 371."

The upshot was that in 1987 the Navy changed the unit's name in the hope that the stains on its reputation would be forgotten. They weren't—not for another decade.

Nor did the new name really enter the lexicon. The Navy may have called the unit DEVGRU, but to most Sailors, and in popular culture, YouTube videos, computer games, and Rogue Warrior boy-book novels, it was—and always would be—SEAL Team Six.

■

0512 Hours

The temperature read thirty-six degrees as Troy turned into the wind and kicked into stride. The cold didn't bother him; he always ran in shorts no matter what the weather, although his body core was protected by three layers of state-of-the-art, virtually weightless windproof and waterproof clothing topped by a fleece watch-cap.

Running had always been therapeutic for Troy. Even during BUD/S, the six months of hell all SEALs go through during their initial selection process, when all selectee candidates run a total of more than eight hundred miles, he had used the running sessions to zone out and let accumulated stress drain from his exhausted body.

Selection for DEVGRU was even tougher. Of the fourteen selectees who entered the six-month training cycle at Green Squadron in the fall of 2007, Troy was the only one to make it through.

But BUD/S—even Hell Week, when Class 237, which had originally numbered more than eighty, was whittled down to a few dozen and ultimately to eighteen—wasn't anything compared to what was happening now.

His career at DEVGRU was on the line, which meant his Navy career was, too. Because Troy couldn't see himself as anything but a SEAL. He'd enlisted in the Navy at eighteen, volunteered for BUD/S at the earliest possibility, and after two years at SEAL Team Four, made the selection cut for DEVGRU.

The bottom line was this: he was fully aware that he was living his dream and he'd never be able to settle for less. What would happen to him if they yanked his security clearance? He'd be out in the cold. With the economy in the toilet, a mortgage, Brittany with only a part-time job, their five-and-a-half-year-old son, Corbin, in day care, and a baby on the way. They'd lose the house. Everything. What would his pastor say? Troy was a devout and committed Christian. He and Brittany were active in their church.

This was not good. Not good at all.

It had been two months ago, almost to the day, when Troy was a member of the SEAL element tasked with rescuing a British national named Linda Norgrove, a thirty-six-year-old aid worker for a U.S. nongovernmental organization. Norgrove had been kidnapped on September 26 in Kunar Province, eastern Afghanistan. U.S. drones tracked her and her three Afghan colleagues as they were taken to a walled compound in Korengal Province. Using technical means—laser technology from the National Security Agency and imagery from the National Geospatial Agency—it was determined beyond a doubt that the kidnappers intended to mutilate and kill the hostages.

A nighttime rescue mission was put together. A six-man assault element from Red Squadron was assigned the task by Task Force 131's commander.

Six of Norgrove's kidnappers were killed in the initial assault, and during the chaos of that firefight, Norgrove managed to break free. But none of the SEALs saw this, and from the roof of one of the huts on the compound, one of the SEALs caught movement and instinctively tossed a grenade. Moments later, a mortally wounded Norgrove was discovered near the shredded body of a kidnapper.

During the mission debrief, the Red Squadron shooters never mentioned the grenade. First reports said Norgrove was killed because one of her captors exploded the suicide vest he was wearing, which paralleled the story the SEALs told during their initial debriefing.

But subsequent questioning by the Joint Special Operations Command task force commander, an Army Ranger lieutenant colonel who'd been watching the mission on Predator video, made it clear there had been no suicide vest. The commander's review of the video showed one of the SEALs lobbing a grenade.

It was only then that the SEAL who had done it stepped forward. He was certain to face an inquiry that could lead to disciplinary action up to and including a less than honorable discharge. But the others were liable, too, because they had committed the sin of omission. They hadn't lied; they had remained silent. Betrayed their honor code. The fact that Norgrove had been killed by mistake troubled Troy, but didn't affect him, or the rest of his shipmates. They had all participated in scores of similar missions and understood that war is messy and that people—sometimes innocents—get killed, often by friendly fire. What was more troubling was the psychological disruption to the team. The incident and the subsequent investigation jarred them out of synch. The dynamics of the inquiry caused them to become individuals, as opposed to acting in unison. For the present, their unit integrity was shattered. Plus, their careers were in limbo. It was not a healthy situation.

Nine weeks later, Troy's career was still on the line. Charlie Troop's deployment had been curtailed. These days he was shackled to a desk at Dam Neck while the powers that be mulled his and his shipmates' fates.

Worse, Red Squadron itself, and by extension all of DEVGRU, was under microscopic examination by some of the Navy's manager-bureaucrats up in D.C., many of whom—ship drivers, Airedales, or submariners—bore no love for SEALs, whom they thought of as cowboys, loose cannons, or worse. And the Norgrove disaster only served to reinforce those negative opinions.

But this was a different Navy and a different SEAL team from the old days. The old days, so Troy had heard, resembled the stuff that went on in the old movie *Navy SEALs*: lots of drinking, fast cars, and faster women. Outrageous behavior was all too often encouraged by SEAL officers and senior NCOs.

Not today. Today a single DUI could cause you to lose your top-secret clearance—and your job with the teams.

So could a morals infraction. Today's SEALs were far less likely than the frogs of the 1980s to spend nights out drinking at one of Virginia Beach's many saloons. For T-Rob and most of his shipmates, it was one beer, maybe two, polished off at home. Because God help you if you got a short-fuse summons on your BlackBerry and you weren't sober and ready to deploy.

But the situation wasn't hopeless. Troy had two aces up his sleeve who might help his cause: JSOC's ultimate commander was one; Troy's close friend and teammate was the other.

COM/JSOC, the man to whom all DEVGRU SEALs ultimately reported, was himself a SEAL. Vice Admiral Wesley Bolin, USNA '76 and BUD/S Class 95 (1978), had commanded SEAL Team Three in Coronado, then DEVGRU itself, and served in the number three position on the staff at the U.S. Special Operations Command in Tampa. Like his immediate predecessor at JSOC, Lieutenant General Stanley McChrystal, Wes Bolin was a lead-from-the-front operator who often accompanied assault elements of Task Force 131, which specialized in capture/kill missions against high-value targets.

Bolin was also a scholar of warfare in general, and of special operations in particular, who understood that what war ultimately came down to was killing people and breaking things. And that winning meant doing it to them before they did it to you.

In fact, in 1994, as a student at the Naval Postgraduate School in Monterey, California, Lieutenant Commander Wes Bolin had inspired his fellow student and SEAL Team Three colleague Bill McRaven to write *Spec Ops: Eight Case Studies*, a seminal work on special operations warfare. The book, published commercially a year later, dissected eight significant special operations warfare ops, including disasters (Operation Chariot, Britain's 1942 raid on St. Nazaire), triumphs (the U.S. Army Ranger raid on the Cabanatuan prison camp in January 1945 and Operation Jonathan, Israel's 1976 Entebbe Raid), and dry holes (Operation Kingpin, the U.S. Army's abortive raid on Son Tay in 1970). McRaven had almost dedicated the book to Wes.

Troy had met Admiral Bolin, an Arizona native and former Naval Academy football letterman, during one of the JSOC commander's frequent visits to Afghanistan. Wes Bolin had even ridden in Troy's helo on two capture/kill missions. So the young SEAL knew he and his teammates would get a fair shake from the boulder-chested admiral with a bone-crushing handshake, whose radio call sign was Slam. It was Admiral Slam, after all, who had, more than once in public, referred to the politically correct, zero-defect Naval Pentagoners currently calling for Red Squadron's heads on pikes as "perfumed princes." And who was one of the few flag officers who regularly displayed loyalty *down* his chain of command as well as demanding that it bubble up from the bottom.

Troy's other ace was Alpha Troop's master chief. Danny Walker was Red Squadron's official Old Man. Now forty-three, he had enlisted in the Navy after five years in the 82nd Airborne. He went through BUD/S Class 203 at age twenty-nine, the oldest candidate by four years. He'd been at DEVGRU for a decade now and was not only Troy's best friend, but also his mentor and coach. They even attended the same church.

Danny's advice had been short and sweet: "Think of this as Purgatory, T-Rob. It'll sort out. And I've got your back. So keep your mind in neutral, your ass in gear, and your hatches dogged."

■

It began to drizzle. Troy glanced up and scanned the horizon. There were gray clouds overhead, but he could see blue sky to the west. The rain wouldn't last long. He picked up his pace, anxious to finish his PT and get to the office.

He hated doing nothing, and he knew the longer he was deprived of the shoot house, the helos, all the training that kept his skills honed, the longer it would take to get them back. But God, Troy believed—believed to his very core— had his reasons. There was a plan. Of course he didn't know what it was, but it was there. Just as surely as God had allowed him to survive BUD/S and Green Squadron selection, just as surely as He'd given Troy the talent that allowed him to jump out of a perfectly good aircraft seven miles above the Earth's surface, fast-rope from a helo, breach a door, and pull the trigger on a high-value target.

Yeah, life sucked right now. But God had a plan, and He would see Troy through. So Troy's faith would keep him on an even keel until God revealed His hand and—dear Jesus, please—sent him back to war.

On the secular side, Troy also knew deep in his heart two of the basic truths that all SEALs know: first, that the suckiest job at DEVGRU or any SEAL team was a bucketload better than anything else the Navy had to offer. And the second? One of Troy's BUD/S instructors had said it best. It was during Hell Week, the evening of the second day. They hadn't had any sleep yet. He'd had them rolling around in the cold surf—it was late February—then in the sand. Back and forth.

They were called whistle drills. First whistle, you hit the surf. Second whistle, you hit the beach. Third whistle, you crawled through the soft sand toward the instructors. Hit the water. Hit the beach. Roll and crawl. It went on for more than an hour. By the time the punishment ended, Troy's soggy, sand-infiltrated camo fatigues weighed thirty pounds and his legs, back, shoulders, and chest were scraped raw. His ankles were bloody from the chaffing sand in his boots. He was sliding past the edge of hypothermia, shivering so hard he almost couldn't stand up.

That was when he saw the next stage of Hell Week torture. Each six-trainee boat crew got its own telephone pole. First, they did twenty-five sit-ups, the telephone pole clutched to their chests. Then the pole got hoisted onto their shoulders. And was carried. For a mile. On the beach. In the wet sand. In the dark.

After less than a hundred yards, with his muscles burning, splinters digging into his shoulder, and half a dozen missteps when he thought his ankle was going to snap in two, Troy seriously, genuinely thought he was going to die.

That was the whole idea of Hell Week. Even though he couldn't enunciate it at that point, Troy understood instinctively that it wasn't the gazelles who would survive Hell Week, or the buffed-out weightlifters, or the me-first high school or college quarterbacks. It was the grunts—he hoped he was one of them—who just . . . kept . . . going. The grunts who drove through the pain and the hurt and the cold and helped their swim buddies make it through, too. The ones who never, ever gave up.

So Troy fought through the pain and the splinters and the swollen ankles. And the cold, the all-consuming, mind-numbing, totally penetrating cold. Cold he'd never come close to experiencing before. And at the end of that long, excruciating mile, when the instructors finally allowed them to drop the telephone poles and collapse, that was when Troy discovered the truth about life as a SEAL.

"Tomorrow," the surfer-tan instructor had barked through his megaphone at the miserable trainees as they lay beyond exhaustion on the cold sand. "Tomorrow I'll have you tad-

poles doing shit that'll make you think tonight was frickin' fun."

"Oh, yeah," he shouted, backpedaling on the beach barefoot, a big fat Cuban Cohiba Siglo VI in his right hand. "Big frickin' *F-U-N!*"

The instructor had almost tripped over himself he was laughing so hard. "Tomorrow, you'll learn the only easy day . . . was frickin' *yes-ter-d-a-a-y!!*"

5

Ty Weaver dropped his cell phone into the secure locker outside the door of the consulate's Regional Security Office, where the facility's Sensitive Compartmentalized Information Facility, or SCIF, was located. He punched the cipher into the keypad and, careful not to disturb the plastic holly wreath, pulled the door open.

Weaver, thirty-six, was listed by the consulate as a technical and security consultant who owned Kronos International, an Orlando, Florida, security company. In point of fact, Kronos was a CIA front, and Weaver, who had spent seven years as an operator at Delta Force, the Army's Tier One hostage rescue and counterterrorist unit based at Fort Bragg, was currently a GS-14 working for the Ground Branch of CIA's Special Activity Division (SAD), the Agency's paramilitary arm.

He'd joined CIA in 2007, shortly after he'd served on a joint CIA-Delta mission in northwest China. Since then, he'd done two six-month tours in Afghanistan and a four-month temporary duty assignment (TDY) at the U.S. Embassy in Islamabad. For the past ten months, he'd been back home in Ashburn, Virginia, with his wife, Patty, working as an instructor at the West Virginia facility the Agency used to train its personnel in evasive and defensive driving maneuvers. It was perfect: a reverse commute every morning out to Summit Point, and home by five.

But in mid-October, Rich Erwin, SAD's branch chief for special operations, had called him in and asked him to volunteer for a second TDY to Islamabad. The Agency needed an operator who knew the lay of the land to get out in the boonies and spot targets for its armed Predator drones. Ty had the experience in-country, as well as the tradecraft capabilities and the technical knowhow. So, would he go?

It was the absolute worst of times, and Ty let Erwin know why. Patty was five months pregnant. She'd had a miscarriage the previous year, and her doctor had ordered her to take things easy this time. This would be their first child. The Agency had promised that he wouldn't have to travel until mid-2011.

He looked across the desk, furious that the branch chief had even brought the subject up.

Rich Erwin shrugged sympathetically. "Hey, I know how tough this is for you," he said. "Problem is, we've just created a joint special program element with the Asymmetric Warfare Group's D Squadron."

That was news to Ty. For years the military's special operations units and the Agency had had a prickly relationship. It was a leadership culture thing: sure, they'd been forced by circumstance and mission requirements to work together, but it was for the most part oil-and-water. The operators were fine; many had come from Tier One units or Marine recon. But at the top, there'd been no homogeneity, no symbiosis, very little of the finish-each-other's-sentences kind of unit integrity practiced by Tier One operators.

But now the D/CIA had formed a tight working relationship with Wes Bolin over at JSOC. They did better than just get along—they actually enjoyed one another's company. Big things were in the works. This TDY was, for lack of a better term, the test program to see if the top-down relationship would transfer to bottom-up.

"Which is why we need you, Ty. You're basically the only guy here who knows both Pakistan and the folks at Meade well enough to integrate on short notice."

Ty had to admit Rich had a point. SAD had its share of SEALs and Marines. But D Squadron, which was one of the two classified mission components of the Fort Meade–based AWG, was staffed in large part by former Delta operators and Airborne Rangers from the 75th Ranger Regiment. Ty had put in three years at the 1-75 before he'd been selected for Delta. Plus, he'd worked closely with AWG's C Squadron in Helmand Province in Afghanistan in 2008 and 2009. He'd helped them refine an effective method for identifying and targeting high-value targets, Taliban bomb makers, and fabricators of the al-Qaeda network's improvised explosive devices (IEDs).

The tactics had originally been developed in Iraq back in 2005 and 2006 by the counter-IED program named Constant Hawk. But they were significantly improved and enhanced in Helmand under the Asymmetric Warfare Group's Whiskey Solo program.

And now CIA wanted to adapt Whiskey Solo to the unique mission requirements of AFPAK, the Afghan-Pakistan theater. The new compartment would be called Whiskey Trio. The main challenge? Whiskey Trio had to operate completely under the radar, because the ultranationalistic Pakis went batshit every time some Jihadi was blown into the well-known smithereens by a Hellfire.

Rich said, "It's only four weeks."

"A critical four weeks, so far as Patty's concerned."

"We'll check up on her." Rich read the skeptical look on Ty's face. "I'm serious, dude. Daily, if you want. Get her full-time care, if that's what it takes."

Ty looked at his boss with pursed lips. "Goddammit, Rich." He stood up. "I'm going down to the cafeteria for some coffee."

Rich's expression remained neutral. "Sure, go on, think it over. But bring me back a cup, okay? Black, no sugar."

▪

Of course he'd volunteered. At heart, Ty was still a Soldier who believed in the old-fashioned values of Duty, Honor, Country. Even so, he'd wrung extra funds out of Rich Erwin so that Patty would be covered 24/7 while he was gone. And on the upside, the TDY would give him a chance to catch up with his old Delta compadre, call-sign Loner, who was running AWG's D Squadron these days. Loner was a lanky, dark-haired chief warrant officer who lived in Maryland about a forty-five-minute drive from Meade. He was the best pistol shot Ty had ever worked with. And one of the hardest workers.

Ty would travel in the same way as on his first TDY to Pakistan: on an official—as opposed to a diplomatic—passport and under the alias of Tim White. His cover was technical security consultant to the U.S. Embassy in Islamabad and the American Consulate in Lahore.

Loner and two other D Squadron shooters, Kent and Gary, would also come in on burgundy (official) passports as contract security personnel detailed to work as drivers for the State Department's regional security officer in Islamabad. The RSO would then detail them to the Lahore consulate.

On paper, Ty would report to the RSOs in Lahore and Peshawar to do security surveys; in essence, he would be the advance man for diplomatic forays. Which he would indeed do, to maintain what is called in the intelligence business "cover for status." Ty needed cover for status because both consulates, as well as the embassy in Islamabad, were chock-ablock with personnel the State Department called FSNs: Foreign Service nationals. FSNs were required because, to be blunt, not very many American diplomats are fluent in the language of the country to which they are assigned. Currently, for example, the entire State Department had only six diplomats who spoke fluent Pashto, and none of them worked in Lahore. It was therefore FSNs, not FSOs (U.S. Foreign Service officers) who actually carried out most of America's diplomacy at the consulate. The Americans were limited to dealing with those Pakistanis who spoke English.

Moreover, CIA was convinced that many of the FSNs who worked as consular staff, visa examiners, drivers, exterior security guards, translators, clerks, maintenance crew, cooks, and secretaries either reported to, or were officers of, ISI, the Pakistani intelligence service.

It was a simple fact of life that every American consulate and embassy was riddled with intelligence operatives from the host country. Which is why Ty and his colleagues had to maintain their covers for status and actually do the work their visas said they were supposed to be doing.

Hostile surveillance and infiltrators were the reasons there were always areas within embassies and consulates that were secure, and where no FSNs were allowed. The regional security officer's office suite was one of those secure areas. The consulate's SCIF was inside the RSO's suite. If the facility was large enough, CIA preferred to have its own

SCIF. But in Lahore, even though the consulate was located in Pakistan's second largest city, it shared quarters.

The regional security officer was a fortysomething smart-talking redhead Second Amendment devotee known around the consulate as Mr. Wade. His radio call sign was Mountaineer, because Mr. Wade had gone to West Virginia University and his blue and gold WVU sweatshirt hung on a coat hook in the office. He wore it as a good luck talisman during football season, and so he was wearing it now, because the 9–4 Mountaineers were scheduled to play in the Citrus Bowl in Orlando in five days. Wade had done tours in Baghdad, Kabul, and Beirut. It hadn't taken him thirty minutes to figure out who Ty worked for.

But since RSOs are Foreign Service specialists, as opposed to Foreign Service officers, and they often have disdain for their caste-conscious FSO colleagues, Mr. Wade had been more than willing not only to play along, but to give Ty his wholehearted support. Besides, Mr. Wade enjoyed the company of the three AWG Soldiers who had dropped in shortly after Ty had arrived. They called themselves Eugene, Gary, and Kent. Wade labeled them The G-Men and The Demon. Demon because Kent, who insisted on opening beer bottles with his teeth, could also do incredible things with the boot knife he invariably carried in his sock.

■

"Yo, Mr. Wade. Merry-merry."

The RSO looked up. "Yo, Mr. Tyster, or should I say Mr. Tim. Merry-merry and a White Christmas to *vous,* too." Wade giggled and jerked his thumb toward the SCIF door. "You got a call from House o' Spooks."

"They say what they want?"

"Yeah. They said NSA just intercepted a secure message and now can confirm that Santa Claus is indeed coming to town."

"Everywhere but here, right?"

"Oh, no. Santa always makes an appearance in Lahore. Instead of a sled he travels in a tuk-tuk, and he brings us dust and rain. Especially rain."

The RSO jerked his thumb toward the Keurig machine. "Coffee? I got a care package today. Wolfgang Puck French Vanilla."

Ty's idea of real coffee was day-old percolator-brewed mud. "I'd settle for Yuban."

"Whoban?

"Yuban." Ty parked himself on the edge of the RSO's desk. "You know, the famous caffeine terrorist, Yuban Bin Laden."

"You ban Bin Laden?" Wade stifled a cackle. "Then you didn't hear him say, 'Wake up and smell the coffee, because Yuban Bin Tryin' for almost ten years.'"

"Don't remind me." Ty slid off the desk. "Wasn't there some CNN report a couple of months back that he was here in Pak, living the life of luxury in some villa?"

"Yeah, I heard it. Total disinformation. Listen, I know this country. He ain't here. He's hiding in plain sight."

"Where?"

"Washington. Driving a cab."

"Funny." Ty plucked a mug off Wade's bookshelf, took it over to the Keurig, and made himself a cup of the RSO's coffee. "Not bad." He blew over the top. "Hot. Langley say what they want?"

Wade stuck his lower lip out. "Uh-uh. But it can't be good news. It's Christmas. At Christmas, all bosses turn into Grinches. You'll see—they'll probably extend you again. Ask you to work right through the holidays."

"Don't even think that."

"You're right. Positive thoughts only. They'll fly you home first class. Give you a month's paid leave. Promote you to the senior service."

"Please," Ty said, "give me some of what you're smoking."

"That would be mistletoe."

They laughed. Then the RSO grew serious. "Truth? The Pakis are the Grinch."

Ty snorted. Wade was right about that. The Paks had been getting real aggressive of late. It was growing more and more difficult to break surveillance and get out into the boondocks, which is how Ty thought of the target-rich environment of North Waziristan, where he and the AWG personnel had spent the past eight weeks slipping tags onto targets that would be surveilled by UAVs (unmanned aerial vehicles) flying at fifty, sixty thousand feet.

Frankly, Ty was exhausted. Between the cover work and his real job, he'd been putting in eighteen-hour days. He was actually looking forward to the three-day Christmas weekend when the consulate would be shut down. "Guess I'd better call home."

"Tell House o' Spooks you want a replacement for Christmas."

Ty punched the cipher lock on the SCIF door, opened it, eased inside, and then closed it firmly behind him.

Wade watched the CIA man open the SCIF door. He hadn't been briefed on Ty's mission, but as they used to say during the Cold War, the RSO had been around the bloc. He knew Ty was working one of Langley's counterterrorist programs, and it hadn't been lost on him that the three other civilian contractors looked very similar to some JSOC personnel he'd run across in Kabul, where they were known as Erasers.

■

Ty set his notepad down, then dialed the number Wade had left for him. It was a Langley number, but one with which he was unfamiliar. The phone was picked up after two rings. Ty said, "Two-one-four-one."

The operator said, "Clearance?"

Ty recited the clearance code.

The operator said, "Go secure."

Ty hit the button on the side of the instrument and waited until the LEDs went from green to red. "Secure."

"I'll connect you now."

There was a pause. Ty heard the phone ring three times. Then an unfamiliar voice said, "Ty Weaver?"

"Yes."

"This is Stuart Kapos. Good to talk to you."

Stuart Kapos? Whoa. Ty estimated that there were eight or nine levels of management between him and the director of the National Clandestine Service. "Sir?"

"Forget 'sir.' Call me Stu. Like the phone."

Ty laughed. STUs was Armyspeak for secure telephone units, an older, more cumbersome predecessor of the instrument on which he was currently speaking. "Sir—uh, Stu."

"Good to have you on the line. Two things, Ty. One: I apologize for extending you in Pakistan. But you have to understand that Whiskey Trio is mission critical. We've killed a large number of HVTs because of you and your colleagues. And we've put the fear of God into many others."

"Thank you . . . Stu."

"You've spoken with Patty—two days ago, I think—and you know that we're looking out for her."

"Yes, sir." Ty's mind was racing. What did the director of CIA's National Clandestine Service want with him?

"So here's the second item."

"Sir?"

"I need you to go provocative."

"Provocative?"

"You and your AWG team have done brilliant work, Ty. The Paks have no idea where you've been or what you're doing. But now that has to change. I need you to get out of the embassy. Lose the official car. Leave a big wake. We want to see how they react. How closely they follow. If they try to impede you or provoke you, and if so, how."

"You want me to blow my cover."

"In essence, yes."

In essence? It was a lot more than essence. Stu Kapos was asking Ty to paint a big red bull's-eye on his back. "So you're using me as bait, right?"

There was a pause on the line. "In a manner of speaking."

In a manner of speaking? WTF. Ty rolled his eyes. Bosses never, ever fricking changed. "Why? For what?"

"Let's put it this way. We're very interested in learning how closely ISI monitors us. And how they do it. More than that I can't say right now." There was a pause. "Does that still work for you?"

"How critical is this?"

"Absolutely mission critical."

Ty thought about what Kapos was saying. "I've got an official passport. They can't arrest me."

He waited for Kapos to agree.

Kapos didn't agree.

This was not good juju.

"I mean, the best they could do is PNG me, right?"

More silence. Then: "It would suit the mission better if you carried your blue passport instead of the official one."

Jeezus H. Why not just ask him to wear a suicide vest? "You're not serious."

"You have your blue passport with you."

"Sure. But I don't have a Pak visa in it."

"Not to worry. We'll cover you."

"Cover me?" Ty paused. "If you don't mind my asking, Stu, what exactly does 'cover me' mean?"

"It means that we will do everything we can to protect you."

"And what if they bounce me around a bit?" The Paks were not known for being touchy-feely.

"They could do that," Kapos said.

Ty considered the possibilities. "Let me ask you a direct question. What if they come after me?"

"You mean if they try to use force?"

"Affirmative."

There was no hesitation in the NCS director's answer. "You're trained. You should protect yourself."

"Including deadly force?" In these politically correct days, when the Justice Department was going after CIA officers and prosecuting contractors, he wanted absolutely specific instructions. No winks and nods.

Obviously Stu Kapos understood the situation as well. "You will do whatever is appropriate to the situation. I'm not giving you permission to be a cowboy. So you do what you have to do—and let me be specific here, that includes lethal force—and we will back you up every way we can."

"Understood." Ty had no idea why they were asking him to get aggressive, or to blow his cover. But Stu Kapos's corridor reputation was better than good. Unlike so many of the backstabbing managers at the Agency, he was, as far as Ty had heard, pretty much a straight shooter.

Moreover, while Ty may have had qualms, he was also mission-driven. Which was why, instead of quibbling, he asked the Soldier's question: "When do you want me to start?"

"ASAP. Use the AWG people as your extraction team. Set up a protocol, so if there's an incident they'll come get you and bring you back to the consulate—sovereign U.S. territory. It's all been worked out with their people."

"And the folks from State?"

"We're leaving them in the dark."

"Even the RSO? I mean, ostensibly I'm working for him."

Ty very much wanted Wade to have some idea of what was going on. He might need the RSO's protection and contacts if things went to hell.

"You can tell him you're planning to get in the Pakis' faces. Nothing more. Nothing about learning how they work."

Ty sighed into the mouthpiece. "Okay. Will do."

"Look, Ty." Ty could hear Kapos breathing. "I know how tough this is on you and your family. But you're doing God's work, here. Believe me."

The former Delta operator cracked a grim smile. "Frankly, Stu, I better be. It's my ass you're hanging out in the cold."

6

Under normal circumstances, the president's daily intelligence brief was delivered by either his national security advisor or the special assistant to the president for counterterrorism at 6:30 A.M. in the residence or 7:30 in the Oval Office. The fourth of January, however, was a travel day, and so the briefing took place at 9 A.M. on Air Force One during the flight to Andrews Air Force Base as the First Family traveled back to Washington from their Christmas and New Year's vacation in Chicago. The one event listed on the president's schedule January 4 other than travel was a 4:30 P.M. meeting in the Oval Office with the secretary of defense, a meeting that was closed to the press. The only thing out of the ordinary about the meeting was that no photographs were released. But no one in the White House press corps, or anywhere else, for that matter, noticed it.

One of the reasons for no photographs was that it wasn't just the secretary of defense who was waiting in the Oval

Office when the president arrived, accompanied by his special assistant for counterterrorism. Waiting alongside SECDEF Richard Hansen was D/CIA Vince Mercaldi. And Mercaldi, at the last minute, had asked that Vice Admiral Wesley Bolin also join them.

Bolin wore civilian clothes so as not to attract attention. He needn't have bothered; there wasn't a reporter assigned to the White House who could identify the elusive JSOC commander, who for years had successfully kept himself under the press's radar.

Mercaldi and Bolin were unhappy when they saw the counterterrorism advisor shamble into the room in the president's wake. Dwayne Daley had gotten the job after retiring from CIA in order to campaign for the president, serving as the campaign's director of intelligence policy. In return, he'd been promised the Agency's directorship. But due diligence showed Daley's record to be spotty at best. As CIA station chief in Yemen, he had been blind to the ever-crescendoing support for Usama Bin Laden. His reporting on what happened in Sana'a was superficial and simplistic, ignoring shifting tribal alliances and their significance. Although he spoke Arabic, he allowed the Yemenis to control his access to anything but the most inconsequential intelligence. When the USS *Cole* attack occurred on his watch, Langley discovered, much to its embarrassment, that he had been deaf, dumb, and blind to the depth of the al-Qaeda threat within the country. Later, as CIA's assistant director for intelligence, he had made a series of misstatements that had caused embarrassment both at the White House and in the intelligence community.

Bottom line: after several media outlets produced exposés on his missteps, the White House was told by several high-ranking Democrats that Daley was unconfirmable for any position that required Senate approval.

And so Dwayne Daley was offered the counterterrorism advisor job in the current administration, with the rank of deputy national security advisor and assistant to the president. Not because he was good, or bright, or even competent. But because of simple chemistry. For some inexplicable reason, the president was comfortable with Dwayne Daley. From the campaign on, he'd golfed with him, played one-on-one basketball with him. Worse, Daley managed to shut out the director of national intelligence and the CIA director after he somehow convinced the president that he, not they, should conduct POTUS's daily intelligence briefs.

It was a chronic Washington conundrum. In many White Houses, this one included, competency all too often took a backseat to affability and chemistry. Otherwise, how else could disasters like Bush 43 staffers Harriet Miers and Alberto Gonzales and the current administration's Dwayne Daley be explained?

■

The president shook hands all around, wished everyone a happy New Year, and then dropped into an armchair in the Oval Office's seating area, his back to the desk where he normally conducted business. The others spread out on the two facing sofas.

SECDEF spoke first. "Mr. President, I asked Vince to come with me today because there have been some developments on the Pakistani front."

The president nodded. "Positive ones, I hope."

"I would characterize them as promising," the secretary answered. Richard Hansen was a naturally restrained individual. He had spent most of his professional career as a CIA analyst, rising to become deputy director of intelligence, and finally director of central intelligence in the long wake of the Iran Contra affair of the late 1980s. But he found his true calling in the mid-1990s as the president of the University of Missouri. SECDEF Hansen may have been the consummate Washington insider, but he was an academic at heart: thorough, precise, and judicious. His scholarly persona, however, also contributed to what many thought a tendency toward too much caution. Indeed, at CIA Rich Hansen had always been notoriously risk-averse when it came to operations.

He'd brought that quality back to Washington as secretary of defense, along with a professorial wit and a deep intellect. In this administration, made up largely of youngsters, ideologues, and political neophytes, he, along with D/CIA Vince Mercaldi and Secretary of State Katherine Semerad, were the troika of adults who supplied the president with sage advice, prudent political counsel, and sufficient necessary institutional memory to give presidential decisions context and gravitas.

Rich Hansen wasn't imposing. He wore nondescript suits, white shirts, and boring ties. But he had one of the sharpest minds of his generation, and he wasn't shy, despite his restrained appearance, at speaking truth to power.

"We are having great success with the Pakistani high-value target program we've been running in partnership with CIA," Hansen said, swiveling to look at Mercaldi, who nodded in agreement.

The president nodded. "Can you bring me up to speed?"

"Of course." The secretary spoke for seven or eight minutes, providing the president with a verbal snapshot of the joint program.

When he concluded, the president said, "Thanks, Rich. It's good to see some positive steps have been taken. I'm only sorry we can't inform the American people about what's being done on their behalf."

Dwayne Daley cleared his throat. "Mr. President," he said, "I don't want to be negative, but there's a downside that could prove perilous to our strategic goals in the region."

"Really?" The president turned toward his counterterrorism advisor. "Give us your thoughts, Dwayne."

"We're in danger of alienating the Pakistanis, Mr. President. These reckless missile attacks are nothing less than provocations. Every attack becomes a recruiting message to al-Qaeda and Pakistan's own extremist elements."

"Every attack takes out the enemies of Pakistan as well as the U.S., Dwayne," Wes Bolin interrupted. "We're killing the same people who are killing Pakistanis by the scores."

The admiral turned toward the president. "Sir, I've been to Pakistan six times in the past eight months, and I can tell you firsthand"—Bolin looked pointedly at the counterterrorism advisor—"that, one, the program is working, and two, the Pakistanis are grateful."

"Well," Daley said reprovingly, "not universally, Admiral. Let's be accurate."

"You're right, Dwayne, not every single Pakistani loves us." Bolin wasn't about to take on the counterterrorism advisor in this venue. But he wasn't going to be stepped on, either.

There was a brief silence. Then the president asked, "What about the other program? The one you're running in Abbottabad?"

"We are making consistent progress," Vince Mercaldi said. "The monitoring base is set up. We have identified eighteen individuals so far as occupants of the villa."

"But," the president interjected, "not our primary target, right?"

"Not yet, Mr. President."

"Can you give me a ballpark?"

The CIA director shook his head. "I'm afraid not, sir. These things take time. We have eyes and ears on scene. We have good resources on the ground—we even sent one of our assets, a doctor, to the compound as part of an inoculation program in the Abbottabad area."

The president looked quizzically at the D/CIA. "CIA set up an inoculation program?"

"We did, Mr. President. Through a false-flag front, which is an organization that doesn't know it's working for CIA, we covertly funded a Pakistan-based NGO that wanted to offer hepatitis B shots in Abbottabad. Then we slipped in our penetration agent, a physician, as a volunteer inoculator. We figured we could get some bang for the buck by not only getting him inside the compound, but also doing some good for the people of Abbottabad."

The president smiled. "That's thinking outside the box, Vince. Great idea."

"Thank you, Mr. President. I wish it had been mine. But it came from one of our Bin Laden Group people."

"Oh, really. Who?"

"We call him Spike."

"I'd like to meet Spike someday."

"Of course, sir."

"So, what finally happened?"

"Our doctor was admitted to the Khan compound, but not the house itself. Nor was he allowed to vaccinate anyone. So we never obtained any DNA samples."

"Too bad," the president said.

"Nor did he see anyone who resembled UBL."

The president bit his lower lip but said nothing.

Mercaldi continued. "Still, we are confident the Pakistanis have no idea about our presence in Abbottabad."

The president frowned. "So, we have not yet enjoyed eyes on target."

"Regrettably correct, Mr. President. For the moment, anyway, that's where things stand."

"Mr. President, perhaps it's time—" Dwayne Daley

started to say. But he caught the expression on Vince Mercaldi's face. It made him stop short. "Sorry, sir. Nothing."

The president rubbed his chin with his forefinger. "Should we get what you call 'eyes on' our target, Vince, how long would it take to mount an operation?"

"It's so preliminary we hadn't discussed specifics yet, Mr. President."

"Not even a ballpark?"

That damn ballpark again. Then the CIA director caught something in the president's eye, an almost indiscernible glint of negativity and reluctance to act, that made him swivel toward Wesley Bolin. "Wes, any ideas?"

Vince Mercaldi knew that Wes Bolin had ideas because they'd discussed them not two hours before. Bolin had told him that a capture/kill strike by Delta Force or SEALs was the most efficient way to take out Bin Laden. He'd mounted more than a thousand such raids over the past year. The only problem was Pakistan. They'd have to make a stealth approach in order to get in under the Pak radar. Otherwise, it was all very straightforward. As Bolin put it, "Vince, we've been doing these sorts of snatch-and-grabs for nigh on thirty years."

The SEAL admiral thought about the question for a few seconds. He'd noted the tension in the room and decided that specificity wasn't a good idea right now. "Less time than you might think, Mr. President. We've already got a pretty good idea about the venue's layout. The question is what we'd like the outcome to be. We could use air assets—repeat what we did in the opening hours of the Iraq war, when we bombed the three locations we believed were the most likely places Saddam would be. But as you know, we missed him then. My preference would be boots on the ground, which—"

"Admiral, as Vince just said, perhaps it's still very early in the process to be discussing specifics," Hansen interjected, cutting Bolin off. The SECDEF had good sources at this White House. He knew that both Daley and the national security advisor had been telling the president that the CIA base in Abbottabad was a risky operation that could end in disaster, and that a manned assault mission would permanently fracture U.S. relations with Pakistan.

Privately, Rich Hansen shared a rare agreement with the counterterrorism advisor about a special operations raid, but for other reasons. Hansen had been at CIA during the Desert One catastrophe. It was his firm opinion that the mission had been designed to fail by a timid, spineless administration led by a timid, spineless president. Still, that shattering experience colored every decision he had subsequently made. There was no way he would allow American lives to be squandered the way they had been in April 1980.

There was another factor as well: *this* president. Hansen and Mercaldi were Washington veterans who had worked for administrations both Republican and Democrat. They had discussed it and agreed that neither had been a part of any administration so lacking in weltanschauung and strategic sophistication as the one they both now served.

They had also agreed earlier in the day that this particular meeting was neither the time nor the place to debate the tactical—or, for that matter, the strategic—issues surrounding a possible Abbottabad operation.

Bolin swiveled toward the SECDEF. "Sorry, Mr. Secretary. You're right: we don't want to get ahead of ourselves."

Hansen was relieved to see the admiral stand down so readily. Besides, there was one more reason the SECDEF didn't want to discuss specific tactics. He knew from previous experience that this commander in chief was a man who possessed very little background in military planning. Neither did this particular president possess a sophisticated understanding about the real-life imperatives of special operations missions—or just about any other military mission, for that matter. It was, Hansen thought, partially generational—this president had been nowhere near draft age when the draft was abolished—but also cultural. This president, Hansen had noted with increasing disappointment over the past twenty-four months, was virtually tone-deaf when it came to dealing with the military, military personnel, or military issues.

Which was why, even though Hansen was personally opposed to a direct assault on the Abbottabad compound, there was no way he was going to argue the case in this venue. He had already discussed the matter with Mercaldi, and they were agreed on one critical item: the Abbottabad mission would never be anything but capture/kill. With emphasis on the kill. Precisely how the mission would be executed, and how the president would be presented with their decision—and convinced to approve it—would be worked out at a later date.

Wes Bolin also knew of the secretary's negative view about a possible assault on the Abbottabad compound. He had spent most of the early afternoon discussing Hansen's opposition with Mercaldi. That was one of the primary reasons the D/CIA had insisted that Bolin accompany him to the White House. He wanted the SECDEF to see Bolin in action, and also allow the SEAL admiral to get a read on the secretary. The D/CIA's advice was classic Vince. He'd advised the former Navy linebacker, "Know your adversaries, and prepare for every possibility."

Which is exactly what Slam Bolin had been doing since before January. At Mercaldi's invitation, on New Year's Day he had assigned Captain Larry Bailey, one of his senior JSOC SEALs, as his personal liaison to CIA's Bin Laden Group and sent him off to Langley. By then he had already replaced the National Security Council's JSOC special war-

fare liaison, an Army lieutenant colonel, with a SEAL rear
admiral. And he'd had elements of his Tier One units—
Delta, DEVGRU, and the 75th Ranger Regiment's Strike
Force—training for an assault on UBL's Abbottabad compound within days of CIA's setting up Valhalla Base.

The troops just didn't know it.

7

Troy Roberts loved to work the shoot houses. Which was a good thing, because now that he was back from Purgatory, he was spending a lot of time in them. He knew it was a cliché, but he still loved the smell of gunpowder, the adrenaline rush of shooting on the move, the unit integrity that came from knowing—really *knowing*—where every member of your team was every millisecond of the scenario, and the satisfaction of putting his rounds exactly, precisely where he wanted them to go.

Another reason he loved working in shoot houses was that they gave him—and the rest of his six-man assault element from Charlie Troop—the chance to practice over and over and over again the intricate, complex, sometimes problematical choreography of snatch and grab and capture/kill executed at close quarters, under high stress, and always contrapuntally against unforeseen events and the omnipresent Mr. Murphy of Murphy's Law.

Because despite all the hours of rehearsals, all the force-on-force scenarios, all the endless repetitions that every man in DEVGRU was responsible for doing, Troy and his shipmates understood—because they'd been there—that no matter how well prepared you were, no matter how many times you'd rehearsed the scenario, no matter how much you honed your body and your mind and prepped your gear, in the real world Murphy's Laws of Combat always apply. Troy's favorite was Murphy's original law: *What can go wrong, will go wrong.* But he was also a firm believer in a few of the others. He understood that no op-plan ever survives initial contact, that five-second fuses always burn just three seconds, and that if your attack is going perfectly, it's an ambush.

And there was the one Murphy's Law of Combat that, at least to Troy, summarized much of the thinking behind special operations: *If it's stupid but it works, it's not stupid.*

■

The shoot houses at Dam Neck, much like the one at top-drawer training facilities like the old Blackwater complex in Moyock, North Carolina, are multilevel structures with moveable walls and adjustable stairwells. They can be rigged to resemble an intricate warren of narrow hallways connecting small rooms, like the ones you'd find in Beirut's southern suburbs or *droguista* hideaways in Bogota, Colombia, or the multilevel Iraqi villas common to the Triangle of Death, where Sunni Jihadis still lived, or walled Taliban compounds like the ones in Helmand Province, or even a couple of floors of the Taj Mahal Hotel and Tower in Mumbai. All you needed was a floor plan and the shoot house crews would build it for you.

Within twenty-four hours you could practice assaulting a Yemeni hovel or a Saudi prince's palace; rehearse multiple simultaneous entries; blow doors with shaped charges or rake-and-break windows. You could work force-on-force using Simunitions—flesh-seeking, red- or blue-dye primer-powered rounds that stung like hell when you got hit—with one of the other assault elements playing the bad guys.

And then there was the occasional dog-and-pony show, when some VIP—the speaker of the house, the secretary of state, Prince Charles and Camilla—would visit the compound, and they'd sit inside one of the shoot house rooms and an assault element would show off all its bells and whistles and stage a live-fire hostage rescue using mannequin terrorists and the VIPs as the hostages.

The shoot house instructors loved to make life difficult. They would add nasty elements—invisible tripwires attached to flash-bang grenades, for example—to keep DEVGRU shooters alert. They'd start a scenario in total darkness and then turn the lights on, watching how the suddenly blinded shooters adjusted to their new situation. They would do their best to introduce Murphy's Laws into every stage of every exercise, so that every single DEVGRU SEAL would be able to think on his feet and realize that rigidity ain't no good and blindly following an op-plan just because it's there can get you killed.

Lieutenant Colonel Pete Blaber, one of Delta's better squadron commanders in the 1990s, had put it this way: "If you fail to prepare, you prepare to fail."

DEVGRU's shoot house instructors phrased it a little more starkly. A stenciled sign nailed above the entrance of Shoot House No. 1 at Dam Neck said it all:

DARWIN SUN TZU MUSASHI
ADAPT, OVERCOME, OR DIE!

This morning's exercise would be a variation of the standard capture/kill template that had been in existence since 1983. It had been refined since then, of course, and DEVGRU's equipment was a lot more sophisticated and its weapons a lot more efficient and reliable. Sure, now mission briefs were done on PowerPoints instead of using chalk on a blackboard, and you had drone and satellite imagery instead of drawings. But the core of capture/kill hadn't changed in decades. In fact, it hadn't changed in more than half a century.

Capture/kill, just like the heart of all special operations, relies on the theory of relative superiority, which was first formalized in 1995 in Bill McRaven's seminal book *Spec Ops*. Briefly stated, relative superiority occurs when a small group of assaulters gains a pivotal tactical advantage over a larger adversary. They do this through the use of six basic principles listed by McRaven: speed, surprise, simplicity, security, repetition, and purpose.

Think Entebbe, July 4, 1976, or Skorzeny's September 1943 rescue of Benito Mussolini, missions conducted by small units that, because of speed, surprise, and violence of action, overcame much larger opposing forces and achieved their objectives successfully. What had worked for the Nazi captain Otto Skorzeny were the same dynamics that allowed Yonatan Netanyahu's Israeli shooters to rescue a hundred hostages from their terrorist captors: the six basic principles of relative superiority.

It was those basic principles that T-Rob and his Red Squadron assault element would hone in their shoot houses at Dam Neck, up north at Fort A. P. Hill, where they practiced fast-roping and assaulting compounds from modified Black Hawk 60-J special operations helicopters, or the one hundred square miles of desert near Davis-Monthan Air Force Base in Tucson, where they dropped out of perfectly good aircraft six miles above the ground and free-fell almost four miles before popping their chutes at eighteen thousand feet and parasailing two miles to their drop zone.

■

Today T-Rob's Charlie Troop and his DEVGRU mentor Danny Walker's Alpha Troop were working a scenario that had been dropped on them at 0630. It was a live ammo drill, their tenth since Red Squadron had been reactivated eight days previously. They'd started with walk-throughs, then progressed to empty weapons. Then, three days ago, they'd commenced live fire exercises. It was all about bringing their shooting and moving skills—frangible skills—back online.

The problem: Stage a helicopter insertion of a twenty-four-member assault element to capture/kill an HVT living in a multilevel villa in an urban environment. It was the same basic scenario they'd worked for the past two days. Only the shape of the target had changed. On the tenth, it was a two-story townhouse; yesterday, a split-level house; today there were three floors.

They'd been supplied with a rough drawing of the villa's exterior and the parcel on which it sat. There was one other structure, a square building that was marked out of bounds, which sat directly opposite the front door. There were no other entrances marked and no windows on the ground floor. They were not given any information about the interior design, but were informed they would be rehearsing a nighttime operation.

This was SOP so far as the SEALs were concerned. Most HVT missions took place at night. That was when the target was most vulnerable and SEALs were in their element, given the array of night-vision, infrared, and thermal equipment available to them.

Charlie's 6-Team of six shooters was the entry team, which would breach the door, then follow 2-Team and work the starboard side of the ground floor. Charlie's 2-Team, which comprised six assaulters, would clear the ground-floor rooms and hallways. One-Alpha's shooters would take the second and third floors, and 3-Alpha's SEALs would be exterior security.

The two dozen men met in Red Squadron's workroom, a nondescript space that closely resembled a large, midwestern high school classroom. Two flags, the Red, White and Blue and the Navy's Blue and Gold, stood on stanchions at the front. The walls bore pictures taken during missions and photographic portraits of Red Squadron's previous commanding officers. There were individual desks for seventy-two on a spatter-patterned linoleum tile floor, a reference library sporting IKEA shelves, an array of AV equipment whose cost probably went into the mid-six figures, a coffee dispenser, and half a dozen each secure and nonsecure computers.

The Red Squadron CO, Commander David Loeser, waited until the Sailors settled in. Then he rapped on one of the front row desks and said, "Okay, guys, listen up. We've got another scenario from JSOC to work."

Loeser, a Marylander who'd grown up on the Eastern Shore near Cambridge, was thirty-nine and would probably make captain by the time he was forty-five. He was pretty happy with the squadron in general, and this particular group specifically. There was a good mix of youngsters and seasoned veterans. They had gelled, too, come together into a real team. They could work in pairs, quartets, half-dozens, or dozens. They were cross-trained and could handle one another's assignments if necessary.

They were, Dave Loeser thought as he looked at them, exactly what Roy Boehm, the maverick Mustang lieutenant and godfather of all SEALs, had in mind when in 1961 he'd conceived the idea of a Navy special operations unit of rugged individualists who worked together like the proverbial well-oiled machine, who could do everything from picking locks, to falling out of the skies holding an atomic submunition, to rescuing hostages, to dropping behind enemy lines to break things and kill people. A team that could go anywhere, do anything, and come out the other side having prevailed against all odds.

Except for one factor. The Linda Norgrove disaster of November. Loeser thought of it as That Horrible Episode. The Norgrove debacle had, if not shattered their self-confidence, certainly dinged it badly. Red Squadron's deployment had been curtailed. Until this past week, they'd been allowed to do nothing but administrative duties.

After Norgrove, the entire squadron—six troops totaling seventy-eight Sailors—had been stood down. Because they were a team, the innocent suffered along with the guilty. There'd been no training, no range time, none of the classes in everything from battlefield medicine to hand-to-hand combat to other skills that kept their unique capabilities in top form.

The day the inquiry ended, with one Sailor dismissed from DEVGRU and the others cleared, Loeser talked about his troop's condition with Captain Tom Maurer, DEVGRU's commanding officer. Maurer was sympathetic, but firm: either your people will get past this, or we'll replace your people. The OPTEMPO, the pace of any operation, he reminded Loeser, was unforgiving. Either Red Squadron would pull its weight, or changes would be made.

Loeser knew he had first-class personnel. Indeed the squadron CO thought the newly redeemed T-Rob and his shipmates were making excellent progress. Their tactical skills were first-class; their problem-solving abilities were good. What they needed now was the self-confidence they'd had prior to Norgrove. That was the nut that had to

be cracked. Yes, they'd screwed up. Terribly. But they had
to learn to live with it, and they had to learn from it. Loeser
understood that the guns, knives, and grenades they carried were only tools. The most dangerous weapon a SEAL
possessed was his brain. Right now, that particular weapon
wasn't operating the way it should. And it was his respon-
sibility to fix the problem. What these kids needed, Loeser
understood, was a nudge, an ineffable and indefinable *something* that would give them back the super edge that the very,
very best of DEVGRU SEALs had. When that happened,
Loeser would have Red Squadron back again.

Loeser glanced appreciatively at the Alpha Troop master chief. Danny Walker had that edge. He was, in Loeser's
opinion, the best master chief in the Navy. Danny epitomized
what Loeser considered Old Navy, the Navy of wooden
ships and iron men. He was rough around the edges, but
he demanded—and he received—110 percent from all who
served under him. He achieved this, Loeser understood, because he led from the front. Led by example.

It was a paradigm that had not been lost on Dave Loeser,
who learned as much from Danny Walker as any of the enlisteds. That was one reason Loeser loved his job so much,
loved Naval Special Warfare so much. NSW was a small
community, a tight community. As an ensign just out of the
Naval Academy he had seen that, just because some officers
made it through BUD/S and wore the trident, they weren't
necessarily Warriors.

But Loeser's goal was to be a SEAL in the Roy Boehm
mold, a lead-from-the-front Warrior. So even at the Academy, he had conscientiously sought out Warriors and tried to
learn from them. He listened to chiefs as they talked about
what they had done and how they had done it. He read Sun
Tzu, Musashi, and Clausewitz; he devoured books on tactics, history, and warfare.

But even then he realized that he still had a lot to learn about both warfighting and leadership. That was why he applied to NSW and went to BUD/S, where he learned a lesson that all too many of his colleagues and Annapolis classmates failed to learn.

It was during BUD/S Class 198 that Dave Loeser came to understand that from-the-front leadership is a two-way street. The Navy of ship drivers and Airedales revolved around a caste system set in stone: it was all about the ward room and the chiefs' goat locker.

In contrast, NSW was collegial. Officers and enlisteds went through BUD/S together. Suffered together, pulled together, and ultimately either prevailed together or failed together. Same in real life—it was . . . the *Team*.

And the officers who didn't pull together, who tried to maintain the caste system and didn't trust their NCOs? Usually they did their fourteen months and then they left. For a staff job somewhere or a slot aboard one of the big gray monsters where they could hide in the ward room, away from all the scoffing chiefs and truculent Sailors, and be officers, managers, bureaucrats. Screw that. Which is why, after talking things over with his senior NCOs, Loeser decided to use shoot house exercises to bring back his squadron's self-confidence.

Danny and Charlie Troop's senior NCO, Kerry Brendel, suggested a basic incremental approach. They'd start with dry runs, then move to live ammo, and finally force-on-force using Simunition training ammo. Loeser realized it was a perfect solution because it combined the SEAL fundamentals of approaching a target stealthily, attacking it swiftly and ferociously, while simultaneously honing frangible shooting skills, with the principle of learning from your mistakes.

■

Dave Loeser projected a PowerPoint slide on the workroom's wall-mounted flat screen. It showed the outline of the villa, an X marking the single entry. "No windows on the ground floor. One door—material unknown. Hostiles? Unknown. Family: wife, kids, and probable relatives." He paused. "Ideas?"

"Pretty straightforward—just like yesterday, except we don't know about the hostiles." Ken Michaud was, like Troy, one of Red Squadron's youngsters; he'd just turned twenty-three. He had the lean, sinewy build of a marathoner, which he was. Tall and bearded, Padre, as the knuckle-scarred veteran of a Catholic education was known, had been top of his class at BUD/S. He'd been spotted as a potential DEVGRU candidate within weeks of his arrival at SEAL Team 2, and he had made it through selection less than a year ago—one of the squadron's newest members. He'd been reassigned from Delta Troop to Charlie's 6-Team to replace the Sailor who had fragged Linda Norgrove.

Loeser asked, "So?"

"Are we working against Jihadis?" Gunner's Mate First Class Len Elliott was Alpha 1-Team. Tall, solidly built, with short blond hair going prematurely gray. His call sign was Rebel, and he'd been at DEVGRU for seven years and two wives.

"Don't know," Loeser said. "All I was given was the layout."

In fact, the colonel from JSOC who'd given them the scenario had told Loeser to be vague about target, location, and occupants. "That'll be pretty easy," Loeser had responded, "because you haven't given me any of that data anyway."

The colonel had laughed. "Ain't life grand when it's full of surprises."

Charlie 6-Team's Machinist Mate First Class Jerry Mistretta, call-sign Cajun, cocked his head in the whiteboard's direction. "You don't know? Then we gotta factor dem Jihadis in."

"That could mean suicide vests." Quartermaster First Class Blair Gluba, call sign Gunrunner, was a round-faced pocket rocket from Michigan's Upper Peninsula. He had four filled-to-capacity gun safes at his home just off London Bridge Road, behind Oceana Naval Air Station, and whether he was on or off duty, he never carried fewer than two weapons on his person.

The tall, angular boatswain's mate first class from Florida, Roger "Heron" Orth, broke in: "Which means we got to get in and shoot them first."

"That would be the general idea, Heron. What'd they say on that TV cop show—'Do it to them before they do it to us.'" Loeser popped another PowerPoint frame on the screen. "Unless, of course, there are women and children." He let that possibility settle in for a couple of seconds, then put a new frame up. "Here's the landing site. The scenario begins with a fast-rope insertion."

Troy's hand went up. "Time?"

"Five minutes or less."

"That's doable, " Padre said.

"I'll break it down, and we'll talk it over," Danny Walker said. "Be with you in a couple of minutes, Boss."

"Works for me." Loeser dropped the remote on the desk. "Work it, then jock up. H-Hour is 0800."

8

It was cold enough in the shoot house that the SEALs could see their breath. The target villa was three stories high, perhaps forty feet to its roofline, and seventy feet in width. There was one door, right in the center, and no windows. There were two circles taped on the shoot house deck to indicate the fast-rope locations; in the center of each, a sixty-foot, soft, thick fast-rope was suspended from the ceiling. The platform from which the SEALs would drop was just over forty-five feet above the deck.

From the left side it was just over ten yards to the single doorway, a straight run at about a 40-degree angle. The right-hand circle was just to the right of a square perhaps twelve feet on each side, built out of eight-foot-high moveable wall sections. Troy walked over and—habit—pulled on the fast-rope. Secure. He checked the angle. From the right-hand circle, the door couldn't be seen.

"Breachers and entry team have to see the door," he called out. "So we drop left, Alpha right."

Rebel grabbed the right-hand fast-rope and hoisted himself a couple of feet off the ground. "Makes sense."

The first two assault elements broke into swim-team pairs and lined up to check equipment. They were jocked up in full assault kit: the newest model light ballistic helmets with dual-tube NODs—night observation devices—and talk-through Peltor hearing protection with boom mikes that were connected to their communications suite M-BITR radios.

Each assaulter had tailored his kit individually. Most favored lightweight plate-carriers with the stand-alone ceramic plates that made them more battlefield agile. Some wore CamelBak hydration-capable vests. Others had subload from which they attached pistols, magazine holders, and first-aid blowout kits. Other pouches held flexicuffs, rolls of tape, and other miscellaneous supplies.

The official issue handgun for the U.S. military is the Beretta M-9, a 9mm semiautomatic pistol. Almost universally, SEALs reject that pistol in favor of one they consider more reliable and accurate, the Sig-Sauer 226 semiautomatic 9mm pistol. At DEVGRU the pistols du jour were Sig 226s, loaded with 124-grain +p+ hollowpoint, and Heckler & Koch's new .45 ACP semiauto, with Speer 200-grain +p hollowpoint. Both pistols were durable enough to survive a maritime environment.

Long guns were either HK416s, short-stroke, gas-piston-driven automatic assault rifles that fired the 5.56 NATO round, or, for working perimeters and stand-off, 7.62 LWRCI REPRs—gas-piston-driven rapid engagement precision rifles with 16.1-inch barrels, or the 12-inch barreled REPR JKW (joint kinetic weapon)—slung off a variety of slings, depending on each SEAL's preferences and the mission requirements.

Altogether the assaulters' gear weighed close to fifty-five pounds. It was bulky, and it could be cumbersome when a dozen SEALs were crammed into the fuselage of a helo. Especially when the goal was to get all twelve out of the helo and onto the ground in ten seconds or less.

The reason for the rush? To avoid vulnerability. As Admiral Bill McRaven wrote in *Spec Ops*, there is an area of vulnerability in every special operations mission during which the probability of mission completion can be compromised—compromised by what Clausewitz called *la friction*, compromised by the fog of war, compromised by Murphy's Law. Whatever the cause, the longer that area of vulnerability exists, the more likely it becomes that things will go south and relative superiority will not be achieved. So, when getting boots on the ground ASAP was key, fast-roping was the most effective insertion method.

Basically, fast-roping is a controlled free fall. The operator goes out the helo and descends a rope using his hands as brakes. Thick leather gloves prevent rope burns—but not always. In fact, some fast-ropers have been known to adapt extra-thick welder's gloves as their descent equipment of choice. The fast rope itself is an olive green, multiple strand, right-hand lay weave, soft-woven, multifilament polyester over multifilament polypropylene, with a diameter of one and three-quarter inches. It is known as a Plimoore fast rope. Plimoores come in four lengths: 30, 60, 90, and 120 feet, the most common being 60 or 90 feet. They have a tensile strength that exceeds thirty thousand pounds.

Today the SEALs would have it easy. They were dropping off a platform on a single rope, not a hovering helo and twin ropes, where the rotor wash could smack them onto the ground if the helo shifted, or toss them into the air as they ran through the wash vortex. Still, between the weight of what they carried and the cumbersomeness of it all, even this sterile exercise could end in injury. Fast-roping is, to repeat, a (slightly) controlled free fall. And the human body free-falls at 180 feet per second—more than 120 miles an hour—once it achieves terminal velocity.

Or, as Boatswain's Mate First Class "Heron" Orth was fond of saying, "Ain't gravity wonderful."

0819 Hours

Dave Loeser came into the shoot house all geared up and carrying a thirty-gallon blue plastic garbage can. He put two fingers in his mouth and whistled to get everyone's attention. "Change of plans, guys."

He dropped the garbage can on the cement deck. "Magazines, please. All ammo please."

He waited as the twenty-four shooters cleared their weapons, extracted magazines from their pouches, belts, and thigh rigs, and dropped everything into the can.

"Check one another, please, and call clear when you're done." He watched as the SEALs patted one another down. Loeser looked over in Blair Gluba's direction. "Hey, hey, Gunrunner, don't get fresh with Rebel."

"Not to worry." Len Elliott towered above the short SEAL. "He can't reach the good parts." He looked down. "Can you, ankle biter?"

Gunrunner rolled his lips back over his teeth and growled.

Alpha 1-Team's Myles Fisher, call-sign Fish, laughed. "Hey, we got our own Jack Russell."

Cajun Mistretta's arms were raised in a surrender position as Troy patted him down. "Hope Gunrunner have his shots."

Fish: "Hope Rebel have *his*."

Three minutes later, Loeser received a thumbs-up from Walker. "All clear, Boss."

"Good." Loeser pulled a BlackBerry out of his chest pouch. Two minutes later one of DEVGRU's armorers walked in, wheeling a mobile storage cabinet.

Cajun was the first to get it. "Oooh, oooh, we gonna get the chance to shoot real people today, ain't we, Boss?"

0824 Hours

The SEALs exchanged their HKs and REPRs for preconfigured Simunitions guns. They were the same size and weight, but the barrels were bright blue and were specially tailored for Simunition's 5.56, primer-powered marking cartridges. Handguns were different. Marking cartridges came only in 9mm, and so Sig-Sauers and HKs were outfitted with Simunition kits that had proprietary barrels and lighter recoil springs.

"Saddle up, gents." Loeser led the way up the ladder attached to the shoot house's north bulkhead.

0845 Hours

Atop the platform the SEALs split into assault elements. Troy's 6-Charlie broke into three pairs: T-Rob and Padre, the pairing Walker referred to as "Kindergarten SEALs," Chief Quartermaster Jack "Jacko" Young with Cajun, and Heron with Alpha's senior NCO, a tall, lean sniper with a wispy Fu Manchu mustache, Chief Gunner's Mate (GUNS) Kerry Brendel, call-sign Rangemaster.

Loeser checked equipment. When he was satisfied, he

called "STAND BY . . ." The shoothouse lights went out. "EXECUTE!"

Troy muttered, "Shit." He dropped his NODs so he could see the fast rope. His left hand was on Cajun's left shoulder; Padre's hand was on his.

Troy was third in the stick. He moved forward as quickly as he could, following the breachers. Jacko hit the rope first. Disappeared. Cajun hit the rope, then Troy followed as Cajun's head disappeared below the platform.

Hit the rope hard.

0.05 seconds. Hands up. As his arms go high, his rifle smacks the back of his head.

0.87. He can feel the heat start to build on his palms as the rope slides past his hands.

1.4. Brake-squeeze—heat.

1.6. Troy's knees buckle as he hits the deck. He lands off balance, his NODs out of position.

Quickly he rolls to his port side, gets his night vision where it needs to be, and scrambles to his feet so he won't get smacked by Padre.

Drops his thick gloves, retrieves his weapon.

4.8. Quick mag check. Senses Padre behind him.

5.9. Move toward door. Scan and breathe. Weapon up. Trigger finger indexed.

8.2. Door breached. Cut the pie. Clear. Make entry.

9.1. In. Go left. Scan and breathe. Furniture. Couch. Movement. "Gun!"

Head. Shoulders. An AK coming over the top of the couch.

Two-shot burst. Never stop moving. Head shots. Advance, advance, advance. Target down. Coup de grace as he goes past.

Keep moving toward the door on the left.

Padre's voice in his ear. "EKIA." Enemy killed in action. "Go door."

Shots coming from their right. Breaching team has made entry and is engaging. Troy can hear their comms in his ears.

13.6. 1-Alpha has made entry and is proceeding to stairwell. Troy allows himself to think, *We're swarming.*

17.4. At the door. No visible hinges. It opens inward. Paneled.

Padre's hand on the knob. Troy's head goes up-down once. Turn.

Locked.

Stand back. Kick.

Wood splintering. Door slams into far side wall.

Instinct: charge.

No: fatal funnel.

21.5. Light. Troy retrieves infrared flashlight from right chest pouch.

Cut the pie. Line of sight?

Clear. Ten-foot hallway. Door left six feet, second door left eighteen feet. Hallway ends in a T.

Troy starts to move forward. Stops. Shines the IR at the deck. "Deck clear." He's been checking for tripwires.

30.9. First room. Cut the pie. Scan and breathe. Troy edges slowly around the door jamb, his 416 up; Trijicon night-vision-capable sight bright. He keeps moving until he can see the whole room. It's empty. "Clear." He backs out of the room.

39.5. Padre leapfrogs Troy's position. They move quickly down the hallway heel-toe, heel-toe, knees slightly bent, bodies angled slightly forward in an aggressive stance, the muzzles of their weapons absolutely rock steady. They are breathing steadily and their eyes never stop moving side to side, down the hall.

Padre's muzzle is pointed directly ahead. Troy's muzzle is parallel to Padre's, eight inches off his right shoulder.

49.9. Second doorway. No door. Padre starts to cut the pie.

Troy's peripheral vision picks up movement on the right side of the T, eight yards away.

Both eyes open, HK muzzle downrange, Troy's left hand squeezes Padre's shoulder.

Padre stops.

01:16.5 minutes. Troy's finger is on the HK's trigger. A hand appears, then an arm. Torso. Burka-clad figure at the end of the hall.

Padre's flashlight is in his left hand. Shines a blue light down the hallway.

Troy: "Step out. Show us your hands."

Burka-clad figure displays both arms, both hands. They are empty. Troy hears gunfire from above.

Can't lose focus. They still haven't cleared the second room. Can't go past it. *Make her come to us.*

His hand on Padre's shoulder. Pull Padre back. Quickly, they move backward until they reach the cover of the first room.

01:43.0. "Walk this way. Keep your hands in the air. LET US SEE YOUR HANDS!"

Burka-clad figure complies. When she is ten feet away, Troy shouts, "Stop!"

She complies.

"Turn around."

She complies.

"Hands out where we can see them."

No reaction.

"HANDS OUT WHERE WE CAN SEE THEM!"

02:30.0. Finally, she shows her hands. There is nothing in them.

"BACK TOWARD US."

She complies. Slowly. Way too slowly.

When she is within arm's reach, Troy grabs her arms, pinions them, slaps flexicuffs on her wrists, forces her to the floor.

He drags her into the cleared room while Padre's eyes and weapon never leave the hallway.

03:30.0. Troy has secured the flexicuffs with tape, bound the captive's feet together, and taped around her legs at the knees. Once she's been secured he pats her down to make sure there are no weapons or explosives. "Clear."

03:55.0. They resume the search. Down the hallway to the second door. Cut the pie. Padre moves cautiously around the arc, HK up.

04:14.0. The muzzle of Padre's HK is just past the plane of the doorjamb.

A burst of fire comes up from floor level. Stitches Padre from his waist to his right shoulder: six nasty pink marking round starbursts.

Transmit: "Padre down. Port side hallway ground level." The sonofabitch was lying prone, up against the hallway wall.

Padre falls back. Troy already has a grenade in his hand. Pulls the pin, reaches around, lobs it into the room, drags Padre to safety.

Waits for the flash and the explosion. Starts to move down the hallway to the T, and then—

5:07.0. A whistle. Then: "Stand down, stand down," in Troy's headset.

The shoot house lights come up full.

The SEALs assemble in the landing area. They clear weapons, pull off their helmets, reach for the hydration hoses secured to their shoulder harnesses, and suck on water or sports drinks. It is forty-six degrees inside the shoot house, but every one of the two dozen SEALs has sweat through his uniform.

Troy shakes his head. "Not great." He and Padre had fallen behind schedule almost from the get-go. There has to be a way to factor in prisoners and still maintain pace. And—worse—his shipmate got shot. In fact, of the twenty-four assaulters, five have telltale pink starbursts on their uniforms. That's more than a twenty percent casualty rate.

Totally unacceptable.

0919 Hours

Dave Loeser dropped his gear on the deck. He'd been watching the exercise from the control room, a cargo container on a catwalk fifty feet above the deck. Night-vision-capable video cameras had taped the entire exercise.

He wasn't happy with what he'd seen. The entire assault force had fallen behind schedule. They'd been slow to react. The Alpha SEALs took forever to get up the stairs—in fact, no one had made it to the third floor, where five role-players were waiting.

And no one in the assault force saw the sentry who was crouched behind the eight-foot-high square structure, and who'd shot two of the SEAL rear-guard security element.

But this was only the first time today they'd run this particular scenario. The role-player positions might change over the next several iterations, but the layout would remain the same. That's what JSOC wanted, and that's what JSOC would get.

More to the point, this was a teaching exercise. The Red Squadron CO understood two of the most basic principles of Warrior training: that what doesn't kill us makes us stronger, and the more we sweat in training, the less we bleed in battle.

Which is why Loeser knew he had to go positive. Everyone knew they'd screwed up—he could see it in their faces. No need to rub it in.

So he started on a light note. "Here's the good news, gents: we are making progress. No one shot themselves or their swim buddies." He paused, looking at the pink starbursts on Padre's multicams. "Although, I do see Padre was . . . blessed. Or is that, as they say in French, *blessé*, Padre?"

He waited for the laughter to subside. "But you know and I know we got a lot of work to do." He paused. "First, let's hear from the role-players, see what they thought of your performances and how they took advantage of you. Then you can critique yourselves, see what lessons we can take away from this. And then we can do it all over again. And again. Until we get it right."

9

Ty Weaver checked the side mirror of his rented white Honda Civic. Shit. The same motorbike and tuk-tuk—one of those three-wheeled scooter-powered minitrucks ubiquitous in Pakistan—had been following him for the past eight minutes. Ty had picked out the vehicles just after he'd pulled cash from the Deutsche Bank ATM on Mall Road, a short distance from the house on E Street he shared with Loner, Kent, and Gary just south of the Lahore American School.

He'd shot video with his cell phone. He would blow it up later, so hopefully they could run a trace on the license plates. Too bad he hadn't been able to get shots of the drivers—two Paks on the motorbike running thirty, forty yards behind him, and one in the tuk-tuk, playing catch-up.

He'd intended to go straight to the consulate. Instead he veered east, circled around Alkman Road, then turned south until he hit Lawrence Road. *Let's see what they do.*

After six minutes, the bike was still behind him. He couldn't find the tuk-tuk.

Ty drove with his left hand. His right eased the Glock 19 out of its Galco concealable and slipped the pistol under his left thigh.

Better safe than sorry.

The question was, who were these assholes? ISI's gumshoes favored Mercedes sedans, Hondas like his, or Toyotas. Ten days ago they'd followed him up to Peshawar in two Toyota pickups.

He'd never seen a motorbike-tuk-tuk combo before. So who were these guys? They could be Taliban or AQNs who wanted a Gringo scalp for their belts. They could just as easily be snatch-and-grabbers who'd seen him at the ATM and were looking for an easy score. Or they could be ISI gumshoes, out to rattle his cage in new sets of wheels.

He snorted. Well, ISI had cause. The past month had been . . . interesting would be an understatement. On Christmas Day he'd given up his consulate vehicle and its diplomatic plates for a rented Honda and local plates.

The local plates lasted less than a week. Currently he had six sets of forged license plates in a sealed envelope in the RSO's safe and a seventh set on the car. They'd been Dippouched to the consulate by Langley. He switched them out every few days.

■

He had stocked the Honda with equipment that said SPY in neon: binoculars, two cameras, a four-foot-nine by three-foot-six 1:500,000-scale National Imagery and Mapping Agency tactical pilotage chart of northwest Pakistan marked "G-6C," a GPS unit, a telescope, a six-power night-vision monocular, four mags for his Glock 19, and two of Loner's 9mm Beretta magazines. He'd also tossed a Paki outfit and a dark wig into the trunk.

The first day back in the office after New Year's, Mr. Wade caught a glimpse of Ty's stash. The RSO's eyes bugged out like a cartoon character's. He thought Ty was nuts.

"What the fuck?" Wade asked when Ty opened the rear door and showed him the pile of stuff behind the front seats.

"They want me out there. So I'm out there."

"Yeah, like a frigging flasher. The only thing you're missing is the raincoat." He gave Ty a strange look. "You know those people you work for are crazy? Insane? Certifiable?"

"Tell me about it."

"I mean, if this were State, you'd be in a grievable situation. Take it to the IG and you'd win."

"Well, yeah—if I was at State, probably."

"So?"

"Bottom line? Bottom line is that's why we're different. You guys at State work within the system. Diplomat to diplomat. You ask 'May I?' Me? My training manual says if I'm not breaking the laws of the country I'm assigned to, I'm not doing my job."

"Isn't that the training manual from the DO, or whatever they're calling the Directorate of Operations these days? I thought you worked for the Security Division."

"National Clandestine Service is what they call it. And I do. But occasionally—" Ty cut himself off. Wade was a friend. And helpful. But he'd been specifically instructed how far the information flow could go.

"Occasionally?"

"Occasionally our paths intersect."

"So these days you go around introducing yourself as"—Wade's voice dropped into a dramatic basso profundo—"Weaver, Ty Weaver, right?"

"No, *dummkopf.* I tell them, 'White, Tim White.'"

Wade laughed. "Oops. Forgot about the alias." Then he grew serious. "But listen, you know as well as I do, Paks are real uptight about snooping. Shit, every time I have to move somebody around, ISI's crawling up my ass because I carry a weapon and a radio and I've got a GPS in my FAV." His fully armored vehicle was Wade's favorite piece of equipment. "And I've got diplomatic plates. What the hell do you think they'll do when they see how you've pimped your ride?"

"Well," Ty said as noncommittally as he could, "I guess we'll find out."

■

Yeah, "interesting" would be an understatement. He'd done exactly as ordered. First week of the year he'd driven right across Pakistan, almost five hundred kilometers, to the North West Frontier provinces. Stopped for lunch in Bannu. Cruised through Isha. Hit a certain bazaar on the outskirts of the rugged frontier town of Miram Shah. Got as far as Kotai Kili before ISI had the Pak National Police stop him and tell him his papers weren't valid in the Frontier, and besides they couldn't guarantee his safety, so he had to turn back.

But not before he'd taken hundreds of digital pictures of the locations he'd been instructed to photograph and emailed them back to the cover address Stu Kapos had given him.

Second week, he'd done the same in the greater Peshawar metropolitan area. Started with the Bala Hisar Fort, the clay-red headquarters of the Frontier Corps, a paramilitary organization with ties to the Haqqani network and also, according to the intelligence data Ty had read, elements of the Taliban.

Ty had waved at the bereted sentry who binoculared him from a guard tower atop the fort's crenellated wall. The next five days he spent in constant motion between P-war and Charsadda, taking pictures of villas, madrassas, schools, and shops, leaving a big fat wake all the way back to the consulate.

His antics made them crazy, of course. They thought he was doing targeting for Predator drone strikes. Or looking for UBL.

Just east of Peshawar, the ISI gumshoes even tried to run him off the road. They didn't know he was a defensive driving instructor. He'd turned the tables on them—made them roll one of their pickups onto its side and forced the other into a ditch. Not a scratch on the Honda, either, except for a couple of small dings in the front fender.

But last week was the best. He drove north and east of Lahore up to the Indian border and took dozens of photos of the bunkers that the Paks were building between Narowal and Shakargarh. He shot with a 300mm lens from a quarter mile away. The soldiers were so mad some of them were actually jumping up and down by the time the local constabulary arrived. But by then he'd switched the memory cards in the Nikon, and the card he handed over held only sixty or so photos. He figured they shouldn't go away empty-handed.

But despite all the success something nagged at him, like a piece of food stuck between his teeth.

The question—and it was a question he could not answer—was *Who was watching the watchers?*

It was a serious issue. He certainly was drawing the Paks out. As of four days ago he had a permanent tail. They'd put gumshoes on him 24/7. The house he shared with Loner, Kent, and Gary was staked out. A *shwarama* vendor had suddenly appeared on C Street, right behind the American School, every day from seven until seven. In the evenings the vendor was relieved by a Mercedes that parked at the intersection of Street 2 and E Street. It was manned by two Paks, who sat and chain-smoked for twelve hours. Ty wondered where the poor guys were relieving themselves. They were probably pissing into bottles.

But he couldn't figure out who was watching *them.*

And yet, wasn't that what Stu Kapos had wanted? To learn ISI's patterns, that's what he'd said. To discover their vulnerabilities so CIA personnel could operate more efficiently in Lahore, Peshawar, Karachi, and Islamabad, where CIA maintained its bases and station.

But there was no sign of countersurveillance. None. Ty was sure of it. Because every Delta operator—and although he couldn't confirm it, probably every other Tier One operative as well—went through an intensive course on countersurveillance and denied area operations run by CIA. So Ty knew what to look for. And he saw nothing. Not a hint. Zip. Zero. Zilch.

It occurred to him one evening, after a couple of beers with Mr. Wade, that no one was watching the watchers. That he was just out there, alone. They were running him around for no reason. They were running him because, well, he had no idea. None at all.

But that made no sense. There had to be a purpose for all this craziness. A reason HQ had pulled him off assignment and turned him into an ISI magnet.

1326 Hours

Ty checked his side mirror. The tuk-tuk was following him again, and now the motorbike had disappeared. He decided to pick up the pace. He gunned the Honda into a skiddy left turn across from the Markaz Mosque, fishtailed, then swung north. The third road was Lovers Lane. He took a quick left, then left again onto Birdwood, then left again onto a one-way street that targeted the driveway of the Royal Garden Hotel.

Glanced back. *Shit*. The tuk-tuk had stayed with him. He

could make out the driver's mustached face. The guy was holding a cell phone to his ear, steering with one hand. He was talking up a storm. Ty could see his lips jabbering.

He accelerated into the hotel's horseshoe-shaped driveway. The tuk-tuk followed. Just ahead, a cab pulled out to pick up a fare under the portico.

Ty floored the Honda, jumped the curb and veered around the taxi, cutting it off, answering the blast of its horn with a friendly wave at the furious driver, who'd stalled out.

Ty kept going. He could still hear the driver cursing. He stuck his arm out the window and waved again as he serpentined around the hotel driveway. As he headed for the exit, he looked across the landscaped median.

The tuk-tuk was trying to reverse. Fat chance. Ty sped up, turned south on Birdwood Road, took his first left, went under the Jail Road overpass, then turned right onto the service road that ran alongside the multilane Jail Road.

It was time to end this stupidity. Just past the Mozang subway stop he'd merge into Ferozepur Road, cut through Quartaba Chowk junction onto Queen's Road, and head north toward the consulate.

Home free. Screw ISI.

1328 Hours

He was stopped at the Quartaba Chowk intersection when the motorbike caught up to him. Ty was in the middle lane. The bike pulled alongside his right door, close enough to keep him from opening it. He could smell the engine exhaust. The driver was maybe late twenties, blue long-sleeve sport shirt, leather vest, jeans, and sandals. He kept his eyes straight ahead. The passenger was a kid in a plaid flannel shirt. Long greasy hair secured with a bandanna, jeans, and sandals. He smiled at Ty. It was a mocking, derisive, smart-ass smile.

Ty's Delta Force instincts sounded an alarm. This was not right. Ty's left hand stayed on the steering wheel. His right slid onto the butt of the Glock.

Simultaneously the kid tauntingly raised his shirt. Displaying the semiauto pistol stuck in his belt. The kid's hand went crossdraw for the weapon just as the light changed.

The motorcycle shot ahead.

It cut off the Honda.

The kid swiveled, that smartass smile still on his face as he brought the gun up to take a shot.

Ty's foot smashed down on the brake to keep the Honda steady. His hand brought the pistol up from under his thigh. He brought it up to eye level much faster than the kid, who was transitioning from a one- to a two-handed grip.

Ty didn't need two hands. He got a quick sight picture and double-tapped the kid through the windshield.

Oh, fuck, that was loud. Even with the window open, Ty's head rang as if he'd been clubbed. He couldn't hear anything.

He focused on the bike. The kid was down, two hits, upper center mass.

Ty put the Glock's front sight between the driver's shoulders and fired three more quick shots.

Now the driver went down, the bike toppling onto him.

Muzzle still on the threats, Ty reached across with his left hand and opened the Honda's door. He exited the car, Glock in hand, his eyes moving left-right, right-left to ensure there were no more threats. No tuk-tuk with an AK-wielding driver. No backup team.

All clear. The tuk-tuk was nowhere to be seen. Incredibly, traffic was streaming around the downed bike and the Pakis on the ground.

Ty advanced on the shooter. The kid was still moving. Twitching. Gurgling. *Neutralize the threat.* Ty kicked the kid's pistol away, then put two in his head, careful to shoot at a safe angle so his rounds wouldn't ricochet off the pavement and come back at him.

The twitching stopped.

Suddenly there was a lot of blood. He had to report this. Had to call Wade. Had to call Loner, too. He lowered the Glock and with his left hand reached for the cell phone on his belt.

As he did so, the dead driver pushed the bike off his legs and struggled to his feet.

He turned toward Ty, screamed something in Pashto, then fled north.

Christ almighty. Ty's eyes scanned the street. Now cars were stopping, the drivers looking at the scene. Pedestrians were watching, too. Some had cell phones to their ears. Some were taking pictures.

Ty realized the driver was still running. He was twelve, thirteen yards away. If he got much farther he'd be in among the knot of onlookers on the near side of the intersection. Unstoppable.

Ty stuffed the cell phone in his shirt pocket, got a two-handed grip on the Glock, took a good sight picture, and fired a triple-tap at the driver. Hit him right in the lung area.

The driver's knees buckled and he fell facedown onto the pavement. Ty walked rapidly up to where he lay and shot him twice more in the back of the head. *Second threat neutralized.*

Reflexively, he ejected the almost-empty magazine from his pistol and dropped it into his trouser pocket while simul-

taneously feeling for the spare, retrieving it and ramming it
firmly into the Glock's butt until it clicked securely in place.

He heard the distinctive "hee-haw hee-haw" of sirens in
the distance. Holstered his pistol, felt his heart pounding as
if he were about to have a heart attack. He lay two fingers
across the inside of his left wrist. His pulse was going warp
speed. *Holy crap. I am so out of condition.*

He forced himself back into alertness. Scanned—moving
his whole head back and forth—and breathed so he wasn't
tunnel-visioning. Amazing, he thought, there were perhaps
eighty, ninety people at the intersection, but not one of them
had tried either to intervene or advance on him.

Yet.

He speed-dialed Loner's phone, and when the AWG Soldier answered, Ty said, "SITREP China Lake." SITREP
was the situation report. China Lake was the codeword for
the get-me-outta-here contingency plan the four men had
created.

Ty continued: "Quartaba Chowk. Cops arriving."

Loner: "You okay? You're shouting."

Ty: "I'm fine. Two EKIAs. I'm fine. There's a crowd." He
wondered if Loner could hear him, because he still could
hardly hear himself. "Cops arriving. I'm okay."

Loner: "On our way."

"I'm okay." Peripheral movement caused Ty to look up.
A knot of Pakis was coming his way. Maybe a dozen men,
maybe a few more, led by a pair of uniformed traffic war-
dens wielding batons. Ty ended the call. His last words: "I'm
okay."

Oh, crap. They didn't look friendly. *This is all going terribly wrong* is what Ty was thinking. He knew he should
jump in the Honda and drive pedal to metal to the consulate,
straight over any Paki dumb enough to get in the way.

That's what you did in places like Pakistan, or Egypt, or

any other place where the cops did their interrogations with the help of electric cattle prods or pliers. That's what he'd been taught to do. *Haul your ass outta Dodge, Soldier*, was how it had been phrased.

But he wasn't a Soldier anymore. He was a civilian, even with his diplomatic status. And he had to document what had happened. And so, instead of burning rubber, he stood there and shot one-two-three-four-five-six frames of the scene and the bodies and the downed motorbike with his cell phone camera.

He was sending them to Loner as the first police car screeched to a stop behind him, and he turned to see the cops coming at him full-tilt-boogie, weapons drawn and screaming instructions he couldn't understand.

PART TWO

FEBRUARY 1, 2011 TO MARCH 31, 2011

10

The news spread through Pakistan like a wildfire. All about the nest of spies at the American Consulate in Lahore and the CIA cockroach who had killed two innocent Pakistanis out of pure racist spite. And the three other American dung beetles who had killed a third brother—run him down in cold blood—as they raced in their Land Cruiser Prado to the scene to rescue the first cockroach. And how the Pakistani authorities had stood up to the Americans and were holding the American assassin in jail even though the other three had made it to the consulate and had been illegally secreted out of the country. And how all over the country tens of thousands of Pakistanis in cities, towns, and villages north, south, east, and west had demonstrated their righteous hatred for the United States, a nation of dogs, cockroaches, and vermin. Demonstrated even in Abbottabad, where the hand-lettered signs read "Stone the American CIA cockroach to death" and "Amerika, Nation of Murderers."

Even Waseem the tearoom owner had closed his business long enough to join in the previous day's protest. He couldn't help but chortle to the beggar about the arrest of the American double murderer and how it had caused the United States great embarrassment throughout the Muslim world. It was a sure sign of things to come.

"Thus will the Infidels be brought down," he said as he offered Charlie Becker a second sweet cake to go with his tea.

"God bless you, brother." Charlie took the cake and stuffed half of it in his mouth. It had been a cold night, and Charlie's entire body ached. His stumps, especially, were sore. And he had a rash on his ass from sitting all day on the fricking dolly.

It was on days like this he missed his legs—even the prosthetic ones. He'd lost his ability to step over things on the street that he now had to muscle his dolly around. The simple act of taking a leak was a cumbersome, drawn-out process. And there was the constant, gnawing, dull sense of . . . loss.

Then Charlie thought, *What crap!* Okay, he'd lost his legs. He knew Soldiers and Marines who'd lost more—their lives. He might have been killed in that tunnel. Never seen his grandchild. Never gone back to work. Never had the chance to give something back for all that America had given him.

Charlie considered his time as a Soldier a paid fellowship. He got to travel. He got to learn languages. He got to meet interesting individuals. And of course he got to break things and kill people. All in all a great life.

And his legs? Yeah, he missed them.

And yes, today was one of those days he would gladly have given his left nut for some Aleve. But he was a beggar. And beggars, he knew, couldn't be choosers. Or possess over-the-counter American pain relievers.

Besides, he was a Ranger. And Rangers Drive On sans

complaints. In fact, during his rehab, Charlie had often worn a baseball cap to his physical therapy sessions that read "NO SNIVELING."

Words to live by.

And so Charlie fed his sugar jones instead of his pain jones. And was okay with that.

"God is great, Brother Shahid," Waseem told Charlie as he watched the beggar chew. "He works in mysterious ways to protect us, even if it requires sacrifice."

"He does indeed, brother," Charlie replied. He displayed his ruined hands. "Sacrifice is what he requires of us, and sacrifice is what we willingly provide."

"We willingly provide because God is great, brother," Waseem sing-songed.

God is indeed great, Charlie Becker thought—but maybe, so is Langley. Charlie couldn't be sure, but he guessed that CIA had something to do with the fact that over the past two and a half weeks, the ISI surveillance teams had been withdrawn from Abbottabad.

Gossip at the mosques had it that the detested Americans were engaging in provocative activities in the Frontier provinces. That they'd been seen in Miram Shah and Shawa and near Peshawar, too, selecting targets for the unmanned but armed Predator drones that killed from above. But ever since the murdering assassin had been caught, there hadn't been a single drone attack anywhere in Pakistan. *Allahu Akbar.* God is great!

Whatever the truth of the matter with regard to Predator strikes (or the lack of them), Charlie was also hugely relieved, because for the past five days he'd seen no sign of ISI activity anywhere near Valhalla Base, an info-bit that he had burst-transmitted the previous afternoon. He knew—he'd received a coded message at the dead drop he checked when Valhalla Base pinged him to do so—that new equipment would be arriving soon, along with one or two new personnel. Given the current situation, there was a better-than-good chance that everything would be accomplished well under the ISI's persistent radar blanket.

All in all, the news was good. Which made Charlie, who'd had twenty-six years as an Airborne Ranger, sixteen of them as a senior NCO, nervous. He had done Grenada, El Salvador, Panama, Mogadishu, and Iraq and was entitled to wear combat jump wings, a Silver Star, a Bronze Star with Combat V device, and three Purple Hearts, so he knew from experience that it was right after the good news arrived that the situation generally went south.

But for the moment, anyway, things were okay. Valhalla was safe; ISI and its bloodhound Saif Hadi al Iraqi were long gone. He'd had a nagging, seed-under-the-gum-line sensation for the past few days that something wasn't quite right, as if his feng shui was out of balance. If indeed he'd ever had feng shui. But today that discomfort had blessedly evaporated. He'd even been given an extra treat. Charlie gave silent thanks for small blessings.

He stuffed the last of the sweet pastry into his mouth, handed the cup back to Waseem, and wiped his lips with his sleeve. "God be with you, brother."

"And with you, Brother Shahid. May God grant you the blessing of watching an American die."

That remark certainly changed Charlie's mood. "He has already done that, my brother," he responded grimly, for once telling the Pakistani an absolute unvarnished truth. "He has allowed me to watch Americans die more than once."

11

"Stu, get your coffee-swilling ass up here right now. This is a hell of a way to start the weekend." Vince Mercaldi was pissed. He wasn't a big man—perhaps five-ten and a half. He was beginning to resemble a pear in shape. And he wore suits that were more than slightly baggy, plain white or blue shirts with French cuffs, and ties that might as well have come from Sears. And the kind of 1970s aviator frame glasses that had been out of fashion for so long now that they were almost, almost back in style, eyeglasses that, sitting on Vince's prominent, rounded Sicilian nose, gave him the bug-eyed appearance of that bee in the Nazonex allergy medicine commercials.

But he was passionate. And eloquent. Indeed, Anthony Vincent Mercaldi had been known in the House of Representatives as a stem-winder when he took the floor. Lucky were those in the House Visitor's Gallery when Call Me Vince, steamed about some matter or another or fulsome in praise for an issue or an individual, would enter the chamber and ask for floor time. He had what is known in the military as command voice, which was linked to an extensive vocabulary and combined with a trial lawyer's ability to spellbind an audience using an articulate, contrapuntal mélange of drama, wit, and eloquence, sprinkled with occasional flourishes of menace or tenderness. He could play a jury like Joshua Bell played a fiddle.

That ability, combined with the fact that as a congressman he'd always felt it his duty to be responsive to his constituents, made him uniquely and forcefully persuasive, a quality he brought to his job as director of the CIA.

There had been much skepticism in the hallways at Langley when Vince's appointment was first announced. The instant verdict from CIA's 42,389 full-time employees (augmented by 30,000-plus contractors), was that Vince Mercaldi was an APP—another professional politician—a spineless puppet who would do the White House's bidding.

Two politicians had previously been appointed CIA directors. George Herbert Walker Bush, who would go on to be the nation's forty-first president and after whom the CIA headquarters would later be named, had served as director for just under a year. Previously, Bush had been a congressman, run for the Senate unsuccessfully, and served as ambassador to the United Nations and chairman of the Republican Party. When he was selected as director of central intelligence by President Gerald Ford he was the head of the U.S. Liaison Office to the People's Republic of China—in effect, our first ambassador there, although without the title.

Bush assumed his role as DCI on January 30, 1976. Five months later, Francis Melloy, the U.S. ambassador to Lebanon, and his economic counselor, Robert Waring, were kidnapped by terrorists and subsequently murdered. DCI Bush was summoned to the White House, where he briefed President Ford and his national security team on the incident. But instead of remaining in the Situation Room, where he could have gotten hours of face time with the president, Bush asked to be excused. "I need to be back in our operations center at Langley with my troops," the World War II Navy pilot told the president.

That act earned Bush the reputation of a man loyal to an agency that had suffered the loss of Vietnam and had been tarred by the stigma of Watergate. Bottom line: George H. W. Bush was well liked by most of the CIA rank and file.

The second politician was Congressman Porter J. Goss, a Florida Republican and former CIA case officer whose short tenure as DCI (September 2004 to April 2005) was judged a disaster. Goss was aloof and vindictive, and he wasn't shy about bringing politics to the seventh-floor director's suite. His acolytes, known as the Gosslings, were largely recruited from his congressional office and composed of Hill staffers and former Agency bureaucrats who settled old scores and drove many of CIA's professionals into retirement. Goss was almost universally detested.

By the time the forty-fourth president sent Vince Mercaldi's name up to the Senate for its advice and consent, the only politician-turned-CIA-director just about anyone still serving at CIA remembered was Goss. The corridor gossip at Langley, therefore, was not favorable to the former California congressman. Some of the more cynical wags in the clandestine service suggested that Call Me Vince should be treated like a mushroom: kept in the dark and fed lots of manure.

Yet Vince surprised everyone. He surprised the White House staff by being his own man and not knuckling under to the strongly partisan Chicago-style politics the rough-and-tumble political staff were used to conducting. He surprised the Department of Justice by fiercely defending his CIA constituents when the attorney general decided to mount a politically motivated witch hunt against those officers who conducted what was labeled enhanced interrogation techniques and waterboarding against captured enemy combatants. And he surprised his Langley skeptics by demonstrating loyalty down the CIA's chain of command, a tectonic policy shift from most of his predecessors, who would—and did—sell out Langley's worker bees at the hint of a crisis or embarrassment.

Indeed by the end of 2009, it was understood almost universally at Langley that if you were straight with Vince Mercaldi, he'd be straight with you. And he'd watch your back.

0748 Hours

"You saw this?" Vince held up a sheaf of newspaper clippings, the CIA's version of the Pentagon's Early Bird, a daily clip file containing all significant news stories about defense policy issues and the armed forces. CIA's version, which was unnamed, dealt with stories on intelligence, terrorism, and world politics. Vince's copy was folded back to a *USA Today* clip that quoted unnamed U.S. Embassy officials in Islamabad on the subject of Ty Weaver. Their anonymous quotes, most of which hinted that he was a rogue operator who didn't enjoy diplomatic status, didn't do him much good.

Stuart Kapos, the National Clandestine Service director, dropped into the armchair facing the director's desk and spoke through pursed lips. "I did. What can I say, Vince? They're assholes."

"Ty's wife, Patty, called Rich Erwin, the deputy at SAD, at five-thirty. She'd just received a call from some idiot reporter in Pakistan asking her to comment. Thank God she hung up on him. Rich called his boss, and John called me. John said Rich told him Patty was in tears, Stu. Tears. She has no idea what her husband is doing out there or why we haven't gotten him out of jail. She knew he left with an official passport and had diplomatic immunity. Now all she knows is he's in jail, and neither we nor the State Department is doing a goddamn thing to help the situation. I'm afraid she'll miscarry again—John told me about last year—and then there'll be all hell to pay."

"Can Kate help us out here?" Secretary of State Katherine Semerad and Vince Mercaldi had known one another for years and had a first-rate working relationship, despite the fact that State—or more to the point, its USAID administrator—was screwing up Afghanistan by allowing the Chinese to steal just about all of that country's valuable mineral assets, like copper and uranium, by shutting American firms out of the bidding process.

Diplomats. They didn't have a clue. "You know how hard it is to rein in those goddamn cookie-pushers," Vince said. "Leak, leak, leak. I swear, that's what they do for a living." He uttered a bitter cackle. "They certainly don't spend much time defending American interests."

The D/CIA continued: "I can talk to Kate—I will, too— but we both know there's no way she'll be able to put the cork in this." He paused long enough to drop the clips on his desk. "The immediate problem here is Weaver's wife. She's frantic."

"We can send someone over."

"I thought we had."

"We did—we do," Kapos said. "But not on a daily basis."

Mercaldi frowned. "Do some spade work. Talk to Rich Erwin at Special Activities. Find Ty's friends—people he's close to—and get them over to help Patty out. Certainly for the weekend. And starting next week twenty-four-seven if you have to."

"Will do," Stu said. He paused. "But can I be frank for a second, Boss?"

"Go ahead."

"Why the big push on this? Ty knew the risks. And he's an adult—he can handle it. I—"

"Hold it right there." Vince cut him off. "There's a lot at stake here. I don't want anyone making the connection between Weaver and Abbottabad. Or Weaver and ISI. Or Weaver and the Asymmetric Warfare Group. Or, worst of all, between Weaver and the BLG, even though we've worked hard to keep him compartmented from anything to do with UBL. We know the Paks he killed were snatch-and-grab guys. They had stolen stuff on their bodies and illegal weapons. Even the bike was stolen. But they still had ties to ISI. So it's a can of worms. Which is why everybody's focused on Ty's diplomatic status and the killings, right?"

Kapos nodded. "Yeah."

"Well, like it or not, and no matter how tough it is on Ty, that's where the story has to stay."

The director looked over at Kapos. "Look, Stu, the media is smart. The Paks are smart. For chrissakes, Bin Laden is smart. Every one of them can put two and two together. I don't want anybody getting anywhere near two."

"Understood."

"Then you understand one way to do that is to keep the Weaver family on our side. I don't want Patty giving tearful sidewalk interviews to Channel 7, *Oh, they sent him out with a diplomatic passport but they asked him not to use it because he was on some sort of secret mission but CIA won't tell me anything*. How do we ensure she won't give that interview? We don't just *tell* her we're doing everything we can, we *do* everything we can. We make sure she sees that we are doing everything we can. We support her. We make sure she is comfortable. And informed."

"And all those leaks from State?"

"Don't you have any contacts in the press after all these years?" Vince gave Kapos a sly smile. "You could pass on a few words to the . . . wise."

Kapos grinned. "I could."

"Then do it. SECSTATE is with us on this. But the professional diplomats at Main State and Islamabad and Lahore think they know better. So make them look like the striped-pants, heel-rocking, change-jingling, equivocating, namby-pamby, mush-mouthed assholes they are. On deepest background, of course."

Vince's expression grew serious. "Look, Stu, when our people visit Ty under consular cover, they've got to be able to give him positive messages from Patty. I want him to know we're doing our damnedest. And I want folks like Charlie Becker to know that, too. And the others. Like the folks you've got hunkered down at Valhalla Base. And Bagram. And Jalalabad."

The director tossed the bundle of news clippings across the table. "This isn't about Ty Weaver. Or Patty Weaver. Or what the goddamn media print. You and I, and Dick Hallett, and Spike, and everybody at BLG, we have to keep our eyes on the prize. Everything we do, everything we say, every action, every reaction, has significance. We have to think about *everything*. Look at everything holographically. Why? So nothing caroms around the table and comes back to bite us on the ass. We have to stay focused. Consider all the angles, all the subtleties, all the crazy intangibles. This is all about the bigger thing, Stu. The Abbottabad thing. It's about getting our hands around the throat of that rotten murdering sonofabitch we've been chasing for ten goddamn years. And putting him in the ground.

"UBL. That's why Charlie's out there risking his life. And the people we have at Valhalla Base, and Doctor Afridi who tried to get DNA for us. And all the others, too—including all those who don't know why they're doing what they're doing. People like Ty Weaver. And the other Whiskey Trio team we used as diversions. And all those SEALs and Delta shooters and helicopter pilots Wes Bolin has in training. We're doing this for a goddamn reason. It isn't because we're going to end terrorism once and for all, or make al-Qaeda or any of its franchises disappear. It's not about bringing democracy to totalitarian regimes, or making the world a better place, or singing 'Kumbaya.' And it isn't about politics or personalities. Not about me, or Secretary Hansen, or Secretary Semerad, or the president even. It's all about KBL—Kill Bin Laden. Put him in the ground because that's where he deserves to be, full stop, end of story. This is about KBL. That's what you and Wes Bolin and I have to stay focused on. That one goal. KBL, and bringing everybody home alive."

He peered over his aviators at the NCS director. "I mean, that *is* the goal, right?"

Kapos sat silent. Stunned. In almost three decades at CIA he'd never heard a director express himself with such passion for the mission and loyalty to the people who were putting their lives on the line to achieve it. Finally, he thought, someone who doesn't consider us chess pieces. Or political pawns. This man *gets it*.

At that instant Call Me Vince reminded Kapos of his football coach at the Naval Academy. Now, he realized in an epiphany, he was lucky enough to have known two leaders for whom he would willingly run through walls. And one of them was a fricking fourteen-karat certified Washington insider. A pol. Who woulda thunk it.

He stood and tossed his boss an offhanded salute. "Aye-aye, sir."

Vince cracked a smile. "You wouldn't be spelling that 'c-u-r,' would you now, Stu?"

"No way, Boss. I save that for the diplomats."

"Then get the hell outta here. You have your sailing orders. Go make the diplomats unhappy. I'll do the same for the Pakistanis."

12

Charlie Becker made a habit of changing his sleeping arrangements every two to three weeks. It was one way of making sure he didn't fall into a recognizable pattern. Patterns were bad juju, because they put you in the same place at the same time every day, which made it easier for your enemies to find you and harder for you to notice your enemies. For example, sometimes he'd be at Waseem's tearoom after morning prayers, sometimes after midday. That way he could watch out for watchers. He did much the same with his other daily circuits. He followed no set schedule or itinerary.

Six days ago he'd taken new lodgings in back of a carpentry shop that sat northwest of the Bilal Mosque, at the edge of Hassan Town, a residential subdivision of smallish villas just off Kakul Road. The location was perfect: about a kilometer and a half from the Khan compound Charlie called GZ, and slightly less than that from Valhalla Base. The neighborhood was quiet, mostly retired Pakistan military and faculty from the academy, along with a few shops that had been there before the development started. It was precisely the anonymous kind of place Charlie always sought out. He'd only begun talking to the carpenter, Mohammed, the previous month, although he'd been wheeling himself past the shop since November.

It turned out Mohammed had a thriving business because of all the development in Abbottabad. He'd even worked on the Khan compound. He also, Charlie noted, had a storage shed that faced the plowed field behind the carpentry shop. And so, when it came time to move again, it occurred to Charlie to ask.

Two weeks ago he'd mentioned that he was losing his accommodations, and while he didn't want to be presumptuous, he'd seen that Mohammed had an unused outbuilding in the alley behind the fence. Perhaps the carpenter would like to rent it for a few weeks?

"It would be an honor, brother," Mohammed had said.

The shed was a rectangle about the size of a jail cell, with a sloping roof and an earthen floor. Charlie borrowed some of the pallets stacked behind the shop, and he and Mohammed created a sleeping platform. The carpenter had offered him a couple dozen burlap bags as insulation and padding.

It was all very comfortable—and a lot warmer than Charlie's previous crash pad, which had no glass in the windows. He'd tried to pay Mohammed a few rupees in advance for his lodging, but the carpenter refused, saying he'd been blessed quite enough by Charlie's request for shelter and didn't want to insult God by taking his money. He even put a door on the structure to give Charlie some privacy.

■

It had been a long and cold day—freezing wind blowing off the mountains that ringed Abbottabad in the northwest. And Charlie had felt unsettled, because the seed-under-the-gum-line sensation was back. It was nothing he could put a finger on, just an instinctive reaction to a stimulus he couldn't identify. He put it out of his mind because the new equipment and crew for Valhalla were coming in. Despite occasional rain showers he had maintained constant countersurveillance from a series of locations way out on the perimeter. He'd been gratified to see that everything seemed to have gone without a hiccough.

On the surface, all that happened was that a family of Pakistanis came to visit their relatives, who lived in one of the newer villas in Bilal Town. Family visiting family. The visitors, a plump, obviously prosperous Pakistani and his equally ample wife, arrived in a Suzuki SUV with Amritsar plates and loaded down with all the essentials you need when you're visiting family for a week or two, you have babies in tow, and you want to be generous to your cousins or brother-in-law. There were suitcases and bundles and lots of economy-size bundles of Pampers and gifts and all the other miscellaneous stuff well-to-do families carry when they travel with kids.

Charlie had to marvel at what the Agency was capable of these days. The babies—dolls, of course—were so animated and lifelike one was crying and actually kicking its little legs as it was bundled into the house.

The prosthetics were also incredible. Langley had come a long way since fake beards and glue-on mustaches. Today Agency disguises were made by the same people who created special effects and makeup for Hollywood's most high-tech movies. There were masks that adhered like a second skin; *Mission: Impossible* stuff that was good enough to make it through checkpoints and roadblocks. From eighty yards away, Charlie, a Jurassic relic from the analog days of Walkman cassette tapes, couldn't tell whether it was real or Memorex.

And NSA's techno-geeks had gotten good about creating equipment that could be broken down into transportable, innocent-looking packages. Gone were the days of shipping a parabolic electro-snooper in a four-by-four-foot wooden crate weighing sixty kilos. Now even the most sophisticated eavesdropping equipment could be concealed in a couple of everyday suitcases—or something that looked exactly like a Costco-size bundle of diapers. Parabolics unfurled like umbrellas and weighed ounces, not pounds. Lasers that used to need power packs the size of beer cases now ran off two or three quarter-size 2032 batteries.

And next week, two of the old crew would leave, wearing the same faces and clothes the visitors had worn. Charlie had no idea who they were or what they did. But he admired them. He was mobile. He could get around. And he'd created an E&E plan very early on just in case the you-know-what hit the fan. But the people who staffed Valhalla, they were sitting ducks. They seldom left the base, even though Charlie guessed that some of them at least had language skills. They'd have to be able to pass—at least on the surface—to get out to the dead-drop sites, shop for groceries, put out the garbage, handle all the details that running a covert base in a hostile or denied area entailed.

Moreover, if they were discovered, CIA would deny their existence. That was how it worked in the real world. And they knew it. Yet, still, they were here.

Not only here, but volunteers.

That, thought Charlie, took real guts. It came to him as he wheeled himself around the corner and crossed onto Hassan Town Road, that today was Valentine's Day. Maybe he should send them all flowers. Bouquets for the Brave. The thought brought a smile to his face.

■

2042 Hours

He worked his way slowly toward the alley between the shop and the house next door. It was very dark. The waxing moon was obscured by clouds tonight. He was wet, chilled to the bone, and couldn't wait to climb into dry clothes, wrap himself in his burlap insulation, and get some sleep.

The dolly almost flipped when it hit a crease in the uneven pavement—what there was of it. Times like these Charlie wanted his Surefire, one of those mini LED flashlights that gave you 120 lumens on one lithium battery.

From sixty feet away he could see a car parked on the road in front of the carpentry shop. His antennas went up. Mohammed drove a Toyota pickup, which was parked alongside the shop. This was something else—midsize, dark. He stopped. Waited for some traffic on the road. After perhaps sixty seconds a car turned from Kakul Road onto Hassan Town Road, its lights hitting the parked car as it drove past, heading northeast. The car's interior was empty.

Charlie pushed off, his sticks scuffing the pathway. He made his way past the parked vehicle, brushing the hood with his hand as he did. The metal was cool. The car had been there for a while. He pivoted his dolly and pushed himself sideways, into the alley.

And sensed someone behind him.

He swiveled. Ducked.

Not fast enough.

He took a strike from something hard. The blow came upward, glanced off his left shoulder, then his head, knocking off the *qarakul*.

Charlie grunted, raised his arms to defend himself. But the guy was just too big. Too quick.

Used a long tire iron. Caught Charlie under the arm.

Smacked him off the dolly. Stomped his hip. Rolled him. Kicked him in the ribs. Knocked the breath out of him.

Charlie flailed at the guy's feet and legs, but couldn't reach them.

Charlie was thinking *knife*. Gotta get to a knife.

He carried three. Two were local. One was special.

But there was no time. No way.

No way because he was being rolled. Like a fricking barrel. Kicked and struck and rolled.

Back out toward the road.

Which is when he caught a glimpse. Saif Hadi's flattened nose and thick eyebrows were all he could see because the sonofabitch was wearing a hood. Just like he'd worn in Iraq for all those beheadings.

It was surreal. All Charlie could think in that heartbeat of shock and recognition was Bogie's line, *Of all the gin joints in all the towns in all the world, she walks into mine.*

Meanwhile, Saif, who had probably never seen *Casablanca* and never would, was grunting and cursing as he kicked Charlie toward the car, careful to stay away from Charlie's arms and hands.

Careful because he understood that Charlie, legless, was a grappler. A ground fighter.

Saif was snarling, growling, muttering as he kicked.

Charlie couldn't make it out at first, because *oh, shit*, he realized through it all, Saif was speaking Arabic and Charlie was thinking in Pashto.

Then it came to him. Saif was saying, "I will kill you Mr. José, fuck you, Mr. José, fuck your mother, Mr. José, I'm going to kill you slowly, kill you, Mr. José."

Over and over.

Charlie thought, *This is not real.*

But it was.

So Charlie knew what he had to do.

Catch Saif's foot.

Twist and roll.

Break his fricking ankle.

Bring him down.

Then kill him.

But it wasn't happening.

Saif was keeping his distance. Dancing around, kicking from behind.

Using the tire iron.

And the blows were taking a toll. Charlie took one at the base of his spine that felt like a Taser hit. Shot numbness right into his brain.

His arms, which had been up around his ears like a boxer's to protect his face, dropped.

Which is when Saif smacked him upside the head. Smacked him good, too.

Because everything went white.

Then black.

13

Charlie struggled back into consciousness slowly. Little pieces of life ebbing and flowing. Like breathing, which was hard to do. And trying to figure out why everything was so fuzzy. And why it was so dark. And what was rubbing against his face, his head, his lips. And why he couldn't feel his hands. And why there was constant noise. And where the fuck was he?

The last question was the easiest. He was in the trunk of a car. The car was moving at a pretty high rate of speed over a paved road that needed work. And it was cold.

Everything else was up for grabs.

He worked his shoulders. There was considerable strain on them. That was because his arms were pinioned. They were bound behind his back, overlapping so that his right palm touched the inside of his left forearm and his left palm the outside of his right forearm. From the feel of things, he'd been secured with duct tape. Lots of it.

He rolled slightly. He'd been dumped facedown. He opened his eyes wide. Nothing.

Of course not. There was a bag over his head. That was the roughness.

He rolled slightly to his left. Came up against something hard and rough and cold. Like a big stone or something. He edged away from it to give himself space. He'd stored one of his knives under his tunic on the left side. Not that he could reach it.

He jiggled. It was gone. The second knife had been attached to his belt, and that one was gone, too.

That left the third. The knife Charlie called his Blaber knife.

Charlie had once worked with an officer named Pete Blaber, who'd gone on to command B Squadron at Delta and afterward had written *The Mission, the Men, and Me*, one of the best books on leadership Charlie had ever read.

When they worked together Blaber was an Airborne Ranger major, and he happened to witness Charlie do something very dangerous for a master sergeant: cold-cock an asshole Ranger captain. Left him prone out on the ramp of a C-130, because the captain had been about to do something that would have cost several members of Charlie's platoon their lives.

Charlie just stood there, waiting for the captain to regain consciousness so he could call the MPs and end Charlie's career.

Then Ranger Blaber, who'd seen and heard the whole thing from the get-go, trotted up to Charlie. "Get the hell out of here, Ranger," he told Charlie. "I'll handle this."

He pointed to the captain, who was rolling onto his stomach so he could puke. "He's an idiot. He shouldn't be put in charge of changing lightbulbs."

Blaber looked at Charlie. "Did you hear me, Master Sergeant? Go! Vamoose. Di-di-mau."

It was Ranger Blaber who later gave Charlie some valuable advice. "Always prepare for the worst-case scenario," he told him. "If you do that, nothing will surprise you, because you've already factored in what to do when everything, absolutely everything, turns to shit."

Charlie had taken Ranger Blaber's words to heart. Both as a Ranger and later, at CIA, he'd always tried to conceive of what the worst that could happen to him would be—and then prepare for it. So he referred to his backup gun as the Blaber gun; his extra water, Blaber water. And his last-ditch when-it-all-goes-to-hell knife was his Blaber knife.

Which is why Charlie now rolled far enough to put himself on his side, but careful not to roll onto his back. He flexed his fingers. Good news: Saif hadn't taped his hands, just his wrists and arms.

2104 Hours

He maneuvered himself so he could get his left hand under his sheepskin vest and rough-knit tunic. He yanked, clearing the cloth from his waistband. Pulled it up as far as he could.

Because duct-taped to Charlie's back, just to the left of his right kidney, was his Blaber knife, a SOG Micron tanto.

It wasn't very big. Forty-eight millimeters long and three millimeters wide, with a forty-six millimeter blade. But taped where Charlie had taped it, it could survive just about any pat-down, which obviously it had.

He pulled a corner of the tape, which he'd affixed before he'd left Afghanistan, and eased it down. It took skin and hair with it, but Charlie didn't give a damn.

Pulled the two-by-two patch of tape off, letting it stick to his fingers so he wouldn't lose it.

And while the knife was still stuck to the tape he used his left thumbnail to open the blade. Pulled it free of the patch. Began to work it against the tape binding his wrists and arms.

The road was getting increasingly rougher. Charlie worked the tiny blade. He could feel himself cutting his arms as well as the tape, but it didn't matter, just so long as he didn't nick a vein.

What felt like a hairpin turn set him back some. He almost lost his grip on the knife.

But he held on.

2107 Hours

His arms were free. He cut the cord holding the bag around his neck and pulled it off. He still couldn't see anything, but at least his breathing was unhampered. His head still hurt like hell. He examined himself. He could feel blood above his ear. His nose was stuffy. He probed and touched coagulated blood.

Work through it, he told himself. Drive on! The main thing is to keep the main thing the main thing.

And the main thing here was Saif Hadi al Iraqi. The main thing was that Saif had to die.

The next question was, *Where were they headed? Was Saif taking him to ISI?*

Charlie doubted it. If that had been the case he would

already be hanging naked, suspended by chains wrapped around his stumps while they used cattle prods on his privates or dunked his head in a barrel of water. Paki enhanced interrogation techniques were seriously enhanced.

No, Saif was doing this solo. Charlie's instincts told him it was personal. So either he was delivering Charlie to the Haqqani Network, or he was going to perform a ritual slaughter. Like during Eid al-Adha, the Muslim festival of sacrifice at the end of the Haj.

Charlie had seen it often enough. The sheep or goat was held down, struggling. Its throat was cut while the slaughterer repeated the name "Allah," as a sign that life is sacred.

Just like all those beheadings he watched videos of in Iraq. Listening to the victims' screams as they realized it was for real, while the slaughterers, like Saif, repeated "God is Great," or quoted the Quran's Sura 8/12: "Behead the Infidels and cut off their joints."

Charlie had watched, even though it made him sick to do so. Watched because *Know thine enemy* was one of his credos.

Lying there, the Blaber knife in his hand, he decided that beheading was the deal. Saif the Iraqi wanted Charlie's head on a platter. Or more likely in a bag: *Look who I found.*

2109 Hours

The knife was comically small. Charlie used Saif's duct tape to build some bulk into the handle, leaving some of it sticky-side-out so he could keep a firm grip. He lay his thumb along the length of the handle, the handle across his fisted index finger, and wrapped tape around both fingers and knife, creating an inch-and-a-half talon that could either slash or stab.

Then he waited. Making himself stronger with every passing second. Making sure he kept the main thing the main thing.

2112 Hours

He didn't have to wait long. He felt the car decelerate, veer to the right. Now he felt and heard gravel under the wheels.

The car came to a stop.

Charlie rotated his shoulders to ease the strain, then coiled himself like a spring.

He'd get one shot at this.

It was all about speed, surprise, and violence of action.

The same three tactical principles, Charlie thought, that Mohammed Atta used on September 11, 2001, against the crew of American Airlines Flight 11 out of Boston's Logan Airport. With a blade about the same size he was holding now.

You can kill with a blade of less than an inch if you know how to use it.

Charlie knew how to use it.

The car shuddered slightly. Charlie felt it shift as Saif got out.

Heard footfalls crunching on gravel.

The trunk opened.

Charlie was ready.

Saif wasn't.

The Iraqi froze, eyes wide open.

Charlie had already launched himself.

He grabbed Saif's hair.

Pulled his head down.

Right hand: blade tip up.

Charlie punched the tanto blade with all the force he could muster, straight from the shoulder.

Into Safi's left eye.

Twisted, slashed, pulled his arm back.

Saif screamed. Instinctively, the man's hands went up to his face.

Which was when Charlie's left hand yanked Saif's head down, smashing the Iraqi nose-first onto the jamb of the trunk.

He lifted Saif's head and twisted, exposing the Iraqi's neck. Stabbed into the carotid artery, worked the blade around real good, then cut his way out the back side of Saif's neck.

Back-sliced across Saif's forehead. Stabbed at the other eye. Missed.

Lost the knife. The tape had come loose.

Saif was struggling now. He was going into shock and he'd probably bleed out in a minute or so, but until then Charlie had to hold on.

So he smashed Saif neck-first into the edge of the trunk *UHuhhh* to crush his windpipe, then yanked his head up, got both his big, knotty thumbs into the man's throat, and squeezed. Squeezed like hell.

Charlie was a strong man. Even with damaged hands. He kept the pressure on until Saif stopped struggling. Stopped moving. Stopped breathing.

Kept it up until the sonofabitch was dead.

14

Charlie let go of the Iraqi and slumped back, breathing hard. His stumps hurt like hell because he'd put all of his weight on them. His hands were sticky slippery from Saif's blood. He leaned over and wiped them on the Iraqi's corpse.

Charlie didn't like killing. He'd done enough of it over the course of his life not to like it. But he also knew, as do all true Warriors, that it was a necessary skill in the real world, and that through training, experience, and instinct, he was quite efficient at it.

He also understood a second truth: that some individuals just deserved to die.

Saif was one of those. Saif, who'd beheaded sixteen Iraqi policemen one after the other only because they were Shia. Saif, who'd disemboweled children in front of their parents to make a political point. Like most of his brothers in arms, Charlie Becker preferred peace to war. But they hadn't started this war. Usama Bin Laden had started it. Charlie was where he was to help finish it.

Quickly Charlie checked the trunk. It held two cinder blocks and a short roll of what looked like fence wire. He tossed everything out, then pulled himself out of the trunk and rolled onto the roadside.

He looked around to get his bearings. Saif had parked next to a river with a pretty fast current. The road was about ten feet above the bank, separated by a low metal guard rail. Charlie looked up and down the road. No lights. No signs of life. Perfect.

First things first. He checked Saif's body—carefully—for documents, papers, ID, pocket litter. He stashed everything in his own pockets. He'd look through them later. He couldn't find car keys, so he scooted himself to the driver's side door, opened it, hoisted himself inside, and checked.

They were in the ignition. Better: Charlie's padded dolly and his push-sticks were stashed behind the front seats. Also tossed in the rear were Charlie's knives and a rolled-up black plastic garbage bag. Which Charlie unrolled.

And discovered a heavy, curved, razor-sharp butcher's knife with a twelve-inch blade. A beheader. Saif was planning to extract revenge and take a souvenir, maybe to his al-Qaeda pals.

Charlie laughed. He couldn't help himself, given the morbid irony that it had popped into his mind that he and Saif shared something in common: a favorite old adage. *Don't get mad. Don't get even. Get . . . a head.*

He crabbed back to the rear, took Saif's body by the collar, trying his best not to get himself all bloody, dragged him to the guard rail, then pushed him under so the body would roll down to the riverbank.

He repeated the trip thrice, with cinder blocks, then

fence wire, then garbage bag. By the end of the third, he was bathed in his own sweat. It was yet another episode during which he thought it would have been *s-o-o-o* much easier with legs.

Hyperventilating, Charlie peered over the edge. The slope wasn't too bad. There was a fair amount of vegetation. He figured he could claw his way back to the car easily enough.

He tossed the cinder blocks and wire over the guard rail. Then he shoved Saif's corpse and watched it slide two-thirds of the way down the scrub-covered incline.

Charlie followed, the big knife stuffed in his vest. He dragged Saif to the edge of the river. Rolled the body so it was parallel with the bank.

That was when he realized that he couldn't do what he wanted to. Sans legs, it was impossible to drag Saif far enough into the river where it would be deep enough to sink him.

But he could do the other thing.

He maneuvered the body so that he could straddle Saif's chest. Then he unrolled the big, sharp butcher's knife and set to work.

When he finished, he tossed the head into the river. A good throw—maybe thirty-five, forty feet. He saw the splash.

He did a quick forensics check. He was leaving behind a headless corpse with no ID. Probably not the first of its kind in this neighborhood, either. Charlie heaved the cinder blocks and the fence wire into the river. Policed the riverbank. Glanced up toward the road. The blood on the shoulder next to the guard rail would stay there. Nada he could do about it. That left nothing else to clean up.

Except himself, and the knife. He washed it first. Then he doused his hands in the cold water, rubbing his face only after they were clean. Then he soaked his vest, tunic, and trousers to get rid of the blood, wrung them out semidry, and put them back on.

He rolled the big knife back in its garbage bag, stuffed it inside his vest, and crabbed his way toward the car. On his way up the embankment, he decided not to report any of what had just happened. There was no reason to. It would just complicate matters. Charlie understood the system, be it Army or CIA: Give them a bone and they will chew on it. Don't give them a bone, and they won't have the opportunity.

He made it to the top, scuttled under the guard rail, and pulled himself inside the car. Only then did he give in to the fact that he was totally spent.

He put his head back and reconsidered his position. Was he doing the right thing in not reporting? Yeah, he was. But what about Saif's ISI contacts? Had the Iraqi mentioned anything?

And if he had, would the Paks be coming after him?

Not necessarily. Charlie had seen this sort of thing in Iraq. The local services treated foreign nationals as disposables. Sure, ISI would make use of Saif, pay him well. But he wasn't a part of their culture, or their clan. They'd use him and then forget him. Unless, of course, he had mentioned that he'd seen one of the Gitmo Infidels sitting outside a *zam-zam* shop.

But all of Charlie's instincts told him Saif hadn't said a word. Not to ISI or anybody else. Saif had said it himself: he wanted to kill Mr. José and do it slowly. He wanted revenge on Mr. José. It had been personal.

Personal. That was Saif's mistake. Too bad for him.

And good for Charlie.

Time to move. Charlie adjusted the seat, maneuvered his sticks—he'd use one in his left hand to control the gas pedal and the brake—and turned the ignition key.

That's when he remembered he hadn't closed the trunk.

"Oh, shit," he said out loud.

The words brought a laugh. They were the first English he'd spoken in more than a month.

As he rolled out and dragged himself toward the rear of the car, he was already thinking about where he would abandon the vehicle. Of course he was. Exhausted or not, Charlie always tried to follow the Ranger's Rule of the Five Ps: Proper Planning Prevents Poor Performance.

He knew a neighborhood on the southwest side of Abbottabad where he could leave it. He'd take the plates. The car would be stripped clean within twenty-four hours.

15

"Kate, we have a problem." Vince Mercaldi was on his secure line to the secretary of state, who was in her limo, just departing Main State for a speech at George Washington University. "That idiot is freelancing again."

"I know, I know." He could hear the exasperation in her voice. "I couldn't order him not to go to Pakistan. You can't tell the chairman of Senate Foreign Relations not to go. Especially this chairman."

"Understood. But all the same—"

"Vince, you and I are on the same page on this. So is the president. I spoke to the senator"—she said the word with obvious disdain—"three times yesterday, when he called to announce he was on his way. I spent this morning with the Veep trying to put a cork in the senator's . . . mouth, and I'm going back to the White House at three-fifteen for a one-on-one with POTUS on the subject. Believe me, I'm doing everything I can. Hold on." There was a momentary pause.

Then her voice came back on the line. "Gotta run, Vince. I'll call him between appointments and see if I can't get him to dial it down."

She hung up before Vince could respond. He slammed the phone back onto its cradle. It was an irritating habit of hers to end a conversation abruptly if she knew she couldn't solve the problem. And fat chance she'd be successful at dialing *him* down.

Him being Senator Jason Fitzpatrick Kelly III. The senior senator from Massachusetts was a former presidential hopeful, the current chairman of the Senate Foreign Relations Committee, and a self-proclaimed expert on all things diplomatic. He was famous for his collection of Hermès ties (most of them courtesy of his millionaire wife) and his monogrammed Turnbull & Asser shirts, whose French cuffs all bore the logo JFK III. As if he could stand in *that* shadow.

He had, two days ago, taken it upon himself to fly to Pakistan in order to, in his words, "do everything I can to ease the tensions between Islamabad and Washington brought on by the unfortunate Ty Weaver incident, an incident over which I was not, as I should have been as chairman of the Senate Committee on Foreign Relations, properly and thoroughly briefed before the fact."

Of course he hadn't been thoroughly briefed before the fact. The good senator was one of Washington's most prolific leakers. Briefing him before the fact was the equivalent of telling our adversaries what our plans were.

Or, as Vince had put it to Stu Kapos and Dick Hallett at eight that morning, "That self-aggrandizing sonofabitch would sell his mother out for thirty seconds of airtime."

And as usual, Vince noted, the good senator was going off half-cocked. He had never bothered to check with Main State or the White House on the matter of talking points. Nor had he called CIA to ask for a briefing, even though he knew, because he had been told, that Weaver worked for Langley and should therefore be protected as much as possible.

But that was as far as the information flow went. There was no way "King Jason da turd," as Stu Kapos was fond of calling him, was going to be given any of the specifics about Ty Weaver's real assignment.

Thus prepped, Senator Kelly flew to Pakistan. Where, not on the ground for even half an hour, he held a news conference to announce that Ty Weaver would be subject to a criminal investigation as soon as he returned to the United States.

Three hours later, at the consulate in Lahore, Kelly met with reporters and repeated the promise, emphasizing, "Mr. Weaver's diplomatic status is, of course, up for negotiation with our good friends the Pakistanis." With that sound bite Kelly managed to contradict not only the State Department spokesman, but also the president, who had said not twenty-four hours previously that Weaver enjoyed full diplomatic immunity and that the Pakistanis were holding him illegally.

Then, not fifteen minutes ago, Vince watched CNN go live to Islamabad, where Senator Kelly was repeating that he, for one, wasn't sure about Weaver's diplomatic status. That's when Vince muted the sound and called the secretary of state.

Now Vince watched the tall, angular, carefully coiffed senator look straight into the cameras. He turned the volume up. "Once again, I must emphasize that Mr. Weaver's status remains to be negotiated," Kelly said. "But I also believe that now that I am on the ground here in Islamabad, my good friend the prime minister and I can come to a satisfactory solution."

"Jeezus H." Vince slammed his palm on the desk. The stupid sonofabitch is sending the whole mess back to square one.

Vince muted the TV. "Get Ty Weaver's wife on the phone for me," he barked into his intercom. At least he could reassure her that Chairman Kelly's antics didn't reflect the views of the U.S. government.

He pulled off his glasses and massaged his face with his hands. It was one of those pile-on days. There had been no contact with Charlie Becker for more than twenty-four hours—and no way to contact him, either. The attorney general had announced yet another investigation of CIA activities. And Senator JFK III was running his mouth overseas. Live.

Vince stared at the ceiling. Yeah, this was one of those days when a nice, quiet law practice in northern California looked pretty damn good.

16

As the crow flies, it is roughly 225 miles from Dam Neck, Virginia, to Fayetteville, North Carolina. The MH-60G Pave Hawk helicopter made the trip in just over an hour. From the Joint Special Operations Command apron, it took Captain Tom Maurer a little more than four minutes to reach Wes Bolin's office. He was dressed, as were many SEALs operating in Iraq and Afghanistan, in desert camouflage utilities and tan boots. The only insignia that separated him from any other SEAL were the eagles on his collar tabs.

Maurer was a bear of a man—ruddy complexioned, dark brown hair cropped close, six foot four, 220 pounds, and at forty-six, young to have been a captain for two and a half years. The Colorado native was the son of a Naval Academy graduate who'd been killed in Vietnam. Tom attended the U.S. Air Force Academy. But he wanted to be up close, not above it all. It was not an easy transition, but the young second lieutenant kept at it until he made it happen. Within six months of his graduation, he'd lateraled to the Navy, exchanging his second lieutenant's gold bar for an ensign's and volunteering for Naval Special Warfare. He graduated from BUD/S in December 1987. From there it had been a tour at SEAL Team Five, followed by a deployment with a special boat unit working clandestinely against Iranian Revolutionary Guard naval forces who were trying to mine the Persian Gulf. And then back to ST5, where he deployed to Kuwait and then Iraq for the first Gulf War as the unit's operations officer. After Desert Storm and Desert Shield, he'd been assigned to the Joint Staff at the Pentagon for three long years, followed by a year at the Naval War College, after which he was promoted to full commander and assumed command of SEAL Team Five.

Maurer made captain in 2007. His initial assignment as an 0-6 was working at the NATO Special Operations Coordination Centre in Belgium. He took command of DEVGRU in 2009. It was his first experience working eye-to-eye with the Joint Special Operations Command, and its commander.

JSOC had been created in December 1980, in the wake of the operational disaster at Desert One. It had been designed to C^2—militaryspeak for command and control—the nation's special operations forces: Delta, SEALs, Rangers, and Tier One units in the execution of counterterrorism missions. By the late 1980s, JSOC's mission statement had been expanded to mounting counter-WMD (weapons of mass destruction) operations, counternarcotics operations in Central and South America, and ops that dealt with helping to secure the nuclear facilities of America's former adversaries, as well as designing operations to deal with the nuclear capabilities of America's potential enemies.

Between its creation and 2003, JSOC had the reputation of being a snake-eater's command: a home for renegades and mavericks, filled with cowboys who lacked discipline. That may not have been the truth, but despite the talent of

JSOC's Tier One units, which included Delta, SEALs, and the Army's 160th Special Operations Aviation Regiment, known as the Night Stalkers, that was how the command was seen by the defense—and the political—establishment.

Then, in 2003, things changed. JSOC's new commander, Major General Stanley McChrystal, transformed the command. McChrystal, an ascetic, lead-from-the-front Airborne Ranger, had spent the majority of his career at the 75th Ranger Regiment. He brought with him the Ranger ethos and discipline voiced in the Ranger Creed:

> *I will always endeavor to uphold the prestige, honor, and high "Esprit de Corps" of my Ranger Battalion. . . .*

> *I accept the fact that as a Ranger my country expects me to move further, faster, and fight harder than any other soldier. . . .*

> *Never shall I fail my comrades. I will always keep myself mentally alert, physically strong, and morally straight and I will shoulder more than my share of the task whatever it may be.*
> *One hundred percent and then some.*

> *Energetically will I meet the enemies of my country. I shall defeat them on the field of battle for I am better trained and will fight with all my might. Surrender is not a Ranger word nor will I leave a fallen comrade to fall into the hands of the enemy and under no circumstances will I ever embarrass my country.*

> *Readily will I display the intestinal fortitude required to fight on to the Ranger objective and complete the mission, though I be the lone survivor.*

> *RANGERS LEAD THE WAY!*

■

McChrystal's Ranger vision brought JSOC into the mainstream. He integrated its disparate component units into multiple task forces that worked to solve problems, from identifying and capturing/killing IED makers in Iraq, to targeting and eliminating Abu Musab al-Zarqawi and his al-Qaeda in Iraq network. He sought out both strategic and tactical relationships with the intelligence community so that it could become an integral part of JSOC operations and JSOC part of theirs. He made sure that JSOC was a nimble, proactive command that used intelligence-based ops to keep the enemy off-guard and on defense. By 2006 JSOC had become a three-star command, with newly minted Lieutenant General Stan McChrystal as its head. There was no region in the world in which JSOC did not operate.

Vice Admiral Wes Bolin succeeded McChrystal in 2008. Bolin insinuated JSOC even further into the system, allowing it to seamlessly function within combatant commands such as CENTCOM, at the Pentagon, at CIA, with the State Department, and even at the National Security Council, where early in 2010 a SEAL rear admiral (lower half) named Scott Moore, detailed by Bolin, added depth and special operations insight to White House counterterrorism, counterinsurgency, and counterproliferation policy making.

Moore's flag rank, Bolin recognized, also gave JSOC a prime seat at a very special table. As well as a pair of trusted eyes to gather intelligence that would help him further his—and JSOC's—mission.

Bolin also ratcheted up JSOC's OPTEMPO, running more than a thousand capture/kill raids against Afghan targets in 2010 alone. He initiated Project Ursus, run by JSOC's Task Force Odin, which used UAV drones equipped with chemical detection sensors to identify large stocks of ammonium nitrate, a key bomb-making component for what the Odin task force commander called "low metallic/non-metallic bombs" in the Afghan theater. He expanded raids by Task Force 131, the hunter-killer unit that worked Afghanistan's border region and even occasionally crossed into Pakistan to snatch or kill a high-value target. He dispatched TF 131 elements to Yemen to provide human reinforcement to the drone strikes that were taking a toll on AQAP, the al-Qaeda network franchise in the Arabian Peninsula.

Like his predecessor, Bolin was a lead-from-the-front commander who spent large segments of his time on the ground with his troops in Afghanistan and Iraq. He would often show up unannounced to accompany them on night raids. Indeed Bolin and McChrystal were the highest ranking American officers in decades to fire shots in anger—and sustain enemy fire at close quarters. The fact that they were not only willing but enthusiastic about sharing every facet of their troops' actions engendered a level of loyalty and a winning attitude virtually unknown outside special operations or the Marine Corps.

■

"C'mon in." Bolin shook Tom Maurer's hand. "Good to see you again." The admiral, who was dressed no differently than Maurer, pointed at the sofa. "I think we'll be more comfortable there." He looked at the hovering petty officer who had ushered Maurer into the office. "Coffee?" He shot Maurer a glance. "Black, right?"

"Yes, thank you, admiral." Maurer dropped himself at the end of the sofa, legs scrunched up. Bolin waited until two mugs had been placed on the coffee table and the petty officer had left them alone. Then he pulled the armchair over and sat adjacent to the younger man.

"How're things going?"

"The only easy day was yesterday, Admiral."

"Ain't it the truth." Bolin sipped his coffee, watching as Maurer took his lead and sipped, too.

"Your people are doing fine work in Afghanistan," he said.

"Thank you, sir."

"I know—I was out with one of Blue Squadron's troops last month—Bravo Troop's Three-Team. A zero-dark-hundred hop and pop near Khost."

Maurer nodded. "I heard." He had indeed. Slam Bolin showed up unannounced and alone. His gear bore no rank. He'd ridden in Chalk Two, sitting squeezed between an AWG contractor and a SEAL petty officer first class, and was eighth in the stick going out. He'd even helped flexicuff the prisoners. Afterward he shared the beer he had brought with him with the assault element, gave them a "Well done," shook hands all around, and departed as low-key as he'd arrived.

"They did good. In and out in seventeen minutes, no collaterals, three prisoners, and two fewer knuckleheads wasting our air."

"That's the way it should be done, sir."

"*Hoo-yah!* Textbook stuff. And effective. We've degraded a whole level, level and a half of Taliban leadership in the past eight or nine months."

Maurer nodded. "Heavy OPTEMPO, though."

"Seventeen hundred HVT hits last year alone. It's a tough pace, but we have to keep it up."

"I understand." Maurer sipped his coffee, wondering where the conversation was leading. He had no idea why he'd been summoned. Certainly not to make small talk about OPTEMPO.

He didn't have long to find out. The admiral put his mug back on the table. "We're not in a SCIF, so I can't talk specifically."

"Sir?"

"I'm going to assign DEVGRU a mission." The admiral paused. "HVT. Nothing your people don't do every day."

Maurer's nose wrinkled. If it was everyday stuff, why did it warrant this special summons? He chose a neutral response: "Can do, sir."

Bolin's big, strong hands went palms down on the coffee table and he leaned toward the younger man. "This particular operation may go, or may not go, depending on what develops"—Bolin's chin nudged toward the ceiling—"in the stratosphere. But I need your people to be ready, drop of a hat."

■

Wesley Bolin had given the matter a lot of thought, and he'd come to the decision that SEALs—DEVGRU—would do Abbottabad. For legal reasons they'd have to be under the nominal control of CIA, but it would be a DEVGRU mission all the way.

Yes, Delta would be pissed. Yes, the Army would be pissed. But it made sense. DEVGRU had been working Afghanistan for the past ten years, while since 2003 Delta had concentrated mainly on Iraq. It was SEALs who had executed so many of those seventeen hundred HVT capture/kill missions in the past year. It was DEVGRU's Black Squadron, not Delta's D-Boys, who made regular cross-border hits with CIA's paramilitary people to take out HVTs in North Waziristan. AFPAK was SEAL turf. They'd earned this mission with their time, their sweat, and their blood.

There was another factor as well. Bolin had commanded SEALs in battle. He knew that SEALs wouldn't hesitate. They'd pull the trigger. There would be no second-guessing, no thumb-sucking. If SEALs got into the Abbottabad compound and Bin Laden threw up his hands and said, "I surrender," he was still a dead man. Full stop, end of story.

Bolin wouldn't have to tell DEVGRU anything except to do what they always do. And they'd get the job done exactly the way he wanted it done.

He understood all too well that the politics of his decision could result in political blowback. SEALs ran both SOCOM—the U.S. Special Operations Command—and JSOC. There was even RUMINT, which was intel community slang for what Bolin called PUG, or Pentagon urinal gossip, that another SEAL admiral was in line to take command of CENTCOM later in the year.

Bolin knew from firsthand experience that the Army's chief of staff and especially his deputy were Machiavellian backstabbers. They'd never been supporters of special operations. In fact, they were currently trying as hard as they could to disassemble several of the Army's most valuable spec-ops components, including the Asymmetric Warfare Group. But he had no doubt they'd go crying "conspiracy" to their friends in Congress once they knew Delta was being shut out of Abbottabad.

And if politics was one reason Wes Bolin had decided he'd keep his decision to himself, op-sec was the other. He would continue to deploy chaff, sending out taskers just as he'd been doing to all the Tier One units. But DEVGRU would work the real scenario: utilizing all the overhead, all the thermal, and all the eyes-on intelligence Vince Mercaldi's people were collecting in Abbottabad. That intel would allow the SEALs to work the kinks out.

He would also insist they red-team the mission—tabletop it against another group of SEALs who would play the bad guys, so that every vulnerability could be tested, every flaw probed, every contingency considered, all before the fact.

Oh yes, starting early was good tactics. The more preparation time a unit had, the more likely it would be to develop a successful op-plan. Starting now would give DEVGRU the time to do just that. Yes, the assault was the easiest part of the mission. But it had to be flawless because, especially in Abbottabad, there had to be an extended time for sensitive site exploitation. Most HVT missions ran on a thirty-minute template. This one would take one-third longer.

JSOC's slurpers, as they were called, would want to go over the compound with the proverbial fine-tooth comb and gather up flash drives, hard drives, DVDs and CDs, laptops, papers, pocket litter, memorabilia, and photos. And meanwhile the JMAU—the Joint Medical Augmentation Unit—would be collecting DNA from corpses and everyone else in the compound. All of that would have to be table-topped, and then run real-time. Bolin's mind was made up. It would be DEVGRU, and Bin Laden would be a corpse. Buried in a secret location. Or better, it came to him in a sudden, dazzling burst of inspiration, put somewhere no one would ever find him.

Let people scream and yell afterward. It wouldn't matter then. Because UBL would be dead—and everything else would be moot.

Vice Admiral Wesley "Slam" Bolin, varsity defensive lineman, USNA class of '76, even had an operational designator ready to go: Operation Neptune Spear.

And yes, he had to admit when he looked in the mirror, maybe there was just a little bit—a smidge, as his wife, Debra, would say—of a "Go Navy! Beat Army!" attitude to all of this.

But guess what? He was also making the right call. And he knew *that* right down to the marrow in his bones.

■

"Sir, how much intelligence will we have for our prep?" Even though the admiral hadn't given him a clue about the specifics, Tom Maurer understood all too well that special operations was not a seat-of-the-pants art. Intelligence was the key to success. If you're going to blow an outer door, you have to know how thick it is and what it's made of (most inner doors can simply be kicked in). You have to know how many bad guys there are and have a pretty good idea of how they'd be armed. You have to know if there will be civilians, and how many. Are there dogs? Geese? Sentries wearing suicide vests?

And more than anything, you have to know what can go wrong—have to analyze your own vulnerabilities, so you can identify most of them them beforehand, and then, when the *merde* hits the fan, you can adapt, overcome, and prevail.

"I can give you this much now." Bolin looked intently at the younger man and ticked off items on his fingers. "Suburban environment, multilevel structure, multiple occupants including women and children, one prime HVT, possibly two others. Security force, unknown."

The admiral paused to consider his next words carefully. "In about five or six days I'll be able to provide you with additional information. *Very* good intel, so you can create a mock-up in a secure location and work out the kinks. And in time—certainly within the next month, I would hope—extremely specific intel with regard to targets, timing, and other matters. My question to you is, who have you got available so you can begin the process ASAP?"

Maurer didn't answer right away, because it was a tough call. Personnel-wise, his unit was stretched thin. Very thin.

The original SEAL Team Six in 1980 had seventy-two shooters broken into two teams, Blue and Gold. By the late 1980s, post-name change, the command was expanded into four: the original two; Green Team, which was DEVGRU's training element; and Red Team, the third action team.

These days there were new unit designators. Instead of

teams, DEVGRU was broken into six squadrons of fifty to seventy SEALs each: Blue, Gold, and Red were the action units; Gray handled technical and equipment test and evaluation; Green Squadron was the training unit; and the smallest, Black Squadron, was the covert group, which did much the same sort of totally under-the-radar work as Delta's D Squadron.

Squadrons were broken down into three troops, which had alphabetical designators: Alpha, Bravo, and Charlie. And the troops were further segmented into numerically labeled assault teams of four to six SEALs each.

Blue and Gold were overextended. Roughly half of Gold was parsed out in two- and four-man SEAL teams in Colombia and Peru, working counternarcotics and going after the FARC. The other half of Gold was in Afghanistan, chasing HVTs. Gray was not action-ready and would take time to bring up to speed. Other DEVGRU SEALs were training, some in shooting schools like Gunsite or Mid-South to hone their skills, others doing advanced language work in Monterey. Blue Squadron, like Gold, was forward-based, although entirely in Afghanistan, some of its people working TF 131 missions in Helmand Province, others in the northeast border regions, still others supporting missions in Kandahar Province, south of Kabul.

That left Red Squadron, which had been stood down following the Norgrove rescue attempt. Red was neither on alert nor deployed.

But Red?

Maurer knew how hard Dave Loeser had been working to rebuild the squadron's esprit de corps and its performance. They had the balls. They had the capabilities. But the Norgrove episode had made them second-guess themselves. That couldn't happen. Not ever. Killing a hostage was tough.

But they had to get past it. Because there were times—as there had been in the past—when they would have to look a woman in the eyes and kill her. Not hesitate.

Because when it came right down to it, DEVGRU was all about killing, full stop, end of story. You had to be able to pull the trigger. That was what the unit was all about.

So Dave Loeser started slow. But in the past few weeks he'd been pushing them balls to the wall. Challenging them. Demanding their best—and then some. Testing every bit of their capabilities, judgment, and skills. Setting them up to fail and watching to see how they dealt with it. Putting them through his own version of Hell Week.

They'd been at it without letup since the seventh of January.

Loeser had told him three days ago that Red was good to go. He had his killers back.

A less secure CO might have asked for specifics. But Maurer trusted his squadron commanders enough not to second-guess or micromanage them. If Dave Loeser said his people were ready, that was enough for him.

Maurer looked COM/JSOC straight in the eye. "Red Squadron's available, Admiral."

17

Lahore's central jail sits in the southern part of this parallel-ogram-shaped city of six and a half million souls. It is surrounded on the north by plowed lentil fields and on the west by cabbage fields and an eighteen-acre, half-empty industrial zone. To its south is the Lahore Race Club. To the east, as far as the eye can see, lies a series of neighborhoods filled with tens of thousands of lower- and middle-class houses and apartment blocks.

The main jail is built in the shape of a wheel, with inmates housed in long, one-story spokes that radiate out from a large, oval inner courtyard. Ancillary buildings housing administrative and other functions dot the grounds on the perimeter of the wheel. A new section of the jail, two square, multistory, high-security buildings built especially for sectarian, domestic, and foreign terrorists and jihadists, sits on a walled, rectangular four-acre plot directly to the east of the old jail.

The old Central Jail is, like all the other jails in Punjab Province, extremely overcrowded. Originally built for fewer than a thousand prisoners, Kot Lakhpat currently houses more than four thousand inmates, ranging from common criminals to mass murderers. It was where the Pakistanis chose to incarcerate Ty Weaver.

The consulate was closed on Sundays, and that was the day its RSO elected to visit so he could do it on his own time and under the radar. Ty Weaver was not the professional diplomats' most beloved of individuals these days, and as far as the consul general and most of her staff were concerned, he could rot in hell—or jail. The RSO, on the other hand, had different views.

Twice the Paks sent ISI teams masquerading as policemen to interview him about Ty's duties and his relationship with the consulate. Both times, Wade had corroborated the CIA man's cover story, insisted that Ty had diplomatic immunity, and even showed them copies of the reports Ty had written as part of his cover for status.

And when the ISI officers told him his story was at variance with the consul general's interview, Wade became indignant. "He worked for me, not the CG. She doesn't have a clue about what he did."

Of course he covered for Ty: Ty had been Delta. Tier One. He'd put his life on the line for the country. You don't give up people like that.

■

At the outer perimeter, Wade waited in line until he was allowed through the main gate. He displayed his diplomatic credentials at the guard post, told them why he'd come, and was asked to wait. After half an hour he was escorted across the five-hundred-foot, poplar-tree-lined driveway to one of the squat, shoebox-shaped administration buildings that flanked the jail's main gate.

Inside he was marched through a series of metal detectors, handed a visitor's badge on a chain, then led to a snot-green office with peeling paint and steel furniture bolted to the floor.

Wade followed the guard into the office and perched on the edge of the cool table. The room smelled of industrial-strength disinfectant. The guard said, "Please wait here," and left, closing the door behind him. When he did, Wade realized that only the corridor side of the office door had a knob on it.

Sixteen minutes later Ty was brought into the office in handcuffs, escorted by a Mutt & Jeff pair of guards in soiled uniforms and Pancho Villa mustaches. He was unshackled, and the guards withdrew.

Wade eyeballed the CIA man. He was still wearing the same clothes he'd had on when he'd been arrested. "You've lost weight," Wade said.

"Prison food." Ty laughed. "Actually, they feed you pretty good here. Lots of lentil and chicken stew."

"How're the accommodations?"

"They've got me in isolation. I've got a small barracks all to myself. Six cells. I could have my pick."

"You've got two more rooms than I'm allowed on my State Department housing allowance. Maybe I should consider a move."

"Only if you like all your locks on the outside of the doors."

"Maybe not." Wade scratched his beard. "Anything I can do for you?"

"Call Patty," Ty said. He recited the number and Wade wrote it down. "Tell her you saw me. Tell her how I look, and that I'm in good shape."

"Will do."

"And let her know I'll be home soon."

"Sure."

"Hell, I would have been home by now, except for that idiot senator."

That was true. Just prior to Senator Kelly's visit, the Pakistanis and the U.S. were close to a backdoor agreement engineered by Prime Minister Yousuf Raza Gilani. The Americans would pay half a million dollars in *diyya*—blood money—to the families of the men Ty had killed. He would be allowed to leave, and the U.S. would quietly spirit him out of the country.

After Senator Kelly's press conferences, however, a Pakistani court decided that Ty would be held at least until March 14. And the *diyya* price had gone up. Now the families wanted just over $2 million.

Wade examined Ty's face. It was haggard, strained, tense. He had a two-, maybe three-day beard. "You look like shit, you know."

Ty gave the RSO a grim smile. "Do I look like that on TV?" The Pakistani news shows regularly aired segments of Ty's videotaped interrogation, which the Paks leaked to their state-run media.

"Naw, on TV you look like that guy on *CSI*."

"If only." Ty ran his hand through close-cropped hair. "I hate not working out. I'm going to flab."

"Don't they have a weight pile here?"

"This ain't San Quentin, dude. No TV, no library, no weight pile."

"The good news is no Mexican Mafia or Aryan Brotherhood, either."

"Yeah, but we've got AQN and Taliban."

"In segregation, right?"

"You better believe it."

The room fell silent for half a minute. Ty took the time to

appreciate the RSO's visit. He looked at Wade. "Thanks for coming, dude."

"You'd do the same for me."

Ty gave the RSO a thumbs-up. "You bet."

The two men fell silent again. Neither was given to small talk.

Finally Wade said, "I pouched most of your professional stuff for you. It should end up at your home base."

"Thanks." Ty had stored a cache of CIA gear—false license plates, IDs, and other equipment—in the RSO's safe.

"No prob," Wade shrugged. "Anything else you need?"

Ty fingered his very ripe plaid shirt. "A fresh set of clothes would be nice."

"I'll bring a package in a couple of days." Ty's belongings had been moved out of the apartment he'd shared with Loner, Kent, and Gary within hours of the shootings. The three AWG Soldiers were long gone, but Ty's two suitcases sat in the RSO's office. "Anything you specially—"

The RSO stopped speaking at the sound of the door being unlatched.

The guards were back. Mutt was holding the shackles. Jeff had a big ring of keys.

"Yeah—skivvies. Mine'll walk out of here on their own." Ty extended his hand. "Thanks, dude."

Wade took it. "Keep the faith, bro."

"Nothing else to do." Ty gave the RSO an upturned thumb before Mutt slipped the handcuffs on his wrists. "Remember—call Patty."

18

Charlie Becker sat outside the Iqbal Market collecting alms, and his thoughts. Tareq Khan was back. Charlie had eye-balled the Bin Laden courier, quite by chance, four days earlier. He was skirting the perimeter of Ground Zero, the Khan compound, when the gates opened and the red Suzuki drove out.

But it wasn't Arshad who was driving. It was another Pashtun, slightly younger, whom Charlie had never seen be-fore, with a woman and two kids in the back, and a young male child riding shotgun.

Had to be Tareq. The Suzuki was the Khans' car. No one else drove it.

Then Charlie had seen him again. Yesterday. At the *zam-zam* stand across from the Kabul Café. No wife, just Tareq and the kids. He bought them all milkshakes: mango, pa-paya, orange, and melon. They had stood next to the stand and drunk them. And Charlie heard the kids ask Daddy how his trip was and how sad they were when he was gone, but what wonderful presents he'd brought them.

And then Daddy told them he wouldn't have to go away again, not for a long time. He kissed them all, telling them he'd be at home, except for one or two very short visits to friends near Peshawar, but it would only be for a day or two.

Bingo, thought Charlie. Gotcha.

Exuberantly, he'd bursted it all to Valhalla Base: the short trips, the kids' presents, the *zam-zams*.

And from there his transmission disappeared into the great void.

And left Charlie hope, hope, hoping, it would do some good.

Because if Charlie had thought about it, which he had— oh, had he ever—he was beginning to wonder whether anything he was doing out here was making a difference.

The reason for this unusual (for him) introspection was that, although he wouldn't admit it to anyone, including and most important to himself, he'd been somewhat depressed of late.

It wasn't anything to do with Saif's death. That sonofabitch deserved everything Charlie had given him. If anything, killing Saif had served to remind Charlie of his *raison d'être:* putting those who threatened the nation in the ground. But even so, for the past week or so, Charlie had been feeling . . . empty. Like he'd been caught up in an existential vortex and couldn't spin out of it. Part of it, of course, was the culture of which he was a part, had been a part for more than three decades, first as a Ranger, then at CIA. Rangers, like other Tier One units, operate in secret.

Tier One Warriors don't talk about what they do, or where they do it, except to other Rangers. Same for SEALs and Delta shooters. Charlie understood secret. But this was different. Undercover was a whole nother universe. Like working in a vacuum. And, as Charlie had lately discovered, depression was a palpable reality; a bona fide part of his life. It was *agnawing*.

Even Waseem noticed it. "You seem very quiet these days, even sad, Brother Shahid," the tearoom owner had said only last week. "Is something wrong, God forbid it?"

And Charlie had thought, as he sat there sipping his tea, *Well, yes, Waseem, I'm quietly debating the state of my world, because I'm hoping that what I'm doing here will help to put one of your greatest heroes in the ground. Bury him with a stake right through his fricking heart. But y'know, I don't actually know if I'm doing anybody any good out here because I'm working in a vacuum and I feel totally isolated. On the other hand, the tea sure is wonderful.*

To be sure, Charlie understood intellectually that the rigors of undercover work require immense, almost ineffable levels of concentration, discipline, and, above all, the ability to be out there with no net, no support, no backup, and, most critical, no one to talk to. Like a hardhat diver a hundred feet down. Alone. In a vacuum.

That last little bit—and he'd learned it on the job because no one had ever discussed it with him before he'd come here—was the toughest part of working a long-term undercover assignment like this one: no one to talk to. No one to bounce ideas off of. To fricking listen to you. To let you vent about your frustrations. About your fears, anxieties, doubts. About your hopes and dreams, and yes, your successes. The aloneness, the vacuum, was debilitating. Draining. Exhausting. Depressing.

Charlie had spent virtually his entire military career in the 75th Ranger Regiment. The Army was collegial. The Army was built to be that way. Squads, platoons, companies, battalions, regiments, divisions. It was all about working as a team. Which was why, when some idiot had come out with the inane recruiting slogan "An Army of One," Charlie had wanted to smack the stupid sonofabitch silly. An Army of One? One *what*?

Well, now Charlie was an army of one. Working in a vacuum. He'd arrived in Abbottabad four months ago, almost to the day. The intervening weeks had not been easy.

Oh, *that* was putting it mildly.

It was tough. It was tougher than tough. It was compartments within compartments within compartments. It was bottling up all your hopes and dreams inside an impenetrable shell, the shell that will keep you alive in this hostile, deadly environment, but the shell that wants to explode out of frustration, anxiety, aloneness.

That was why catching sight of Tareq was so important to him. It was the first time in weeks, certainly since he'd killed Saif the Iraqi, that he felt he was making forward progress.

But there had been no reply to his message. And it would have been oh so wonderful to hear someone say, "Thanks, we needed that."

Yeah. It would.

But then it occurred to him, sitting there on the street by the Iqbal Market, not six rupees in his bowl. It occurred to him, like *Boing!* The Proverbial Lightbulb. An epiphany.

Having put Saif in the ground was thank-you enough. Interdicting a threat and neutralizing it? That was what he *did*. He didn't need a thank-you. He was a Ranger.

Always would be. Even in Abbottabad. Because what was Abbottabad?

It was a target. It was his job to be here.

And what was his job?

Recon. Spotting Tareq was his job.

Because he was on Point.

Of course he was. Because *Rangers Lead the Way!*

Charlie refocused. Remembered the Ranger Creed.

I will complete the mission, though I be the lone survivor.

Airborne Ranger. That's who he always was and would always be.

He pushed off and rolled down the street toward his next checkpoint.

Energized. Recommitted.

Thinking, *Hoo-ah, Ranger Becker, Drive ON!*

19

Brittany Roberts slid the pasta salad onto the big folding table, careful not to crease the tablecloth. Troy and Ken Michaud had moved the table up against the wall in the family room to give everybody a little more space. She gave the table an approving glance. Pasta salad, pot roast, and a big green salad followed by homemade apple pie and vanilla ice cream made for a lovely dinner. Plates, napkins, and flatware were laid out. There were even flowers. There was a fire in the fireplace, sports on Fox Soccer channel, and the mini fridge that Troy kept under his bar on the other side of the room was full of Corona, Coors, and Michelob Light.

She was barely showing, her figure still slim in skinny jeans and a long-sleeved flowing top. She ran a hand through long, dark hair and looked around the room, delighted that everything was shipshape. The word brought a smile to her face.

Brittany loved the house. They'd bought it a year and

a half ago, at a fire-sale price. The basement family room
had a beamed ceiling and a fireplace. The front garden was
framed by a white picket fence that Troy and Ken had put
up last summer as a birthday present for her. The neighborhood was lovely, the schools were good, and she was less
than fifteen minutes from the Lynnhaven Mall, across from
which she worked part time as a billing clerk at a printing
company.

She turned and headed for the stairs, bringing the gravy
for the pot roast, which was even now out of the crock pot
braising liquid and being sliced by Danny Walker.

There were nine of them for dinner. She and Troy and
Corbin, who was being allowed to stay up later than usual
because of the guests, and Ken Michaud, who just about
lived with them since he'd broken up with his long-time girl-
friend. Master Chief Danny Walker and his wife, Christine,
had come, and Jerry Mistretta, who was also stag, and Kerry
and Jama Brendel.

She glanced at Jerry and Ken as they sipped their beer,
deep in conversation with Kerry, the tall, lanky SEAL
known as Rangemaster. Hopefully, she thought, they'll find
someone soon. But in the special operations community,
relationships, Brittany had come to understand, could be
rocky. There were the long deployments—months of separation. There was the constant gnawing comprehension that
your boyfriend or husband earned his living by jumping out
of aircraft at heights measured in miles, or looking out of nuclear submarines, or spending long periods of time in groups
of two or four or six, living unannounced and unwelcome
in the midst of people who would just love to behead him,
shoot him, or blow his limbs off with an IED. She and Troy
had visited SEALs at Walter Reed. Wounded Warriors, they
were called. Missing limbs. She cried every time she left the
wards, thinking but at the same time trying not to think how

she would feel if Troy was like one of his wounded brothers in arms. And of course there were the constant stories of SEALs and their wandering eyes and testosterone overdrive.

She was lucky. She and Troy had their church and their faith. And she knew how much he loved her. Loved her enough to take her on with a three-year-old child and tell her straight out, "Corbin's my kid just as much as he's yours."

■

The dinner was sort of an impromptu thing. They'd run into Danny and Christine at church, and Brittany suggested they do something together later, because the guys were scheduled to TDY out west for some training first thing Monday morning and Ken was coming to dinner anyway. Christine said she and Danny asked Jerry over so he wouldn't have to eat by himself, and so why didn't Bri and Troy just join them. And then they saw Kerry and Jama, and asked them if they were free—and they were.

But Brittany's baby sitter wasn't available this weekend, and so to make it work she and Troy would host and Danny and Chris would bring the main course and Jama and Kerry the dessert.

Or, as Danny'd put it as they all walked out into the March sunshine, "Hey, guys, it's Darwin, Sun Tzu, Musashi. Adapt, overcome . . . or starve."

Brittany loved the closeness of Troy's team. It was very much like having a big, extended family around. Danny's wife was like an older sister. So was Roger Orth's wife, Barbara.

It was the first extended family she'd ever known. Brittany was an only child, a Chesapeake, Virginia, native who had left home at nineteen, using marriage as a form of rebellion against her loving but distant only-child mother and orphaned father. Her intended, who had just turned eighteen, worked at a Jiffy Lube.

Four years later, she was abandoned, miserable, and living back in her parents' house, her seven-month-old Corbin cared for by her mother while she worked at Dick's Sporting Goods in the Lynnhaven Mall and took classes toward an associate's degree in business technology at Tidewater Community College.

She met Troy at Dick's. He'd come in to buy the latest Under Armour cold-weather compression gear. They had talked, and as he was fond of telling anyone who would listen, he'd fallen in love with her glorious green eyes in about, oh, five seconds. Fifteen minutes after they had first spoken he asked her out, and she said yes.

That had been two and a half, almost three years ago, when Troy was still at SEAL Team Four. But ST4 was an overt team. The team partied as a group, went out to restaurants, held picnics. Troy could even talk about his work—or at least some of it.

Where he worked now—Brittany was hesitant even to *think* the word DEVGRU, though it wasn't classified—everything was secret.

Like tomorrow's deployment. All she knew was what he had told her: he was going out west for some training. It might last a week, it might last a month. He didn't know.

Sometimes, she'd come to realize, his explanation was actually true. Sometimes, however, "out west" or "down south" could mean Afghanistan, Iraq, Yemen, Colombia, or some similarly dangerous place. Like the time a year ago January when he'd said he was going up to Fort A. P. Hill in northern Virginia for a week and came home with a deep suntan. Or last March, just about a year ago, when he told her he was going to do a week of HALO—high-altitude low-opening—parachute certification in Arizona. Four days later she turned on the news and saw that the president had made a secret trip to Afghanistan to meet with troops at Bagram Air Base, and also with the Afghan president, Hamid Karzai. In one of the shots, she caught a glimpse of Troy. He was dressed in Afghan clothes and a funny-looking hat, standing at the edge of the contingent of bodyguards escorting Karzai to the meeting.

That was an eye-opener. When she asked him about it, he just smiled and kissed her and said, "Aw, sweetie, you know we shouldn't talk about that stuff."

Then she understood: working at DEVGRU meant Troy could end up in some place he could never talk about, doing something he would never be able to talk about. Like the months of November and December, when he came home from an assignment and told her he might have to leave his job.

He never said why. But she'd read in *Navy Times* that a SEAL team had killed a hostage by mistake during a rescue attempt. She asked Troy if that had something to do with his situation. He looked at her with his big brown eyes, hugged her, and said, "Baby, I can't say anything. But it'll be okay."

Indeed secrecy was omnipresent in their lives. He had a Navy cover job and a Navy cover unit, so they had answers for the times people asked about his work. And if, God forbid, anything happened to him, because his deployments were classified all that would come out publicly was that he was a petty officer second class working in support of Naval Special Warfare Group Two. If that: the real names of two of Troy's shipmates killed in Afghanistan had never been released. Their deaths were reported, but under pseudonyms.

If something happened to Troy, there would be no yellow ribbons or public grief. It wasn't done. Not at this command. DEVGRU's mourning was done in private.

That was all on the one hand. On the other hand, she knew that Troy had the best training and the best equipment and worked with some of the best intelligence the United

States could provide. She knew that very, very few candidates made it into his unit. BUD/S was tough; what Troy had had to go through to make it into DEVGRU was even tougher. He was the real tip of the spear. The best of the best. And knowing that made her very, very proud of him, of the unit, and of what they could accomplish.

■

Coors Light in hand, Troy wandered over to the corner of the family room, where Kerry, Ken, and Jerry were talking, their voices masked by the English Premiere League game he had TiVo'd. He paused long enough to check the score. In the forty-first minute, Liverpool was up two-nil over Manchester United. That brought a smile to his face. Although he appreciated the robotic relentlessness of Man U, he was delighted to see that once in a while the underdogs kicked some butt, too.

He'd gotten to appreciate English Premiere League Football—he still called it soccer—during cross-training with the Royal Marines the previous year. At its best—he realized this the first time he saw Chelsea play Arsenal—it was all about *team*. The pace of the game also floored him. He marveled at the accuracy of the passes, often made blind, with the passer just knowing that his teammate was going to be exactly where he needed to be. In many ways, watching the best of the EPL reminded him of the seamless way he and his shipmates in Red Squadron worked.

In fact, when he thought about it, there were some strong similarities. Like the EPL, Troy and his shipmates were professionals who were expected to excel every time they played the game. No excuses. No woulda-coulda-shoulda.

The difference, of course, was the game, and the stakes. Troy's team played for life-and-death stakes. If Man U or Chelsea or Tottenham lost one, it affected their standing in the league and their chance of winning the championship.

If DEVGRU lost, it meant someone died, or that the results could have huge implications for the United States.

Troy clapped a hand around Ken Michaud's shoulder. "Padre—ready to eat?"

The tall, thin redhead took a pull on his Corona. "In a bit." He nudged Kerry. "So, Rangemaster here thinks we're setting up to snatch Ahmed Wali Karzai."

Ahmed Karzai, the head of the Kandahar Provincial Council, was the half-brother of Afghani president Hamid Karzai. AWK, as he was known, had his finger in every pie in the province—taking a slice of the trucking revenues, drugs, and protection. You didn't move in Kandahar unless you gave AWK a piece of your action. More than one American general and a couple of ambassadors had tried to dislodge him. None was successful.

"AWK's back on our team," Troy shook his head. "Petraeus loves him these days. So does State, because he helps USAID's people move around. Besides, we're working a three-level house. The big house on AWK's compound is two stories, remember?"

"Shit, you're right," Padre blinked. "When we were there with Petraeus, he held the Jurga or whatever they call it on the top floor, and it was up just one flight." Their troop had pulled bodyguard duty for the International Security Assistance Force commander the previous year.

"So who does that leave?" Cajun Mistretta leaned behind Troy's bar and dropped his bottle into the recycle bin. "Today's frog is a green frog, T-Rob," he grinned. "My guess is Cyclops." Cyclops was the code name for the one-eyed leader of the Taliban, Mullah Omar.

Troy suggested, "What about The Doctor?" That was Ayman al-Zawahiri, the Egyptian who was Usama Bin Laden's Number Two.

Cajun pulled the other three in close and whispered conspiratorially. "Or maybe even the big guy: Crankshaft." He opened a fresh bottle of Corona. "Boy, would I love to pull the trigger on him."

"You're nuts," Rangemaster scoffed. "There's no solid intel on UBL."

"So what? There's no solid intelligence on the other two, either. And what about the NATO story last whenever it was?"

Padre squinted at Cajun. "That he was living in Pakistan?"

"That the one."

Troy said, "It was debunked. CIA, the White House. They all denied it."

Cajun frowned. "I wouldn't trust anything the White House put out. Remember how long they took to green-light the Maersk op when that container ship captain was taken hostage?"

"And tried to get us to wound, not shoot to kill," Rangemaster said.

"Did they actually do that?" Troy asked.

"That's what I heard, too," Cajun said. "But y'know what, all White Houses are the same. They're filled with politicians. Me? I say just let us do our jobs. Don't tell us how to do them."

"Agreed." Troy took a pull on his beer. "Sometimes I can't figure out why they don't understand we're doing God's work."

Padre laughed. "That we are—helping all those AQN and Taliban scumbags get their seventy-two virgins."

Rangemaster grinned. "I hope we help Crankshaft on his way, too."

"If we can find him," Troy said. "C'mon, we see some pretty good stuff. Any of you guys read anything credible anywhere about Crankshaft living in Pakistan?"

The four SEALs looked at one another. All of them shook their heads no.

"Y'know what?" Troy finished his beer and dropped the bottle into the blue bin behind his bar. "We'll know when we get out there. Eyeball the target, then we'll Google Earth it and see what matches. That should give us some clues."

"Good idea," said Cajun.

"I have a better one," said Rangemaster. He pointed at Danny Walker coming down the stairs carrying a huge platter of sliced pot roast. "Chow time."

20

Shortly after 0700, Alpha Troop's 1- and 2-Teams, Charlie Troop's 2- and 6-Teams, and Commander Dave Loeser and his Red Squadron executive officer, Lieutenant Commander Joey Tuzzalino, assembled in the lobby of the Landmark Inn, the only hotel located on the Fort Irwin grounds. They were all dressed in Army combat uniforms (ACUs) patterned in tan, green, and brown multicam. The ACUs bore an ID strip on the chest of their combat vest and infrared-readable American flags sitting on their right shoulder above the tab that identified the men as members of the Twenty-Seventh Civil Affairs Company, a unit that does not exist. Their rank tabs were all the same: E-5.

The only visual elements that differentiated them from regular Army troops were their appearance—they wore their hair longer than most Soldiers, and a few had facial hair—and the weapons they carried: instead of Colt M4s, they had suppressed piston-driven HK416s and the short-barreled LWRCI 7.62 rifles known as JKWs, and instead of Berettas, Sig-Sauer and HK semiautomatic pistols. You had to look twice to pick up on those subtleties.

Which was the idea. Clad as they were they looked no different from the thousands of Soldiers who used the Fort Irwin National Training Center for their predeployment urban combat training. The NTC, a hundred miles west of Las Vegas in California's vast San Bernardino Desert, comprised roughly one thousand square miles of sand dunes, flatlands, and mountainous terrain in many ways similar to the topography of Iraq and portions of Afghanistan. Its airspace was restricted. Communications were ideal owing to the uncluttered electromagnetic spectrum in the sparsely populated region.

The site had been used by the military on and off since 1940, when President Franklin D. Roosevelt first established an anti-aircraft range there. In 1942 the location was named after Major General George LeRoy Irwin, who commanded the 57th Field Artillery Brigade during World War I.

During the Cold War, Fort Irwin was one of the Army's key armor and artillery training sites. The NTC was activated in 1979, and a resident opposing force was brought in to challenge incoming units. In the early 1990s, with the realization that much of future combat would occur in urban environments, unlike the great land war against the Soviets, the NTC instituted a curriculum dubbed MOUT (Military Operations in Urban Terrain) in December 1993.

Since 2005 Fort Irwin and the NTC had been designated the Army's main training facility for urban operations training. Many of the local residents had been hired to role-play during the field exercises. Visiting Army linguists got to practice their language skills by donning Afghan or Iraqi dress and confronting the trainees in Pashto, Urdu, Dari, Arabic, and Farsi.

Today troops can train in Afghan villages and Iraqi towns, or wire-strewn urban warrens of alleys similar to the ones the Marines fought through meter by meter in Fallujah. There are clusters of buildings that can be adjusted to reflect the Middle East, Southeast Asia, Africa, or Central or South America, giving troops the ability to practice the urbancentric combat that is known as the "three-block war" in venues that mimic Cairo or Kandahar, Lagos or South Lebanon, Jalalabad or Abbottabad.

On March 8 there were more than five hundred Soldiers on predeployment exercises at Fort Irwin, as well as fifteen hundred National Guard personnel training for urban and border-surveillance operations. The twenty-six SEALs went completely unnoticed.

The fact that Fort Irwin is a busy venue was precisely why Tom Maurer and Dave Loeser had selected it for the initial training site. It was, they understood, far easier to get lost in a crowd than to be the only game in town. And so, near the outer edge of the northernmost urban warfare training area, nestled behind a faux apartment block and down a thirty-foot-wide paved road leading to a Potemkin Village marketplace, they'd created an irregular, pentangled site roughly 225 feet in length and 150 feet at its deepest point, delineating the outer borders with telephone poles laid end to end. Within the irregular pentangle were six structures. One was three stories tall, one had two stories, and the remaining four were single level.

With Loeser's vehicle in the lead, the SEALs parked their five Humvees a hundred feet beyond the site and dismounted.

The squadron commander and his XO stepped across the telephone poles. Loeser waited until the SEALs gathered around him. He pulled a small spiral notebook from his ACU breast pocket and opened it, checking the notes he had written.

"Here's the mission," he said. "Capture/kill a high-value target living in this"—Loeser indicated the three-story structure behind him—"location. Insertion by no more than two helos, which have to land and take off within the confines of the area indicated by the telephone poles." He paused while the SEALs looked over the layout.

"The HVT will be living with family members and friends who may or may not be armed. The HVT may be wearing an explosive vest or have weapons within close proximity. There will most certainly be children, some of them young, who may or may not be used as human shields. The political implications of collateral damage are huge, especially where it comes to the children." Loeser paused. "In other words, do *not* shoot any kids unless they are shooting at you. Everybody with me so far?"

Heron's hand went up. "Hey, Boss, what about wives? I—"

Gunrunner's hand shot up. "I know a couple of wives I'd like to shoot."

Followed by Troy's: "Okay, what about armed teenagers?"

Loeser waited for the laughter to subside. "Give me a break, guys." He paused to look at Troy. "T-Rob, you know as well as I do there's no bag limit on armed teenagers. You bagged enough of them last cycle in Helmand to know that. Wives, on the other hand . . ."

Padre: "There's a three-wife limit."

Gunrunner: "Then Rebel better watch out, he's approaching it."

More laughter as Rebel's face flushed red.

Loeser called for order. "Okay, c'mon, guys, back to business. Constraints. Like all HVT templates, we have to be in and out within thirty minutes. We will infil and exfil on helos, so weight will be a factor. Insertion element will be twelve, secondary will be twelve. Assaulters are One-Alpha and Six-Charlie."

"How many in the command element?"

"Three," Loeser said.

He did *not* say, "Including me and Captain Maurer." He and Maurer had discussed the assignment immediately upon the captain's return from JSOC.

Maurer was not naive. There were only one or two HVTs in the world who met the criterion "devote a Tier One squadron for a couple of months to one single objective." Usama was at the top of that list. And if it was going to be UBL, there was no way either Tom Maurer or Dave Loeser was going to miss the op. Even if one of them had to go as the K-9.

Rangemaster rubbed his upper lip. "And intel people?"

"Try to factor for two, but one is definite." Loeser was being vague on purpose. If he had mentioned supplemental helicopters and a Ranger blocking force, the proverbial cat would have been out of the proverbial bag.

Loeser looked around to see if there were more questions. There weren't, thank God. "Okay. Here's how we're going to go about this. Today I want you to walk the site. Discover it, learn it, measure it, war-game it. Look for vulnerabilities—its and ours. Work on identifying potential problems and possible solutions. Then come up with a preliminary action plan keyed to this one problem. At eighteen-hundred hours, we'll assemble in a SCIF—we've been given use of one while we're here—and talk things over."

One-Alpha's Geoff Ziebart looked surprised. "A SCIF?"

"Affirmative, Z. What we're doing here is compartmented." He scanned the SEALs. "Everybody hear that loud and clear?" He waited for a chorus of "Aye-aye, sirs."

When he got it, he said, "Good. Understand, gentlemen, this is very close-hold. And it has to stay that way."

Loeser paused. "Any final questions?"

Heron's hand went up. "Who's the target, Mr. Loeser?"

Loeser was ready for this one. He could answer it truthfully, if not honestly. "I can't say, Roger, because I haven't been told."

Gunrunner: "Any time restrictions on getting this planned, Mr. Loeser?"

"Timing's indefinite, Blair."

It was, too. Sort of. A full-scale copy of the Khan compound and the surrounding area in Abbottabad was being constructed on a ten-acre section of land adjacent to the rifle ranges at Fort Knox in Kentucky. Fort Knox was more than a gold repository. For the past decade it had been used as a training site for Tier One units. It was close enough to Fort Campbell so that DEVGRU could stage at Fort Campbell, at a site built for the 160th Special Operations Aviation Regiment (SOAR), a site that could be configured to look like Jalalabad or Bagram.

They would load onto SOAR's MH60-J and MH-47 helicopters and fly to Fort Knox as a complete assault element and rehearse the entire scenario at night under the same blacked-out conditions they'd face in Pakistan. Another plus: the Fort Knox site was isolated enough so that, unlike some other, more commonly known military bases, it seldom drew any media attention. So while Red Squadron's final training iteration would take place where pilots, assaulters, the command element, and the Ranger blocking force could train together in what is known as a BILAT, or bilateral, exercise on a full-size doppelganger of the Abbottabad compound, for now Fort Irwin was the perfect place to start working out the kinks.

"You're here for the immediate future," Loeser said. "But our plans and prep time may be cut short any minute, so you gotta work as quickly as you can. The objective right now is to get this specific tactical problem worked out to my satisfaction, and Captain Maurer's."

He cracked a smile. "Hope you like the accommodations, gentlemen, because you're going to be here for a while."

21

It was, all things considered, the perfect day for this particular meeting. Secretary of State Kate Semerad was in Paris to host a G8 ministerial dinner as well as bilateral meetings with French President Nicolas Sarkozy, UAE Foreign Minister Abdullah bin Zayed, and Japanese Foreign Minister Takeaki Matsumoto. But if necessary she could use the embassy SCIF and join by secure phone. The secretary of defense had no public schedule at all, and so he and the chairman of the Joint Chiefs of Staff were able to slip out of the Pentagon and be driven into the White House complex unnoticed. The president's public schedule included a trip to a middle school in Arlington, Virginia, to talk about education, a visit with ISAF commander General David Petraeus, and a separate meeting with, as the official schedule put it, "senior advisors." In the evening, POTUS would attend a fundraiser for the Democratic National Committee.

At the daily White House press briefing, questions to

the new press secretary, Jay Carney, focused on Japan's nuclear disaster, gun control, gay marriage, the antigovernment demonstrations in Bahrain, and military intervention in Libya. The subjects of Usama Bin Laden and al-Qaeda were never raised.

The focus on those other problems made it a lot easier for D/CIA Vince Mercaldi and a trio of his aides, as well as Vice Admiral Wesley Bolin and Rear Admiral Scott Moore, Slam Bolin's detailee to the National Security Council—and the other members of the Restricted Interagency Group to enter the West Wing and make their way to the Situation Room on the West Wing's basement level unnoticed by pesky reporters. By the time the president arrived six minutes late, everyone was seated at the long rectangular table.

As POTUS entered the room, Vince rose. The others joined him, and there was a ragged chorus of "Good afternoon, Mr. President," which brought a brief smile to the commander in chief's face.

The president took his usual chair at the door-end of the table, facing Vince, who anchored the opposite end. The national security advisor sat to the president's right, Dwayne Daley to his immediate left. The secretary of defense, the chairman of the Joint Chiefs, and Admiral Wes Bolin held down the table to the president's left, and Rear Admiral Moore sat next to the NSC chairman on his right. The president looked down the table at the CIA director, who was flanked by three individuals wearing blue CIA staff badges on chains around their necks. "Vince," he said, "you asked for this meeting, so why don't you begin."

"Thank you, Mr. President." The CIA director adjusted his glasses. "I'd like to introduce my colleagues." He looked to his right. "Some of you may know Stu Kapos, who is director of the National Clandestine Service. Across from Stu, to my left, is Dick Hallett, who runs our Bin Laden

Group. And next to Dick is the BLG's chief analyst, a former Marine whose staff badge reads George S. Nupkins. I can assure you all that the name is a pseudonym. For those of you unaware, it's one of CIA's venerable traditions that all of our covert people receive in-house pseudonyms. And George here—we prefer to call him Spike—selected his own pseudonym from a character in Charles Dickens's *The Pickwick Papers*."

Vince peered over his aviator frames at Spike, a tall, rumpled, beer-bellied, double-chinned, curly-haired fiftyish fellow in a rumpled gray suit, white button-down shirt, and striped rep tie. "George Nupkins was the mayor of Ipswich in that book, wasn't he, Spike?"

"Yes, sir, 'e was," the CIA analyst answered in a badly bogus Cockney accent. "'Appily married, too, just loike me."

Everyone laughed.

The D/CIA continued. "I brought Spike with me today because he probably knows more about UBL than anyone in the world except UBL himself." He waited for the murmurs to subside. "And also, Mr. President, because Spike's the chap who came up with the inoculation program I mentioned in January. You said you'd like to meet him. Well, here he is."

The president's eyes lit up. "Congratulations, Spike. Great idea."

Spike nodded appreciatively. "Thank you, sir. I just wish we'd gotten a positive on the DNA."

"I do, too," the president said.

"But I must also add, sir," Spike continued, "that I am nonetheless convinced that UBL is in residence at the Khan compound."

"Even without conclusive evidence?"

"Yes, Mr. President."

"Why are you convinced, Spike?" The president massaged his chin.

Vince frowned. The CIA director had spent enough face time with POTUS to know the chin massage meant he didn't like what he was hearing. Now the president was tapping the table with his pen, another bad sign. "We have no photographs, Spike. No confirmed sightings. No armed bodyguards. No solid evidence at all. Everything's circumstantial. Wouldn't hold up in court."

Vince was happy to see Spike hold his ground. "That's not quite true, sir."

"Not quite true?"

"Yes, Mr. President, not quite true. There's solid evidence. It may be what you call circumstantial, but it is nevertheless evidence—and it is, to my mind, conclusive when taken as a holographic entirety. The Khan brothers, for example, are known to be UBL's most trusted couriers. We've been tracking them in earnest since 2004. Arshad Khan—his nom de guerre is Abu Ahmed al-Kuwaiti, but his real name may be either Maulawi Abd al-Khaliq or Ibrahim Saeed Ahmed, we're still working on that one—bought the Abbottabad property in 2003 and built the residence in 2004. At that point in time it was on the outskirts of the city. Isolated. Surrounded by big, open plowed fields. The perfect spot for a hideout. And Arshad—I'll call him that so it won't be confusing—built it differently from any other house in Abbottabad. It is three stories, so three families can live comfortably. But here's what: the two Khan families live on the first floor—the ground floor, that is—and in the guest house. The second and third floors are reserved for a VIP occupant and his family. This we know for sure through eyes-on surveillance, as well as thermal imagery from drones." Spike paused long enough to drink from the bottle of water in front of him.

"The third-floor balcony," he continued, "has a seven-foot-high privacy wall. Bin Laden is somewhere between

six foot four and six foot five. There is Sentinel footage—"
The analyst caught the blank look on the president's face.
"Sentinel, sir, is the RQ-170 stealth drone we have dedicated
to the Khan compound and overflights of Abbottabad—of a
male, six foot four or six foot five, judging from the shadow
he threw and the time of day, walking in the courtyard of
the compound. We do not have a picture of his face, but
he resembles photos we do have of UBL. His gait is much
the same, and his shoulders are stooped exactly like UBL's
shoulders. And finally, there's the food."

The president looked surprised. "The food?"

"The food," Spike continued. "Arabs eat lamb and rice,
emphasis on rice. Pakistanis eat chicken and lentils. Whoever lives in that compound eats lamb and rice. Regularly."

"Oh, yeah?" Dwayne Daley said. "How do you know
that?"

"We did some dumpster-diving."

"Oh, *yeah*?" Daley rapped the table triumphantly. "I read
reports that they burn all their garbage inside the compound.
How could you dumpster-dive that?"

"They do burn the garbage," Spike said. "We got hold
of the ashes. More than once. The forensics are solid. The
occupants of that compound eat like Arabs, not Pakistanis."

SECDEF broke in before Daley could argue any more.
"Okay, Spike, let's say for argument's sake you're right. Bin
Laden lives in that compound. The question then becomes,
how do we get him?"

"That *is* the question," Spike said. "And I am not a military strategist." He looked across the table at the SECDEF,
the Joint Chiefs chairman, and Wesley Bolin. "I can tell
you for a fact that both Khan brothers are in residence. The
younger one, Tareq, recently returned from an overseas trip.
And according to one of our eyes-on assets in Abbottabad,
he will be in residence there for the foreseeable future. It is

my opinion that UBL is also currently living in that house on that compound, along with at least one of his wives and some of his children. I am convinced of it. How you get him is for you-all to figure out."

"Indeed it is." Vince Mercaldi opened the folder he'd brought with him. "Seems to me we have three alternatives here. One is an air strike: we flatten the compound and kill everyone inside. Two is a boots-on-the-ground mission, which you, Mr. President, have already heard about in general terms from Admiral Bolin. And third would be a joint mission with the Pakistanis."

The chairman of the Joint Chiefs nodded. "An air strike by B-2 stealth bombers is doable. We could also employ Tomahawk missiles."

"Alternatives that we should explore, Mr. Secretary," Vince said. "I'd like to suggest right now, however, that we do not consider a joint mission with the Pakistanis."

Daley frowned. "And why would that be? They are our allies."

"Because in some arenas they are not our allies," Vince said. "Not at all. Last month, we shared with the Pakistanis intelligence about two capture/kill missions we were about to launch in northeast Afghanistan against the Haqqani Network and a Taliban commander who travels back and forth between Afghanistan and Waziristan. I had the Paks' communications networks monitored, and I can tell you without a doubt that elements of the ISI warned the people we were planning to hit."

The president's eyes widened. "They did?"

"Yes, Mr. President, they did. We went through with the raids, of course, so as not to alert the Pakistanis, and we were, quote, 'surprised' when we came up dry. But it is conclusive that elements of ISI and segments of the Pakistani military as well are collaborating with our enemies. If you would like, I would be happy to supply you with the relevant CDs and transcripts. We have it all documented."

"How did you handle the problem?"

"We've stopped sharing all but the most innocuous information with Pakistani intelligence and the military," Vince said. "We help them if we come across something that affects their domestic security. But everything else these days is close-hold. And the Pakistanis have retaliated. In the wake of the Ty Weaver incident, they started holding up diplomatic visas for both military trainers and diplomatic personnel. Ever since the two snatch operations failed, they also have tried to impede our efforts to identify, isolate, and neutralize other threats. The situation is not good."

Vince took a long pull from his water bottle. "Institutionally, therefore, our position is that any joint operation in Abbottabad would be compromised within hours—perhaps minutes—of discussing it with the Pakistanis and that Bin Laden and his couriers would disappear."

The room fell silent.

The president rapped the table with the end of his pen. "Then a joint operation with the Pakistanis is a no-go," the president said tersely. "So let's drop it from the list right now."

"Of course, Mr. President." Vince looked at the chairman of the Joint Chiefs. "Admiral?"

"We should certainly explore all the remaining options," the chairman said. "At the moment I have no opinion."

Of course you don't, Vince thought. Like most of his immediate predecessors, the current chairman had never taken the leadership bit in his mouth. His role on paper was to be chief military advisor to the commander in chief. It was, sadly, a role very much underplayed by this chairman.

That was not the case with the SECDEF. Vince turned to Rich Hansen. "Mr. Secretary?"

"My opinion," the secretary of defense said, "would be

to examine both remaining options. Explore all the pros and cons, the strengths and weaknesses. Weigh every possibility and then reach a consensus. We would then be making an informed decision." He removed his glasses and set them on the table. "As we all know, there are strategic consequences." He nodded toward Dwayne Daley and National Security Advisor Don Sorken. "Our long-term relations with Pakistan. Our long-range strategic goals in the region. And of course our estimation of a successful outcome." He paused. "Most important, we cannot, in my opinion, tolerate failure here."

The NSC chairman's head bobbed in vigorous agreement. Don Sorken was a veteran political operative who had served the previous Democratic administration both as State Department spokesman and as chief of staff to the secretary of state. As the top NSC advisor he felt it was his job to protect the administration's political requirements while simultaneously working to uphold the nation's national security interests. It was often a tough balancing act.

From Sorken's perspective, any strike on the Abbottabad compound was a two-edged sword, with the potential to produce a supersized political disaster or a tectonic positive shift in public opinion. If it succeeded, the president would be more than a hero. He'd be as electable as the man who shot Liberty Valance. If it failed, the U.S. would look weak and the president's reelection chances would plummet to zero.

Even if the strike succeeded, but there was one iota of nasty collateral damage, the administration would be beaten around the head over its callous insensitivity toward human life, and once again the president's reelection chances would nose-dive. And if, God forbid, Bin Laden were taken alive, he'd become a bolt of political lightning that would blind everything and everyone on a global level, not for days, weeks, or months, but years—perhaps even decades. And make it much, much tougher to reelect the president.

Politically, Sorken would rather see no raid than commit to anything that might result in political embarrassment for the administration, its eclipse by an iconic terrorist, or the possibility that Bin Laden's capture would result in retaliatory attacks within the continental United States, attacks that would hurt, perhaps fatally, the president's chances of a second term.

But of course he couldn't say any of that. Not publicly.

Instead he turned toward the president, his expression grave. "I think Secretary Hansen is correct, sir. My suggestion would be for the chairman, Admiral Bolin, and Director Mercaldi to war-game all the possibilities with their staffs, and come back to us at some point, perhaps late next month, with a series of suggestions that we could listen to, evaluate, and then debate within the White House."

With luck, Sorken thought, we can talk this thing to death. And he wasn't being cynical, either. Don Sorken considered himself a realist. It was simply a matter of priorities. Getting Bin Laden was, to be sure, important. But getting the president reelected in 2012? That was absolutely, critically imperative.

Sorken had been in politics his whole professional life—as a lawyer, a lobbyist, and an operative. The lesson he learned from Jimmy Carter's Desert One debacle in April 1980 was that reelection considerations have to trump everything else, even rescuing American hostages. In 2011 similar considerations might have to take precedence over capturing the terrorist who had caused the deaths of thousands of Americans.

22

Mr. Wade lined up the three-car consular convoy so it could make a fast getaway from the jail. The RSO had been told—"ordered" was probably more accurate—to drive directly from the jail to the military section of Lahore's international airport, where a State Department Cessna Citation twin-engine jet would be waiting. Aboard would be the American ambassador to Pakistan and two unnamed American officials.

Wade guessed the mystery guests were CIA. But it really didn't matter, did it? Whoever they were, they would escort Ty Weaver to Bagram Air Base in Afghanistan, where he'd be checked over by an Air Force doctor, then picked up by a CIA aircraft for a direct flight to Dulles.

Mr. Wade knew the fix was in. CIA had paid a couple of mil-plus in blood money. Not directly, of course. The United States does not pay ransom. So CIA slipped the Pak government the cash, and the Paks paid the two victims' families, although Wade figured a couple of ministers and a few folks from ISI probably took a cut, because that's the way the Paks did business. But whatever the split may have been, the cash had been paid, the papers had been signed—rumor had it that the two families were ordered to sign by ISI—and now it was time to hustle Ty out of the country.

Wade could only shake his head in awe of American diplomacy.

Speaking of which, Lahore's U.S. consul general, whom Wade called, though not to her face, "Her Royal Highness," insisted on being a part of the diplomatic charade.

Of course she had: she wanted thirty seconds of face time with the ambassador, as if it would do her career any good. Her participation was a mistake. The idea of this transfer was to keep everything low key. But with the CG, it was all about grandeur, pomp, and circumstance. And so she just had to get out of the car, introduce herself to the jail administrator, and make small talk while they waited for Ty Weaver to be brought out.

Plus, she'd insisted on having her own vehicle. There was no way she was going to ride in the same car as Ty, to whom she'd been referring for the past month and a half as "that CIA criminal."

So not only had the two-car below-the-radar transfer convoy become a three-car motorcade, but the CG had insisted that they fly the American flag on her limo.

Wade could only scratch his head in bemusement. Yanquis were not big favorites in Pakistan these days. Why not just paint "Throw rocks at me" in visibility orange on the side of the car?

■

Ty finally appeared at 1623. He looked better than expected, though thinner, wan, and unshaven. But then, he'd been a

VIP prisoner, treated with the proverbial kid gloves, instead of the ones whose knuckles contained lead shot.

Wade clasped his shoulder and shook his hand. The CG acknowledged Ty's presence by nodding vaguely in his direction, then hand-signaled Wade to open her car door. Instead the RSO ushered Ty into the front seat of his own vehicle, walked around the hood, climbed aboard himself, and started the engine. He watched smiling in the rearview mirror as the CG scrambled into her car and slammed the door. He looked over at Ty and grinned. "I'm gonna catch hell for that," he said, "but it was worth it."

Ty said, "Thanks for coming, dude."

"No prob." Wade steered through the jail's main gates and turned north. The traffic was already heavy. "Got your bags in the back, by the way. Your friends came for what was in the safe." That was Ty's backup pistol, which had been left behind the day he was arrested.

"Thanks."

Wade checked to see that the CG's driver was tight on his tail and that the chase car was keeping up. "So, what you gonna do first thing when you get home?"

Ty stretched his arms in front of him. "Take some downtime with Patty," he said. "Then? Then, I don't know." He swiveled in Wade's direction. "They didn't fill me in," he said. "They played me. At least, that's the way it seems right now."

"They?"

"Everybody. That fricking senator. Islamabad. My people. The Paks."

"Ain't it the way it always happens?"

"I just wish . . ." Ty raised his hands palms out. "I dunno. I'd just like to know why—how this mess happened. It's almost two months of my life, stolen."

Wade didn't say anything. Sometimes, he knew, there's nothing to say.

Ty finally said, "Think I'll ever find out? I don't. At least not for a while."

Wade snorted. "I think you're probably right." He waited for a light to change, then swung the big SUV east, then north. He checked the digital clock on the dash. They were sixteen minutes out if there was no gridlock. "But you never know, Ty. Miracles happen."

"I guess." Ty cracked his knuckles. "But then, you believe in Santa Claus, don't you?" The former Delta Soldier sat silent for a while, staring through the windshield. Then he swiveled toward Wade. "You heading home anytime in the near term, dude?"

"I get two weeks' leave in June."

"What's your home base?"

"Fairfax, Virginia."

"Got a pen and paper?"

"Notebook's in the console. Pens, too."

Ty retrieved them and wrote in the notebook. "We're in Reston. Come on by and lemme buy you a beer."

"Count on it. But really? Just *a* beer? After all we've been through?"

"*We? We*, Kemo Sabe?" Ty laughed—really laughed—for the first time in almost two months.

23

"We're ready for you, Boss." Bin Laden Group Chief Dick Hallett stood in the partially opened door to the director's inner office. The former Marine was a big man, barrel-chested. A weight lifter and a skier with a vacation house in Idaho. He hadn't had much time for the latter in the past eight months, although he was religious about bench-pressing three days a week in the CIA gym to relieve stress. Stress had been a big part of Hallett's life since early the previous August. That was when his top analyst, George S. Nupkins, a.k.a. Spike, had painstakingly laid out his argument about UBL and the Khan compound in Abbottabad, and suggested that once eyes-on had been established, CIA's paramilitary Special Activities Division should mount a covert capture/ kill mission to take Bin Laden out.

Spike made sense, too—at least the part about UBL's location. His rationale answered all those nagging questions about how and where, and why Bin Laden was leaving so few ripples, such weak spoor, and such sparse footprints.

Spike's conclusion: there were no footprints because UBL wasn't moving. He'd gone to ground. He wasn't transmitting. He was static. No electronic signals intelligence signature. No Internet. He was obviously passing messages through his two trusted couriers. The selfsame couriers who had bought land and built a huge compound on the outskirts of Abbottabad, a house large enough to hold at least three families: Arshad's, Tareq's, and a third one as well. With a privacy wall surrounding the third-story balcony tall enough to shield the six-foot-five Bin Laden from prying eyes. And the Khans were always there. Except when they traveled, to the Gulf, and Yemen, and the Maghreb, and Europe.

Only last week, Spike noted wryly, Arshad had flown from Lahore to Abu Dhabi, and from there to Frankfurt. He stayed one night there, having dinner with the publisher of an Islamist magazine, then took a train to Paris, where he caught the Chunnel train to London. And then it was on to the coast and a ferry to Dublin.

Spike paused. "And between the time his passport was stamped at Frankfurt and he climbed off the ferry in Ireland, guess what: no one checked his passport. Because it was all EU-centric. Because despite a real threat, the Euros are either lazy or just careless."

In Dublin, Spike continued, Arshad checked into The Fitzwilliam, a fashionable hotel on St. Stephen's Green. It was, Spike noted, the same hotel Tareq had stayed at in 2005, when he'd made that significant phone call back to Abbottabad. On this trip it was the same hotel, as it turned out, where a trio of young British citizens of Pakistani descent were also staying. The Brits, two from Manchester, one Londoner, were on an MI-5 watch list and suspected of terrorist activity. They and Arshad had gone out to dinner at a neighborhood restaurant called Hugo's, where they'd spent hours talking in code about possible operations. "Thank God," Spike said, "MI-5 was on the case."

There was more. "All those places Arshad visited?" Spike asked rhetorically. "Al-Qaeda has operational cells. One wonders from whom he was bringing messages, since the villa he lives in has no phones, no Internet, no comms at all. There's been only one incoming call in months—and that was Tareq again, when his kid was sick. And we know neither of the Khan brothers is an operator. They don't do bombs or explosives. They're couriers. They carry messages face to face.

"Imagine. No incoming information. And yet, they certainly have lots of information to take away. And to deliver face to face. How . . . coincidental." Spike's eyes glistened. "How . . . *asymmetric.*"

"Gotcha." It struck a chord. Dick Hallett knew that in the intelligence business there are no coincidences. And he understood "asymmetric" not just because he was a Marine, but because he was a Marine who studied Marines. And one of the Marines he'd studied was a three-star Marine general named Paul Van Riper.

In 2002, then-SECDEF Donald Rumsfeld ordered a major war game, the largest war game the Pentagon had ever put together. It was called Millennium Challenge 2002 (MC02), a $250 million multilevel, multitheater multiexercise that ran from July 24 to August 15. MC02 included live, tabletop, and computer battlefield simulations. The reason for the war game was Secretary Rumsfeld's desire to test his theories of "force transformation" and "network-centric warfare," in which U.S. forces, continuously linked by data, information, and joint operational tactics, defeat an enemy by employing overwhelming technological superiority: precision-guided munitions, automated C^3I (command, control, communications, and intelligence), overhead surveillance systems like satellites and UAVs, and sophisticated SIGINT, IMINT, and MASINT (signals intelligence, imagery intelligence, and measurement and signatures intelligence) to spy on an enemy's communications, capabilities, and positioning. Rumsfeld's theory was that by relying on technological superiority, you could wage warfare, if not on the cheap, then certainly in a more efficient, digitized manner, resulting in victory less dependent on old-fashioned analog warfare, that is, boots on the ground.

The United States was represented by the Blue Team, and the Blue Team had the best capabilities that the science of war could produce. The bad guys—an unnamed Middle East country that should have been called Iraq—was represented by the Red Team. Lieutenant General Paul Van Riper was in charge of the bad guys. Van Riper is a big proponent of the art of war, not the science of war. As he himself once put it to an interviewer on the PBS science show *NOVA*, "The art of war and the science of war are not coequal. The art of war is clearly the most important. It's science in support of the art."

Bottom line: Van Riper employed the art of war against the Blue Team. How do you defeat an overwhelming enemy? You employ the art of war, following dictums written three thousand years ago by Sun Tzu. You go asymmetric.

So Van Riper's messages were delivered by motorcycle messenger or F2F (face to face), not via cell phone or radio. He used small boats, like the ones used by Somali pirates, to gather intelligence on the Blue Fleet. And then, while his Blue adversaries were still trying to get a fix on him, he launched a massive, preemptive strike combined with suicide attacks.

In the first seventy-two hours of MC02, Van Riper sank

one Blue aircraft carrier, ten Blue cruisers, and five Blue amphibious ships and caused more than twenty thousand Blue Force casualties.

As the story goes, Rummy hit the ceiling. Van Riper had hit him where it hurt the most: right in the transformation. At that point, MC02 was suspended. The Blue Fleet was refloated, and the war game was resumed. With certain changes, changes that guaranteed a Blue victory. The Red Force would henceforth follow a predetermined script. It was like the field maneuvers in the movie *Heartbreak Ridge*, in which the idiot major's force always beats the Recon platoon, until Gunny Highway uses unconventional methods to shake things up and Recon comes out on top.

But real life ain't Hollywood, and the good guys don't always win. Real life is politics and hundreds of billions of dollars in defense contracts, and if all those expensive technological goodies like littoral combat ships and F-22 fighters can be defeated by guys in small boats and raggedy-ass insurgents with RPGs, then why are we spending all this $$$$$ on crap that doesn't work against asymmetric adversaries?

The answer is simple: because we rig the war games so the military-industrial complex can prosper.

Except: Paul Van Riper was more concerned with the art of war than the art of making money. He resigned from MC02. He retired from the Marine Corps. Then he went public. He told anyone who would listen that having overwhelming force and cutting-edge technology doesn't mean you're going to win against an asymmetric enemy who can adapt, identify your vulnerabilities, and exploit them.

Van Riper's theory was proved correct in Iraq by AQI and by the thousands of IED attacks against our forces.

So when Spike came to Dick Hallett with his Abbottabad theory, and Hallett spent two days arguing devil's advocate but couldn't shake the keep-it-simple-stupid, makes-sense logic of Spike's arguments, he and Spike took the case to Stu Kapos, who listened, and then called up to the director's office and asked for an appointment.

Within twenty-four hours, Hallett had been instructed to commence an operation that would result in a covert CIA entity, Valhalla Base, being established in Abbottabad. From that base an undercover team of CIA spooks would observe the Khan compound from afar and penetrate it utilizing the latest state-of-the-art eavesdropping, thermal, and optical equipment available. The goal: lay eyes on UBL. Then find a way to kill him.

24

Valhalla Base had been operational since October, without results. Immediately in the wake of the March 14 Restricted Interagency Group (RIG) meeting, NSC Chairman Sorken had started making noises about closing it down. Of course he had. Vince Mercaldi was con*vinced*—he laughed and said "Of course I am" whenever he pronounced it that way—that Don Sorken wanted the entire Abbottabad mission to go away.

Sure he did: Abbottabad was risky. And risky was bad politics. Closing down Valhalla Base would kill the Abbottabad mission.

Vince had already spoken to the secretary of state on the subject. Kate Semerad agreed that CIA's outpost should be kept operational. And she would be happy to make that argument to the president. If, that is, her colleague at Defense was also on board.

"We've got to present a united front," she insisted. "This is a president, and you know this as well as I do, Vince, who tends to go with the last person he talks to. And Don's in the goddamn office ten times a day, and you and Rich and I are not. And you also know the president's a purebred political animal. First, last, and always."

She laughed, a tinge of bitterness in her voice. "Shit, *I* sure know it, the way he creamed me in the primaries in oh-eight."

Vince knew enough not to say anything.

"Bottom line? He'll talk to Don and his Chicago people and they'll tell him 'Stay away.' Will that be final? I'm not so sure. I think he'll do the right thing if we can find a way to . . . *encourage* I guess would be the most printable word I could use . . . encourage him to do it. But we can't accomplish that unless you and Rich and I are on the same page."

Vince promised he'd get her a definitive response from SECDEF within forty-eight hours. That had been forty hours ago.

■

So now it was Spike's turn to make his argument about UBL and Valhalla Base to the secretary of defense. But SECDEF Hansen was in Cairo—and seven hours ahead. Moreover the SECDEF's Cairo schedule was chockablock full, programmed to the minute. He had a meeting scheduled with the Egyptian military chief Field Marshal Mohamed Hussein Tantawi, a session with Essam Sharaf, the interim prime minister, as well as visits to Army headquarters and the Mukhabarat, a Q&A press availability, a short meet-and-greet with Cairo's sizable group of U.S. military personnel, and a dinner with members of Egypt's interim government.

It took half a dozen phone calls between Vince's chief of staff and the SECDEF's military assistant before arrangements could be made for a secure, fifteen-minute teleconference at 2315 Hours Cairo time, 1615 at Langley.

Vince Mercaldi knew Rich Hansen was not in favor of a spec-ops assault on the Khan compound. But he was also sure that the SECDEF would want Valhalla Base kept operational. He knew that because Hansen had had the Joint Chiefs chairman go through the Air Force chief of staff to come up with attack plans using stealth bombers flying eight and a half miles—just under fifty thousand feet—above the target. The strike would be flown by the Air Force's 509th Bomb Wing from Whiteman Air Force Base in Missouri by B-2 Spirit bombers. The weapons would be the Joint Direct Attack Munitions.

JDAMs are tail-kits that incorporate global positioning systems (GPS) and inertial navigation systems (INS) onto a wide range of general-purpose munitions. The problem for Abbottabad was that under normal circumstances JDAMs had a thirteen-meter CEP, or circular error probability. In English, that meant that their accuracy was only within a forty-two-foot-three-inch bull's eye.

Nowhere near good enough for this particular mission.

For JDAMs to be accurate within three meters (just under ten feet), they would need what is known as a terminal seeker. The point of impact would have to be "painted" on the target by a forward air controller utilizing an infrared beam that the munitions' guidance systems would key on. Only then could the strike use five-hundred-pound bombs to surgically flatten the complex but still ensure that the six homes across the ten-meter-wide road that ran past the Khan compound's front gates went unscathed.

For that kind of pinpoint accuracy, a pair of FACs—forward air controllers—would be needed to paint specific parts of the villa. The FACs would need to be infiltrated prior to the bombing raid. They'd also require a safe house in Abbottabad as the Air Force had no Pashto-capable FACs. CIA had a safe house. And the language-capable people to run it.

1612 Hours

Dick Hallett punched the cipher combination into the door lock and waited until the latch was released. Then he pushed it inward. He'd insisted, despite OSHA regulations, that all the exterior doors to BLG areas open inward, because that meant the hinges were inside, and thus protected. Hallett had broken into more than a few locked-down locations overseas by tapping out door-hinge pins.

He and Vince proceeded into BLG's SCIF, where Spike and BLG's two AV technicians were waiting.

Hallett introduced Sue and Jessica, the technicians, then ushered the director to a conference table. Vince eased into the center chair of the three that had been prepositioned and opened his jacket so Jessica could affix the mike to his lapel and give him an earpiece. Spike, rumpled as ever, clipped on his own microphone and sat on the director's right. Hallett dropped into the remaining chair.

Sue focused the camera. "Hey, it's the Three Amigos," she said as she brought their pictures up on the four-foot-wide screen.

"Amigos, Sue? 'Wherever there is *eennjustice*, you will find us,'" Hallett bellowed theatrically, "'wherever *leeberty* is threatened, *ju* will find'"—he spread his arms wide—"'*los Three Amigos!!!*'"

The SECDEF's face suddenly lit up the screen. "*Hola, amigos!*"

Hallett's face reddened. "Sorry, Mr. Secretary."

Rich Hansen broke into a wide smile. "It's okay. After all the pomp and circumstance here in Cairo, a little levity is just what's called for." He paused. "How's it going, Vince?"

"Hot and heavy," the CIA director replied. "We've got a little problem here, and we need your help."

"Shoot."

"There's been talk at the White House about closing down Valhalla."

"So I've heard."

"We here don't think it's a good idea, because it limits our options."

The secretary said nothing.

"So I thought you might like to hear from Spike about why we need to keep those options open."

"Thanks," Hansen said, "but I don't need to. I'm with you on this, Vince. As you know, I've been working on some options of my own."

"Yes."

"And they would necessitate having a forward-basing opportunity available."

"Gotcha."

"Plus, I had a chat with Kate about an hour ago. I don't think I'd be violating any confidences if I told you we talked both strategy and politics."

"So you—"

"Let's not take it any further," the secretary said. "We all have our note-takers working. Let me just use her words and say I'm on the same page as you-all."

Vince gave Dick Hallett a quick glance. "Thank you, Rich."

"We have the same goal here, Vince," the secretary said. "One target. One objective. Where we opine differently is about how to go about achieving that goal."

"Mr. Secretary?"

Hansen squinted. "Is that you, Spike?"

"Yes, sir." The analyst pressed forward against the conference table. "One point I'd like to make."

"Go ahead."

"I've red-teamed your air option with some of my colleagues here, and there's something I think you should know."

"Yes? Go ahead."

"We've never been able to do a complete forensic evaluation of the site."

The secretary's forehead wrinkled. "Forensic evaluation, Spike?"

"What I mean to say, sir, is that the Khans bought the compound and built the house before it was on our radar. We have overhead from before it was built, and overhead from after it was built. But nothing from *while* it was being built."

"What's your point, son?"

"Sir, for all we know, they could have put in a bunker below the house." He paused. "A deep bunker. We've got soil samples from adjacent land. The ground there is perfect for it—no rock layering, so no blasting would have been necessary. And there's no way to absolutely confirm or deny without inspecting the interior of the villa. Which we are not capable of doing. So we must assume that they built a bunker to protect UBL."

Spike looked at the screen. The SECDEF's eyes showed surprise—even shock.

Spike said, "Sir?"

There was a long silence. Then the secretary said, "Good catch, son." He said it without enthusiasm and then he grimaced into the screen. "The Air Force hadn't considered that factor, Vince."

Vince kept a poker face. Because neither had he. Or Hallett. Or Stu Kapos. But Spike had. And it was huge. Significant. A deal-breaker. If UBL had a bunker, five-hundred-pound bombs would do no good. Two-thousand-pound penetrator munitions would have to be employed—at least a dozen of them, perhaps more. Which would absolutely have lethal collateral effects on the surrounding area.

And more to the point, there would be virtually no way to confirm Bin Laden's death. The site would be obliterated. Sure, Bin Laden DNA might be obtained. But it could be DNA from one of his children. No way to know for sure. Because the Paks were certainly not going to allow a CIA forensics team to go combing through the rubble.

Bottom line: the mere prospect of a bunker beneath the villa effectively killed the air strike option.

Which meant the one remaining possibility was a stealth approach using helos, a fast ground assault, and a rapid exfil. Exactly what Wes Bolin first suggested and was currently rehearsing. And what Rich Hansen would argue against.

Vince cleared his throat and said, "That's why we have folks like Spike here, Rich. And thank God we do."

"Agreed." The secretary stared into the camera. "I'm still not convinced that Wes Bolin's plan will work," he said. "But given today's development, I want to hear him out. I'm back in three—no, four days. Can we arrange something early next week?"

Vince nodded affirmatively. "We're scheduled for our next RIG briefing at the White House on the twenty-ninth. We'll meet before then, and you can hear how Wes would put this thing together. I think you'll be impressed."

"If anyone can pull it off, it would be Wes."

"I agree." Although he made sure not to show it, Vince Mercaldi was mildly surprised. It was the first positive reaction to a special operations raid he'd heard from the defense secretary. He'd have to call Wes Bolin right away. Prep him for the pre-RIG session with the SECDEF. But Vince's face betrayed nothing. Instead he smiled at the camera. "Safe travels, Rich."

"Thanks, Vince. I like getting out of the office once in a while. Now Kate—she's on the road *all* the time. She's this administration's Flying Dutchman."

It was true. The secretary of state had logged more than half a million miles since she'd been confirmed by the Senate. In fact, there were those who believed—and Vince was one of them—that the president was keeping Kate Semerad on the road to ensure that she wouldn't present a threat to his reelection efforts in 2012. She'd been his most formidable opponent in 2008.

Vince chuckled. "Well, thanks for your time, too, Rich. I know how precious it is."

"*De nada.*" The defense secretary waved offhandedly into the camera. "*Hasta luego . . . amigos.*"

The screen went blank.

Hallett looked at the tech behind the camera. "We clear, Sue?"

"Yes, sir," she said.

"Mikes turned off?"

She checked her console. "Mikes are dead."

The director said, "Great." He dropped his mike on the table, grinned, and high-fived Hallett and Spike. "We're in business, gents. Magnificent work, Spike."

The analyst beamed. "Thank you, sir."

Vince looked at him strangely. "By the way, what you told the SECDEF."

"Yes?"

"About the bunker." Vince had to reach up to put his

arm around the younger man's shoulder. He tiptoed toward Spike, stage-whispered "C'mon, Spike, you can tell me" conspiratorially, then stood back.

"Tell you what, sir?" The analyst looked confused.

"What you told the secretary. About the bunker," Vince reiterated.

"Yes, sir?"

"Was that actually *true*, Spike?"

"I believe it is." Then the big man whose pseudonym was George S. Nupkins took a long and uncharacteristically theatrical pause. "But I guess we'll only find out for sure when our people are in the house, sir," he finally said, a sly smile creeping across his face.

25

Charlie Becker lay back on the pallet he used as a bed and massaged what was left of his legs. His whole body ached. But it was a good ache. A Ranger ache. The kind of ache that told him he was alive and well and had used his body to its limits. A Darby Queen ache.

Ranger candidates spend ten days at Fort Benning's Camp Darby, where, among other things, they get to run the obstacle/confidence course known as the Darby Queen. The Queen is twenty-four stages that test your fear of heights and challenge your balance, your upper-body strength, and your ability to keep going no matter how badly you're being dinged. Tonight Charlie felt as if he'd done three circuits on the Darby Queen.

But the news was all good. His message, bursted half an hour previously, was that Abbottabad had gone back to being the sleepy little garrison town it always had been.

There were no ISI gumshoes trolling. Arshad and Tareq Khan were both in residence.

But the main point of his message was that today he'd gotten a glance inside the gates of Ground Zero. He'd gone by the perimeter just after noon. From the smoke and the smell, they were burning trash behind the wire-topped wall.

As he rolled past, Charlie paused to watch half a dozen youngsters playing street soccer on the road that ran parallel to the compound wall. He'd just started up again when one of them sliced the ball over the wall. So he paused to see what would happen.

A couple of minutes later, the gate opened just a crack, an arm and a shoulder protruded, and the ball was dropped into the street.

And Charlie, on the opposite side of the road, saw something as the gate cracked open. He saw a strap diagonal across the sliver of chest of whoever had opened the gate. And the butt of an AK.

It was just a flash, but it was important. Yet another sign. There were no other villas in Abbottabad—at least among the ones Charlie had seen—where people came to the gate carrying assault rifles.

Was it proof of anything? Of course not. But Charlie also knew intelligence isn't like, wow, here it is: everything. Intelligence is finding little pieces of a puzzle and sending them on to folks who understand how to put those pieces together—folks who know that they may not be working on one puzzle, but five or six or ten puzzles simultaneously.

So far as he knew, no one had ever seen anyone in the Khan compound who was armed. Now Charlie could report for certain that there was at least one AK-47 on the premises.

Did it prove that UBL was living there? Not exactly. It proved only that there was at least one person living in the villa who was wary enough to arm himself when he burned garbage. But it was . . . an info-bit. Something that might turn into an indicator.

Charlie blew out the kerosene lamp, covered himself with the lumpy pad that served as his blanket, and snuggled in for the night. He would sleep well. Today he had earned his pay.

26

The RIG had to be scheduled for nine o'clock because the president was traveling to New York just after noon to dedicate the U.S. Mission building. He was not the only one on travel. SECSTATE Kate Semerad was in London. She had promised to call the White House at precisely six minutes past nine from a secure phone in her limo as she traveled between her meeting with British Prime Minister David Cameron at 10 Downing Street and her appearance at Lancaster House, the neoclassical Bath stone palace on Stable Yard just off St. James's, where she would meet with contributors to the Libyan opposition.

The president arrived precisely at nine, a black leather folder tucked under his arm like a football. The secure teleconferencing equipment had already been positioned on the long conference table. Under normal circumstances, no phones, BlackBerrys, or other devices were allowed in the room. POTUS was trailed by National Security Advisor Don Sorken and Rear Admiral (SEAL) Scott Moore, the JSOC detailee to the National Security Council. The CIA director, the secretary of defense, the chairman of the Joint Chiefs, and Wes Bolin were all waiting for him.

They rose as he came into the room. POTUS indicated they should sit down. He took his own seat and the others followed suit.

When they had settled, he opened the leather folder embossed with the Presidential Seal. "I hear we have some news today."

"Yes, Mr. President." Vince Mercaldi spoke. "Two significant developments. The first is that we've had a sighting of an armed individual in the Khan compound."

"Really? When?"

"Two days ago."

"What was the source?"

"One of our CIA assets in Abbottabad."

"And they were sure?"

"Absolutely, Mr. President."

The president stared at his CIA director. "That's the first indication aside from the overhead stuff that may point toward UBL being in that house."

"Yes, sir. We think so, too. Spike took it as a very strong sign that UBL is there."

The president nodded, but said nothing.

So Vince picked up where he'd left off. "The second is that our options have been reduced to one: a unilateral helicopter assault on the compound."

"That's a nasty surprise." The president, obviously stunned and fuming, looked at the CIA director. Then he turned to the secretary of defense. "What about the air strike option, Rich?"

"It's a no-go. CIA cannot confirm beyond a reasonable doubt that there isn't a bunker under the compound. Therefore, the only way to guarantee mission success would be to go with two-thousand-pound enhanced munitions—bunker-busters—which certainly will cause major collateral damage."

"Major collateral damage." The president frowned. "We can't have that."

"No, sir, we can't. Moreover, the destruction would be so total that even if we recovered Bin Laden DNA at the site there would be no way to prove it was from Usama and not one of his children."

The president frowned again and massaged his chin.

Don Sorken cleared his throat.

The president noted the look of concern on his National Security Advisor's face. "Don, you look worried."

"Not worried, Mr. President. But apprehensive, yes. And nervous about a mission that could very easily be compromised." The NSC chairman looked around the table until his gaze fell on the secretary of defense. "And I was led to believe I wasn't the only one nervous about a ground assault."

"I still have concerns," Rich Hansen said, "but in this case, where our options have been severely limited by the situation on the ground, the need for zero collateral damage, and current intelligence estimates, I think we have to listen to Admiral Bolin, whose people have successfully pulled off more than seventeen hundred of these types of missions in the past year alone. And—"

The teleconference unit in front of the president buzzed. Don Sorken pressed the receive button. "Kate, is that you?"

The room fell silent. Within a few seconds, Kate Semerad's voice said, "Can you all hear me? Good morning, Mr. President."

"Good morning, Madam Secretary."

They could hear her hearty laugh on the speaker. "It's

a lovely day in London. By the way, David Cameron sends you best wishes."

"I hope you gave him mine." The president peered at his folder. "Kate, we were just discussing the Pakistan matter, and it would seem that we've had our options narrowed to a boots-on-the-ground thing. Where do you stand on that?"

There was a pause, then Semerad's resonant voice filled the Situation Room. "I'm fine with it, Mr. President. To be honest, I was always a little nervous about the air strike option, as it's so easy for something to go wrong and cause collateral damage. That was something my husband's administration found out in Serbia back in the nineteen-nineties. You may have missed this in Chicago, but despite the best intelligence and precision weaponry, CIA got some of its map coordinates wrong, and we mistakenly bombed the Chinese Embassy in Belgrade."

There was a pause. Then she continued. "I know Vince's people would never do that—he's really brought the Agency back. But mistakes happen, and there's always Murphy's Law."

The president leaned toward the speakerphone. "But what about the Pakistanis?" He looked at Sorken. "The latest NSC estimate is that if we continue to aggravate relations they might renege on many of our bilateral agreements regarding counterterror programs and, more important, our supply chain to Afghanistan."

"Frankly, Mr. President, I think that between myself and Secretary Hansen, and the chairman of the Joint Chiefs and Vince, we can handle the Pakistanis and deal positively with any potential blowback. I don't doubt that they will not receive this well. But to be blunt, we are largely keeping their country afloat. Pakistan's economy is in the cellar. The per capita GDP there is just over a thousand dollars a year. There's a fifteen percent unemployment rate—that's almost thirty million people without work. If not for the United States they'd be virtually destitute. The Pakistanis lack India's entrepreneurial spirit and they don't have Afghanistan's natural resources." There was momentary static on the line and the secretary's words were garbled.

The president said, "Come again, Kate?"

"I was just summing up, Mr. President. I'm certain that if you as commander in chief decide to go ahead, the mission will resolve successfully. And I believe that Admiral Bolin's scenario is both the most practical and the most efficient."

"You are. You do."

"I am and I do."

"Well, then." The president tapped his pen on the open folder in front of him. "Thank you, Madam Secretary. Safe travels." He waited as Sorken disconnected the line and the equipment was removed. The president looked pointedly at the CIA director. "That certainly was another surprise."

Vince said, "I think she's spent a lot of time thinking about this. After all, she's lived through similar situations before."

"Hmmm." The president massaged his chin with his thumb and index finger. He swiveled toward Wes Bolin. "Admiral," he said, "it looks as if the ball is in your court by default." He looked at Vince and then back to Bolin. "How soon can you present us with an op-plan?"

Wesley Bolin had worked his answer out long before the question was asked. And he knew enough to cut himself some slack. "I'll need three weeks, Mr. President. I want to red-team every piece of this operation."

"Red-team?"

"Yes, sir. As my people work out our operation plan I'll have a red team—a cadre of my most experienced operators—challenging every one of their decisions. We'll try to uncover our vulnerabilities so we can adapt to mitigate and overcome them. We will also integrate every element of the operation into a seamless, holistic totality. Then we'll do it all again, and again—until I am convinced we have it right."

"And who will you select, Admiral, to get the job done?"

"Navy SEALs, Mr. President. DEVGRU's SEALs, to be precise. They've got the most experience in Afghanistan and Pakistan, some of them have language skills, and they are used to working high-risk clandestine and covert assignments."

"DEVGRU. The Naval Special Warfare Development Group." The national security advisor scowled. "Wasn't that the unit involved in the killing of a civilian hostage during a rescue attempt recently?"

"Yes, sir, it was."

The president interjected, "And you still want to use them?"

"Mr. President," Bolin said, "I trust DEVGRU's SEALs to do the right thing. I believe that the ones involved in the incident Mr. Sorken mentioned have been disciplined—and at least one of them has been separated from the unit. But let me be emphatic, sir. I have commanded this unit. They have protected you, they have protected the secretary here and also the chairman. And I would trust any of these DEVGRU SEALs with my own life—and have done as recently as a month ago."

"You have?"

"In Afghanistan. Accompanied them on a mission near Khost. They operated flawlessly. And they will operate equally flawlessly when it comes to Abbottabad and Usama Bin Laden."

The president's pen tapped rapidly on the folder as he

spoke. "I defer to your experience, Admiral, as to the units used, their tactics, and the technologies you employ. But"—his face grew somber—"I've spoken about this . . . possibility in the most general of terms—let me emphasize that again—the *most general of terms*—to some of those whose opinions I trust." He paused. "And universally, reaction was negative. Negative!" He scanned the table. "We, you and I, have had our differences about the direction of national security policy and about the conduct of military operations, both in Iraq and Afghanistan. But everyone here should understand that I have no preconceptions. Nor do I hold any prejudicial thoughts one way or the other about whether to go or not to go."

Stroking his chin, the president looked directly at Vince Mercaldi. "I will not be railroaded or steamrollered by anyone. *Will not!*" He scanned the rest of the attendees. "But I won't be close-minded, either." He tapped his pen on the table for emphasis. "If you can make the case, Admiral, I'll consider—*consider*—a helicopter strike on the compound. If you cannot, then as commander in chief I will turn thumbs-down, and both the issue and the mission will be over. Finished. Dead."

He paused, barely able to conceal his anger. "And we'll pray that no one at Fox News ever finds out how much money we have spent drilling a dry hole in a two-bit town in Pakistan that very few people have ever heard of."

Vince spoke so quickly he almost cut the president off. "That's fair enough, Mr. President. We couldn't ask for more."

The president said nothing. He just glared at the CIA director.

Vince looked across the table at Wesley Bolin. "Well, as the president said, looks like the ball's in your court, Admiral."

Bolin's face was impassive, but his response was instantaneous. "I'll have something for you in twenty-one days, Mr. President."

"That would be the nineteenth of April." The president slapped his folder shut with a noise like a gunshot and rose abruptly. "I'll be waiting, Admiral. Good luck." Then he wheeled toward the door and exited without acknowledging the rest of the room.

27

"He's setting us up to fail, you know," Vince Mercaldi said.

"Of course he is. Did you see the look on his face when you told him we're down to one option?" Wes Bolin settled into the armchair in the director's hideaway office. "He so very much wanted B-2s. No up-close-and-personal. No eye-to-eye. That's why he's willing to approve all those drone strikes. It's all remote-control. Sanitized. Impersonal." The admiral paused to peer over at the CIA director, who was staring at the ceiling. "Tell me, Vince, how do we play this?"

Vince focused on the SEAL. "I think Kate Semerad put it best. She believes he can be nudged into action."

"Easier said than done, don't you think?"

Vince removed his aviator frames, pulled a handkerchief from his pocket, and polished the lenses, slowly, methodically, and in silence.

Wes Bolin laughed.

The CIA director looked at him. "What's so funny?"

"You always do that."

"What?"

"Polish your glasses when you don't want to answer the question."

"Guilty," Vince grinned. "Lemme tell you a story. Remember Anwar Sadat?"

"Sure. President of Egypt. Signed the peace treaty with Israel in seventy-nine. Assassinated in October nineteen eighty-one by the Muslim Brotherhood."

"An assassination in which our pal Ayman al-Zawahiri, UBL's Number Two, played a part," Vince said.

"Yeah, he did. But I remember Sadat. Smart dresser. Natty Savile Row suits. Smoked a pipe. Very distinguished guy. I've seen film of him."

"Well," Vince continued, "he was one of ours." He caught the look on the Admiral's face. "CIA's, I mean."

"No shit."

"Nope. No shit. This was the mid-seventies. Oil embargo right after the Yom Kippur War. Bill Colby was director of central intelligence—just took over for Jim Schlesinger. So CIA starts to recruit Sadat. The initial goal was to drive a wedge between him and the Soviets, because he'd already shown some independence by tossing out all his Soviet military advisors in the wake of the Six-Day War in sixty-seven.

"Amazingly, he was receptive. It was probably the money, but you know, maybe it wasn't—maybe he really wanted peace in his region. But it didn't matter. In this trade you take 'yes' for an answer and go with it. So anyway, once Sadat took the bait, it was Henry Kissinger's idea to turn him into a sophisticated, peace-seeking American ally. He got Bill Colby to send a team over there. With a suitcase full of money, of course. Set up an account for Sadat, the whole deal. Sorta what we did in Jordan, but on a larger scale."

"Jordan?" Wes Bolin looked surprised.

"Well, yes. King Hussein."

"Never heard that."

Now it was Vince's turn to look surprised. "Never? Hmmm." He drummed his fingers on the desk. "Well anyway, at that point—we're talking late seventy-four, early seventy-five, right after Jerry Ford became president—Sadat looked pretty much like a tin-pot dictator, dressing in Nehru suits and loud plaid jackets when he wasn't wearing his uniform. And Kissinger thought no one would take him seriously if he looked like a schlemiel. So the CIA team helped create him a whole new persona. They bought him clothes and taught him how to dress. He was a cigarette smoker. They broke him of that and gave him a pipe. Why? Because, as they told him, it looks sophisticated. Plus, any time you need to think about a question you've been asked but you don't want to look as if you're being evasive, you just relight your pipe. Take your time. Sit there and suck on it. Think about the question. You'll look smart. Academic. Considered. Wise."

"A psy-op team to make him over. No kidding."

"Nope. And Sadat was no fool. He took our money and he took our advice. And five years later he signed a peace agreement with Israel, and Egypt became the biggest recipient of U.S. aid in the world. And by the way, in September nineteen eighty-one, just a month before he was assassinated, he threw all the Soviets out of Egypt."

Bolin said, "All very fascinating, Vince. But what's your point?"

Vince brandished his eyeglasses. "These, Slam, are *my* pipe."

"They must be, Vince, because you still haven't answered the question. How do we play this so we—Kate's words—nudge him?"

"Smartass." The CIA director put his glasses back on. "I'm not sure 'nudge' is the right word. I think we're going to have to . . . *induce him* somehow to paint himself into a corner. And how do we do that? Pincer movement. You're one. You're going to present POTUS with a great op-plan and show him, not tell him, how you'll accomplish it."

"Show him."

"Exactly. We'll have a scale model of the compound built out here. We'll be able to show him precisely how your people will take it down, step by step. You'll bring the DEVGRU commander with you. Put a face on the mission, something POTUS can get a physical handle on. Y'know—exude confidence. Make it all sound inevitable. All that *oourah* stuff you SEALs are supposed to be great at."

"*Oourah*'s Marines. We're *hoo-yah*."

Vince blinked twice. "Hoo-yah. Got it. Navy. Maritime unit. Cheer sounds like a foghorn." He sing-songed it like a two-toned foghorn. "Hooo-*yaaah!*"

Slam Bolin broke up. "Y'know, Vince, I went through BUD/S in seventy-eight, and I've been a frogman ever since, and I've never, ever, thought of *hoo-yah* that way."

"Of course," Vince laughed. "It took a Sicilian boy from a landlocked part of California to open your eyes to the obvious." The CIA director grew serious. "Okay, so Pincer one is your show-and-tell. Then I come around the flank with new information, new intelligence. For that, by the way, we're going to need a second Sentinel drone over Abbottabad between now and the nineteenth."

Bolin nodded in agreement. "I'll get a Blue one assigned." JSOC had six Sentinels at its disposal. DEVGRU's RQ-170s were known as Blues.

"Great—your budget, not mine." Vince had already spent tens of millions on the one Sentinel he'd had overflying the city since Charlie Becker's insertion.

The expenditure was well worth it. Lockheed Martin's RQ-170 stealth drone had a loiter time measured in days, not hours, because its engine could be shut down and the bat-like craft would glide, riding the thermals, saving fuel. Its flying-wing design was invisible to radar. It had the ability to jam Pakistani radar, monitor their communications, and if necessary reduce them to unintelligible verbal burble. It could send clear color photos and pinpoint-sharp video from fifty-thousand-plus feet. CIA's Sentinel may have been fly-ing more than five months, but the Pakistanis didn't have a clue about its existence, even though it was remaining well within the Islamabad Exclusion Zone—the air defense inter-cept umbrella the Pakistanis had permanently unfurled over and around their capital region.

"No problem, Mr. Director. And if things get too busy, I can get us a third one to stream unilateral video to the JOC in J-bad, to you at Langley, and to JSOC's Alpha and Bravo op centers." JSOC maintained a JOC, or Joint Operations Center, in Jalalabad. That was the location from which Wes Bolin and the task force commander, a huge Ranger one-star nicknamed McGorilla, would run the Abbottabad strike. And Bolin's command had within the past few months also established its second U.S. command and operations center. It was located in Pentagon City, Virginia. The low-profile site, known in-house as JSOC Bravo, sat not half a mile from the Pentagon.

Vince pursed his lips. "All good. Another thing: I'm going to lay low for the next few days while we red-team all our existing intelligence. You saw his face. POTUS is pissed at me because he thinks I'm caballing behind his back. Maybe that's what his politicos are telling him, maybe he's getting paranoid because his approval ratings are in the toilet. Well, whatever it is, they're all wrong. This is no effing cabal. But those guys at the White House have got to get past politics and start behaving like adults when it comes to national security policy."

"Amen, Mr. Director. You're preaching to the choir."

Call Me Vince smiled wryly. "Yeah, but just because I'm right doesn't mean the Chicago gang likes it. So my instinct is that it's probably best not to go over there for a while. I've got my sources. They'll let me know. And when I do go, I'll make sure I'm well armed with irrefutable information. So we'll take some time now. Build ourselves an unshakable case."

"And on April nineteenth?"

"I think we should use a Powell Doctrine template. Overwhelming force, followed by inescapable conclusions. But no PowerPoints, no memos, no briefing papers. Like I said, it's all 'show me' and no 'tell me.' You gotta make POTUS visualize how your SEALs and Rangers will get in, do the deed, and get out before the Paks even know you're there. Tell it like it's a movie. Captivate POTUS. Make him see it in his head."

"Gotcha."

"I'll get our technical support people to build a scale model of the compound. Better yet, not just the house, but the whole area. Where the helos will land, how the SEALs will make their assault."

"Agreed. It's perfect."

"Exactly. All 'show me,' no 'tell me.' That's how you'll convince him—by making it impossible for him to do anything except give us a go."

"Aye-aye, Mr. Director." It was good counsel, and Bolin intended to follow it.

Vince scratched his nose. "Where are your SEALs now?"

"California. Training." Bolin paused. "I'll bring them

back. Give them a couple of days off while we finish the full-scale replica at Fort Knox."

"Knox?"

"Yup." The admiral saw the quizzical expression on the director's face. "It's close enough to Fort Campbell, where TF One-sixty, the Army's Night Stalker unit, is based so that they can stage at Campbell and rehearse the approach in the helos they'll use on the mission. Plus, Knox is big enough so that we can build the entire five-hundred-yard street and the houses as well as the compound. That way the pilots will learn the layout. We'll bring in the Ranger blocking force, the supplemental helicopters, the whole Assault package. And no one will notice, because we're constantly training there."

"Great." Vince was impressed.

"The helos are the important thing here, Vince. The flight and the air assault are the elements that can most easily go awry. For these SEALs, this is just another capture/kill mission. They've done hundreds. Thousands. Sure, there may be wrinkles inside the house. Bodyguards, suicide vests, human shields. But those are nothing these guys haven't faced on a regular basis for the past ten years. Nah—this is nothing special for them. Except who they're going after. Only the target is special."

"So are you gonna tell them who the target is?"

"Yeah," the admiral said, "at some point. I don't want them surprised when they stare the sonofabitch in the face." He grinned. "Shock can affect accuracy."

"Can it now?"

"You better believe it." Bolin stretched. "I'll leave for J-bad within the next couple of days to start the ball rolling on the support side and make sure our JOC is up to snuff."

"Jock? Like athlete?"

"Nope. JOC, like Joint Operations Center. It's where the Ranger commander and I will be situated when this goes down."

"Ah—just like our OC. But joint."

Bolin caught the wry look on the director's face. "Yes, Vince. You say OC and I say JOC." He paused. "Anyway, I want to make sure all the elements are there ready to roll. That's something best done face to face."

Vince nodded. "Agreed." Then, silence. All that Bolin could hear right then was the muffled hiss of the white sound piped between the quadruple panes of window glass, making them impenetrable to eavesdropping devices or lasers.

"Wes," the CIA director massaged his nose with his thumb and his index finger, "there's one question that's been nagging me for weeks now. And I think we have to have an answer ready for the nineteenth."

"And that is?"

"What are we gonna do with UBL's body? I mean, we don't want a Che Guevara situation." In October 1967, a Cuban American CIA contract agent named Felix Rodriguez had been instrumental in capturing the Argentine communist revolutionary and terrorist Che Guevara in Bolivia. Rodriguez even interviewed Che before the Bolivians executed him, amputated his hands, and ultimately sent them to Fidel Castro as proof Che was dead. Shortly after Che's execution and autopsy, the Bolivian Army buried his body in an unmarked grave near the small Bolivian mountain city of Vallegrande. But by the early twenty-first century, someone who had been in Vallegrande and seen the burial talked, and Che's body was exhumed. Vince understood all too well something similar must not happen with Bin Laden. "We gotta get rid of it before it becomes an icon or a relic."

The admiral looked at the CIA director with mock shock.

"You mean you've already assumed he won't be brought back in cuffs, so your good friend the attorney general can try him in New York federal court?"

"Y'know, the sorrow of it all is that Eric Holder would probably try to do exactly that." Then Vince gave Slam Bolin a wicked smile. "But gee, Wes, somehow I just don't get the feeling Usama'll be taken alive, y'know?"

"Well, in the infinitesimal case that he's KIA," Bolin said, pointing up toward the ceiling, as if a Department of Justice microphone might be concealed there, "I've given the matter some thought. Here's what: the *Carl Vinson* is on station in the vicinity."

"The aircraft carrier."

"Correct."

"What are you gonna do, launch the sonofabitch off the main catapult?"

"Only if he's still alive." The two men roared with laughter. "That's exactly what I'd like to do," Bolin said. "But as my Irish friends say, the proprieties must be observed."

"So—burial at sea."

"Precisely. Within hours of the takedown. No body. No way to find it. No iconic memorabilia, no relics." Bolin imitated his version of a Brando-esque New York City Godfather. "Usama's gonna sleep wit da fishes."

"I love it," Vince chortled. "It's perfect. It answers all the questions. It solves all the problems."

"And if the White House insists, we'll even do the burial according to Islamic tradition."

The CIA director nodded in agreement. "Sure. Why not." He took a few seconds to make some quick notes. "Okay, we can check that box off. And as for anything else that might come up on the nineteenth, I'm going to bring Spike. From the intelligence side, if there's anyone who can make the president paint himself into a corner, it's him. Because there's not a question POTUS can ask that Spike can't answer."

Vince scratched behind his ear. "Meanwhile, I'll see what we can do on the ground in Abbottabad to make life easier for your guys getting in and getting out. High time to make those folks at Valhalla Base earn their hazard pay, right?"

28

"Oh, crapola." Matt Nassar read the burst transmission a second time. "This is not good."

"Whassup?" Attila Harai peered around the doorway. "Who's it from this time?"

"The Zoo—headquarters. Who else? We have to find Archangel." Archangel was Langley's call sign for Charlie Becker.

"And?"

"They're sending a package. We have to dead-drop it to Archangel. And they're sending us equipment, too. They want us to take soil cores." Matt Nassar was a big, bulky, thirty-seven-year-old second-generation American of Lebanese descent who'd applied to CIA directly out of the University of Tennessee, where he'd majored in Arabic literature. Currently he spoke 5-level Arabic, and 3+ Farsi, Pashto, and Dari.

"Equipment? Soil samples? Tell them not to send anything. I'll buy a shovel. They'll get soil samples." Attila Harai was an Ivy Leaguer—Cornell—who'd begun his career at CIA in 2001, shortly after 9/11, as a security officer.

"Cores, not samples. We've been sending samples for months." Matt had been chief of Valhalla Base since Valentine's Day. He'd volunteered to stay until either it was all over, he got pulled out, or the Paks killed him. He was, to say the very least, passionate about his work.

Attila, Valhalla Base's junior officer, laughed, "What's the difference? It's dirt, right?" In 2005 Attila was accepted into the National Clandestine Service and took the six-month case officer's course at The Farm, the Agency's training facility near Williamsburg, Virginia, followed by immersion in Pashto and Dari, languages spoken fluently by fewer than two dozen of CIA's forty thousand employees prior to 9/11. He'd been picked for this assignment because of his language skills, as well as the fact that he could pass for Pakistani, right down to his thick, black Pashtunwali mustache.

Matt ignored Attila's comment. He stuck his head into the stairwell. "John, when can you burst Archangel?"

Valhalla Base's third occupant was John Brasseux, a Navy communicator assigned more or less permanently to the National Security Agency at Fort Meade, Maryland. He'd been cooped up for Valhalla Base virtually since it opened. A chief petty officer at twenty-nine, he was an honors graduate of Corry Station Navy Technical Training Unit in Pensacola, Florida, where he'd been top Sailor in his cryptology section. He had been looking for a slot in the fleet, but Corry Station, a low-profile installation located adjacent to Pensacola Naval Air Station, through which just over seven thousand students passed annually, was where

NSA trolled for the best communicators, cryptologists, and SIGINT (signals intelligence) slurpers. No Such Agency snapped up the petty officer second class with the promise of a signing bonus and a kick up the ladder to chief within twenty-four months if he mastered Pashto. Brasseux, never one to turn down a challenge, accepted on the spot.

Of course, no one at NSA ever mentioned that the MA in Information Warfare might ultimately volunteer for an assignment that kept him sequestered in a safe house for five-plus months, setting up and operating a half-dozen sophisticated eavesdropping devices that targeted the walled compound that sat 265 yards away. Nor had they bothered to explain, when he did volunteer, that there was no decent food in Pakistan. None at *all*. And that the water sucked. And that, due to security considerations, he would have to live entirely on local products because, as he'd learned during the three-week indoctrination course called "Denied Area Operations," which he'd taken at a CIA training site in Rosslyn, Virginia, even your shit can betray you.

And absolutely no one—*no one*—had told Brasseux that he'd have to wear a fricking man dress, which is how he referred to the traditional Pakistani *shalwar qameez,* the knee-length tunic and baggy trousers he thought of as harem pants, to make his infil to Abbottabad.

"John?" Matt climbed the stairs and walked into the second-floor bedroom the NSA tech used as his lab. "C'mon—when can you burst Archangel?"

Comms with Charlie Becker were complicated. The Paks were sophisticated—and good. And they had decent equipment, some of it from the U.S., some of it from the Russians, and some from the Chinese. If Valhalla Base bursted Charlie at a regular time, the transmissions would be discovered. And so John had worked out a pattern that, unless you were really looking, appeared to be random.

But it wasn't. Brasseux checked the clock on his console. "He won't be looking to receive for another five hours."

Matt double-checked the message. "When you send, tell him there'll be a dead drop in twelve days. And a package he'll have to cache for a while."

"'For a while?'" The tech looked over his shoulder. "That's real specific."

Matt shrugged. "That's headquarters. That's why it's the Zoo. 'Cause it's filled with dumb animals." Matt watched the Sailor's expression change. "What's up?"

"We've got movement." Brasseux tapped the thermal reader. "Somebody started a vehicle."

"I'll get on it." Matt scrambled for the stairs. His single-lens reflex camera and its 300mm lens were on the top floor of the villa. The house was roughly 250 yards from the target and slightly higher. From the third floor, he could see about two-thirds of the exterior of the compound and its structures, and a slash of one of the compound's interior yards. Unfortunately it was the yard where they burned the trash, not the one the occupants occasionally used for walking and conversation.

He'd set up the third-floor room just like a sniper would. The entry door had bedspreads nailed to the top of both the interior and hallway door frames so they could function as light blocks. No one would ever be silhouetted going in or out. The camera was on a tripod that was screwed into the floor to keep it stable. The window facing the compound was permanently open. But suspended a foot behind the window frame was a light gray gauze net. From the outside, anyone peering up would see nothing but a darkened room. The netting did not affect the quality of the photos.

Matt slipped behind the exterior drape, opened the door, closed it behind him, and stepped around the inside drape. He squinted into the Canon's viewfinder, focusing the long lens first on the third-floor balcony's privacy wall, then dropping to the exterior gate, squinting and squeezing off frame after frame as the gate opened inward and the red Suzuki nosed out onto the unpaved road. Tareq got out, closed the gate, and climbed back into the vehicle. The driver turned left and accelerated slowly southward.

Matt zoomed in, catching the driver. It was Arshad. He was laughing at something Tareq had said. He couldn't read the Pashtun's lips, but he hoped that Brasseux, one floor below, was getting audio. NSA's techno wizards—they were known as NSA elves, NSA being Nasty Santa's Assistants, had built what appeared to be two of the boxy, exterior ductless air-conditioning units common to Southwest Asia. They'd been affixed to the exterior wall of the safe house that faced the Khan compound. But the lines running inside weren't carrying refrigerated air. They were attached to an array of listening devices, some of which could be manipulated remotely in order to pick up conversations up to five hundred meters away, and others that were fixed on portions of the three-story structure in the hope of hearing a voice that could be identified as Bin Laden's, or someone referring to him either by name or one of the codes he used.

Matt panned as the SUV disappeared out of frame. He pulled the memory chip out of the camera, replaced it with a fresh one, and headed for the first floor so he could download the pictures, examine them closely, and then transmit anything new to HQ. On his way he stopped by Brasseux's workspace. "Get anything?"

"I'm just filtering now, Matt. You'll have it by the time you're downstairs."

"Thanks, dude." Matt galumphed down the narrow stairs to the ground floor. "Attila?"

"Yo."

"Check these out." He handed the memory chip to Attila. "If you see anything new, lemme know."

"Roger that." Attila inserted the chip into his computer. "What's with the soil samples?"

"Soil cores. I told you. They're sending a corer."

"A what?"

"It looks like a pipe. It takes a core sample. You drive it into the ground—straight down. You pull it out, and you send the whole thing back for analysis."

"We're gonna do that?"

"Yup."

"How we gonna do that?"

"We're going to put on our Cloaks of Invisibility, walk out at high noon, take our samples, and—"

"C'mon, Matt."

"We'll figure it out, okay? Do it at two in the morning or something. We're operations officers. We're supposed to be good at this stuff."

"Shit, we are good at this stuff. But we've never done something like that before."

"Can't be any worse than filling a mailbox or servicing a dead drop. And we've done that half a dozen times since we got here."

"True." The younger man paused. "Why do you think the Zoo wants soil samples—cores?"

"Dunno." Matt scratched his cheek. "Could be they want to see if the ground near the compound would support weight."

"Weight?"

"Weight." Matt's brow wrinkled. "Weight. Like a plane." He pumped his thumb toward the compound. "That field to the south? You've got more than five hundred yards of flat, plowed land back there. They could land a STOL—a short takeoff and landing aircraft."

"Or a big helo," Attila said. "Or a couple big helos." He considered what he'd said. "Think something's up?"

"Could be."

"Think they'll fill us in about what's up?"

"Who," Matt snorted, "the Zoo? Fill us in? You gotta be shitting me. You probably believe in the Easter Bunny, too."

"Oh, dude, say it ain't so." Attila pouted and kicked the ground. "You can't tell me there's no Easter Bunny."

PART THREE

APRIL 1, 2011 TO MAY 2, 2011

PART THREE

29

"Sweetie, I'm home." Troy Roberts dropped his duffel in the hallway, headed for the kitchen, and swept his wife into his arms.

"And about time, too, because I'm smoochless." Brittany Roberts threw her arms around his neck. "I have been smoochless for weeks now," she said, dropping her arms, stepping away, and adapting a serious tone. "Petty Officer Roberts, I want the situation corrected. Immediately."

"Aye-aye, ma'am. Execute-execute Operation Repair Smoochless." He kissed her long and passionately, mindless of their son Corbin's "Eeewww, gross."

He turned toward the five-and-a-half-year-old, picked him up, and hugged him, disappointed when he didn't get as big a hug back as he'd expected. Corb was like that just about every time he came home from a deployment. It was as if the bonding had to take place all over again. He kissed the top of his son's head. "Good to see you, too, trouble-maker." And he put the kid down.

"Where were you?"

"Cali-four-knee-ah." The SEAL pronounced it Schwarze-negger-style.

"Uh-huh." The kid shrugged.

"That's all the way on the West Coast." Troy struggled to make the kid understand. "Havin' fun in the sun." Indeed, the SEAL had gotten a fair amount of desert color.

Corbin looked up at his father. "Was there a pool?"

"You bet there was. And boy, did I do cannonballs. You remember cannonballs, Corb."

Finally, a smile that Troy felt lit up the room. "Cannon-balls are great. And you do them biggest of all." The kid's arms went wide. He screamed, "Spuh-LASH!"

"Shhh." Brittany knelt and cradled the boy in her arms. "Good trip?"

"I guess. We learned some stuff. Got a lot of range time. Improved skill sets. You've heard it all before, sweet: same old, same old."

They'd spoken almost every day. But of course, he'd never been specific. It was always "Hot here," or "Got a long run in this morning," or "Food's not bad, hon, but I sure do miss your cooking." No specifics. In point of fact, she had no idea whether he'd called her from where he said he was calling from, which was Fort Irwin, California, or whether he'd been in the desert, but a desert in Yemen, or Jordan, or Saudi Arabia.

He grinned. "Brought you back something, trouble-maker." Troy scampered back to the hallway and half a min-ute later reappeared holding a fair-size cardboard box. He set it on the kitchen table. "Where I was, they train in these," he said, slitting the wrapping tape with the big blade of the Emerson CQC-8 combat folding knife that he habitually carried both on and off duty. He pulled out a scale model of an Abrams M1A2 battle tank in desert tan, complete with the TUSK (Tank Urban Survival Kit), side skirt reactive armor, reinforced slat armor on the rear, and gun shields for its 7.62mm top-mounted machine gun.

"These are the same tanks they used in Fallujah in Iraq, Corb," he said, manipulating the model to demonstrate that all the parts moved. He looked at his son's blank stare.

"Fallujah is a city in Iraq. Iraq is far, far away." He laughed and looked at Brittany. "Forgot—he wasn't even born then." Troy tousled his son's hair. "Anyway, I figured you'd want your own tank, kiddo. Whatta you think?"

He handed the model to the boy, and the kid's face told him everything he needed to know. But to make it all the sweeter, Corb leaped into Troy's arms, nearly crunching the tank between them. "Dad, this is so awesome!"

It still sent the best kind of chill up Troy's spine whenever Corb called him "Dad." He'd never thought of himself as a father, only a son, until Bri and Corb had come into his life. Sometimes it scared him more than his work, the dad thing did. But he loved it, because the dad thing was like . . . free fall.

He put the kid down. "Go have fun."

Troy watched as the boy scrambled toward the stairs to the rec room. He went to the fridge, unholstered his weapon and set it on top, then grabbed a beer, twisted the cap off, and took a long pull. "Ahh." He scanned the kitchen appreciatively. "Oh, it is wonderful to be home." He looked his wife up and down and smiled proudly. "You're beginning to show."

She blushed. "I feel like a balloon. I want to be a lot slimmer."

"You look just fine to me." He took her in his arms. "I'm blessed."

She looked up at him. "We're blessed." She kissed his neck. They stood, embracing for a long time, rejoicing in the feel of each other's bodies, in the closeness, the touching. She could feel the coolness of his beer bottle on her back. "How long will you be home this time?"

"Don't know." He released her and took another swallow of beer. "We're on call, so it may be three, four days, maybe a week, maybe more."

"I hope it's more." Her brow wrinkled. "Any idea about a deployment?" She didn't want to go any further.

"Nope. But I get the feeling we're gonna head out some time in the near term." He looked at her. "It's our turn for AFPAK. You know about the rotations."

Indeed she did. She knew that two rotations ago, the squadron Troy's was replacing had lost one SEAL and suffered three wounded, including one double amputee. Then there was the retired DEVGRU SEAL who had been killed in December 2009 in Khost at Forward Operating Base Chapman, while working for CIA.

"Whatever," Troy said. "We do what we do. In the meanwhile, I'm home, we're together, and you're beautiful. God's looking after us."

"Yes, He is." She beamed. "Go up and take a shower," she said. "I'm going to finish down here." She looked at him. "Hungry?"

"Nah. We grabbed pizza during the debrief." He looked at her. A broad smile spread across his face, reacting to the warm, inviting smile on hers. "Maybe I'm psychic, but something tells me if I'm good I may get lucky tonight."

"Y'never know about luck, sailor." She grinned. "But if you're very, very, very lucky, you may get . . . lucky." She giggled. "Quite lucky."

"That's one way to put it."

"What's the other?"

"You know what they teach us, Bri."

She laughed. "That luck has nothing to do with it. That it's all training." She looked at him slyly. "Muscle memory and all that stuff."

"Oh, yes, muscle memory and all that stuff, Mrs. Roberts. Emphasis on the muscle." He watched her cheeks turn bright red. "And I have been training. Oh, have I ever."

She took the beer bottle out of his hand and kissed him on the lips. "Begone," she said. She pointed at the fridge. "Secure your weapon, then make sure Corb's in bed and lights out. I'll be up to conduct an inspection in exactly six minutes. We'll see just how much memory your muscle has."

30

"I'm gonna need me a full Sentinel countermeasures package—two, maybe three birds, sometime in the near future. You tell me." Wes Bolin wrapped his size ten-and-a-half hands around a big coffee mug emblazoned with the sword and shield of the KGB. The mug was a gift from Vince Mercaldi, who had bought it at what he liked to call "the *real* Company Store." Which would be the CIA employee gift shop that sat between the Northwest Federal Credit Union branch and the unclassified cafeteria, the one used by overt employees and Agency guests, as opposed to the classified cafeteria, which was reserved for covert operatives only. The fourteen-ounce mug was half-filled with lukewarm, weak coffee. Bolin had come of age on U.S. Naval Academy coffee, brewed so thin, the admiral liked to say, that you could see the bottom of the mug even after you added milk. It was a habit he'd never outgrown.

"Three more? As of last night you already got a second

bird over Abbottabad. Must be something real big." Brigadier General Eric McGill was a big man, a huge man, who,
as a varsity offensive lineman at West Point, had earned
the nickname "McGorilla" for his intimidating three-point
stance. Currently he was Wes Bolin's point man in Afghanistan and commander of Task Force 131, JSOC's J-Bad-based
hunter-killer group, whose mission was to find and eliminate
al-Qaeda and Taliban high-value targets on both sides of the
AFPAK border. He had SEALs, Delta shooters, Rangers,
and Air Force special operations personnel under his command as well as an array of technological resources whose
value ran into the eleven figures.

"Y'never know, Mac. 'Be prepared: That's the Boy
Scouts' marching song,' remember?"

"Only too well." McGill retrieved the big Cuban cigar
he carried in his breast pocket and stuck it in his mouth.
"What's the goal?"

"I need the Paks to be deaf, dumb, and blind. On command. But without making ourselves obvious." Bolin pulled
a tactical pilotage chart out of his briefcase and unfolded
it on the conference table. He drew a line with his finger.
"Coming from here, I run southeast, skirt to the north of
Shahi Kowt," he tapped the map, "then cross the border
at Tawr Kham and run the corridor between the Pak West
ADIZ and the Peshawar no-fly zone." ADIZ stood for Air
Defense Identification Zone. All flights entering an ADIZ
are required to file a flight plan with the Pakistani military
and remain in constant two-way contact during their transit.

For the past month, Bolin had examined satellite imagery and pored over pilotage maps. There were more direct
routes to Abbottabad than the one he was leaning toward,
but they also overflew some populated areas and, more to
the point, came dangerously close to Pakistani military
installations. Bolin wanted to thread the needle, flying the

lowlands that skirted the demarcation line between several Pakistani commands.

He'd studied the Paks. Most of their military commands were stovepiped; they did not interact. So if Colonel Ahmed happened to catch a glimpse of unidentified choppers flying in Colonel Walid's sky, that would be Colonel Walid's problem, not Colonel Ahmed's.

Then he'd had his intelligence people work the problem. They discovered that the Pak military didn't even have a universal communications system. Each region had its own. Which made it even better odds that the Paki left hand would have no idea what the Paki right hand was doing, and Bolin's SEALs and their Night Stalker stealth MH-60J and MH-47 helos could skedaddle hi-diddle-diddle straight down the middle. Invisible to everyone.

If it was dark enough. "Mac?"

"Sir?"

"Punch up moon phases for the next couple of months, will you?"

"Starting when?"

"Tomorrow would be good. And take it through fifteen May." If POTUS hadn't signed off by then, it would probably be too late.

The Ranger hunt-and-pecked at his laptop keyboard. "We're in new moon now through the tenth."

"Next new moon?"

McGill squinted at his screen. "Zero-three May."

"And May tenth?"

"First quarter."

Too much light. "Send me those dates, will you, please?"

"Yes, sir." McGill did some typing. "Heading your way, Admiral." He closed his laptop. "Sir, how big's the package?"

"Six, maybe seven birds, to include a JMAU and an SSE in the secondary, and a FAARP backed up by a couple of

Ranger platoons." JMAUs were forensics-capable Joint Medical Augmentation Units; SSEs were sensitive site exploitation groups, more colloquially known as slurpers. FAARPs were forward area arming and refueling points positioned no more than thirty-five miles from the target.

"I could invade a country with six, maybe seven birds, a couple of Ranger platoons, a JMAU, and an SSE. Where you going?"

"Can't say yet, except that it's not an invasion. But I'm going deep on this one, Mac. I'll need every fricking Pak air defense radar between the border and Islamabad north to go sightless for three, maybe four hours." Bolin looked at the Ranger. "Can we do that?"

"Depends."

"On?"

"Time, conditions, maybe a little bit of luck." The big Ranger tapped the four-by-six-foot area map on the wall. "Most Pak radar faces east, toward the main enemy, India. There are Pak Air Force fields at Risalpur, Kamba, and Islamabad. Each has radar and missile defenses, and some of them come back this way. We've spoofed every single one except Islamabad on previous missions—and they never noticed a thing. But we've never smacked all the sites at the same time. That's the unanswered question: Can we silence every site simultaneously?"

"And make them think nothing's wrong. That's the key, Mac. They have to believe everything is situation normal."

"Sitnorm, sitnorm." McGill paced back and forth, cigar chomped between his teeth, muttering the word like a mantra. He looked, Bolin thought, like a caged animal or a crated attack dog, winding into tighter and tighter circles as, brow knit, he scowled at the floor.

Then: "Here's what."

"What?"

"Every weekend they run maintenance."

"And?"

"One at a time they shut down for about three hours, sometimes a lot more. Which one shuts down depends on the traffic, so it's not as if they maintain a specific schedule."

"And?"

"So take Islamabad. When I-bad goes dark, they signal Peshawar, Risalpur, Rawalpindi—all the other stations that they're going dark. If we can screw with their comms, maybe we can make them think it's okay to go dark. Not all—but some. And the others, we maybe capture signal, then tap their lines and rebroadcast it back to them—like a tape loop. Or we could spoof a power outage. Most of those installations rely on substations we know about—Sentinel should be capable of taking down the power grids."

"Ever tried it?"

"Nope. But it's well within their ROC." ROC was military shorthand for range of capabilities.

"Who can you put on this right now?"

"Got some signals intelligence squirrels, and some MA-SINT contractors with cyberwar experience who maybe could program the algorithms we'd need to bore inside the power grids. Plus the Sentinel people and their contractors."

"Make a compartment." Bolin understood that secrecy was everything. "Read in those you have to. Get the proper paperwork. And maximum op-sec. No conversation except in SCIFs. You're point, and you report to me, or to Joe." Joe was Air Force Brigadier General Joseph Bradley Franklin, Bolin's deputy back at Fort Bragg.

"Got it." The Ranger's gaze settled on the admiral. "Timeframe?"

"I need to know you've solved the problem by the sixteenth of the month, and I will need on that date a couple of paragraphs telling me exactly how you did it—and in non-technical language, Mac."

"Can do." McGill stuffed the cigar back in the breast pocket of his ACU. "Anything else you'd like to tell me, sir?"

"Not right now." Bolin took a long swig of the cold coffee. "But let me speak plainly, Mac: if you think you know what's going on, or if you even think you think you know what's going on, forget about it. No whispers, no RUMINT, no gossip. I can't have it." Bolin squinted at the Ranger general. "Got it?"

"Hoo-ah, Admiral. Heard, understood, and acknowledged."

31

Dick Hallett yawned, stretched, and scanned the message from Valhalla Base. Charlie Becker had been alerted, and the soil sampling was under way. He pulled a green pencil out of the mug of writing instruments on his desk, flipped open a spiral notebook, and drew two neat green lines through the appropriate portion of his to-do list. The notebook was two-thirds filled. Green lines stood for tasks accomplished successfully, red lines stood for screw-ups, and blue-highlighted items were requests or orders from Vince Mercaldi and were to be dealt with ASAP.

Hallett's work schedule had been turned on its head ever since he'd become chief of BLG. Abbottabad was nine hours ahead of Washington, so he lived on a Pakistani schedule, coming to work just before midnight and dragging himself home somewhere between five and six the next evening. Unless there was a crisis, in which case he'd grab a combat nap on his couch and remain until it was solved.

His schedule had been like this since the previous August, and Hallett was exhausted, physically, mentally, and emotionally.

His wife, Sara, worked at the National Clandestine Service's logistical support group, which created legends for CIA's covert operations personnel. They kept regular hours. She wanted him to hang it all up. He had twenty-nine years in, four beyond what was necessary for full retirement benefits—more if you counted his five years in the Marines. And he was an SIS-2, senior intelligence service and holding the equivalent rank of a two-star general. She had only nineteen months left until she was eligible to retire. Why didn't he just go now and spend the time fixing up their lodge in Idaho? Hunt. Ski. Play with the grandkids. Sleep.

But he couldn't—he wouldn't—quit now. Hours be damned, they were on the cusp of ending an almost ten-year hunt, and Dick Hallett was not about to leave before the mission was completed.

He scanned the never-ending, ever-expanding to-do list. Blue-highlighted was the terse note **KHAN MODEL.** That would have to wait. CIA's technical services people worked normal schedules. They wouldn't appear until seven.

He flipped the page. Picked up the phone. Dialed.

The phone rang twice. "Bailey."

U.S. Navy Captain (SEAL) Larry Bailey was Wes Bolin's detailee to the Bin Laden Group. Vince Mercaldi and Bolin had an eye-to-eye relationship, but down the chain of command, there was liaison. In JSOC's case, liaison meant Larry Bailey.

"Larry, Dick Hallett. Morning."

"Same to you." Hallett heard the SEAL slurp his ever-present coffee. The tall, dark-browed Texas SEAL was a caffeineado. "What can we do for you, Dick?"

"You guys were supposed to get me a package for my guy in Abbottabad."

"The Ranger you've got on the ground. Roger that."

"And?"

"Arrival within the next twenty-four hours."

"Super." Hallett sipped from his mug. "What's in it?"

"Fireflies."

Hallett hadn't heard the term before. "And they are?"

"We used to call them Phoenix Beacons."

"Gotcha. We had 'em in Central America." Between 1984 and 1987 Hallett had been deputy station chief in San Salvador and a trusted advisor to the government when it fought for survival against Soviet- and Cuban-supported communist FMLN guerrillas. Phoenix Beacons were miniature infrared flashers powered by 9-volt batteries. They were easily concealable and could be seen from hundreds of yards away. He'd supplied the Salvadorans with beacons over the protest of the State Department, some factions of which, Hallett believed then and now, had wanted the communists to win. The Salvadorans were basically blind after dark. The beacons helped guide their helicopters at night. The only problem back then had been short battery life. He mentioned the flaw to the SEAL.

"You probably had the nine-volt version," Bailey said. "Today, they're LEDs, powered by 2032 batteries—the ones about the size of a quarter—and they can blink away for a couple of weeks, maybe longer. Besides, today we remote-control them."

Hallett heard the SEAL pour himself a fresh cup of coffee from the ever-present thermos on his desk. "We're sending twenty, more than enough for your guy to lay out our approach."

"Super."

"He'll do box-and-ones." That was the five-flasher pattern favored by the Night Stalkers for a hot approach.

"Gotcha," Hallett paused. "So you want Charlie to position the fireflies adjacent to the compound."

"Affirmative. We'll give him positioning data."

"Clandestinely."

"That's the usual procedure."

"You do know," Hallett said, "Charlie's a double amputee, right?"

There was silence on the other end.

"Larry?"

"Ah, Dick, I, uh—"

"Gotcha." Hallett did some mental scrambling. "Tell you what," he said. "Lemme run it by Charlie."

There was a pause.

"Listen, Larry, Charlie's a Ranger. He's tough as nails, and so far as he's concerned, we're the ones with disabilities, not him. So let me check. If he feels comfortable, then it's a go. Because we're not talking about whether he can or can't physically, it's whether he can get in and get out clandestinely. If he tells me he can, then he can. If not, we'll get one of the people at Valhalla to lay 'em down for you."

"What kind of operational experience do they have?"

"They're case officers."

"Dick, I'm talking the sort of stuff we do."

"Neither has a military background."

There was another pause on the line. "Then I'd really like Charlie to get this done for us," Bailey said emphatically. "Rangers know all about box-and-ones and where they should go, and how to compensate if things don't work out perfectly."

"I agree, Larry. I'll get back to you." Hallett rang off, put a question mark next to the line in his notebook, and eyeballed the next item on his list. Which caused him to stand up and look around the bullpen of an office.

He'd set the place up so there was no overt hierarchy or caste structure implicit in its design. He sat in the middle, in the same sort of cubicle everyone else worked in. Well, maybe a little larger. He had a couch in his workspace, and a coffee table, and two armchairs. BLG also had its own conference room, an AV room for teleconferencing, and a SCIF. Hallett, who'd done a tour in Buenos Aires and come back as an espresso addict, had also made sure the unit had a grade-A coffee machine, an industrial-strength, computer-driven gizmo that made a wide array of coffees, espressos, mochas, teas, even hot chocolate.

Hallett saw who he was looking for, grabbed his mug, which was emblazoned with the eagle, globe, and anchor of the Marine Corps, and zigzagged to the outer edge of the bullpen. The analyst known as Spike was setting up for the day. He was already in shirtsleeves, sans tie, his sport coat hanging precariously from the top of the cubicle wall.

He looked up as Hallett approached and dropped the cruller he was eating onto a paper napkin. "Morning, Chief."

Hallett swallowed coffee and peered over the cubicle wall at the chaos on Spike's desk and work table. "If clutter indicates success, then you gotta have a lot of good news for me, Spike."

"Then I'm glad I finally cleaned my desk up," the analyst deadpanned. He finished the cruller, wiped his fingers, locked them behind his head, and stretched. "Nothing's changed, Dick." He held up a transcript. "This is Arshad and Tareq in the car, thirty-one March. They talk about 'the Diamond,' *al mas*, which is one of the codes for Bin Laden. But the conversation in and of itself is no absolute confirmation that UBL is living with them."

"Could you read it, please?"

"Sure.

TAREQ: Did you lock the gate, brother?

ARSHAD: Of course. It is important to protect our jewels, our diamonds.

TAREQ: Indeed, brother. That is why we keep our valuables behind locked gates.

The transcript says Arshad laughs at this point." Spike shrugged. "The earlier part of the conversation they didn't get. And subsequently, until they got out of earshot, it was all about family—kids, wives, the normal stuff."

He looked at the disappointed expression on Hallett's face. "Boss, there's no smoking gun. Never has been. Frankly, I don't think there ever will be."

"Why, Spike?"

"Because he's smart. Because he's disciplined. He knows how to keep himself below our radar. And so are the Khans, or whatever their real names are. But I'm as certain that he's there in that building, on that compound, as I've ever been about anything. The food, the couriers, the way the house was built, the overhead we've seen, the full-court press ISI staged in Abbottabad—and, more significantly, nowhere else—in the wake of the NATO leak. Each piece itself doesn't mean much. But take them all together?"

The analyst threw his hands into the air. "Dick, the guy is there. But if we don't go in and find out for ourselves, it may be another ten years before we get this close again."

Hallett mirrored Spike's gesture of futility. "I agree. But as the director has made very clear, it's POTUS's call."

"And more's the pity," the analyst sighed. "Y'know, we had him in our sights as far back as Khartoum in the nine-

ties. The Saudis tried to kill him back then—and screwed it
up. Billy Waugh, the retired Special Forces guy who was in
Khartoum working surveillance on Carlos the Jackal, was
there when that happened. He surveilled UBL in K-Town in,
what, ninety-two? ninety-three? Could have killed him back
then. Billy even suggested it and drew up an op-plan. But he
was turned down. In the light of the Church hearings in the
seventies, when Congress almost destroyed the Agency, the
Ford administration buckled. Ford signed Executive Order
12333 and lethal findings became a no-no. Billy once said
that for the price of a ten-cent bullet we could have saved
ourselves the pain of 9/11 and a bunch of other stuff. And
he was right. But the Seventh Floor said no—claimed they'd
never get it past the White House and it wasn't worth going
to the mat over.

"Or the time we found Imad Mugniyah aboard the *Ibn
Tufail*." The analyst saw the question mark in his boss's
eyes. "It was a Kuwaiti-flagged ship, in the Gulf. This was
ninety-six, around the time of the Atlanta Olympics. I remember that op because I was at the CTC back then, working Mugniyah. The op was called Golden Ox Returns. We
had SEALs and Force Recon Marines ready to go, and an
amphibious task force straining at the leash. I mean, this
was the guy who'd bombed the U.S. Embassy in Beirut in
eighty-three. Who killed two hundred forty-one Marines
and Sailors when he bombed the Marine barracks at Beirut
Airport at the behest of the Iranians. Who killed the Navy
diver Bobby Stethem aboard TWA Flight eight-four-seven.
Dumped his body on the tarmac in Beirut. But Clinton's fur-
shtunken NSC and the goddamn DCI—I think it was John
Deutch—got in the way. Wouldn't permit it. 'Abort abort
abort' was the message from the White House. Not enough
evidence, their people told us.

"Not enough? We had a fricking ninety percent probability. They said ninety wasn't good enough." The analyst shook his head. "Ninety percent? Nothing in this whole place"—he gestured around the room—"is ninety percent. Ninety percent? Jeezus H. If I get sixty-five, seventy percent probability I'm in heaven. They even had his fingerprints on file. Back in ninety-six, this guy was the most wanted terrorist on the face of the earth. But the White House said it was a risky op. It could have made the Kuwaitis mad. Or the Saudis. Bullshit. The bottom line was the White House had no balls. No one had any balls."

"I can't argue with any of that, Spike."

"Same thing happened in ninety-eight. JSOC set up an op—it was called Rhino, as I recall. We had Delta and Rangers training out at Edwards Air Force Base. Bin Laden was in Kandahar. We had solid intel. But the Clinton National Security Council people said no. Too risky. We were told that if we didn't have one hundred percent surety, we had to scrub. We had eighty-eighty percent surety. So we scrubbed. And Bin Laden? He walked away again.

"There's more. In oh-seven, somebody saw Ali Atwa walking the streets of Beirut." He saw the quizzical look on Hallett's face. "Ali Atwa was Imad Mugniyah's accomplice on the TWA hijacking. He's still on the FBI's most wanted terrorist list. So somebody fingers him, and we know he's in Beirut. But nobody wants to go get him. CIA? We're too busy with the Valerie Plame case and defending ourselves because of all those enhanced interrogations to actually perform our core mission. State's against it because it'll stir up the Syrians. FBI? They can't be bothered. Ancient history, they say."

He looked at Hallett. "That's why *we*, or, okay, we and JSOC, *we* gotta go to Abbottabad. Break into the goddamn compound. See for ourselves. And if it is him, put a bullet in his head then and there." Spike slammed the desk in frustration. "Every time we have these guys in our sights, every fricking time, POTUS says no. Or the Seventh Floor says no. Or State says no. You can't get anywhere. And where did all those nos lead us? Khobar Towers. The embassies in Kenya and Tanzania. The *Cole*. The World Trade Towers. Bali. Madrid. London."

He looked up at Hallett. "Jeezus H, Dick, what's next? Does he have to kill another three thousand Americans before we get serious about putting him in the ground?"

Hallett had heard it all before. And the man was right. Spot-on.

But Spike was an absolutist when it came to UBL. It was all black-and-white to him. But here and now, there were politics involved. There always are. And Richard Hallett understood a few truths about politics. One of the most important was that politics weren't black-and-white absolutes but various shades of gray. Another was that, once every decade or so, it was actually possible to shame, or coerce, or even blackmail a politician into doing the right thing.

Blackmail? Well, yes. For a while Hallett had been one of CIA's legislative affairs liaison officers, lobbying Congress, and he had seen how the Pentagon dealt with the politicians. Some senators or representatives would go on a Pentagon CODEL, or congressional delegation, to someplace overseas. And being senators or congressmen, they'd get into trouble. Sometimes it was women, or booze. Sometimes they'd put themselves in compromising positions with the locals, or hit on some State Department officer who'd scream harassment or attempted rape. Or tap their toes in the wrong men's room. And the Pentagon liaison officer traveling with them would open his briefcase filled with cash, pull the right strings, and everything would be covered up.

Until there was a budget hearing the Pentagon deemed critical. At that point, that selfsame liaison officer would show up at the hearing and make a point of saying hello to every one of the people whose asses he'd saved. And tell them how much he was counting on their support.

The lesson hadn't been lost on Hallett. Which was one of the reasons he was an optimist now. A pol was a pol. There were ways they could be . . . convinced. Not the president, but perhaps some of those around him.

But he didn't say any of that to Spike.

"Spike," Hallett said, "I'm persuaded this time will be different. There's only one person you have to convince. Not the Seventh Floor. Not State. Not Defense. Just POTUS."

"And that, chief, is why there's a problem. POTUS is so fricking political he won't do anything that might hurt his chances of reelection."

"You don't think he's capable of nonpolitical actions?"

"I haven't seen any so far."

"You think it's pretty much Mission Impossible?"

"Probably."

That gave Hallett the opening he'd been waiting for. "Then your mission, Spike—and by the way, you don't get a choice—is to change POTUS's behavior pattern and convince him to do the right thing."

"Very funny, Dick."

"No, I'm serious. You're going to the April nineteen meeting with the director. You and he representing all forty-three-plus thousand of us. Sit Room. Bells and whistles."

"You're shitting me."

"Call it Vince's specific request." Hallett brandished the notebook. "He wants you to close the deal."

"Close the deal. Me."

"Affirmative. You know UBL better than anyone. Who better?"

"So I get to make another Haj to the White House. Make the case for action with all those pols sitting in the room.

Y'know what that makes it? Eid al-Adha." The younger man bit his lower lip. "And I'm the sheep whose throat gets slit.

"That meeting on the fourteenth?" he said. "Dick, I took the course on nonverbal behavioral indicators. I read body language. Y'know what all that massaging of chin and tapping of pen told me? It told me the president is looking for ways not to act. And how SECDEF's arms were crossed, uncrossed, crossed again? Means SECDEF is real iffy. And the frigging politicos? No friggin' eye contact and pushing their wheeled chairs back from the table every time somebody mentioned a strike. That meant they're all looking for excuses, and scapegoats to blame when something goes wrong."

He looked up bitterly at Hallett, whose arms were resting on the cubicle wall. "We're being set up, Dick. We are so screwed."

Hallett had heard enough. "Get off it, Spike. First, we're not being set up—at least not yet. The director's got our political back. And we're not screwed, either. Not if we do what we're capable of doing—which are. Second, you're the best man for the job. I know it, the director knows it—and frankly, you know it, too. You did great last time. Yeah, the president is shaky. Wishy-washy. Blows with the wind. We all know that. But we also believe he can be convinced—you can call it shamed or whatever else you want to call it, but 'convinced' is the most positive—to do the right thing. Whatever the term, you're the one the director believes can get POTUS to give us the go. Why? Because you're passionate, because you know your stuff, and because you're the best informed. Trust me—you'll close the fricking deal."

He peered into the younger man's eyes, searching for confirmation. There was none there.

How to make him commit? Sure, Hallett could order Spike to go—and the analyst would have to obey. But Hallett understood he needed a passionate, committed emissary, not a by-the-numbers bureaucrat in the Situation Room. "Spike, you're a Marine, right?"

"For a while," the analyst nodded. He patted his ample belly. "Course I was just a bit thinner when I did my four in the Corps."

"So was I," Hallett said. "And I did seven." He looked at the analyst. "So what do we Marines do, Spike? We take it to the enemy. When ambushed, we counterambush. We do not retreat."

"And your point?"

"Is that you need to think of April nineteenth as a counterambush. Yeah, Sorken and that asshole Dwayne Daley are laying for us. Screw 'em. We don't retreat. We attack, attack, attack."

"No retreat, eh?" The analyst cocked his head. "Attack, attack, attack." He cracked his knuckles. "Y'know, that actually makes sense." He massaged the back of his head, then fixed Hallett with an uncharacteristically steely stare. "But hear me out. Then it's going to be 'take no prisoners' so far as I'm concerned. Screw the NSC. Screw the politicians. The director has to understand that going in."

"He already does, Spike. That's why he wants you with him."

The analyst's face told Hallett all he needed to know. The BLG chief opened his notebook, pulled a pencil from his pocket, and drew a green line through the appropriate entry. "'No prisoners.' You hold that thought, Spike, and you'll enjoy every single minute of your Haj."

32

Charlie Becker wheeled himself south on Narian Link Road in the darkness, past the girls high school, heading for the graveyard. He'd received a bursted message telling him to clear the cemetery dead drop, so he was on his way. It had to be done early, before the city started waking up. No problem: he'd left Hassan Town at four. The moon was a sliver obscured by clouds and there was a slight chill to the air, a welcome breeze coming off the mountains to the north.

The street was silent. No traffic, no pedestrians. He rolled up to the graveyard and pushed himself through the open gate as a lone truck passed him, spewing diesel fumes as it headed north toward the main highway. He listened to its engine decrescendo into the distance.

Charlie was energized. No—it was far more than that. He was motivated, galvanized, invigorated. *They're coming. They finally made up their fricking minds. They're going to take the sonofabitch down.*

A message had arrived last week, asking if he could physically drop fireflies—position them—adjacent to the compound. His response was an immediate and unconditional affirmative. And here they were. He'd collect them. Hold them. And set them when ordered.

Charlie maneuvered through the open gateway, working his dolly down the rough path. Three rows south, two rows west. Second grave on the right. The dead drop was ingenious. One of the stones at the bottom of the memorial had been chiseled out and replaced by a hollow container made of some sort of composite. A perfect match for the stones used in the memorial. Rap it with a stick and it felt like stone. How the technical people back at Langley had accomplished this, and how they'd installed it, Charlie neither knew nor cared. All that mattered was that it worked.

He reached down, moved the false stone, and pulled out a small wrapped package about the size of a paperback book. He knew what the packet contained: fifteen Phoenix Beacons, thirty 2032 batteries, and fifteen positioners, mini-stakes just a little bit bigger than golf tees that affixed with waterproof adhesive to the bottoms of the infrared flasher casings. Charlie secreted the package in his tunic, replaced the stone, scattered dust to hide his tracks, and made his way back toward the empty street.

They were coming. Soon. Charlie smiled to himself as he headed south on the empty roadway. He glanced at the dark sky. It would be light soon. The muezzin at the Umar Mosque two hundred yards away would be calling the faithful to morning prayer.

Charlie would be there, too.

Facing east.

Reciting the proper words.

But praying for an entirely different outcome.

Allahu Akbar. God is great.

Subhana rabbiyal ad-heem. Glory be to God almighty.

Sam'i Allahu liman hamidah, Rabbana wa-lakal hamd.
God listens to he who praises Him.

And Charlie would be thinking *inshallah*—God willing
that my particular prayer will be listened to and answered.

Answered in the near term.

And most important, answered with extreme prejudice.

Allahu Akbar!

God, Charlie knew, is indeed great.

But so, Charlie knew, is a Barnes 70-grain TSX bullet.
Or a Match King 77-grain. If Bin Laden wanted to recite *ka-
limah shahada* on his way to martyrdom, either one would
help him along the path equally as well.

33

Commander Dave Loeser and Captain Tom Maurer surveyed the mock-up. It had been built by CIA contractors and Army carpenters and excavators over the previous five days. They'd used just over ten acres of cleared land behind the eight-hundred-meter rifle range and built a road from west-southwest to east-northeast, 430 meters long and 9 meters wide. At its northeast terminus, the road dead-ended into a narrower road that ran almost due north-south. Sixty-five feet from the T, an eight-foot chain-link fence ran for two hundred feet. Halfway down the fence was a twelve-foot-wide gate. Then the fencing continued another hundred feet.

Behind the fence sat four structures. Three of them were one story; one was three story, with terraces on its second and third floors. The third-floor terrace, which faced roughly south, was enclosed by a seven-foot privacy shield. All the windows on the north side of the three-story structure were opaque. Behind the structures and enclosing the compound, making it into a five-sided compound, just over an acre, ran another 485 feet of fencing.

Across the road from the compound sat three houses. One faced the three-story structure; the other two sat farther southwest. Behind the houses lay a six-acre, rectangular plowed field. The field behind the compound was also plowed into neat rows.

Behind the twelve-foot-wide gate were a pair of 125-foot-long, twelve-foot-high walls built of plywood, creating a twelve-foot-wide alley, at the rear of which, on the eastern wall, was a twelve-foot-wide steel gate. On the western wall, a four-foot-wide doorway had been cut and fitted with a steel doorframe, on which hung a steel door secured by a hasp and lock arrangement. The western yard, which held only two small boxlike structures twelve feet tall attached to the plywood wall and enclosed by the fencing, was roughly one hundred by one hundred feet.

Tom Maurer paced off the courtyard. "We can get one helo in here easily." He pointed at the flat roof of the three-story structure. "The assaulters on Chalk One can fast-rope onto the roof, drop onto the terrace, and blow through the windows. Then Chalk One drops the Rangers on the road to act as a blocking force. Chalk Two lands here. Assaulters blow the wall or the door, blow the wall opposite, and hit the guest house and the main house simultaneously. Rangers in Chalk Two are perimeter security inside the compound, and the K-9 and handler follow the assaulters."

He turned to face south and pointed to the plowed field beyond the compound. "Enabler helo comes down there. SSE group, JMAU, and us, plus another Ranger platoon, maybe a small CIA element, a translator." He looked at the Red Squadron commander. "Piece of cake, right?"

"Yeah, until we do it for real." Tom Loeser pointed at the third-floor terrace. "No visuals, are there?"

"Nope. We have no idea what's inside. The doc CIA sent in never made it past the main gate. No one's been in there. Thermal readings give us zilch."

"So we have no idea at all what the interior of the house looks like?"

"None at all. But we seldom do, and houses are houses, right?"

"Yeah, but Murphy is Murphy, too. So when we red-team this, let's make sure we put some iron doors inside—something they'll have to blow."

The DEVGRU CO nodded in agreement. "Good idea." He looked at the squadron commander. "When do the boys get in?"

"Tomorrow. I switched things around a little. Six-Charlie and One-Alpha are my assault element, with Five-Charlie and Three-Bravo as my backup. Do you want to stage a walk-through?"

"No," Maurer said. "No walk-throughs. And no daylight. They'll bunk here, but we stage at Fort Campbell, fly ninety minutes—contour stuff to shake them up a little, then come in from the north, just like we will when it's for real."

Loeser said, "When do we tell them?"

"When we're airborne," Maurer replied. "When we're across the Pak border. On the approach. Not before. I don't want them worked up. I want them to think that this is just another HVT capture/kill."

"It ain't, though."

"It is but it isn't. I just don't want them thinking about it for very long. I want them sharp. I want them thinking hop and pop, shoot and loot, not who the target is. Because he may not even be there. Besides, fact is, there's still no decision. The admiral's slipping this stuff to us under the table so we can make ready and cut Mr. Murphy's participation to a minimum."

"You think POTUS will give the go?"

"Admiral says he's sixty-forty—maybe even seventy-thirty—against an op right now."

"What does Director Mercaldi say?"

"Vince." Maurer smiled when he said the name. "I like that man. Asked me to call him Vince when I met him with the admiral ten days ago. Said, 'Tom, you leave the politicking to me. You just show up wearing all that stuff you have on your chest, tell the truth, and show POTUS what SEALs are all about. Show him how you do what you guys do best—all that *hoo-yah* stuff. Then I'll get you the green light. And then you nail the op and make me look good.' He actually sang 'hoo-yah.' Made it sound like a fricking foghorn."

Loeser laughed. "Foghorn?"

"Affirmative. Where he got *that* I'll never know."

"But, so, you believed him? I mean, he's a pol."

"Yeah, he is a pol. But he's . . . different. Pols will look you in the eye and lie to your face. This guy? Gotta tell you, Dave, I actually did believe he meant what he said."

"Ain't that a first."

"Is in my experience." Maurer turned north. "Let's walk the other side—pace off the field south of the compound. The admiral wants to know where we want the box and one on that side for the enabler helo. He says they've got someone already in place over there who'll lay 'em out for us. "

"Service with a smile from CIA." Loeser followed his CO across the dusty road. "So what's the cut-off?"

"There's a meeting with POTUS and the national security staff on the nineteenth. I'm scheduled to participate."

"Hangin' out with the big dogs, eh?"

"If you consider the dog-and-pony aspect, yeah."

"Will we get a green light on the nineteenth?"

"We'll see. If Vince delivers what he says he can deliver, then maybe yes."

"Incredible." Loeser wagged his head in disbelief. "A pol who keeps his word."

34

The president's deputy executive secretary knocked twice, then cracked the door of the hideaway office and stuck her head inside. "Mr. President, the secretary of defense is here."

"Thank you, Linda." The president pushed himself out of his armchair, wrestled into his suit coat, and checked the mirror to see that his tie was straight. From the desktop he plucked the leather folder embossed with the gold Presidential Seal. And he patted his shirt pocket to make sure he had a pen with him. "Let's go."

She held the door open. He turned left and walked the fifteen feet to the Oval Office door and waited as she opened it.

The president walked inside and strode directly to where Richard Hansen stood. "Rich, good to see you."

"Good to see you, too, Mr. President."

"Ready?"

"And waiting, sir."

"Then I think we should get this under way." The president headed back the way he'd come, trailed by SECDEF and two Secret Service agents. They wound their way through the West Wing, stopping momentarily as a presidential aide snagged the president for ten seconds of whispered conversation, then proceeded to the stairway leading past the Secret Service Operations Center, down the stairs. They turned left, then right, then left again. At the Situation Room a Secret Service agent opened the door and the president walked inside.

He looked at the full house, smiled, said, "Good afternoon," and grinned broadly at the chorus of greetings he got in return. Then the smile faded. "Let's get on with it," he said, and assumed his seat at the head of the table.

"Mr. President." Vincent Mercaldi rose, walked to the center of the conference table, and stood behind a tall naval officer. "I'd like to introduce Captain Tom Maurer. Captain Maurer is the commanding officer of DEVGRU, the unit Admiral Bolin has chosen to perform this mission, which will be called Operation Neptune Spear. The operation will be conducted by Navy SEALs, Army Rangers, and Task Force 160, the Army's Special Operations Air Regiment, with additional input from the Army's Delta Force and other military support units. All of these JSOC personnel, however, will for legal reasons be signed over to CIA and become for the duration a part of our Special Activities Division."

Vince paused momentarily, picked up a bottle of spring water, opened it, and drank. "This," he continued, "has been discussed and worked out between CIA and the Pentagon." He looked at the secretary of defense. "There are no legal issues, right, Rich?"

"That is correct."

"I've asked Captain Maurer to come so he can take you through the mission step by step, sir. We believe that once you see how it will be accomplished, you'll realize that it is not only doable, but can be smoothly and safely executed. Then CIA's senior Bin Laden analyst, whom you all know as George S. Nupkins and whom we call Spike, will present the case for going."

The CIA director looked at the president and got a neutral response. Undeterred, he pressed on. "And so, Captain Maurer, if you would." Vince returned to his seat.

Tom Maurer stood six-four in bare feet. He towered over the room. He looked down at the president. "Sir," he said, "let me take you through it." Maurer signaled. A young enlisted SEAL whose uniform bore three rows of ribbons topped by a Bronze Star with combat "V" and two Purple Hearts wheeled a table with a green felt cover adjacent to where the president sat.

Maurer removed the cover. Underneath was a scale model of the Khan compound and the adjoining area, as well as three model aircraft: two MH60-J Black Hawks and one MH 47 Special Operations Chinook.

"First, Mr. President, I'd like to tell you this operation is nothing special. In fact, I'd call it low-risk. My men have done almost two thousand similar operations in the past year alone. In fact, on any night we have a dozen or more capture/kill high-value target, or HVT, ops going on simultaneously. So for us, this is just another night's work."

Maurer paused and scanned the room as the information sank in. He was pleased to see the analyst Spike give him a slight smile and a brief nod.

Maurer picked up one of the Black Hawks. "We'll come in from the north, having fish-hooked from our flight path, and come down here." Maurer manipulated the model so it sat just above the roof of the main house. "These are stealth helicopters, Mr. President. We can mask their signatures, so they look more like a flight of birds than an aircraft to enemy radar. In fact, their signatures are so low that anything less than state-of-the-art will miss them altogether. And the Paks don't have state-of-the-art radar.

"The helo will hover above the main house. Six SEALs will fast-rope onto the roof, then drop onto the terrace nine feet below, go through the windows and doors, and make entry into the master suite—here." Maurer removed the roof of the structure, revealing a master bedroom with three miniature figures inside.

"As they are doing that"—Maurer took the the second Black Hawk out of the young SEAL's hand—"simultaneously, the second Black Hawk will drop eight SEALs and five Rangers in the courtyard." He set the model down in the far courtyard. "They will blow through two walls, then split into two assault groups. One will enter the front door of the main house, the other will clear the guest house." He looked up. The president's face was all rapt attention. "As they are doing that, the Rangers will—"

"Captain?"

Maurer stopped short and shifted his gaze from the president.

Dwayne Daley ran his tongue across his lips. "Captain, how can you be so sure that the Pakistanis won't see or hear you? I know from exper—"

"Dwayne," Wes Bolin interrupted, "we have been overflying Abbottabad since last July and the Pakistanis haven't seen or heard us."

"But you're overflying with Sentinels," the counterterrorism advisor insisted. "We're talking about helicopters here. Three of them."

"Dwayne."

The counterterrorism advisor turned toward the president's voice. "Mr. President?"

"Let the captain finish. We can discuss specifics afterward."

The room fell silent. The president looked at Maurer. "Please," he said, "continue."

"Yes, sir." Maurer shifted the Black Hawk's position. "One element of Rangers will set up a blocking force on the road. The others will provide security on the compound. Twenty-five seconds after the second SEAL element is on the ground, the enabler aircraft will touch down in the field to the south of the compound." Maurer watched as the young SEAL dropped the miniature MG-46 into position. "That aircraft will hold the command element, the JMAU and SSE elements, a Ranger platoon, and one reserve SEAL assault team."

"Captain?" It was the White House chief of staff.

"Sir?"

"That's a lot of gobbledygook. Can you tell me in English what you were saying?"

"With pleasure, sir. JMAU is the medical team. They'll do the on-scene forensics and ID Bin Laden and take DNA from everyone in the compound. SSE stands for our sensitive site exploitation team. We call them slurpers. They'll remove all the intelligence we can get our hands on—hard drives, flash drives, diaries, notes, papers, pocket litter—the sort of detritus that can become a treasure trove for analysts and also provide actionable intelligence. The Rangers will provide security. And the SEALs we hold in reserve."

The chief of staff smiled. "Thank you for the translation, Captain."

The president pointed at the six houses adjacent to the compound. "What happens if people from those houses come out because of the noise?"

Vince Mercaldi spoke. "Mr. President, we will have a Pashto-speaking CIA officer dressed like a Pakistani plain-clothesman on the ground with the assault team. He will deal with nosy neighbors."

The president pursed his lips. "You've thought of everything, Vince."

"I sure hope so, sir," the CIA director said. "Admiral Bolin and Captain Maurer have put a lot of time and thought into this particular operation. Even though it doesn't differ in tactics or methods from the thousands of operations they do annually, it does have, shall we say, a much deeper significance. The results could trigger a tectonic shift in our overall fight against terror. And because of that, we have had to ensure that all of our bases are covered."

"Agreed," the president said. He turned back toward the model of the compound. "Captain, please continue."

"Of course, Mr. President." Maurer's hands went to the two model Black Hawks. "Our template for HVT operations like this is thirty minutes on the ground. This one shouldn't be much different. We should complete our sweep through the house within six minutes after we've touched down," he said. "The SSE and forensics will take another twenty minutes or so. And then we take our prisoners—or bodies—load them in the Chinook, and head for home." He and the young SEAL lifted the Black Hawks and the Chinook off the table, then the young SEAL withdrew to the corner of the room.

The DEVGRU commander looked at POTUS. "Any questions, sir?"

The president made a tent of his hands. "Isn't there any way that you can get to your target without flying in over the city?" He paused. "What about landing outside Abbottabad and convoying in, hitting the compound, and then convoying back out to the aircraft?"

"I'm glad you asked that, sir. In special operations we try to keep things simple. That means the fewer stages we have to make it through, the easier our job will be and the higher our chances of successful completion. We have designed this operation in three steps: insertion, assault and site exploitation, and extraction. We red-teamed the truck possibility—had a working group looking for vulnerabilities. And we learned that with trucks, we have added two more steps to the mission, steps that include a lot of dangerous unknowns."

"Unknowns?"

"Factors over which we have no control. Controlling the situation is critical, Mr. President. But if we were to convoy in, we'd have to contend with a wide range of uncontrollable factors."

"Such as?"

"Traffic lights. Police patrols. Unscheduled roadblocks. Flat tires. Mechanical breakdowns. These are all distinct possibilities." He looked at the president. "Too many nasty opportunities for Mr. Murphy's laws to come into play, sir. We rejected this option."

"Captain?" The national security advisor raised his hand. "What is your estimate of the Pakistani response time? After all, the compound is within a mile or so of their national military academy."

"I'll take that one." Wes Bolin spoke. "There are no sizable Pakistani military installations capable of ground combat response within thirty-five miles. Further, we will use electronic countermeasures against all the west- and north-facing Pakistani radar installations. They will be deaf, dumb, and blind. I have had these countermeasures tested— and they work. Response time is almost one hour for ground troops. Aircraft will not be an issue."

"But if the worst happens?" Dwayne Daley bit his lip. "The Pakistanis are not third world. They have good equipment."

"I have allocated air assets in Afghanistan. We will have air cover. Response time will be less than ten minutes because the planes will be airborne."

Bolin stared down the counterterrorism advisor. "This is elemental, Dwayne. We protect our people. We plan for contingencies."

The president said, "What if we lose a Black Hawk? What if one crashes?"

"We have the Chinook," Bolin said. "We can put everyone aboard it for the extraction. And we would simply blow up the Black Hawk. The crews carry tools to destroy the electronics. We'd also have explosives to destroy the aircraft itself."

"And if it was the Chinook? Would you have rescue aircraft available?"

"I will plan for it, Mr. President. I can keep two more MH-forty-sevens on the Afghan side of the border. Combined with air cover, we could get our people out safely no matter what happens."

"Good." The president made a notation on his legal pad. "Admiral, what happens if we capture Bin Laden instead of kill him?"

Bolin shrugged. "That's up to you, sir. We are the tip of the spear. We do not make policy. We just carry it out."

"You schooled him well, Rich," the president winked at the secretary of defense. "Good answer, Admiral."

He paused. "And what do we do with Bin Laden if he resists and you do kill him?"

Bolin turned toward the CIA director. "I think Director Mercaldi has an interesting piece of history to tell you," he said. "About Che Guevara's death, and the lessons it teaches us today. I myself believe it is hugely instructional with regard to our current situation."

Bolin looked at Vince. "Sir?"

35

The president looked down at his notes. "That was very instructional indeed, Vince. Thank you. And I am convinced that what you have planned for our target's final resting place is the perfect solution to what might have been a thorny problem."

The president's face displayed relief. "I must say that you, and Admiral Bolin, and you, Captain Maurer, have made a very convincing argument that a helicopter operation could be successful. You have thought of what could go wrong, and you have come up with innovative ways in which to mitigate potential problems. And after listening to Captain Maurer, I have no doubt that his team of SEALs, airmen, Rangers, and other specialists—including the K-9 team, which I'd never in my wildest imagination factored into this scenario—can get the job done."

The president sipped from the bottle of water in front of him, then faced the secretary of defense and the Joint Chiefs chairman, who sat side by side halfway down the big conference table.

"Rich, Mr. Chairman, I think your people deserve our gratitude, our respect, and of course, our best wishes for your success."

The SECDEF nodded deferentially in the president's direction. The chairman stared straight ahead.

Wes Bolin's face showed both surprise and delight. "Thank *you*, Mr. President."

The president let his remarks sink in, his eyes never leaving Vince Mercaldi.

That was when Secretary of Defense Rich Hansen caught the whiff of a smirk on Dwayne Daley's face. Instinctively, he knew what was about to happen.

And there was no way to prevent it.

Because the president continued speaking. "But here's the problem," the president began. "We do not know beyond a shadow of a doubt that UBL is in that compound. Not after"—he ticked his fingers—"nine months, Vince. *Nine months!* Not a single solid piece of evidence. Nine months. And close to one billion, with a *b*, dollars spent. And for what? For nothing. Nothing, Vince."

The room fell silent.

"No results." The president's face grew somber. "Not one shred of decisive evidence." He fixed the CIA director in his gaze. "And now you want me to stage a raid. Violate the sovereignty of an ally. Break the law. Without a shred of evidence. Is that it, Vince? Is it?"

It was Spike who rose to his feet. He was close to six feet tall and his girth gave him a certain Falstaffian presence despite the rumpled appearance. "Sir," he said, his voice low, steady, and unexpectedly aggressive, "with all due respect, Mr. President, you are incorrect."

You could have heard a pin drop.

"What?" The president's face flushed in anger.

"I have tracked this man for almost two decades," Spike said. "I have had him in my sights three times before. Once in Khartoum in the early nineties, when no one but I and a few other crazies—as we were called at the time, Mr. President—thought he was dangerous. Once in Kandahar in ninety-eight, when the White House was unwilling to launch Operation Rhino even though we'd confirmed UBL's presence and despite the fact that he'd issued a fatwa calling for war against the United States. And once at Tora Bora, when both the White House and the Pentagon refused us the assets we needed to put this, this murderer in the ground."

Spike caught his breath. "Yes, sir, you might—indeed you did at our last meeting—call the evidence that UBL is in Abbottabad 'circumstantial.' I choose to define the evidence as empirical. Because there is a difference. 'Empirical' evidence is based on observation and/or experience. That, sir, is what we have been doing since last August. Observing, and taking what we learn and folding it into our experienced overview of UBL. In other words, we have been obtaining empirical evidence. And taken as a whole, it becomes prodigiously, overwhelmingly, convincingly conclusive.

"UBL has gone asymmetric against us. We use cutting-edge technology; he uses face-to-face communications carried by trusted couriers. We use listening devices; he plays his stereo or TV set loudly. We feel we need to see him; he stays indoors. So what do I do to counteract his asymmetry? I look at his world. I look at the food he eats—Arab food in a house that is supposed to be occupied only by Pakistanis, Pashtuns. I look at the occupants of that house: two men who we know for sure—*for sure*—are UBL's most trusted couriers. I look at the way the house was built. It is a house built to hide one tall—six-foot-four or more—individual from public view. How do I know this? From the opaque windows and the seven-foot privacy wall on the terrace, to give you two examples. And I look at the whole picture. Surveillance cameras on the outer wall. Concertina wire on top of walls that go as high as eighteen feet. No wires coming in, no satellite communications capability, no telephones, no mail delivery, no garbage pickup, nothing delivered." He paused. "No visitors. Ever."

Spike caught his breath. "So, sir, the question is, who lives like that?"

The president sat mute.

The analyst swept the room with his gaze. "Anybody? Who lives like that?"

The chief of staff said, "Well, either a recluse, or a fugitive are the obvious choices."

"Yes, sir," Spike said. "Recluse or fugitive. Except this recluse has two families living with him. Five children. Three wives. Two cars. It's the families who do the shopping, clean the house, and slaughter the sheep. Oh, and the menfolk? They are armed. Or at least one of them is, because we've seen the weapon."

He paused. "So, recluse or fugitive, sir?"

"Reclusive fugitive, maybe?" The chief of staff shrugged in response to the muted laughter his answer provoked.

"Good call," Spike interrupted. "That's exactly what I think, too. And who would be the logical fugitive living in the same house as the two individuals Usama Bin Laden trusts the most in the whole wide world?"

The analyst turned toward the president. "Sir," he said, "I will be honest with you. In my mind, there is about a seventy-six, seventy-seven percent possibility that UBL is in that house. Not one hundred, or ninety, or even eighty percent. But in the real world, in *my* real world, that is enough of a possibility to justify action."

"It's a long shot," the president said after a pause, "What you want to do is very risky."

"Mr. President," Spike said, "you can fire my Irish behind for saying this, but for too damn long our policy with regard to cases like this one has been based on risk aversion, not proaction. We could have killed UBL in Khartoum. As one of our CIA people said at the time, for the price of a ten-cent bullet we could have averted nine-eleven. The powers that be back then didn't want to take the chance that the Sudanese might be offended. Why? Because there was all that Sudanese oil." He paused. "Which the Chinese are currently getting all of. We had another chance in ninety-eight: Kandahar. But once again, we didn't launch. The Clinton administration considered it too risky."

The analyst looked the president in the eye. "Bin Laden is there, sir. All the empirical evidence points to it. And if you miss this opportunity, it may be ten years before we get the chance again. How many more Americans can he kill in ten years?" Spike's eyes glistened. "You cannot let this opportunity pass, sir. It would be—"

"What?" the president cut the analyst off. He looked straight into Spike's eyes, daring him to speak.

Spike's focus was unbroken. *Attack, attack, attack.* "Wrong, sir. It would be wrong. Morally wrong, politically wrong, and strategically wrong not to do this, and do it now. It may not be the safe and political thing to do, but, sir, with all due respect, politics can only do so much."

The president drew breath, as if he was about to speak.

But Spike cut him off. "Mr. President, it is time. You have to draw a line in the sand. For yourself, for the nation, and for the future. Because if you don't, it will come back to haunt you."

The president sat silent for perhaps half a minute.

"If *you* are wrong, Spike," he said, "this administration will be sorely embarrassed in the world's eyes."

Spike knew it wasn't the administration the president was worried about. But for the first time that day he held his tongue. "It won't be," he said diplomatically. "He is there, Mr. President. He is. As much as I know anything, I know he is there."

The president said nothing. He sat, hands clasped in front of him, staring into space.

Finally he spoke, addressing himself to Wes Bolin. "Admiral, you have my provisional—repeat, provisional—approval to proceed with Operation Neptune Spear."

He looked down the table at Vince Mercaldi. "Mr. Director, I want an intelligence brief from you and Spike one week from today."

"Yes, Mr. President."

"After which I will, or I will not, sign off on this . . . undertaking." He stared at Vince Mercaldi. "Mr. Director, remember that it is I and no one else who can sanction this operation."

"That is well understood, Mr. President."

"It better be." The president slapped his folder shut. "Then that is all." He got to his feet. "Thank you—thank you all for your hard work."

He looked toward Spike. "And thank you for voicing your strong convictions. You, especially, have given me a lot to think about."

"You're welcome, Mr. President."

"And good luck to all of us—we'll need it." POTUS turned and left the Situation Room, trailed by the secretary of defense and chairman of the Joint Chiefs.

The chief of staff, NSC Chairman Don Sorken, and Dwayne Daley followed grimly in their wake, their faces reflecting anger and defeat.

Wes Bolin could hear Sorken's voice imploring "But Mr. President" as the door closed behind them.

There was ten seconds during which no one said a word.

Then: "Oh, merciful God." Vince Mercaldi sagged back in his chair and groaned.

Concerned, Tom Maurer looked at the CIA director. He'd sweated right through his shirt. "You okay, Mr. Director?"

"Call me Vince," Mercaldi croaked. He wiped his perspiring face and neck with a wrinkled handkerchief. "Don't know about you guys, but I could use an adult beverage right about now."

"Oh, Vince," Wes Bolin said, "I could use about six."

Said Spike, "Semper Fi, Admiral, so could I." He jerked his thumb in Vince's direction. "And he's the one who should be doing the buying."

36

"Geoff, it's for you. Langley."

"Thanks, Courtney." Geoffrey Woodward—the name was an alias—was CIA's much beleaguered station chief in Islamabad. It was not a good place to be. The Taliban and the Haqqani Network had a price on his head. So did al-Qaeda. His relations with ISI, Pakistan's bipolar intelligence service, were tenuous at best and of late had become permanently fractious.

Only two weeks ago, ISI's director general, Ahmad Shuja Pasha, had ordered Woodward to notify ISI in advance whenever any of his people planned to venture beyond the limits of the cities—Islamabad, Lahore, Peshawar, and Karachi—in which they were stationed. The origin of that edict was *l'affaire* Ty Weaver, over which ISI was still smarting.

Woodward had smiled and answered noncommittally. Oh, yeah, he was really gonna comply with that one.

Another was the ridiculous demand that he forthwith identify all CIA personnel in Pakistan as well as their agents.

Moreover, the nasty relationship with ISI was only one of the fronts on which he currently had to fight. The other war pitted Woodward against his self-important, meddlesome boss, the U.S. ambassador, Cletus Winthrop Hampshire IV. Clete was one of those Foggy Bottom elites who believe that talking equals diplomacy; results aren't important. And it didn't help matters that he also insinuated himself into CIA's aggressive drone campaign in Waziristan by taking the Paks' side. To Clete, killing terrorists was undiplomatic and therefore, as the ambassador was fond of saying, "to be eschewed."

Tall, prematurely gray, and bearded, Woodward had been on station for only nine months. His predecessor's true name and address had been bandied all through the Pakistani press, leaked by ISI because the American had aggressively built a successful network of Pakistani agents right under ISI's nose. Langley was taking no chances of the same thing happening again; Woodward had therefore reported to the embassy bearing a diplomatic passport in which the only true fact was his first name. He'd arrived in early October, just in time to coordinate the setup of Valhalla Base. Between the Abbottabad operation, Ty Weaver, and ISI's double-dealing, it had been nonstop since then.

He picked up the receiver. "Woodward."

"Geoff, it's Dick Hallett."

"Hey, fella. Good to hear from you. What's goin' on at BLG?"

"Busier than a one-legged man in an ass-kicking contest around here. Listen, I got some good news and some bad news for you."

"And your point?" Woodward heard Hallett's hearty laugh and chuckled himself.

"Good news is we're about to break down Valhalla, so please gear up and let the lads up-country know."

"Will do." Woodward paused. "And the bad news?"

"We're about to break down Valhalla, so please gear up and let the lads up-country know."

"Very funny. What's the schedule?"

"That's the real bad news. Don't know. But get them started now, because we could be shutting them down and extracting on twenty-four-hour notice."

"Geez." Woodward exhaled. "We've got a ton of equipment up there. Moving it is gonna be a bitch. ISI's all over us, y'know."

"Affirmative. But the schedule's out of my hands. Seventh Floor stuff."

"Understood." Woodward's mind was already churning, trying to figure out the logistics of a covert repositioning that included packing and hauling millions of dollars' worth of delicate surveillance equipment out of Abbottabad and getting it inside the embassy without the Paks or the ambassador knowing. "Anything else?"

"What are you, a glutton for punishment? How many migraines do you want simultaneously?"

"This one is enough, believe me."

"Then my work here is done," Hallett boomed. "Thanks, Geoff. Gotta run."

"Take care, Dick. Have a Hendrick's for me at Charley's." Charley's was a restaurant on the corner of Chain Bridge Road and Old Dominion Drive, about seven minutes from headquarters. It operated under another name these days, but CIA veterans always called it Charley's. They had reliable food, a decent wine list, and the afternoon bartender made perfect, ice-cold Hendrick's martinis.

Hallett laughed. "Will do. In fact I'll have two."

"Yeah—rub it in."

"Stay safe, brother. Talk soon."

The phone went dead. Woodward stood, hitched his pants, and headed for the communications shed. He had to burst Abbottabad immediately.

37

It was dark enough inside the aircraft so that life was easier with NODs down. And it was cramped. There were six 6-Charlie SEALs, five Rangers, the K-9 and its handler, and the helo's crew chief all in there, with full gear.

They'd been airborne for fifty-seven minutes, the Night Stalker pilots twisting and banking as they contour-flew a route that would set the SEALs and Rangers on target within thirty seconds plus or minus. Tonight was the third Joint Readiness Exercise, or JRX, for the SEALs and the Task Force 160 aircrew, flying 160-plus miles from Fort Campbell, where the 160th was based, to Fort Knox, where the target site was located.

The target tonight was "Muhammed Maulavi," code-named Tombstone, a high-value target who was described by Red Squadron CO Dave Loeser to the assaulters during the evening's BUB (Battle Update Brief) as a Haqqani Network captain. M2, as Loeser referred to him, would be portrayed,

as would his family and bodyguards, by life-size mannequins dressed in Pashtun clothing and placed strategically in
the target house. Those mannequins bearing weapons were
hostile and could be killed. The others could not.

The flight from the 160th's home base at Fort Campbell,
which sat on the Kentucky-Tennessee border, to the training
area at Fort Knox, located close to the Indiana border, was
164 miles as the crow flies. But it would take ninety minutes
because the aircraft wouldn't fly a straight course. Instead,
they'd take an irregular route, allowing them to contour-fly
the topography at extra-low altitude. The SEALs and Rangers didn't know it, but the distance from Fort Campbell to
Fort Knox was just about equal to the distance between Jalalabad, Afghanistan, and Abbottabad, Pakistan. Which was
precisely why Wes Bolin and Tom Maurer had selected the
two sites for the assault package's predeployment JRXs and
had ordered the 160th to take a circuitous route that would,
although the pilots didn't know it, more or less resemble the
flight path they'd be using on the real mission.

For Troy, Padre, Jacko, Cajun, Heron, and Rangemaster, however, it was just another night's work. These drills
were really for the aircrews. Flying formation at night, with
no lights, following a complicated, evasive flight plan, and
doing it in formation so that both Black Hawks arrive on target simultaneously and within thirty seconds plus or minus
of H-Hour, with the MH-47G Chinook enabler aircraft coming in precisely twenty-five seconds later, takes precision,
confidence, and above all, practice.

Which is why the three-craft assault package, the backup
package of Rangers and SEALs who'd be held in reserve, as
well as the tertiary arming and refueling package known as
FAARP, positioned no more than thirty-five minutes' flight
time from the target, would practice infiltration, assault, and

exfiltration in real time repeatedly. Until they all got it right and they all got it smooth. Until the aircrews could fly while compensating for the weights they were carrying, maximize their speed and stealth while keeping a minimum separation between the aircraft so as to minimize signature, and get the entire assault element, blocking force, command package, JMAU and SSE sections delivered exactly where they had to be delivered, all while making sure that Mr. Murphy of Murphy's Law fame hadn't snuck aboard any of the aircraft as a stowaway.

Oh, yeah, and also do it with on-time delivery right down to the second, Mr. Murphy notwithstanding.

The most decisive element was weight. Where the weight was, and how it balanced out, was absolutely critical to the ability of the helicopter to perform at the outer limits of its capabilities. Edge-of-the-envelope flying was what Task Force 160 pilots did better than anyone else in the world. And if the situation called for it, they could fly their helos unbalanced. But they preferred to trim out as much as they could because it made doing the impossible just that much easier.

All three aircraft in the assault package were equipped with avionics suites and multimode radars that allowed them to evade detection. The Black Hawks—top-secret stealth model MH-60Js—were specially configured with radar-spoofing composite exteriors and silencing-configured main and tail rotors that cut operational noise by forty-six percent. If they made an into-the-wind approach, they couldn't be heard until they were virtually on top of the target. The MH-47G wasn't anywhere near as silent, but it too was equipped with a huge array of sophisticated electronic countermeasures that gave it the ability to operate in the most hostile of environments and survive.

0054 Hours

"Six minutes." The pilot's voice played inside Rangemaster's head. He was senior SEAL on the Chalk One aircraft. As Chalk leader he was plugged into the aircraft's system.

He swiveled, made a megaphone of his hands, and shouted loudly above the jet engine noise and wind. "Six minutes. Six minutes!"

The SEALs and Rangers turned their radios on, made sure the wires were plugged into their Peltor talk-through hearing protection, and pulled on their helmets.

"Three minutes." In the cockpit, the pilot brought the airspeed down to ninety knots. His eye on the mission clock, the copilot activated the PAIT, a secure passive airborne interrogator transponder, which turned on the infrared firefly devices that indicated the landing zones.

"Two minutes." The SEALs double-checked their weapons, ensured the magazines were seated, yanked the charging handle, which slammed a round into the chamber, performed press checks to ensure the rounds were seated properly, then made sure the safeties were engaged. They secured the weapons so they wouldn't get in the way during the fast-rope, and checked their safety harnesses.

Some pulled on the Outdoor Research gloves that were thick enough for fast-roping if the drop was under forty-five feet, and thin enough to use as shooting gloves. Others felt, to hell with rope burn, and went with Oakleys, or the unit's new favorites, classic mechanic's gloves.

The aircrew, also wearing night vision, adjusted their safety harnesses, then took their positions by the open port and starboard hatches where the thirty-foot fast-ropes were coiled. Just as the helo approached and flared above the target, the crew would drop the thick lines, get out of the way so the SEALs could drop unimpeded, then pull the pins and drop the lines.

The Black Hawk was bobbing and weaving now, slaloming as it careened toward the target.

"One minute!" sounded in Rangemaster's ears. Counting backward silently, he disengaged from the aircraft system, pulled on his own hearing protection and helmet, and dropped his NODs.

"Thirty seconds!" Rangemaster shouted into his boom mike. "Thirty!" he repeated. The Rangers unsnapped their safety lines and pulled themselves away from the doors as the helo rapidly decelerated from ninety knots. They, the K-9, and its handler would not fast-rope, but land inside the compound's western courtyard. Two of the Rangers would blow through the walls; the others would clear the courtyard, provide security for the helo as long as it stayed on the ground, and back the SEALs if necessary. The K-9 would be deployed if anyone tried to run or if one of the target's occupants decided to play hide-and-seek.

In the cockpit, the copilot yelled, "*Fifty knots!*" The pilot could see the box-and-one infrared flashers that would line him up with his target.

"Forty knots." He maneuvered the helo.

"Thirty knots" came in above the three-flasher line.

"Twenty knots." Dead on.

He pulled up, his eyes fixed on a point in the sky.

The ground drops away.

The helo's nose flares up, forty-five degrees.

The aircraft stands on its tail. Motionless for an instant.

Ropes go out.

Helo's nose drops almost horizontal.

Rangemaster yells, "*Go!*"

■

0:02. NODs down, Troy clears the dangling rope, Padre and Jacko behind him.

0:03. Troy rolls over the edge of the roof.

0:04. Drops onto the terrace nine feet below. Lands.

Weapon up. Safety off.

0:06. Scan and breathe.

Behind him, a shout: "Oh, shit!"

0:08. "Go!" Padre's hand on his shoulder, pushing him on.

0:10. Kick the door. It collapses inward.

Into the darkened room. Scan. Sweep.

Nothing.

Empty?

Scan.

Something behind the bed. Top of human head.

AK muzzle visible. "Gun!"

Troy: three quick shots.

Closes on target.

Fires a double-tap.

0:13. Cajun and Heron leapfrog Troy and Padre. Cajun's hand on hallway door.

Troy checks the bed. Hostile target is down. Dead. "Go."

0:16. Door opens inward.

Cacophony of voices in Troy's headset: "Gun" "One down." "Clear" "Go left!" "Gun!"

0:21. Heron cuts the pie. Sweeps the hallway. "Third floor clear."

Move.

Scan and breathe.

Moving fast.

Stairs ahead.

0:25. Shit.

Rangemaster: "Gate."

Heron: "Got it."

Troy's muzzle sweeps the far end of the hallway because he's rear security. No threats. He calls it: "Hallway clear."

Heron smacks small shaped charges on hinges. Pulls primer from the kit on his chest. Places shock tube initiator. Backs off unspooling wire.

6-Charlie backs up into the bedroom.

Heron plugs the igniter.

Padre: "Burning!"

Heron hits the igniter. Concussion and smoke. Screws with NODs. Shit.

1:21. Rangemaster kicks gate out of the way.

Padre into his mike: "Six-Charlie moving down to level two."

From outside the target building: explosions as Alpha 1 blows the outside wall and moves to clear the smaller target building.

Rangemaster repeats the call. "Repeat: Six-Charlie down to level two."

Rangemaster understands Murphy's Law of Combat Number 8, which goes, FRIENDLY FIRE ISN'T.

1:59. Second floor has two doorways. 6-Charlie splits up. Cajun, Heron, and Rangemaster go left, Troy and Padre right. They're one man light.

Troy: "Where's Jacko?"

Rangemaster: "Jacko's down."

2:49. Troy checks the hinges. Can't see them. Door opens inward.

2:52. He kicks it. Smashes the lock.

Cuts the pie. Makes entry. Hooks left back to wall. Sees . . .

Padre: "Target right." Three quick shots.

Troy: "Friendly left." The target is a life-size woman holding a baby.

The 6-Charlie SEALs hear call-sign Jackpot, Master Chief Danny Walker, the mission assault leader, in their ears. "One-Alpha—entry first floor. Burning!"

Followed by a massive explosion. They feel the concussion through the soles of their boots. Probably a Spider Charge.

Smoke and cordite smell floods the second story. Gotta love it.

Padre: "Cuff her."

Troy: "Roger."

4:05. Jackpot's voice in 6-Charlie's heads: "Tombstone EKIA. Repeat: Tombstone EKIA."

That didn't mean the SEALs stopped. Until every inch of the site had been cleared, until the K-9 had swept the house to make sure no one was hiding under floorboards or behind a false wall, until the JMAU had taken DNA samples, fingerprints, and digital photos of both corpses and survivors, and the slurpers had scooped up every bit of intelligence-related material they could lay their hands on, 6-Charlie's antennas were up, and they were on guard.

29:42. The helos sweep back from the logger site, a safe, secure predetermined location within three minutes of the target. Tonight they had set down and idled for the duration of the assault. Other times, they might loiter airborne. It depended on the mission parameters.

30:45 The exhausted SEALs, Rangers, and enabler personnel clamber back aboard their various aircraft for the ninety-minute flight back to Campbell. It has been what is known as a full mission profile: run as if it was for real. There has even been one casualty that morning. Jack Young, the ebullient chief quartermaster, call-sign Jacko, broke his ankle when he rolled off the roof onto the terrace nine feet below and landed badly. It was a clean break and would heal in time. But he'd be out of action for the next two months.

Nor was the night's work over. Back at Fort Campbell, the entire assault package—pilots, SEALs, Rangers, as well as command element, JMAU, and SSE crew—would go through a thorough debrief. The raid had been captured by a dozen night-vision-capable video cameras. Tactics would be evaluated and tweaked, rough edges smoothed. The hot wash, as the after-action critique was called, was never personal, but it could be brutal. The goal, after all, was perfection: total speed, surprise, and violence of action resulting in the capture/kill of an HVT, the exploitation of intelligence materials, and the identification of all those on-site.

But it was the killing part that lay at the core of everything the SEALs did. Because they knew, every one of them in their own heart, exactly what Charlie Becker knew in his: that there are some people on this earth who just deserve to die.

38

"What's the latest from Abbottabad?" Vince Mercaldi peered across his desk at Stu Kapos and Dick Hallett.

"No change," Hallett said. "The brothers Khan are in residence. The mystery guest, if there is one, is also on the premises. The families are maintaining radio silence, and the food is still Arab as opposed to Pakistani."

The director looked at Stu Kapos. "So whatta we do?"

"First? First we break down Valhalla Base. Today and tomorrow. However POTUS decides, we gotta get out and get out clean before the Paks get wise."

Vince nodded in agreement. "Do it."

"Second, Wes Bolin wants a Paki-speaking native on site during the operation. In civilian clothes. To play the part of an ISI agent or a cop. Just in case any of the neighbors come around."

"Good idea. I wish we'd thought of it."

"Actually," Hallett broke in, "we did. I discussed this

with Larry Bailey, the SEAL Wes detailed to BLG, last week. Been looking for a candidate."

"And?"

"And we already have one." Hallett saw the quizzical look on the director's face. "Charlie Becker. And we save one-way air fare."

The director laughed. "Brilliant." He looked at the BLG chief. "Does he have his legs with him?"

"No. They're down at SAD in his locker. Well, they were. Now they're on their way to Fort Campbell, because the package is departing tonight. Moon phase determines operational window, and the moon phase—last eighth—starts on the twenty-ninth and lasts until the fifth of May. Go or no-go, Wes wanted his package prepositioned before the window opens."

The director bit his lip. "Did you send someone Charlie knows?"

"Affirmative. Paul Fedorko, his section chief."

"Then make sure our guy makes it onto the assault package to deliver 'em. That way Charlie doesn't get himself shot."

Hallett made notes in his secretarial notebook. "Will do."

"Also, he should be there because we need at least one senior Agency officer present. After all, on paper at least, JSOC's package is under CIA control."

Hallett looked at the director. "Is that it?"

"Affirmative," Vince said. "You get moving. I need a little time with Stu."

Hallett slid his notebook into a folder. "On my way," he said. "Thanks, Boss."

Vince waited until the door closed behind the BLG chief. "Stu, we may be in trouble."

"Trouble?"

"This whole project may be scrubbed."

"You're not serious."

"I am. And this is very close-hold. But I got a call from someone at the White House at my home last night. Landline to landline. The individual was very, very nervous."

"And?"

"I was told as follows. The president's political guy, the guy who took Axelrod's place, my source heard whispers that he's supposedly conducting a secret poll—outsourcing it to give the White House very deep cover. And one of the questions they're allegedly asking is, 'If a military raid failed and American soldiers were killed, who would you most hold at fault?'"

Kapos's face fell. "Oh, shit."

"So don't be surprised if I get a call tomorrow or the next day."

"Does Wes Bolin know?"

"Nah. He's got enough to worry about. He's sending the package out tonight. Three or four Globemasters from Fort Campbell."

"Godspeed." The clandestine service chief cracked his knuckles. The sound made Vince wince. "Sorry, Boss." Kapos sighed. "Do you see POTUS today?"

"No—I asked and was turned down. Too busy, they say. Not tomorrow either. It's evidently a full day of travel. Chicago—Oprah's show. Then New York—all politics and money. They want Wes and me in the Situation Room on Thursday morning, eleven-thirty." He stared at the ceiling. "Wes will be gone by then. I'll take Spike. Dammit, don't do that!" He gave Kapos a dirty look because the NCS chief had cracked his knuckles again. "I think they're putting us off."

"Because?"

"You want my honest opinion?" The CIA director looked grimly at his top spy. "I think because they're waiting for the goddamn poll results."

39

Charlie Becker scooted off the road opposite the compound he called GZ, moving as quickly as he could, his arms and gloved hands doing most of the work. The instructions were simple: a box-and-one of the Phoenix Beacons that lined up with the center of the ten-foot-high wall bordering the western courtyard, the one where they burned the trash. Then five more fireflies in a straight line running east-west, aligning with the southernmost edge of the plowed field just to the east of a newly built white-roofed villa.

Charlie had been given a deadline of April 28 to complete placing the beacons. Then he was to stand by to go active on the twenty-ninth. He was hardly able to contain himself. He'd be a part of it—whatever it was.

He'd surveyed the locations over the past three days, but there had been too much moonlight. Tonight was overcast, with rain supposedly coming early in the morning. Then clear all day on both the twenty-eighth and twenty-ninth. Perfect operational weather.

He'd done all the prep work. Batteries had been installed and the beacons themselves attached to their spiked bases. He didn't have to turn them on. The helo pilots would do that as they approached because the beacons would respond to PAIT signals. They'd been preset to a specific frequency—217.32, for example. All the pilots had to do was dial that frequency, transmit, and the fireflies would go active. They'd be visible for about three-quarters of a mile through the pilots' night-vision goggles. On final extraction, the pilots would turn the beacons off, and, hopefully, the next time the fields were plowed, they'd be plowed under.

What made the op so easy for Charlie was the fact that the furrows in both fields ran perpendicular to the target, ensuring that all his lines would be straight. His only obstacle: not leaving a trail.

He solved that problem by cutting two pieces of three-foot-long by foot-and-a-quarter-wide board from the scrap at Mohammed's carpentry shop. He had set the first down, crabbed onto it, set the second in front, crabbed a second yard, and kept repeating the process. The three-foot length—ninety-two centimeters was how Charlie had measured it at the shop—ensured that the beacons would be set uniformly. The boards themselves kept him from disturbing the furrows too much.

Charlie laid the first three Phoenix Beacons adjacent to the low wall of the rectangular compound that sat across the road from GZ. He stuck them in the ground at fifteen-foot intervals, then made his way back to the road, dragged himself and his boards five yards east, lined up with the first flasher, then repeated the process with two beacons. The result? After twenty-eight minutes he'd laid out a perfect box-and-one. Then it was time to run the second set.

0445 Hours

Exhausted, Charlie made his way through the tree line adjacent to the ten-foot wall on GZ's southwest side so he could stow his boards on the furniture dolly and wheel himself home. It had begun to rain, and he was soaked clear through to the skin. He was cold. And sore. Sore? He hurt like hell. But hurt was part of Charlie's life. He'd accepted it when he was wounded in Mogadishu. He'd accepted it when he lost his legs to an al-Qaeda in Iraq suicide bomber in a tunnel outside Mahmudiya in 2004. Shit, hurt was part of his job description. And, just like every other Tier One operator, he never allowed it to affect his performance. The mission was everything. It was at the core of the Ranger Creed.

So, yes, he hurt. But he was also energized. Energized the way Rangers are energized when they complete their mission. Rangers like Charlie know there are only two ways to go home: complete the mission and smoke a great cigar and maybe enjoy some single malt, or be shipped home in a body bag.

He would burst Valhalla the good news when he got back to the shed in Hassan Town: Mission accomplished. Standing by to stand by.

Standing by to go home.

40

"Mr. President, the optimum time for Operation Neptune Spear is the next twenty-four hours. The assault package is in position in Jalalabad. The weather is cooperating. The moon is almost new, so there is little ambient light. The targets are all in one place, and we can fly protective cover without the Pakistanis knowing anything." The CIA analyst known as Spike paused to look at POTUS's face.

He didn't like what he saw. The president's nonverbal reaction was impassive at best. Certainly not positive.

"Even though there has been no 'eyes-on' identification, every bit of empirical evidence points to UBL being there." The analyst looked directly at the president. "And that is something we can't guarantee much longer."

Vince Mercaldi decided it was time to put the situation in even starker terms. "Mr. President, the window of opportunity is closing. It is closing fast."

The CIA director would have liked Wesley Bolin to be

with him this morning. But the admiral was gone. He'd left at zero-dark-hundred for the long flight to Jalalabad. The strike was planned for 0100 local time on April 29. The moon phase was perfect, the weather also: clouds, preceding a cold front with rain. The perfect environment for a successful stealth mission deep into Pakistan.

The president frowned at his CIA director and Spike. The public schedule released by the White House told the world that at 1050 Hours the president would be receiving a national security briefing on the Libya crisis in the Situation Room.

And frankly, the president wished he was receiving just that.

Libya was a positive. Both his national security chief and his counterterrorism advisor had assured him that Libya was a win-win for the U.S. and for the administration.

Yes, sure, said Don Sorken, they'd made mistakes with regard to Tunisia, Bahrain, and Egypt. Yes, they'd missed a few signals in Yemen and hadn't quite read the politics on the ground in Tripoli correctly. But, the NSC director insisted, he and Dwayne Daley were convinced the Libya crisis gave the administration the chance to show the world how well the United States understood the Arab Spring. The U.S. had successfully led the opening days of the bombing campaign against Qaddafi's air defenses; tomorrow, April 29, representatives of forty countries were meeting in London to coordinate anti-Qaddafi efforts. It would, Daley said, all be over in a matter of weeks and NATO's going to get all the credit. Even though the U.S. had supplied drones and satellite intelligence. It was time, he said, to get out front.

Oh, sure, CIA's defeatist analysts insisted on saying the Libyan situation could deteriorate; that Qaddafi was well entrenched and financed; that the situation could drag on for months with no clear winner; and that in any case, there was no clear picture of who the rebels were, what they'd do when and if they prevailed, and what their relationship with the U.S. would be. Worse, CIA recommended a clandestine approach: stealth support of supplies, intelligence, and quiet military assistance for the Libyan insurgents channeled through NATO.

"But on the other hand—and it is a big 'but,' Mr. President," Dwayne had growled to the president not an hour ago, "what has CIA done for you lately? Forty-three thousand people at Langley, a budget in the tens of billions, and they can't even prove Usama Bin Laden's living in Abbottabad. And now Vince Mercaldi, your handpicked CIA director, is trying to force your hand into approving an operation in Abbottabad. With no proof."

Abbottabad, Abbottabad, Abbottabad.

The president was sick and tired of Abbottabad.

And yet all Vince wanted to talk about was Abbottabad and Bin Laden. A risky mission. A possible embarrassment for the administration. There was no up-side unless Bin Laden was there, and he was killed.

Seventy-six, seventy-seven percent chance he'd be there. That's the figure Spike had quoted. There were no guarantees about that, either. It could be fifty percent. It could be zero. That was the point. *They didn't know.*

And the president was a man who liked guarantees. Sure things. Sure things were his modus vivendi. It was how he'd campaigned; it was how his whole political career had been engineered. Create the proper conditions, build an organization, develop wide grassroots support, and do it all under everyone else's radar. Make sure you had it in the bag, then make it all look like a surprise. And if those prerequisites weren't met, then kick the can down the road until they were.

Except this was one instance when the president couldn't

kick the can down the road. They would need a decision. Go or no-go.

Vince wanted a decision today. The president could see it in the CIA director's face. And Spike's.

It was Spike who'd told him point-blank that he would be morally, politically, and strategically culpable if he didn't do this. Not going to Abbottabad would come back to haunt him, the analyst had said.

Those were challenging words addressed to the Leader of the Free World. Words to box him in. Paint him into a corner.

Because they were, the president understood, absolutely true.

Which is why they were the precise questions the polls he'd secretly ordered the day after that Sit Room session were supposed to answer. The polls—two of them, both close-hold—that he'd had his top political consultant conduct.

First: Would he be held accountable if it was discovered he hadn't gone after UBL when he had the chance?

Second: If a risky military operation became a disaster, would he be held responsible?

And third: If the answers to those questions were yes, how deeply would they affect his chances of reelection?

The president had to know the answers before he could act. It was Litigation 101: never ask a question to which you do not already know the answer. Otherwise he was just rolling dice.

Not his style.

He'd said just over a week ago that he would give them an answer today. And he'd meant it.

But the polls weren't completed yet. There'd been screw-ups. That unfortunate info-bit had been whispered in his ear by the White House political director as they made their way down here from the Oval Office.

Results wouldn't be in until early Friday. Tomorrow morning.

Today he had nothing to give them.

The president stroked his chin. "Spike, you make an overwhelmingly convincing argument." And the analyst had, too. The only possible answer to Spike's presentation was "Go," and the president knew it. So did everyone else in the room.

"Thank you, Mr. President."

"And so . . ." The president paused.

He could see them anticipating.

But he was the president. The CINC—commander in chief. They couldn't do a thing without him. That was the law.

There was no reason to hem or to haw. "You'll have my final decision tomorrow." The president hoisted himself out of his chair and left without another word.

Vince Mercaldi sat stunned. Tomorrow?

Tomorrow was a travel day. The president was scheduled to leave the White House at 8:30 for Tuscaloosa, Alabama, then fly to Cape Canaveral for the launch of Space Shuttle Endeavour, followed by an event in Miami. POTUS wouldn't return to the White House until shortly before midnight.

The CIA director had no idea what was going on. And he didn't like it one bit.

But there was nothing he could do to fix the situation. Or force it.

He hadn't boxed the president into a corner.

Not at all.

It had been the other way around.

41

"Stand 'em down, Mac." Wesley Bolin wiped his face with his hands. "We got a hurry-up-and-wait from POTUS. Won't hear anything until tomorrow." He muttered something inaudible under his breath.

"Sir?"

"I was just thinking. Get hold of the Sentinel crews and ground the drones we put over the flight path. Let's keep the two over Abbottabad in a loiter. How much more flight time do they have?"

McGill checked his BlackBerry. "Eighteen hours.

"Relieve them tomorrow afternoon with fresh ones. Hopefully we can go tomorrow night."

"We got a front coming in about three tomorrow afternoon," Brigadier General Eric McGill frowned. "Probably have a weather hold even if we do get the go."

"Crap."

"What do we tell the troops?" The assault package personnel were well into their alert sequence. They'd been awakened at 5 P.M. By six they were working out and having breakfast. Currently they were in the SCIF, the bugproof room where they'd assembled for their Battle Update Brief, where they were being told that the night's target was an HVT named Hamid Gul Muhammed, a Taliban bomb maker responsible for the deaths of more than twenty American Soldiers and Marines. They would learn that Gul had fled deep into Pakistan and that the raid was therefore under CIA control.

It was nothing they hadn't heard before. All of JSOC's cross-border raids came under CIA control, because so far as the JAG lawyers were concerned, while it was illegal under international law for the U.S. military to invade a sovereign nation, clandestine cross-border incursions were dead-center in the CIA's mission statement.

"Tell 'em weather. Tell 'em target's moved. I don't fricking care." Wes Bolin was pissed. He almost would have preferred to have the president scrub the mission than drop it into a vacuum.

Worse, when the admiral had asked Vince what happened, the CIA director responded with a stony silence. He couldn't—or wouldn't—supply a reason for POTUS's indecision.

It didn't really matter. The CINC was the CINC. Full stop, end of story.

The Joint Special Operations Command was a strange animal. It didn't report to the Pentagon hierarchy or to one of the combatant commands, even though most people thought it reported to USSOCOM, the U.S. Special Operations Command at MacDill Air Force Base in Tampa. No, JSOC came under the National Command Authority, which translated to the president and the secretary of defense. Without a go from the NCA, nothing moved.

Still, this delay wouldn't do the shooters any good. Tier One units are like Thoroughbreds. You don't keep Secretariat in the starting gate overnight.

Secretariats—military ones like Red Squadron, anyway—operate differently, train differently, work differently than conventional units. They shoot tens of thousands of rounds a year honing their skills. They can operate singly or in pairs, squads, teams, platoons, or troops, depending on the situation. Even the way they shoot is different. DEVGRU SEALs and Delta shooters may carry automatic weapons, but on direct-action missions they almost never fire in any mode but semiautomatic. All those bursts of automatic fire by Delta and SEALs happen mainly in movies. DEVGRU SEALs and Delta Soldiers don't need full auto mode on ninety percent of their operations because they can fire a double or triple tap at virtually the same speed as an automatic weapon does.

And it wasn't just the human factor that worried Wes Bolin. Tonight all his operational ducks were in the proverbial row. Troops were fresh and primed; weather was perfect; targets were exactly where they were supposed to be. Tomorrow the conditions could change. It could thunderstorm for the next week. Crankshaft—the code name for Bin Laden—could switch locations. Any number of variables could result in additional layers of Murphy factors, which, taken all together, could screw things up. Not make the hit impossible, but make it a lot more difficult. "Better get on it, Mac."

"Roger, sir." The big Ranger general stowed his unlit cigar. "By the way," he said, "the CIA guy—their liaison?"

"Fedorko."

"Yeah, Fedorko. He's got a set of prosthetics with him?"

"Affirmative. They're for Archangel—he's the undercover CIA's had in Pakistan since late November."

"Archangel?" McGill scratched his head.

"That's his call sign. He's a double amputee, and we'll bring him out. But during the mission we need him ambulatory because he's fluent in Pashto."

"Know his name?"

"I can find out. Why?"

"'Cause I had a master sergeant working for me at the 175 when I was an O-5 whose radio call sign was Archangel. Charlie Becker. Big guy. You didn't want to fool with him. Hell of a Soldier. Silver Star recipient. Two combat jumps. Yup. Hell of a Soldier. He retired in oh-one or oh-two. Somewhere I seem to remember somebody telling me he'd gone to Langley."

"Could be. I'll check," Bolin said. "Meanwhile, you stand 'em all down, Mac. We're in hurry-up-and-wait mode until we hear from the CINC."

"Aye-aye, sir."

42

"Mr. Director, I've got the president for you on the secure line."

Vince Mercaldi blinked twice. "Got it, thank you." He picked up the phone and watched the green light illuminate. "Mr. President?"

"Good morning, Mr. Director. This is a conference call. Admiral Bolin is on the line as well."

"Yes, sir. Morning, Admiral."

Wes Bolin's voice boomed in Vince's ear. "Good morning from J-Bad, Mr. Director."

Vince shuffled the papers on his desk, found the sheet he needed, and ran his index finger down until he found the item he wanted. "Just taking off for Tuscaloosa, I see, Mr. President?"

"Just about to. Then we head on to the Endeavour launch—the girls are really looking forward to that. I hate to disappoint them, but I think it'll be scrubbed. Weather's being uncooperative over there."

"Well, I hope things turn out otherwise, sir. Those shuttle launches are truly impressive." The president's mood certainly has improved, Vince thought.

There was a four- or five-second gap when no one spoke.

Then the president said, "I'm calling to officially inform you and Admiral Bolin that Operation Neptune Spear is a go. I've signed the Finding."

Vince got "Thank you, Mr. President" out a millisecond before Bolin. It must have sounded like an echo chamber on the president's end.

Bolin's voice was strong. "We'll do you proud, Mr. President. We will prevail."

"I know you will, Admiral." There was a pause on the line. "God bless you, Admiral. You and all of your people. And God bless America."

"Thank you, sir. And God bless you, too."

The line went dead.

Vince sat, transfixed.

They'd gotten a go. The president had done the right thing.

Vince's mind was churning. Why now? Had the polls come in? Had they changed his mind? Had—

"Hot damn." Vince slammed the desk with his palm.

Because it didn't fricking matter. However POTUS had come to the decision didn't matter. He'd signed the Finding. The president hadn't said it on the phone, but the full designation of what he'd put his signature on was Lethal Finding. A Lethal Finding is a document that gives the CIA authority to launch an operation in which they cause fatalities. In this case, the Finding gave CIA permission to use military assets to fly into Pakistan and kill Usama Bin Laden.

How POTUS got to that point was completely unimportant. What mattered was that they were finally in business. And as for the poll, well, it was supposition on Vince's part that the president had one taken: secondhand intelligence. RUMINT. Certainly, Vince wasn't going to talk to anyone about it.

Besides, poll or no poll, it didn't fricking matter anymore.

What mattered was that POTUS had signed off on Neptune Spear.

Keep your eyes on the prize. That's what he'd said to Stu Kapos back in February. This had always been about KBL. Nothing else.

He hit the intercom. "Get Kapos and Hallett up here, please. And get me Admiral Bolin on a secure line. Pronto."

■

JSOC Joint Operations Center, Jalalabad, Afghanistan
April 29, 2011, 1759 Hours Local Time

"Yeah, Vince, we're in business. But not for twenty-four hours. I've got a weather hold here. Huge weather front. Thunderstorms running all night right across our route in Pakistan. Can't risk the electronics." Wes Bolin held the receiver to his ear with one hand while he flipped through papers with the other. "But the good news is that the weather's bad enough so that Crankshaft probably ain't going anywhere tonight, either."

He listened to the CIA director's hearty laugh. "Couple of things. First, your man Fedorko will go out as part of the package. He'll ride with Tom Maurer in the enabler aircraft. Second, what's the true name of your undercover? McGill thinks he may know him—worked with him at the Regiment." Bolin scribbled a note. "Becker. Thanks. I'll pass it along."

He paused. "Vince, what was the hang-up? Why did he make us wait?"

The admiral frowned. "C'mon, whatta ya mean you don't know. You run a fricking intelligence agency. You're supposed to know everything."

The CIA director's answer made Bolin roar with laughter. "No, you're not J. Edgar Hoover, Vince. At least I've never seen you in a dress." He grew serious. "Please make sure your guy's there to rendezvous. Zero-one-hundred hours, plus or minus thirty seconds. Make sure he's holding a firefly. That way he won't get shot.

"Yeah. Me, too. We'll talk later—set up the comms network so the White House will get the Sentinel video. Joe Franklin, my deputy, will handle it. Okay, bye." Bolin dropped the receiver back onto its cradle. There was nothing to do now but wait.

He pressed the intercom. "Get General McGill, Captain Maurer, and Commander Loeser up here, please." He'd schedule PT—a lot of it—over the next few hours. Bolin knew that idle minds were the devil's workshop, especially the devious, cunning, resourceful minds of DEVGRU SEALs, hormonal Rangers, and TF 160 aircrews. Exercise would keep them all occupied, their bodies challenged and their minds in neutral. He would need them to be sharp tomorrow. Might as well work 'em hard and put 'em away wet. That would guarantee they'd get a good night's sleep.

■

Abbottabad, Pakistan
April 29, 2011, 2352 Hours Local Time

Charlie Becker scrunched away from the water that was dripping onto his bedding and read for the third time the text he had received two hours ago. Valhalla Base had been closed down for good at 2100 Hours. Their final text to him:

Meet for morning prayers at nine in four days at the Big Mosque. Bring one of the little brothers.

The codes were simple. Subtract one day and eight hours from text messages; subtract three days and add an hour and a half to all burst transmissions. That meant 0100 Hours on May 2. The big mosque? That was the Khan compound.

And the little brothers? Had to be the leftover fireflies. Charlie knew what they wanted—they wanted him to be able to identify himself.

They were coming. And about time, too.

By Monday, Shahid would be no more. Gone. Vanished.

And about fricking time. After six months and countless cups of tea and scores of *zam-zams,* Charlie allowed himself to think of an ice-cold beer and a good cigar and the thought made him smile.

Tomorrow was going to be as tough a day as he'd ever had. Not displaying anything—not anticipation, nor joy, nor relief, nor impatience for that first fricking beer—as he made his normal rounds. But he'd do it. He'd give the performance of a lifetime.

43

"Execute CONOP Hotel 53." That was the official language that set everything in motion. It was generic-sounding language, too, no different from the dozens of CONOP, or contingency operation plans, released every day.

That way, no one would know what it stood for.

Indeed, at the same time CONOP Hotel 53 was released, other elements from JSOC Tier One units—SEALs, Delta, and Rangers—were receiving their CONOPs.

Hotel 53 was not the only high-value target CONOP executed the night of May 1. It may have been the most important, but fewer than a dozen people knew its significance. To most in the JOC, it was just another of the eleven other high-value target capture/kill operations Admiral Wesley Bolin and General Eric McGill had scheduled that night. They were, after all, simply following Sun Tzu's dictum that all warfare is deception.

At 1535 Hours, DEVGRU CO Tom Maurer picked up the

mission brief from the JOC and went over it in detail with Red Squadron's CO, Dave Loeser, Ranger element commander Lieutenant Colonel David Brancato, and Task Force 160 lead pilot Chief Warrant Officer Tom Letter.

The only unusual detail about Hotel 53 that Letter and Brancato noticed was that Maurer said he'd do the BUB himself. Two nights ago, the Battle Update Brief had been Dave Loeser's chore.

■

1700 Hours

Troy Roberts's iPhone foghorned him awake. He rolled over, got his bearings, and stretched.

One-Alpha's master chief Danny Walker didn't waste any time. He switched the overhead lights on, then drill-sergeanted, "All right, ladies, drop your cocks and grab your socks." He received a barrage of pillows and "Screw you's" in response.

Troy could hear the others next door. It was a bigger space. The remainder of 1-Alpha as well as Heron Orth and Cajun Mistretta were bunked down there. He peered over at Walker. "This gonna be more hurry up and wait?"

Walker shrugged. "Can't say."

"Hope not." Troy moved side to side, then bent over, placed his palms flat on the deck, held the position for fifteen seconds, then released. "Oh, that felt good." He watched as the master chief did the same. "Not bad for an old guy."

"Old enough to kick your ass, baby-face."

"You and all of AARP?"

"Yeah—assault with a deadly Walker, and that would be me."

"Very funny."

The master chief cracked a grin. "I think so."

Padre shrugged into his ACU trousers and, yawning, shuffled off toward the head. Like the others, his biological clock was still on U.S. time.

It had been a long few days. Late on the twenty-sixth, the entire package, including three of the 160th's MH-60J stealth Black Hawks, had loaded onto a quartet of Globe-master-IIIs at Fort Campbell for the long, long ride to Jalalabad. They'd arrived, inventoried gear, checked weapons, and begun premission preparation only to be stood down twice, last night because of weather.

Padre was anxious to get to work, finish the job, and go on to the next one. Like most of his shipmates, he'd completed more than fifty capture/kill missions in the past nine months—and that included the two-month shutdown after Norgrove. And he hadn't worked as hard as some people he knew. Towel in hand, he headed down the hall, yawning as he went. Maybe a shower would wake him up.

■

1816 Hours

They could have been eating an early breakfast or a late dinner at an IHOP or Denny's. It didn't matter—the mess hall had it all. Bacon, eggs, toast, coffee, steak, hamburgers, chicken nuggets, and French fries. Yoghurt in individual containers, hot and cold cereal, orange and apple juice, and fresh milk and butter flown in from Germany.

As usual, Cajun had double-stacked his tray. So had Heron, Padre, and Troy. It was a tradition: bulk up because you never knew when you'd eat again.

"On the usual diet, I see." Rangemaster's tray held a single bacon and egg sandwich and a cup of black coffee.

Cajun gave the lanky SEAL a hurt look. "You need some

meat on them bones, sailor." He pointed to his own over-loaded tray. "The condemned man ate a hearty meal."

"And you've been condemned to?"

"Eat with you, man. You eats like a bird. Ain't good." Cajun scrunched his chair to make room for his shipmate. He nodded toward a table by the far wall where Tom Maurer sat with Dave Loeser and a huge Soldier with a single star on his ACU blouse tab. "Wonder what they're up to."

"That's McGorilla with the boss." Rangemaster cut his sandwich into two perfectly equal portions. "Probably doing what the brass always does: Figure out how to get us in trouble. Complicate our lives. Toss a few hurdles in our direction."

"That's what I love about you: you're always so optimistic." Heron yawned. "Full of Christian love and trust."

"If I weren't an atheist, or a Buddhist, or a Wiccan, I'd be full of Christian love and trust," Rangemaster said. He cut each half of his sandwich into two more precise portions, picked up one, and devoured it in a single bite. "But I'm not, and I ain't." He looked at Padre. "Which one am I again, Padre?"

"Pagan. I keep telling you. You demand human sacrifices, therefore you're a pagan."

"I thought human sacrifices were a SEAL thing."

"They are—that's why they invented Hell Week." Fish elbowed his way toward the table bearing a tray of steak and eggs and hash browns.

Rangemaster made room for the newcomer. "Pull up a throne, your lordship."

"Don't mind if I do." The SEAL set down his tray and scratched at his beard. "Anybody seen Gunrunner?"

Cajun: "He's working out, Fish. Says he has to lose weight."

"Good," Fisher grunted. "Because he was behind me

on that last stick at Knox. Came down the rope and pan-caked me."

Heron: "Gotta be faster, Fish."

"I do better in a maritime environment." He stirred sugar into his coffee. "Don't like to be a fish out of water."

Rangemaster: "Original. I'll bet you've never said that before."

"Absolutely." Fish held his left hand up in a three-fingered salute. "Scout's honor." He glanced over at the table of officers. "Who's the supersize general?"

"McGill."

"The Ranger? Seventy-fifth Regiment?"

"That's him."

"How can he be a Ranger general? He's too big. Looks like he needs a cargo chute." Fish hooked a thumb in McGill's direction. "That man does not eat only one meal a day." Wes Bolin's predecessor, the ascetically thin Ranger General Stanley McChrystal, was legendary for eating only one meal a day.

"Let the truth be told," T-Rob said. "Not all Ranger generals eat only one meal a day."

Fish laughed. "And here I thought that was the Army's latest deciding factor for general officers rank."

44

"Okay, listen up." Captain Tom Maurer stood in front of a three-by-five-foot flat screen to conduct the BUB. Taped to the wall and surrounding the screen were photographs of the Khan brothers and their wives and children that had been taken by the crews at Valhalla. There were also ground-level photos of the compound gates and the concertina-topped walls with the main structure rising behind them. "Tonight our CONOP is Hotel 53. It's a deep end-run into Pakistan, so nobody get lost and miss the tour bus on the way back, okay?"

He waited for the laughter to subside. He punched up the first PowerPoint slide. "Because it's a deep run and there's the possibility that we may have to fight our way out, weapons tonight will be four-sixteens for the assault package. I want us to be able to reach out and touch people should we have to. If the Rangers want to bring some seven-sixty-two stand-off weapons, that's fine with me. And we'll be breaching, so prepare for up to six doors or gates.

"As usual, an HVT. Name: Hamid Gul Muhammad, code name Undertaker—same target as two nights ago. And still just as nasty a piece of work. Bomb maker, trained in Iran. Responsible for more than twenty American KIAs." Maurer looked out at the faces of the SEALs, Rangers, and aircrew. "So how about let's put his head on a pike tonight. *Hoo-yah!*"

He waited for the *hoo-yahs* and *hoo-ahs* to subside, then he hit the remote and the second slide popped up. It was a surveillance photograph of the Khan compound. "He lives here, with his family and two other families. So watch out for wives and children. We don't want collaterals tonight. You see a weapon in a woman's hand, or her hand reaching for one, you shoot her dead. Same for the kids. Otherwise, cuff 'em and stow 'em."

Maurer pulled up the third screen. There were a pair of X's at positions on the south side of the outer wall. The one on the right had a green circle. "Clean zone. That's for people we know and have searched and identified." The next screen had a red circle. "Dirty zone: everybody else."

He looked toward the back of the room. "We have two Soldiers from Delta's intelligence package with us tonight. They'll ride with me in the enabler helo. They speak Pashto and Arabic, so they'll handle the on-site TQ and lead the SSE." TQ was tactical questioning and SSE was sensitive site exploitation: mining for intelligence materials and taking DNA samples and photographs of prisoners, corpses, and leave-behinds. The more you could learn, the more effective your hunt.

He continued with screens that showed photographs and diagrams of the locations where the helos would land, where the walls had to be breached, and where the Rangers would set up their blocking force and security perimeter. "Because it's Pakistan, we're worried about neighbors," he continued. "So we'll link up with an OGA asset at the target site." OGA stood for "other government agency," which is how most of the military referred to CIA. "He's an undercover and looks like a local, but he'll be holding a firefly, so nobody shoot him, okay?" Maurer paused. "The slim guy with the white beard sitting in the back of the room—stand up, Paul—is Paul Fedorko, who works at OGA's Ground Branch. He knows the asset and he'll provide him with a vest, a cover, and NODs. The OGA guy will handle the neighbors."

Maurer looked over the room. "Any questions?"

There was silence.

"Okay," he said. "Dismissed. Let's go get the job done."

■

2030 Hours

By 2000 Hours the assault package was broken into smaller working groups, studying overhead imagery of the target, marking overlays, and making up their grid reference guides, or GRGs, which many of the assaulters would wear on their wrist the same way NFL quarterbacks write their plays on their wrist.

Rangemaster traced the distance from J-Bad to Abbottabad. "Captain said we were going deep?" He shook his head. "This is fricking halfway to San Francisco."

"Asshole's killed more than twenty Americans," Geoff Ziebart said. "Worth the trip."

"We've never gone this deep before, Z," Rangemaster said. He rubbed his mustache. "Strikes me funny."

"Me, too." Padre tapped the map. "Plus, all our prep? Not normal."

"Neither are the sixty-Js," said Gunrunner. "This smells funny to me."

"You smell funny to me," Cajun said. "But it makes sense. Maybe Gul is a cover name. Maybe they found Cyclops." Cyclops was the code name for the one-eyed Taliban chieftain, Mullah Omar.

"Or the Doctor. Just like we said at T-Rob's that night." Doctor was Ayman al-Zawahiri, Usama Bin Laden's Number Two.

"Or the big guy himself." The SEALs looked at one another. Padre whispered the code name: "Crankshaft."

Danny Walker had been off with the brass. Now he walked up to the knot of SEALs. "Gents?"

T-Rob: "Master Chief. You know anything special about this mission?"

"Yeah, I do: you guys are on it."

"That's it?"

"No. I actually have some information you might want to know. Like our call signs tonight. Troop leader—that's Commander Loeser tonight, although he'll be riding in Chalk Two, replacing Jack Young—will go by X-ray India One. Captain Maurer's call sign is X-ray Romeo One. I'm the assault leader, call-sign Jackpot." He watched as the men took notes. "We clear?"

Rangemaster: "Crystal, Master Chief."

Walker: "Good. TLPs are in effect as of now." TLPs, or troop leading procedures, were the overall term for ensuring that the assault element was properly jocked up and all their equipment was checked, double-checked, and triple-checked before the load out.

The master chief checked his watch. "Listen up. PCI at twenty-one hundred and PCCs starting at twenty-one thirty." PCIs were the precombat inspections during which the assault leader and officers checked the troops' equipment. PCCs were precombat checks, an ongoing procedure of SEALs checking one another's equipment to make sure everything was functional and nothing had been forgotten. It was during the PCCs that they'd clone their radios, synching one with the other to ensure that everyone in the assault element was on the same frequency.

"Questions?" Walker scanned his SEALs.

They were silent.

Of course they were: they'd been through this sequence hundreds of times. "Great. Okay, you guys go jock up."

■

Joint Operations Center
2145 Hours

Wes Bolin checked the live video feeds from the two Sentinels that were loitering twelve thousand feet above the Khan compound in Abbottabad. Thermal imagery indicated that both the guest house and the main house were occupied. Three other Sentinels were already in position above Peshawar, Hasan Abdal, and Rawalpindi, where they'd spoof the Pakistani radar sites and shut them down if necessary, as well as monitor all of Pakistan's secure communications networks.

If the Paks sounded an alarm, Bolin would know it. And he'd scramble air assets immediately to protect his people.

He ambled back to his office, sat at his desk, and stared at the big clock on the opposite wall ticking off the seconds. This was the one part of being an admiral that he didn't much care for. Tonight he'd be in the JOC, watching from the sidelines and relaying information back to Washington. He would much rather have been on one of the chalks as an assault leader, or at the very least a part of the command element riding the enabler helo.

He did, of course, occasionally accompany his troops. And once in a while he even saw action. But not as often as he would have liked. He envied his junior officers, the kids like Dave Loeser and the up-and-comers like Tom Maurer and Scott Moore. They could still be a part of the rough-and-tumble, edge-of-the-envelope stuff, the kick-ass take-names part of Warriordom that had made them become SEALs, or Rangers, in the first place.

Rangers. Crap. He hadn't passed on the identity of the Ranger that McGill had asked him to check on. Frantic, he checked every sheet of paper on the desk. But he couldn't find his note or remember the name. "Dammit."

He picked up the phone and waited for the lieutenant colonel manning the operations desk to answer. "Gary, ask Captain Maurer to find the OGA guy on CONOP Hotel 53 and get me the true name of their Abbottabad asset." He listened. "His call sign is Archangel. And ASAP, will you? It's urgent."

45

Charlie Becker rolled off the pallet he'd been using as his bed and onto the rug-topped dolly. He patted himself down in the old "spectacles, testicles, watch, and wallet" mode. Knives, check, check, check. Phone, check. Fireflies, check.

That was it. The begging bowl would be left behind. Charlie didn't want any extraneous souvenirs from this particular TDY. The memories, he decided, would be quite sufficient.

Especially if tonight's festivities went as planned.

He flipped his phone open and checked the time. It would take him one and a half hours to reach the end of the four-hundred-plus-meter street on which the Khan compound stood. He'd been instructed to be on-site at 0100.

Piece of cake. In fact, he planned to get there early, so he could check the compound and make sure nothing was amiss, then watch them come in. Charlie pulled himself onto the dolly, took padded sticks in hand, and cast off into the night.

46

"Dave, you're replacing Jack Young on Chalk Two, right?" Tom Maurer checked the watch on his left wrist. "We're twenty minutes from Start Point."

"Aye-aye, Captain." Dave Loeser grinned as he headed toward the stealth Black Hawk to check that everything was shipshape. He'd ridden Chalk Two during most of the Fort Knox JTXs and could easily step into the injured SEAL's position. He was pumped. He had expected to be included, but as part of the command package on the enabler helo. Now he'd been made an assaulter. It didn't get any better than that.

Even though he was Red Squadron's commanding officer, tonight Loeser would be working for Master Chief Danny Walker, Hotel 53's assault leader, call-sign Jackpot. It made sense. Loeser had gone on perhaps a dozen capture/kill missions in the past year and a half. In that same timeframe, Jackpot had almost a hundred under his belt.

The SEALs were all jocked up now: lightweight ceramic

body armor in hydration-capable carriers, Gen-III helmets with NODs. Their 416 magazines were loaded with heavy, solid 70-grain Barnes TSX rounds that worked so well in the AFPAK theater, their Sig-Sauer 226s held +P Speer Gold Dot 124-grain loads. The two breachers, 6-Charlie's Heron Orth and 1-Alpha's Myles Fisher, wore their breacher kits high on their chest, above the magazine pouches, as did the two Ranger breachers.

The assault element personnel would be cross-loaded. Each of the Black Hawks would have breachers, Rangers, snipers, and assaulters. That way, if one of the helos went down, there would still be enough personnel and equipment to get the job done and get out safely.

Maurer checked his watch again. Things were going relatively smoothly. The FAARP was ready to fly to a safe location within thirty-five minutes' flight of Abbottabad. There were a total of five Sentinel drones in the air. He could get the secure feed from the one dedicated to the Khan compound on the tablet computer in his thigh pocket.

He watched as the assault package made its way to their respective aircrafts. Their radios had been synched so that the entire group could talk back and forth. Their comms would be piped back to the JOC, where Wes Bolin and Eric McGill would watch the Sentinel feed.

The Sentinel feed would also go straight to the White House, where Air Force Brigadier General Joseph Franklin, Bolin's deputy, was set up in a small annex adjoining the Situation Room. And the feed went to Langley, where Stu Kapos and Dick Hallett would monitor it in the CIA operations center, and to JSOC's National Capital Region Task Force Command Center in Pentagon City, Virginia.

Maurer turned back toward the JOC to see Wes Bolin and Eric McGill coming at him. The admiral was carrying a secure phone, which he handed to the SEAL.

"Call for you," Bolin said.

Tom put the unit to his ear. "This is Captain Maurer."

Wes Bolin enjoyed watching the younger man's reaction. It was, he thought, wonderfully genuine and also well-deserved.

Maurer said, "Thank you, Mr. President. We will. Yes, sir. Thank you, sir." He handed the phone back to Bolin, his eyes still wide with surprise.

"Go to work, Tom," Bolin said. "Do it right. Make it look easy."

"The only easy day was yesterday, sir."

"Hoo-yah, Captain. Good hunting."

Special Operations Apron, Jalalabad, Afghanistan
May 1, 2011, 2330 Hours Local Time

Chief Warrant Officer Tom Letter, the lead SOAR pilot, started the mission clock at precisely 2330, as he lifted Chalk One off the ground. Delivery in Abbottabad would be 0100, plus or minus thirty seconds. Chalk Two followed immediately. Less than half a minute later, the enabler aircraft, an MH47-G containing the command group, JMAU, SSE, and OGA contingents, lifted off. It was followed by a non-stealth Black Hawk holding four SEALs and nine Rangers. The security craft would drop off when the assault package crossed the border and head for the FAARP.

The stealth MH60Js headed almost due south at an altitude of four thousand feet, until they passed over the U.S. Forward Operating Base at Shahi Kowt. That was Hotel 53's first checkpoint.

2337 Hours: Tom Letter spoke into his secure radio. "Buick." He banked the aircraft left, running parallel to the power lines eight miles to his north and gradually gaining altitude as he headed for his second checkpoint at Tawr Kham, thirty-three miles southeast. It was a natural border: a mountain range that formed the crooked spine between Pakistan and Afghanistan. Thirty miles south of Tawr Kham, the mountains reached more than eleven thousand feet. Here there was a natural dip. Letter climbed to ten thousand feet, and the top of the ridge passed safely, thirty-three hundred feet below the helicopter.

2359:37 Hours. "Cadillac." Letter grinned inwardly. They would cross into Pakistan in twenty-six seconds. Whoever had given the checkpoints these names certainly had a sense of humor.

They'd go stealth now, running fast and low, threading the needle between Pakistani air defense zones and military commands. Far behind, the FAARP aircraft were leaving Jalalabad for their forward basing location. Thirty-three miles to the southeast lay his third checkpoint. The mountain ridge was dropping fast. Letter descended slowly so he could hug the ground.

0002.33 Hours. Master Chief Danny Walker listened to the pilots' chatter on his headset. As the assault leader, he was the only non-aircrew on the helo who was wearing one. The SEALs and Rangers were holding their helmets and hearing protection as they sat, crammed together on the Black Hawk's deck. Because this was a stealth aircraft, it flew with its hatches closed. Normally, between the engine noise and the wind, it would have been impossible to hear anything. Tonight, however, the SEALs could shout in one another's ears and actually catch a word every now and then.

He'd heard Tom Letter call "Feet dry" when they'd crossed the border. They were in Pakistan now. He checked his watch. Less than an hour to target.

Then, in his ear, another voice. It was Captain Maurer, transmitting from the enabler.

"CONOP Hotel 53 this is X-ray Romeo One. Target Undertaker was incorrect. New Target tonight is Target Geronimo, also known as Crankshaft." There was a pause on the line. "Please confirm."

Danny Walker: "Hotel 53 Jackpot confirm."

From Chalk Two: "Hotel 53 Rangemaster confirm."

For one of the few times in his life Danny Walker was actually surprised. He unplugged his headset from the bulkhead, knelt down, and shouted at the troops. "New Target! Call-sign Geronimo." He saw their puzzled reactions through his NODs, grinned, and shouted, "That's Crankshaft, gentlemen!"

"UBL! We're gonna hit UBL!"

■

"Pontiac." T-Rob put his red-lensed flashlight on the GRG map he wore on his left forearm. They had passed the third checkpoint. They were just about a hundred miles deep into Pakistan now. Just south of Campbellpore. East of the Indus River. Soon they'd be swinging north, passing Checkpoint Chevy, threading the needle between Islamabad, hiding in narrow valleys between the mountain ridges. That's where it would get bumpy.

But he didn't care if half the package heaved big chunks. They were going after Crankshaft. This wasn't just another mission, it was the mission of a lifetime. Son Tay. Eagle Claw. Entebbe. All the special operations he'd read about in *Spec Ops*. This is what he and Padre and every single SEAL in Red Squadron lived for, had become SEALs for, endured Hell Week for.

Not that the other missions weren't special. They were. But this was something else. This was a whole fricking different universe. This was the asshole who'd killed thousands and thousands of Americans. The guy the whole world—

well, a good part of it, anyway—had been hunting for ten-plus years. The high-value target that scores of SEALs, Rangers, and other special operators had given their lives trying to find.

Now it was payback time. And—luck of the draw—it was Red Squadron who'd gotten the call, and 6-Charlie and 1-Alpha who'd be the assaulters.

Troy sat there in that incredible aircraft noise, his mind churning.

And then he prayed.

He thanked God for giving him the chance to be in this particular spot, at this exact point in time.

Thanked God for his great shooting skills and the strength of character to have made it through BUD/S.

Thanked God for the blessing of these incredible shipmates, who were also being blessed with His bountiful generosity tonight.

And for an incredible wife and a glorious child and another on the way.

A child who'd be born into a safer world because on the day his new baby drew its first breath, months would have elapsed since Crankshaft drew his last.

It was . . . incredible.

God, Troy thought, is indeed great.

And yet, when he thought about it, there was something else going on that was even more incredible.

Which was this: CONOP Hotel 53 was just another three helicopters full of anonymous SEALs going out to do one of eight, nine, ten, a dozen HVT capture/kills tonight. Except for the significance of the target—which was, he had to admit, a pretty cosmic damn thing—this was just another mission. Another night he couldn't talk about to anyone—except the other people on this Chalk and his shipmates back at Dam Neck. But bottom line? UBL was just another HVT who wouldn't be breathing anyone's oxygen tomorrow morning.

And then reality smacked T-Rob upside the head. Smacked him good.

Holy mother of God. They were probably watching this one live from the White House.

And the Pentagon.

And Langley.

So it had to go perfectly. No Mr. Murphy. No screw-ups. None at all.

T-Rob nudged Padre, turned, and shouted in his ear. "Great news, huh, bro?"

Padre's head went up and down like one of those toy dogs you see in rear windows. "Frigging awesome." He steadied himself against his shipmate as the helicopter started to swerve evasively.

Troy: "We're about to head north." He tapped the GRG on his wrist. "Islamabad."

"Roger that." The pilot was flying low and fast now. Padre hoped they were slipping past the Pak air defenses without leaving so much as a hint of a signature. Padre had lost friends in helicopter crashes. They were nasty.

Then he thought: Nah, not tonight. Tonight, *inshallah*, they'd get in and get out without a hitch. Tonight it would all go the way it should. Textbook. And end with Crankshaft's head on a pike. UBL would stand for Used to Be Laden.

Padre punched his shipmate's upper arm. "Whoever blows a shot at Crankshaft buys the beer. Pass it on."

"Right on." Troy gave his shipmate an upturned thumb. "Ain't gonna be me, bro."

"Or me either, dude."

47

The National Security Staff started arriving just after 1 P.M., notified that something big was going on. Some carried fast food from the Old Executive Office Building's machines; others carried coffee in white paper cups embossed with a gold Presidential Seal. Those cups came from the entity that in the Mesozoic Age had been known as the White House Mess, but these days was called the Presidential Food Service.

Shortly after 2, the president arrived, dressed informally in an open-neck white shirt and a windbreaker. He'd been playing golf. He was accompanied by the White House chief of staff, his national security advisor, and Dwayne Daley. By 3, he'd been joined by the vice president, the director of national intelligence, Secretary of Defense Rich Hansen, the Joint Chiefs chairman, and Secretary of State Kate Semerad. Vince Mercaldi arrived at 3:45, accompanied by Spike.

On arrival, each of the principals was handed a white

three-ring briefing binder. On the cover, printed in bright red, was the legend

TOP SECRET CODEWORD NOFORN
For Use In White House Situation Room Only

By 2 P.M. Wes Bolin's deputy, Air Force Brigadier General Joe Franklin, had set up his laptop in the small annex adjoining the Situation Room so he could feed the live video from the Sentinel loitering over the Khan compound to one of the Sit Room's four wall-mounted flat screens. The Air Force special operations officer was receiving the same live audio feed that Wes Bolin and Eric McGill were getting in the Jalalabad JOC. While the other officials gathered in the Sit Room, Call Me Vince and Spike stood behind Franklin, watching the video feed and listening to the radio chatter.

There wasn't much of it. Until 3:54.

Then the audio feed speaker came alive.

"Six minutes." Vince didn't know it, but he'd heard Chief Warrant Officer Tom Letter's voice announcing that Chalk One was six minutes from target.

The CIA director said, "What's happening?"

Joe Franklin: "They're going into their final onboard prep, Mr. Director. Turning their radios on, pulling on their helmets, inserting mags in their weapons, and loading rounds in the chambers." He turned toward the director and gave him a smile. "The usual sphincter-tightening stuff."

"Sounds about right." Vince turned and pointed toward the Sit Room. "You gonna feed that in there?"

The general shook his head. "No capability to do sound," he said. "But I can relay the video."

"Hmmm." Vince ambled next door. The big flat screen facing the head of the Sit Room conference table showed an overhead of the Khan compound taken by the Sentinel's infrared camera. There was no movement inside the compound walls and no sound. He looked at the president and said, "The assault package is getting close, Mr. President. They're about five minutes out right now, and if you want to hear what's going on as well as see it, you'd better go next door, sir, to General Franklin."

The president stood up. "I gotta see this," he said, and headed to the annex.

The vice president jumped to his feet. "Hey, this is a big fuckin' deal. I wanna see it, too." He elbowed a national security staffer out of the way and headed next door, the secretaries of state and defense, the director of national intelligence, and the Joint Chiefs chairman in his wake. Within seconds, the small annex was crammed full of VIPs.

■

4.25 Nautical Miles southwest of Abbottabad, Pakistan
May 2, 2011, 0057 Hours Local Time

"Three minutes." Tom Letter's voice exploded inside Master Chief Danny Walker's head. Jackpot unplugged the aircraft headset, settled the olive drab Peltor talk-through hearing protection around his ears, and pulled the boom mike toward his lips. Then he crammed the helmet onto his head, fastened the straps, and dropped his NODs.

He turned his own radio on. "Jackpot's live. Everybody hear me?" He looked at the upraised thumbs. "Roger that. Three minutes."

They could feel the Black Hawk decelerate. They were only doing ninety knots now, which Tom Letter would hold until they were thirty seconds out from the target.

At that point, the copilot would start calling both speed and altitude as Letter slowed the aircraft down for his flare above the roof of the main structure. At thirty seconds, the aircrew would open the hatches. The instant the Black Hawk flared, the fast ropes would go out. Followed by the SEALs.

In the cockpit, Letter banked the Black Hawk in a steep right turn, fishhooking into his final approach to the target. He looked down. Below him was the main highway that led north to Mansehra. He glanced at the mission clock. They were eighteen seconds ahead of schedule. Frickin' A. He glanced at the copilot: "Hit the fireflies."

The copilot dialed in the frequency he'd written on his cuff and activated the PAIT. "Fireflies burning."

■

Abbottabad, Pakistan
May 2, 2011, 0059:44 Hours Local Time

Charlie Becker never heard the Black Hawks until they were right over the compound. Never saw them, either. They were just . . . there. Coming from the north.

The first Chalk came in fast, started to flare just above the third-floor roof of the main house. And then—holy shit, it banked off south and disappeared. Chalk Two veered sharply southward and gained altitude. He couldn't do anything but stare.

Talk about your fucked-up approaches. Welcome to Abbottabad, guys.

■

45 Feet above Khan Compound, Abbottabad, Pakistan
0059:55 Hours Local Time

"I can't hold it." Tom Letter knew exactly what was happening—he just couldn't do anything about it. He had no lift. It was everything going wrong at the same time. He was settling with power.

No way was he going to hit the roof. That could kill them all. He fought the vortex of negative pressure, brought the nose around.

The big aircraft hovered, nose facing south, above the rear wall of the compound. Letter recovered enough control to turn it north. Ahead of him was the large, open western courtyard. He could bring it in there.

He'd almost cleared the wall, when the big bird pancaked. Letter struggled with the controls to keep it from flipping and killing them all.

The tail smashed violently downward into the wall and they were all pitched forward, rotors slicing into the ground.

And then—contact. They'd hit. Instinctively, Letter killed the engine. He turned, wrenching his back as he did so. "Get out get out get out!"

■

The White House Situation Room Annex, Washington, D.C.
May 1, 2011, 1559:55 Hours Local Time

"My God, it's going to crash." Secretary of State Kate Semerad clapped her hand over her mouth.

"I warned you, I warned you," Dwayne Daley said to no one in particular. "It's going to be another Desert One."

The president's eyes were glued to the screen. He hunched forward. The overhead video was too one-dimensional for them to figure out what was happening. But they'd seen the Black Hawk's erratic movements and now, as they watched, its tail hit the southwest wall of the compound and the aircraft pancaked in, its rotors churning up so much dust that it disappeared completely.

After what seemed an eternity, the dust settled and the Black Hawk came back into view. And they could see the

SEALs and Rangers scrambling out, heading for the compound wall.

The president exhaled audibly. So did almost everyone else in the room. Vince Mercaldi muttered "Thank God" under his breath.

The Joint Chiefs chairman glanced in Vince's direction from across the room and mouthed, "Amen."

Now the second Black Hawk came into the picture, its rotors whirring as it disgorged thirteen SEALs and Rangers, the K-9—a Malinois named Cairo—and its handler, in the field just southwest of the compound.

"The entire assault package has just been been delivered successfully," General Franklin said. He swiveled in his chair until his eyes fell on Dwayne Daley's petulant expression. "We've come a long way since Desert One."

He stared coldly at the presidential terrorism advisor. "A long, long way . . . sir."

48

Danny Walker had already scenarioed this particular clus-terfuck in his head. They all had. They'd red-teamed the entire assault, coming up with everything that could go wrong and war-gaming the adjustments needed to overcome Mr. Murphy. Shit, the exact same thing had happened to 6-Charlie's helicopter during a mission in Helmand not nine months ago. For these SEALs it was just another day at the SNAFU office: situation normal, all fucked up.

So Jackpot opened his mike and called "Execute Hotel 53" onto the net. Everything would go as planned. Then he yelled, "Ranger breacher with me, NOW!"

And rolled out of the aircraft followed by his SEALs.

Yeah, they may have been shaken. But not stirred.

And the clock was ticking.

0101:29. Jackpot knows they have to smack two walls to get to the main house. He points the Ranger toward the gate in the ten-foot-high wall. "Blow it."

The Ranger pulls a pre-primed Spider Charge out of his chest bag, fixes it on the metal gate, slams the shock tube initiator home, and then runs backward, unspooling line as he goes. He backs off twenty feet next to a shed, plugs in his igniter, shouts, "Burning!" and hits the igniter.

The gate blows. Jackpot tells the Ranger, "You stay here. See anything unfriendly, you kill it."

One more gate to blow before they reach front door.

0102:55. Two and a half minutes behind schedule, the SEALs are set to make entry into the main compound. As they do, they hear another explosion. It's the Chalk Two element blowing through the compound's southwest wall. The Chalk landed in the pasture, disgorged its SEALs, Rangers, and the K-9 team, then banked off into the night, heading for the predetermined laager site three minutes away, in the valley west of the highway and just north of Abbottabad. They'll stay there, rotors turning, until they're called back.

0103:40. Jackpot is first through the smoke into the fifteen-foot-wide alley. The SEALs fan left and right. Scan north and south. All clear. Gate ahead.

Jackpot: "Heron—blow it."

■

0105:15. The enabler aircraft lands once Chalk Two clears the pasture. Rangers charge down the ramp, heading toward the road, where they'd set up a perimeter. They are followed by Paul Fedorko, who hits the ground running, carrying a vest with plate carrier, helmet with NODs, and two prosthetic legs.

0106:37. "Burning!" Heron blows the front door. Jackpot and Gunrunner make entry.

Jackpot: "Gun, right!" Two quick shots followed by three more. "EKIA."

Troy: "Going left."

Padre's voice: "Gate. Breacher!"

Gunrunner in their headsets: "Kids on the left. Babies. No shoot!"

0107:25. In Jackpot's headset: "Vest, left!"

Followed by shots fired from the guesthouse on the south side of the compound.

In his ear: "EKIAs." Multiples.

The 6-Charlie SEALs swarm swiftly through the ground floor. Unlike police SWAT teams, which move deliberately and in formation, these operators function on the run, working quickly in pairs or trios.

It looks like organized chaos. They call it violence of action.

At the edge of his NODs' field of vision Padre sees Z's got two squalling kids wrapped up in his arms.

Padre likes that: kids running loose equals no booby traps.

On this level.

0109:35. Heron blows the gate protecting the stairwell.

Rangemaster busts through the smoke and runs up the stairs, suppressed 416 in high ready position, both eyes open as he works the wall, scanning and breathing, the red dot of his night-vision-capable Aimpoint sight bright through his NODs.

0109:55. Rangemaster sees movement. Shouts, "Landing! Gun!"

He fires two rapid shots.

Calls, "Hostile down. Stairwell."

Keeps moving up to the second-floor landing.

Jackpot follows.

0110:25. Heron's muzzle is pointed up the stairwell. He sees something on the third-floor landing through his night-vision sight. Face. Gray beard. "Hostile!"

The target looks down at him. Heron squeezes off two quick shots.

Misses. "Shit."

T-Rob hurdles the corpse, a bearded kid in his twenties wearing a white T-shirt. He drops his muzzle and puts a round in the kid's head as he goes by.

Insurance. When in doubt, double shoot the sonofabitch. You don't want them coming up behind you.

0111.00. T-Rob and Padre have already leapfrogged Rangemaster and Jackpot, who are clearing the second floor.

Heron's close behind. He, too, puts a bullet in the corpse's head. He hears: "Second floor clear." Keeps going.

Padre's voice from above: "Gate—Heron."

Heron reaches into his breacher kit for the prefabbed charge.

■

0111.00. Charlie Becker is sitting on the ground, wrapping Ace bandages on his stumps. Satisfied, he takes one of the prosthetics from Fedorko and attaches it, tests, then reaches for the second one.

When it's on, Fedorko and a Ranger pull him to his feet. "How they feel?"

Charlie wobbles like a drunk. "Guess it'll take a while to get my sea legs." He stands unsteadily. Takes a tentative step. Then another. "Kinda like riding a bicycle, huh?"

He steadies himself against Fedorko. "Thanks, bro."

"CIA. We deliver." The Agency man reaches into the breast pocket of his ACU blouse and hands Charlie a big cigar in a silver aluminum tube. "Humongously big one-star at J-Bad gave this to me for you."

Charlie: "One-star?"

"General McGill. He works for Wes Bolin at JSOC."

"Eric McGill." Charlie laughs. "Humongous is right. We used to call him McGorilla. Shit, we were in Iraq together in ninety. And at the Regiment." He opens the tube and lets the cigar slide out halfway, puts it under his nose, says, "Ahh," then looks down at the tube through the NODs Fedorko had given him.

"See that? That's a frickin' Cuban Romeo and Julieta Churchill." Charlie holds up his ruined left hand and mimics Churchill's famous "V for victory" sign, except on him it looks more like a checkmark. "Best cigar ever made." He grins at Fedorko. "Thanks. I think I'll save it for later."

Charlie looks up and down the empty street. "So, now that I'm standing on my own two legs again, who do you guys want killed?" He puts his head back and laughs. It feels great to be vertical.

Fedorko says, "Charlie, I have something that's better than killing." He looks at the bemused expressions on the two Rangers' faces. "Okay, okay, there's nothing better than killing. But tonight . . ."

Fedorko pulls a set of counterfeited ISI creds out of his thigh pocket and hands them to Charlie. "You are hereby deputized as an officer in the Inter-Services Intelligence service.

"Here's the way it works: You patrol out here with the Rangers. If the neighbors get nosy, you tell 'em it's an ISI op in cooperation with the Americans and to go back to bed before they get arrested."

"Can do." Charlie peers at his CIA colleague's green face through the NODs. "What's my rank? Do I get a weapon?"

"You're already rank enough, Charlie," Fedorko says. "And we all know you don't need a weapon, you *are* a weapon."

49

Troy's first onto the third-floor landing. Movement to his right. Runner disappearing.

Door slams.

He's there. Kicks it open. It slaps inward, bouncing off the wall.

Heron's right behind him.

0112:29. Troy makes entry. "Going left."

Two women in front of a man.

Tall man.

Bearded.

Perpetual scowl.

Crankshaft.

Troy calls "Geronimo, Geronimo, Geronimo" into his boom mike.

0112:31. The women charge. Screaming "Sons of whores!"

From behind Troy, Heron shoots the closest one in the leg.

She goes down squealing.

Troy hears Padre's voice: "Going right."

0112:33. Second woman keeps coming.

Heron rushes them.

The big SEAL swats the charging woman, clubbing her onto the floor.

He catches the wounded woman's clothing and drags her toward the far wall.

0112:35. The tall bearded man turns straight into Troy. He's wearing a light-colored *shalwar qameez* and a Fellaheen knit cap.

0112:36. T-Rob's crosshairs are on Crankshaft's center mass.

The women are screaming bloody murder.

T-Rob squeezes off two, three, four quick shots.

Crankshaft's knocked backward.

Starts to go down.

0112:37. Padre's 416 is up. He makes a single shot at the guy's left eye.

Crankshaft's head snaps back.

He's dead before he hits the deck.

Heron's trying to keep the screaming, cursing, flailing women out of the way without killing them.

0112:42. Padre crosses to the corpse, the HK416 in low ready, finger on trigger.

If the sonofabitch even twitches, it'll be two more in the head.

But the motherfucker doesn't twitch.

He's dead.

The hunt had consumed more than a decade. But the finish? Less than ten seconds in a pigsty of a room in a backwater Paki town no one back home has ever heard of.

Until tonight.

Padre calls "Geronimo EKIA" into his boom mike.

Then he and T-Rob help Heron flexicuff the screaming

bitches so they can move 'em downstairs to the Dirty Zone.

0113:45. The three SEALs take a look at Bin Laden's corpse. The sonofabitch's hair and beard are all gray. His face is distorted from Padre's head shot. But it's him. No mistaking that face. That nose. Those lips.

T-Rob thinks, *Thank you, Jesus, for allowing me to be a part of this and not screw up.*

Padre thinks, *Ten years we've been after this asshole, and after all the hype, he looks like every other piece of shit we've killed.*

Heron thinks, *I missed the motherfucker. How could I have missed the motherfucker? Now I'm stuck for the fricking beer.*

■

The White House Situation Room Annex, Washington, D.C.
May 1, 2011, 1613 Hours Local Time

"We got him," the president said solemnly. "We got him."

"It's been a long time," Secretary of Defense Rich Hansen said. "A long hunt."

The president nodded in agreement. "Now," he said, "we have to make sure it's really him."

He looked at Vince, standing at the back of the anteroom out of camera range. "That's being done, isn't it, Mr. Director?"

"As we speak, Mr. President."

The president rose. "Then I suggest we all go back into the Situation Room, where it's a lot more comfortable, and wait for absolute identification."

He looked for his chief of staff. "Bill, let's start drawing up a statement," he said. "I'll want to address the nation at some point tonight, as soon as we have a hard confirmation it's Bin Laden."

■

1617 Hours

Vince Mercaldi waited until they had all left. He walked over to Joe Franklin and put a hand on his shoulder. "Nice work, General."

The Air Force officer looked up. "Thank you, sir."

"Call me Vince." Mercaldi peered over Franklin's shoulder at the images on his split screen. He knew what Wes Bolin was doing right now: checking on the other twelve HVT missions that were under way. They'd talk soon enough, so there was no need to call him now. Besides, there wasn't much to say. The sonofabitch was dead. That was the goal, and they'd achieved it. Time to move on.

Behind him he could hear the chatter in the Situation Room. They'd all be fighting for the credit now. Crowing to their news sources who did what and when. Demonstrating how important they were, what they knew, and how much inside information they'd been given.

Some would; some wouldn't. Kate Semerad would keep her mouth shut. So would Rich Hansen and the Joint Chiefs chairman. They were professionals. They knew better. But that idiot the vice president, a man who never engaged his brain before he put his mouth in gear, or the president's political aides, people like National Security Advisor Don Sorken and Dwayne Daley—Vince knew they'd be spilling their guts. So would the clowns on Capitol Hill. Sourcing their friends in the media. Telling everything that shouldn't be told: who, what, when, where, and especially how.

Except they'd either misstate the facts or spin the truth. Some of it because they didn't know much about either the facts or the truth. Or they'd spin the facts because they didn't care much about the truth. Only the legend.

A legend that was being created even now in the Situation Room.

Vince removed his glasses and polished them on his handkerchief. There was a line from an old John Wayne movie, appropriately titled *The Man Who Shot Liberty Valance*, that came into Vince's head just then: "When the legend becomes fact, print the legend."

In this case, the printed legend would just happen to dovetail nicely with the White House's political goals.

Because 2012 was, after all, right around the corner.

Vince hoped Wes Bolin and Tom Maurer could protect their SEALs and Rangers from the tsunami of publicity that was about to wash over everyone. Those young men worked in the shadows, and to be successful they needed to continue working in the shadows.

He knew damn well that he, Dick Hallett, and Stu Kapos could protect Charlie Becker, Spike, Ty Weaver, and the kids who had staffed Valhalla Station. Because they would never talk about them. Or reveal their roles. And because Charlie and the rest of them were professionals, they'd keep silent, too.

Because *they* knew, just as Vince did, that you never know when you'll have to do it all over again.

"Vince?"

The CIA director blinked and put his glasses back on.

It was the White House chief of staff.

"Yes, Bill?"

"The president would like to congratulate you."

"Thanks. I'll be right in."

Vince sighed and clapped Joe Franklin on the arm. "And so it begins," he said, and walked out of the room.

50

Commotion on the stairwell. Troy turned to see who was coming.

It was Mr. Loeser, Jackpot, and the captain, fluorescent and specter-like seen though his NODs.

Tom Maurer was first into the bedroom. Looked around at all the mess. "What a shithole."

He checked out the flexicuffed, screaming women and turned toward Danny Walker. "Master Chief, get someone up here to transfer them downstairs for questioning."

The DEVGRU commander stared down at Crankshaft's body. There was a lot of blood.

He looked at Padre. "Who killed him?"

"We did," Padre said. "All of us."

The CO bent over and examined Crankshaft's wounds. "Well done. Bravo Zulu."

Padre gave his commanding officer a brief smile. "For God and country, right, sir?"

"You got it, son. God and country. That's why we wear the white hats."

Troy asked, "Who was the kid on the second floor?"

"Khalid Bin Laden," Loeser said. "One of the sons."

He stared down at the body, trying to think of something pithy to say. But there was nothing to say. The corpse said it all.

He looked at his men. "Well done."

Maurer turned to Loeser and Walker. "We've already got the slurpers working," he said. He pointed at the corpse with his thumb. "Get him tagged and bagged, and let's get the JMAU started on DNA and the other identifiers."

"Aye-aye, Captain." Walker had been at war most of his adult life. Most of it had been either clandestine or covert—and kept that way. This hit, however, would make news. Global. Cosmic. He hoped the unit would stay in the black. The master chief scanned his troops. They'd keep their silence. He hoped the pols would, too. But that was asking a lot.

Well, it wasn't his problem. "T-Rob, Padre, tag and bag this scumbag."

Maurer checked the big watch on his left wrist. "We have twenty-two more minutes on the ground, and we still have to blow the damaged Black Hawk. But the Paks have no idea we're here, so I want to exploit every fucking second we have."

He paused. "Hey, you guys, clear out and let the slurpers in so they can start picking up."

"Lots of intel, sir?" Heron asked.

The CO nodded affirmatively. "Goddamn place is a treasure trove. Hard drives, flash drives, laptops. This is going to keep the intel squirrels busy for months—and make our schedule even rougher."

Troy said, "You mean we got job security, Captain?"

"Job security?" Maurer grinned. "Hell, son, you'll be working twenty-four-seven, three-sixty-five right up to the time you do your thirty."

The captain looked through his NODs at his men as they headed down the stairs.

He was proud of them. They'd had a rough start, but they had surmounted it.

They'd followed the credo above the Dam Neck shoot house front door: ADAPT, OVERCOME, OR DIE.

They'd done the first two—and Crankshaft had obliged them with the third.

Maurer regarded his SEALs, the Rangers, and the rest of his package in the way the best commanding officers think of their troops: with a combination of pride, humility, and intense gratitude that he had been allowed to lead these incredible Warriors into battle.

And bringing all of them home alive? And killing Crankshaft? Icing on the fricking cake.

What had gone on tonight, he understood in the marrow of his bones, was one of the most totally awe-inspiring experiences an officer can have. Now he understood why the great Warrior Commanders like Stan McChrystal, Wes Bolin, and Bill McRaven had insisted on going out on CONOPs not as flag or general officers but as just one more shooter in the package.

Gives you perspective. Keeps you honest. And humble.

51

Charlie Becker stepped up to the body bag on the plowed wheat field just as two young SEALs were about to load it into the big enabler helo. He put his arm up like a traffic cop and shouted over the whine of the big twin idling Lycoming jet engines, "Hey, dude, lemme see him quick."

The SEALs started to give him a dismissive once-over. Then they saw Charlie's seven-month beard, matted hair, and filthy clothes, topped off by the helmet, NODs, and the Ranger vest. By the time they got to the vest, their expressions had morphed into holy-shit wide-eyed.

Because this was him.

Archangel.

The double amputee who'd been in fricking Abbottabad undercover for months. Working without a net. No support. One tough motherfucker. The bearded OGA guy had called him The Lone Ranger.

"For sure, bro." They lowered the bag back onto the deck and the baby-faced one unzipped it from the top. Charlie hit the button on his green-lensed Surefire and peered down. It was him, all right, even though the face was distorted. Bullets tend to do that. Especially Barnes 70-grain TSX fired at a distance of under fifteen feet.

One round had hit just above the left eye. Crankshaft's head must have been turned toward the shooter because the heavy bullet exited out behind the right ear, taking a fair amount of skull and brain matter with it. Between the green light and Charlie's night-vision equipment, the blood and brain goo registered black. But that wasn't all. The shock and kinetic energy had ballooned the head itself so it looked almost hydrocephalic.

Nasty stuff, those hand-loads.

Even in the green light he could see that the corpse's unkempt scraggly beard and kinky hair had turned mostly gray. So the sonofabitch had dyed his hair to make all those videos. That brought a smile to Charlie's face. He thought, *Wonder what it says in the Quran about using Just for Jihadis.*

He reached down and pulled the zipper to waist level.

Whoa, Crankshaft had taken a wholesome burst dead-center mass. Three, four, maybe five, maybe even more rounds. Turned most of his chest cavity into squishy, blood-colored jelly. Faint fecal scent told Charlie maybe they'd even nicked the colon.

No way Washington was going to admit to any of that. Charlie made himself a bet that the official report would read something to the effect of "one round to the chest and one round to the head." After all, we wear the White Hats. Turning the architect of 9/11 into hamburger? That would be worse than politically incorrect. It would be . . . un-American.

Still, the sight brought a smile to his face. The kids did good today. No embarrassing arm or leg wounds.

A clean kill.

The best kind. Next to a dirty kill, that is. Charlie Becker, he knew all about dirty kills.

He turned toward the youngest-looking SEAL. The kid had such a round baby face he looked like the Spanky Mc-Farland character in those 1930s *Our Gang* comedies.

Charlie shouted above the jet whine, "He say anything?"

The SEAL shook his head. "Not a word. Sank like a sack of you-know-what. But the wife, boy does she have a potty mouth."

"Women, huh? Can't live without 'em, can't live with 'em." He laughed and pointed at the corpse. "Well, *he* sure can't anymore." Now they all laughed.

The other SEAL adjusted the sling on his suppressed short-barreled rifle as the Ranger hitched up his long, baggy trousers, trousers that covered a quarter-million-dollars' worth of prosthetic legs. The kid seemed lost for words. Finally, he pointed, awkwardly, like a teenager, somewhere in the vicinity of Charlie's knees. "Where'd you lose 'em?"

Charlie pulled the Velcro tighter on the vest and body armor he'd been given. It was way too big. He'd lost twenty, twenty-five pounds in the past half year. "Iraq."

"When?"

"Oh-four."

"*When?*"

The retired Ranger used his hands to reinforce the message. "Zero-four!"

The SEAL caught sight of Charlie's hands. His expression showed respect. He pointed at the prosthetics. "How they work?"

"Pretty good. They're low mileage, though. Tell you in about ten years and fifty thousand miles." Charlie gestured toward the women and children, all flexicuffed and sitting against the compound's outer wall atop a clump of wild cannabis. "What are they gonna do with them?"

"Leave 'em here for the Pakis."

Charlie nodded his head approvingly. "Way it should be."

He pivoted the flashlight to illuminate his way toward the chopper's lowered ramp and half-turned.

Then turned back. "Hey, you guys, thank you. Real nice work," he told the SEALs. "Bravo Zulu. Now, go put him on board."

The kids beamed. "Aye-aye, sir."

Charlie: "Oh, I'm no sir, Sonny."

The SEAL said, "Then who *are* you, Pops?" He said it smiling.

"Who am I?" It was a good question.

Charlie didn't quite have an answer yet.

So, instead, he preceded them up the ramp, gritting his uneven, ruined teeth during the short climb because he hurt like hell but wasn't about to show it. He strapped himself into one of the canvas benches that lined the MH47's fuselage and massaged the tops of his prostheses. He hadn't worn them in more than five months, and they were killing his stumps and the muscles in his ass.

He pulled the big Cuban cigar General McGill had sent him out of its tube, bit off the end, and lit up, regardless of pilots, crew chiefs, and any rules or regulations there might be about smoking on a U.S. military aircraft.

Because he'd earned *this* one the Ranger way.

He got the stogie going, took a couple of huge puffs, then held the cigar in front of his nose to admire the leathery, peppery perfume of the vintage Churchill.

The SEALs got the body bag on board, stowed it against the port side bulkhead, and strapped it down.

The baby-faced SEAL started to leave, but stopped in

front of Charlie. "C'mon, Pops, you can tell us. You gotta be real special to be here, and you're here. Which makes you like, *real-real* special. So, who are you, anyway?"

Charlie took a *l-o-n-g* pull on the Churchill. He held the smoke in his mouth so he could really taste it. Then he blew a perfect smoke ring.

Oh, the pleasure. All that wonderful sweet, spicy stuff you get with only the best *Habanos*.

That's when he gave the kid a big, shit-eating grin.

And told him the truth: "I'm an Airborne Ranger going home, Sonny, is who I am."

EPILOGUE

The lieutenant commander who signed his emails EyeSpy because he served as the *Carl Vinson*'s deputy intelligence officer watched from the captain's bridge as two CV22B Special Operations tilt rotor Osprey aircraft came in low across the North Arabian Sea. He looked up and saw the MC130J Combat Shadow II tanker from which they refueled during the long flight circling lazily overhead.

The flight deck had already been emptied of all but the few senior deck crew necessary to land and tend the Ospreys. Way before noon the Captain had ordered all the ship's audio-visual equipment to be turned off. No closed-circuit TV of the deck, the island, the bridge, the bow, or the stern. In fact, for the past twelve hours the ship had been in lockdown. There was no phone, internet, or email service; the crew—except for a few senior personnel—was sequestered below decks. There would be no iPhones, BlackBerrys, or smart phones sending home snaps, videos, or texts of the day's events. There would be no blogs, no emails, no letters, no phone calls. No Skype. No Facebook or YouTube. No Hushmail. Nothing. Not today, especially between 1200 and 1330 Hours. Hopefully, not ever.

The Admiral himself made the announcement himself just before noon. There would be visitors. What went on during and after their arrival was no one's business, and would not be talked about, whispered about, written about, blogged about, or gossiped about. Violations would lead to severe—he repeated the word twice for emphasis—disciplinary action. Whether now, or in the future.

Being an intelligence officer, EyeSpy understood something was up for the past twenty four-plus hours. He'd been one of the few to know that VIPs were coming; that something big was in the wind. But nothing more specific than that.

Oh, he had inklings, because he saw just about all of the secure traffic. And he had friends at JSOC. So he had . . . thoughts. Yeah, it could be *him*. UBL. The Grail. But you couldn't be sure. Operations like this always used deception—make 'em think you're going to the *Carl Vinson* when in fact you're going to another carrier, or just going to lower the ramp and oops, jetsam Usama from ten thousand feet.

And so he hadn't nailed it down. Until now.

Because now, in a heartbeat, he realized what was happening. Who—no, *what*—had been flown to the *Vinson*.

It was the Grail. Bin Laden. Or, more accurately, Bin Laden's corpse. They were going to bury it at sea. From his vessel.

Transfixed, he watched as the two tilt-rotor craft settled onto the gently pitching deck. They shut down quickly. Of course they did: the downward exhaust from their engines might injure the flight deck surface.

Then the ramp of the first Osprey dropped. EyeSpy raised his field glasses. It was a group of operators—Navy SEALs in full battle gear. They spread out and moved toward the second Osprey as that craft's ramp lowered onto the deck.

Two SEALs debarked the second aircraft. Then another pair. Then another. Then a bearded guy in what looked like Pakistani clothes, wearing a bulletproof vest and a US-issue helmet. Then another bearded man in blue jeans and a blue button down shirt.

EyeSpy squinted, forehead wrinkled in puzzlement. Then: *Ahh: they must be the Imams.*

EyeSpy watched as the SEALs joined up. Then two of them went back inside the Osprey.

They emerged carrying a dark body bag, which they set down on the aircraft's ramp.

A master chief approached. He spoke to one of the SEALs, obviously the senior guy. EyeSpy trained his glasses on them but couldn't read their lips.

The master chief pointed toward EL 4, the aft, port-side elevator. The senior SEAL nodded. He spoke to the man in blue jeans and then to the two SEALs who'd carried the body bag.

They lifted it again. When they did, EyeSpy caught his breath. The bag had left a dark smudge on the aircraft's ramp. It had probably been lying in a puddle of oil during the flight.

Then he focused on the stain. No—it was dark red.

The entire retinue, led by the master chief, walked onto the elevator, where they set the body bag down again. After about sixty seconds, the elevator slowly dropped out of sight. EyeSpy had his glasses trained on the body bag. And yes, there was a puddle underneath it, too.

EyeSpy watched the elevator disappear to the hangar bay. Then he trained his glasses on the horizon, until he saw the C-130 about five miles out, circling the carrier. *Y'know*, he thought all of a sudden, *that's strange*. Strange that they used

EL 4, because that elevator was port side, adjacent to the stern, and customarily, bodies are buried at sea amid-ships.

Garbage goes off the stern.

Not to mention the fact that the big nuclear-powered carrier had four big, nuclear-powered screws and each screw had five big blades. Drop something off close to the stern and there was a chance—remote but still a chance—it would be turned into chum. Fish food. Shark bait.

Just deserts.

Desserts for sharks, that is.

The thought brought a grim smile to EyeSpy's face. He'd lost friends because of the corpse in that body bag. He was feeling no pity. None at all. He swiveled and looked at the others on the bridge. There were no smiles, no cheers, no high-fiving. Of course there weren't: they all knew the war wasn't over. Not by a long shot. But this single battle—a significant battle, too—had just been won. For good.

EyeSpy, USNA 1998 and third generation Navy, sighed, and gave thanks. *God bless the Blue and Gold.*

■

It was almost 1300 when EL 4 reappeared on deck with the full complement of SEALs and the Imams. The one wearing the helmet had an unlit cigar in his mouth. EyeSpy focused on the guy. He was smiling as he climbed aboard the aircraft.

EyeSpy turned and swept the elevator with his glasses. Every trace of blood had been completely washed away.

ACKNOWLEDGMENTS

I couldn't have had a better colleague on this project than my editor, Adam Korn. Adam's suggestions made this a better book, something for which I am eternally grateful. The team at Morrow, its publisher Liate Stehlik, Associate Publisher Lynn Grady, Marketing Director Jean Marie Kelly, Associate Director of Publicity Danielle Bartlett, Managing Editor Kim Lewis, Production Editors Lorie Young and Andrea Molitor, and Editorial Assistant Trish Daly have been wonderful to work with: innovative, energetic, and hugely, hugely supportive of this project. I think of you all as my own Asymmetric Warfare Group.

The Sun Tzu of agents, Paul Fedorko, got behind the idea for this book from the get-go.

I started writing about SEALs and CIA operations more than two decades ago, and I'm proud to say that many of the people who helped me through the Rogue series, as well as *SOAR, Jack in the Box,* and *Direct Action,* are still around to backstop me in matters tactical, operational, and military. I've also had the opportunity to know a fair number of the folks who either work or have worked at CIA over the years, and for this project I depended heavily on their counsel and their experience.

Writing about the military and the intelligence communities can be tough. Writing about what goes on in military and intelligence operatives' minds can be nigh-on impossible. I'm grateful to an elite corps of enablers who helped me through the rough spots and provided wise counsel over the years. Especially Major Kent Bolin, USMC (Ret.), Captain Bob Stumpf, USN (Ret.), Admiral James A. "Ace" Lyons Jr., USN (Ret.), Christopher Michel, Myles Fisher, Lieutenant Colonel Gary Bloesl, USMC (Ret.), Richard Hallett, Duane Clarridge, Geoffrey Hancock, Dr. Roger Orth, M.D., Kevin Gors, "Mr. Wade," Lionel Bourgeois, Buz Mills, Robert K. Brown, John F. Musser, Eliot Jardines, Paul R. Collis, Jerry Glazebrook, Kerry Brendel, Mauro DiPreta, Hardy Ernsting, and last but not least a couple of dozen folks who, because of where they currently work or what they do, cannot be mentioned by name or even initials.

But you unindicted co-conspirators all know who you are. And we will laugh as we sip wine, Jameson, or good single malt, smoke Padilla 1932s or Montecristo Petit Coronas, break off pieces of marble bars, watch Navy beat SMU, and hang out at the U-Club, the Cosmos, the screen porch, or the backyard deck, depending on our mood and/or whim.

A major portion of this book is about character. Bob Corbin of Prescott, Arizona, serves as the template for the Doing What's Right sections of KBL. Bob, the former three-term attorney general of Arizona and a past president of the NRA, has always lived by the credo that the law is the law, what's right is right, and politics shouldn't enter into it. It's a credo more politicians, cabinet secretaries, and attorneys general should live by. Come to think of it, the rest of us should, too.

And finally, thank you, thank you, Deb Corbin, for getting me through this marathon in one piece.